"*Alibi* is a slice-of-life story with a significant romance subplot and then it's also a murder mystery. The mystery itself does not drag out for all that long. The protagonist is a primary suspect (though really there are any number of suspects). Sharon Shinn is outstanding at powerful metaphorical imagery that captures emotional truth. That's the case here as well. [Her] characters are vivid, distinctive, real people, all of whom are unique and appealing. It's the characters that make this story sing."

RACHEL NEUMEIER
author of the Tuyo series

ALIBI

ALIBI

SHARON SHINN

FAIRWOOD PRESS
Bonney Lake, WA

ALIBI

A Fairwood PressBook
November 2024
Copyright © 2024 by Sharon Shinn

First Edition

Fairwood Press
21528 104th Street Court East
Bonney Lake, WA   98391
www.fairwoodpress.com

City cover image by Blue Planet Studio
Silhouetted couple by Chris Tefme
© Getty Images

Cover and book design by Patrick Swenson

ISBN: 978-1-958880-25-8
Fairwood Press Trade Edition: November 2024

ALIBI

PROLOGUE

"**Please tell me what's going on.**"

"Someone teleported into this house around one a.m. this morning, went into Duncan Phillips' study, and shot Mr. Phillips dead. From what we can tell, this individual came to the house with a single agenda—to commit murder."

"Who are you considering suspects?"

"People with access to the house. Specifically, those who live and work at the Phillips mansion, and those who had their own door codes."

"That includes me."

"It does. The last time you were here—the last time anyone knows that you were here—you had a nasty argument with Mr. Phillips. Which was witnessed by five other people and caught on security monitors. We have had an opportunity to view the recording. It looks like an unpleasant encounter. Is that the last time you saw Duncan Phillips?"

"Yes, it was. No, I didn't come back to the house in the middle of the night and kill him. I don't even know how to use a gun."

"There are a lot of fingerprints and DNA traces on this particular weapon. Possibly some of those are yours. You'll need to be printed and scanned before you leave today."

"But I—I didn't kill him. I wasn't even in Chicago last night. I was at a party in Atlanta. There must be fifty people who can give me an alibi."

"Atlanta's not so far away by teleport."

CHAPTER ONE

Four months earlier

THE IRONY OF AN EVOLVING CIVILIZATION IS THAT THE MORE DE-pendent it becomes on a certain form of technology, the more likely it is that the tech will break down.

I was already late for dinner at my mother's and I could tell, by the throngs of frustrated and angry commuters, that I was going to be later. Atlanta's Olympic Terminal was always crowded, since it was the third-largest teleport facility in the world, but there were so many people here tonight that I had to suspect a complete breakdown in the system.

Nonetheless, hoping it might only be a local issue, I headed for the Chicago gate. There, several hundred commuters milled about, expressing outrage and disbelief and arguing with the attendant about the superiority of teleport terminals in New York, London, and Hong Kong.

"So what's the problem?" I asked a well-dressed woman about my mother's age, who seemed resigned rather than furious. She looked up from her tablet and gave me a tired smile.

"I'm not sure. But no one can teleport into or out of the city, and phone calls and texts aren't going out either."

I tried to suppress a groan. "Any idea how long it will take to fix?"

"Somebody said an hour. But who knows?"

I nodded, thanked her, and moved away, looking for a semi-quiet corner. Not that I didn't believe her, but I had to verify for myself that communication was truly impossible. EarFone technology basically meant you could connect with anybody, at any time, and the idea of complete silence in my head was almost inconceivable. Hunkering down by some storage lockers near the restrooms, I cupped a hand over my right ear, where the implant was, and spoke my mother's code. Nothing. Same when I tried my brother Jason and my best friend, Marika.

Sighing, I came to my feet and looked around for entertainment. Though a teleport terminal is not the place to find that. The whole point of teleport, after all, is immediate transmission, so most people don't expect to have to hang around too long. The Atlanta facility is a model of efficiency on most days. It's laid out like one huge multi-pointed star, and each point represents one of the major cities of the world. The local system dumps travelers into gates at the middle of the star, and from these central pads they can walk the shortest distance to their next destination.

I've always been fascinated by, but too cheap to pay for, one of Atlanta's so-called direct terminals. These allow you to make the leap to any other terminal anywhere in the world that's equipped with a reception port, even a private residence. I mean, teleport itself is essentially instantaneous, but traveling between destinations can take forty-five minutes or so by the time you add up all the short walks between gates and portals. But given the state of my finances, I'd rather spend the time than the money.

After pausing to buy a few snacks against the possibility of a long wait, I returned to the Chicago point of the teleport star. But my luck was in. Just as I was looking around for a place to sit, a collective sigh of relief went through the assembled crowd. The whole irritable mass of people seemed to surge to its feet in one convulsive movement and cram itself toward the gate. Looked like we were operational again.

It wasn't all that long before it was my turn to step into the closet-sized booth and shut the door. To me, the long-distance jumps always feel smoother and faster than the local ones. Within seconds, my body seems to dissolve and my mind, for the briefest moment, goes absolutely blank. Then I suddenly come to, standing in an identical gate a few hundred miles away.

Today, that gate opened into the clean white lines of O'Hare. I stepped out and fought through the crowds toward a local portal, already calling my mother. She didn't answer, so I tried Jason again, since I knew he had come in from Denver to join us for dinner.

"Hey, it's me," I said, a little breathlessly. "Sorry I'm late. Is Mom worried?"

"She would be," he said, "but I was smart enough to check the news and learn that all of Atlanta was blanketed by some mysterious electrical storm."

"I'm at O'Hare now. I'll be there in a few minutes."

"Better have your alibi ready," he said and hung up.

I couldn't help grinning as I fell in place behind a line of people waiting to use the gate to my mother's neighborhood. Since we had been children, Jason and I had spent much of our time diverting our mother's concern. She feared that we would be devoured by rabid dogs, kidnapped by malevolent strangers, vaporized by malfunctioning teleporters. Because Jason had an adventurous spirit and I chafed at confinement, we spent much of our time trying to slip her cautious leash—and then devising stories about the harmless pastimes that had kept us away for all hours.

More than once, when he was in high school and I was in college, I had encountered him entering the house in the morning just as I was leaving. At least as often, when I was dating Danny, Jason would find me sneaking home at midnight just as he was about to go off to bed. We would always issue the same challenge: *What's your alibi?* and then offer ludicrous explanations. We never failed to find this routine hilarious.

After we moved out of the house, of course, we no longer had to soothe our mother's fears. But it had become a joke with us, a habit. If I called him and he did not answer, he had better have a good excuse ready; and if he saw me in public with someone he did not recognize, he would want the full background story. The less likely it was to be true, the better.

It was finally my turn to step into the gate that would take me to a booth a few blocks from my mother's house. Local portals are more complicated than dedicated long-distance ones, because they contain keypads where you have to punch in your destination. In most big cities, helpful lists are posted on the interior walls, displaying the codes for popular attractions. In Chicago, those include Wrigley Field and Watertower Place. In Houston, where I work, they include the Space Center and the museum district.

I keyed in the code for my mother's Northbrook neighborhood, and seconds later I was stepping out onto the street. It was cold in Chicago, of course—it's always cold in Chicago, no reason to expect anything different on this early March night. I had worn a sweater in Houston, where it had been too hot, and now I wished I had brought something warmer. I'd have to borrow one of my mother's coats before I left.

A very brisk walk and I was at her house, a cute two-story brick building with an indifferently kept lawn and a small garden, just now brown with leftover winter. Jason met me at the door, which otherwise would have been triple-locked against the possibility of intruders.

He was dressed as usual in pressed khakis and a white shirt. His best friend Domenic always said he looked like a "laker," one of the rich kids from the moneyed suburbs that border the northern edge of Lake Michigan. He was also good-looking in the way rich kids often are, with even features, straight blonde-brown hair, and an easy, athletic carriage that bespoke complete self-assurance. He had inherited all of our mother's Scandinavian genes, so his skin was fair and flawless, a shade or two lighter than my own. Except for the money part, what you saw with Jason was what you got—a handsome, happy, boyish, charming guy.

"Ninety minutes late. I'd call that a new record," he greeted me, handing over a glass of wine. "What's your alibi?"

"Some kind of electronic interference. I thought you knew."

He made a face. "Not very interesting."

"Marika accidentally overdosed on that new designer drug—what are they calling it?—"

"Chelsea."

"And it's scary that you know that. And I had to rush her to the hospital."

He considered, but rejected it. "Don't think you can tell Mom."

"I was consulting with a hit man about doing away with my brother—"

My mother's voice called from the other room. "Tay-Tay? Is that you? Honey, you must be exhausted. I managed to save the meat, but the potatoes are so overdone, I hope you don't mind. Jason's already eaten his salad, but you come on in and get something in your stomach."

Jason gave me a brief malicious smile. "And don't forget to say hi to Dad on your way in."

I grimaced and followed him out of the half-lit foyer, through the darkened living room and toward the big kitchen. And, though I would have preferred not to, I could not help but look over at my father as we passed him in the living room.

Well, not my father. A hologram of him—a fairly high-caliber one, too, because it incorporated some minimal movements and facial expressions. Most of the time it sat, glowing and stuporous, in the big wing chair he had loved so much, facing the oversize video monitor always turned to the news. Now and then, it would turn its head in response to some nearby motion, and its radiant face would break into a welcoming smile. Once the visitor had moved out of its sensor range, it would return its attention to the screen.

I suppose my mother found this comforting. She'd purchased and installed the hologram about ten years after my dad died, using a windfall she'd gotten when one of his stocks took off. They're wildly expensive, holograms, particularly variable ones, and this one was both detailed and accurate. I mean, the artist had exactly caught the contours of my father's face and the slightly ridiculous way he looked when he was truly happy.

Personally, I found the whole setup creepy in the extreme. For one thing, my dad hadn't been around that much when he was alive, since he was a workaholic who spent fifteen hours a day at his office. For another—well, he was dead. This ghostly representation did not make him feel any more alive to me. Mostly it made me want to avoid the living room.

A few quick steps and I was past him, into the much more cheerful space of the kitchen. This was a large, gracious room of white tile, red curtains, bright copper pans, and fabulous aromas. Food always smells better at my mother's house, probably because she insists on cooking everything in her antique stove and oven. Me, I flashfry everything or use the hotbox for baking, so I can put a meal on the table in five minutes, but my mom just doesn't believe such rapid-heat methods cook a meal properly. Sometimes, eating at her house, I agree.

My mother set a generous portion of roast on my plate and directed Jason to pour me a glass of water, "or another glass of wine, I'm sure she needs it, poor thing." To hear the concern in her voice, you'd have thought I was just home from firefighting or demolition work.

Despite her claim that the food was probably burned, everything was delicious, and we all ate with appreciation. My mother, a delicate frail-boned woman, took dainty bites that managed to conceal just how much food she could put away when she set her mind to it. I swear she could eat more food than her two children put together, even though she didn't appear to have gained an ounce since she was thirteen. Combine her ethereal features with carefully styled white-blonde hair and you got the picture of a sweet older woman of textbook grace and elegance. An accurate picture, for the most part, though her constant fussing can make me want to scream with vexation.

Jason loves her close attentiveness. Cannot get enough of it. The man is thirty-one years old, and the first person he calls when he's sick is his mother. Any time he gets a cold, he scoots himself over to her house so she can smother him in concern. I can hardly imagine what kind of woman his own age could compete with that kind of affection.

Tonight, her gentle fretting helped relax my frayed nerves, and I accepted the extra helpings of broccoli and the second piece of German chocolate cake that she had made especially for me. Still, I had arrived so late that the hour was pretty far advanced by the time dessert was served, and I was ready to go the minute I put down my fork.

"Now, Taylor, you call me when you get in," my mother said, following Jason and me through the living room past my father's glowing presence.

"I'm thirty-four years old, I don't think I need to call my mother to let her know I'm safe."

"Just so I don't worry. Jason will call me from Denver when he gets in, too."

"Sure thing."

"Jason, why don't you go all the way to Taylor's apartment with her? Make sure she's okay."

My brother and I locked eyes. "Okay," he said. He bent to kiss her on the cheek, and I gave her a quick hug. I buttoned up my borrowed coat, and a minute later we were out the door, walking as fast as we could through the icy night.

"What are you doing tomorrow?" I asked as we huffed along.

"Class at noon." Jason's a part-time student at the University of Colorado; I sometimes think he will never graduate. "And then Domenic and I might go out to California to see a ballgame."

"Give him my love."

He fished in his pocket. "Here. New book."

I wished I had on gloves, but I took it in my bare hand, squinting at the cover in the inadequate streetlights. It was a small, square volume, probably not much more than a hundred pages, though the type, when I flipped

16 SHARON SHINN

through it, looked very small. "*Sociological Theory in Mid-Millennium Urban Centers.* My God. Where did you pick this up?"

"Class, of course. As far as I can tell, I'm the only one who read it."

"So I'm supposed to throw away *Pillars of the Earth*?"

"Too limiting. Not enough modern references. This one even talks about EarFones and how they've revolutionized communication. Actually, it's much better than it sounds. You might enjoy it if you sat down to read it."

"I don't think so. I'll just scan it for pertinent words."

When we were kids, Jason and I read all the same books. Science fiction, boys' adventure books, girls' adventure books, horse books, whodunits. Everything. In one of the juvenile mysteries, the young detectives communicated with each other by designating a book and working out a numerical code that corresponded with the page numbers, the lines on a page, and the words in a line. So 57-5-3 would be the third word in the fifth line on page fifty-seven. *Dinner*, maybe. Or *served*. Eventually you could construct a sentence like "Dinner will be served in the dining room at seven."

Well, Jason thought this was the most wonderful thing ever. He bought each of us identical copies of some realbook that he'd picked up in a used-book store—*A Wrinkle in Time,* I think, which comes in a zillion editions, so he had to make sure publication dates matched exactly. And then he proceeded to leave me folded scraps of paper, tucking them into my shoes or my coat pocket, with mysterious sets of numbers penciled on them. I can't resist Jason's particular brand of lunacy, so I would instantly grab my copy of *Wrinkle in Time* and decode whatever pointless message he had sent. It was more fun than I can convey.

At least once a year, he changed the source texts, just in case any spies were onto us and were carrying around the same tattered realbooks that we were. And, once we were into our teens, we found we had to modify the code, since some of the modern words we wanted to use were not readily available in old-fashioned novels. For instance, *Pillars of the Earth* did not have any references to "teleport," so we had to assemble it from the skeletons of eight other words, adding a fourth digit to our string of numbers. Therefore, 57-5-3-6 would isolate the sixth letter in the highlighted word. You can imagine how complicated.

You would think that, as we entered our sober adult lives, this particular diversion would have palled, but I can't say that it has. While I was married to Danny, Jason would often send me texts or emails that were nothing but a series of numbers and I would have to dig out my current book and track down words. Once his message was, "Your husband is a shithead." Another time it was "Divorce is an option in modern-day America." I learned to decode his messages when Danny wasn't home.

Ancient history.

Anyway, I was happy to get the new book. "Hey, it's small enough to fit in my dainty purse," I said, tucking it in next to my comb. "I'll carry it with me always."

"I'll be in touch," he said in an ominous voice, and we laughed as we ducked into the little stone housing for the teleport gate.

No one else was there waiting; not much traffic in this part of town past eight in the evening. Jason stepped back to allow me first access to the gate. He had no intention of following me home.

"'Night, Tay-Tay," he said.

"See you," I replied, closing the door and punching in my code. Moments later I was in my own neighborhood. A few more minutes and I was home. Within an hour I had called my mother, checked my EarFone log for messages, mentally reviewed my wardrobe so I'd have a clue what to wear in the morning, and climbed into bed.

CHAPTER TWO

WEDNESDAY MORNING FOUND ME IN HOUSTON. I TEACH ENGLISH at Sefton University, where students are required to attend classes in-person unless health problems or personal emergencies are keeping them off campus. Teleport makes it easy for them to attend from anywhere in the world, though the majority of our students come from Texas or the rest of the U.S.

On this, my last working day of the week, I was facing my Basic Lit and Composition class, which consisted of a rowdy group of freshmen who had little interest in the great literature of the past several centuries. Me, I loved the depth and detail of the 19th-century novelists and the changing poetic form of the 20th-century writers, but my students were frequently bored by some of the mandated texts.

So every year I let my classes vote on novelists they'd like to study in addition to the required ones. I can't tell you how many Stephen King and Stephanie Meyer books this means I've been compelled to read, not to mention the stray science fiction author from the past thirty years. But we've worked our way through *Misery* and *Twilight* and *All Systems Red*, discussing character development, foreshadowing, denouement, and intertwining themes, and I haven't minded one bit. There is no frigate like a book, as Emily Dickinson says, and my students and I have all enjoyed our eclectic travels.

The other thing I've done is make the students compose essays—about each other—in the style of the authors we've studied, then take turns reading these out loud. If they're too shy to pick out a classmate to describe, I'll let them turn their powers of observation on me. My favorite was written by a girl who went on to win all sorts of poetry awards and now works in publishing somewhere in New York. I kept it, of course; I keep all of them. She wrote:

"Taylor Kendall entered the drab room with her usual air of calm self-possession and cast one appraising look at the inhabitants clustered at its inhospitable desks. She had pulled her dark hair back from her face with a bright scarf that brought a wash of color to her olive cheeks. Her clothes, though serviceable, were far from the first height of fashion, and seemed to have been chosen to lend her an air of dignity rather than beauty."

I mean, I did not think I would ever stop laughing.

No one in this particular semester was nearly as talented as she had been, but I loved the class. The students had been together a full year and developed that synergistic personality that you occasionally get with some great groups of kids. They laughed, they asked questions, they challenged me, and they read almost everything I assigned them, which was about the best I could hope for.

This Wednesday, we were discussing *Break of Day,* hailed by every critic of the '00s as "the first true classic of the millennium." It was probably my least favorite book on the syllabus, a dreary post-apocalyptic treatise of savagery in the face of failed civilization (haven't we done that kind of book in every generation, and wasn't it just as dreary then?), and the only thing to like about it was that it was just two hundred pages long.

"Man, what a piece of crap!" was the first admirable critique offered by Devante Ross, a tall, burly, Black athlete who could always be counted on to open any discussion. Other voices were soon raised in support.

"That was even more depressing than *Lord of the Flies.*"

"You know, maybe I'm naive, but I really think that if all the computers failed, we'd manage to live without turning into, whatever, beasts. Okay, I mean, first I think we'd be able to fix the computers, because why couldn't we, but even if somehow all that knowledge evaporated, couldn't we come up with other survival techniques?"

"I don't like the book, either," I said when I got a chance. "So let's examine it. Why is it considered a classic? Why does it appear on every 'great book' list of the century? What are its strong points? Plot, character, description?"

"Character," said Devante.

"That woman—Georgina—the way she reacts when she comes across her daughter's body—see, I started crying then. That seemed so genuine to me, like that's how I would have felt," said Nancy Ortega.

"So, descriptive writing?" I hazarded.

"No, I think Devante is right. Her character seemed so real that I believed this was what she felt. Because we'd seen her interact with her daughter just the chapter before. I mean, I hated it, but I believed it."

We managed to get through an entire hour dissecting *Break of Day,* a feat I always believe is going to be impossible. As always, we were fueled by our overwhelming dislike of the story and the style of the novel. Then the inevitable questions: What would happen to humanity if technology broke down? How long before law and order failed, how long before chaos erupted? To those who said it couldn't happen, I spoke of spectacular riots sparked by any number of events—miscarriages of justice, natural disasters, and political upheavals, both inside and outside of America.

"Yeah, but those were contained," Dave Zirster argued. "A few days, a lot of looting, but the good citizens lock their doors, and the cops arrive on the scene, or the army—"

"That's the point, heezling," scoffed one of the other students. "If communications break down, no one knows what the problems are. If the teleport systems fail, the cops and the army can't get to the problem spots anyway."

Devante's smiling face had turned sober. "And sometimes the cops and the army are the ones causing the problems."

"And sometimes you don't even need a systems breakdown to create a disaster," I said. "What about Back Bay? What about Boulder? What about South Side?"

This quieted them a moment, and they all looked thoughtful. Most of the kids at Sefton came from families of at least moderate means; while we prided ourselves on welcoming first-generation college students and those from less privileged backgrounds, I'm not sure we'd ever admitted anyone directly from the Hot Zones. These lawless communities, which could be found at the edges of almost every major city in America, were essentially war zones overrun by violence and disconnected from the civilized grid. How to eliminate the Hot Zones was the urgent question facing every major regional and national politician, but no one had ever solved the problem.

Every year, I posed the same questions to my class. Were the Hot Zones templates for the breakdown of society? Were they the beginning of a disease that would infect and destroy the society we knew today? If we could not reclaim this one fraction of the population, with all resources still functioning and at our command, how did we think we could halt the onslaught of savagery if all our systems suddenly and cataclysmically failed?

"I see you have no easy answers," I said, after everyone had sat a moment in silence. "So that's today's writing assignment. A five-page essay on what you think would happen if we had sudden catastrophic meltdown. What would we fix? What would we lose? And give it some thought—no easy answers like computer engineers come in and reprogram everything. And make it read like fiction."

Devante raised his hand. "Can I use real people as characters in the story?"

For the life of me, I couldn't stop a grin. "Sure. For all I care, you can set it in this classroom on the day the meltdown occurs. In fact, extra points if you do."

Everyone laughed a little nervously and looked around, envisioning their ordinary classmates turning into heroes and savages. I thought this might be the most fun paper I'd assigned all year.

"It might have to be longer than five pages," said Nancy Ortega.

"So be it," I said, as the bell rang to signal the end of the hour. "Essays due in two weeks."

As always in this class, the students seemed loath to leave. Almost everyone lingered a few minutes to exchange stories with the others, joke about how they were going to portray their best friends in their post-apocalyptic stories, and discuss some new music release by a group I had not even heard of. Two of the girls came up to ask me about classes they were thinking of taking next year, and Evan Stodley loitered behind them, no doubt prepared to explain why he had missed both classes last week. Out of the corner of my eye, I saw my department chair stick her head through the door, realize I was not alone, and then look over at me. I raised a hand to signal that I'd come to her office as soon as I could, and she nodded and withdrew.

It was another ten minutes before I could leave the classroom, and even then, Evan trailed behind me, still apologizing. Finally, I just gave him an extra assignment and told him if he turned it in by Monday I'd erase the absences. Maybe I should have been tougher on him, but, you know, the hell with it. Evan was a little frail, emotionally speaking, but brilliant, gifted, and sweet-tempered. Nancy had told me last week that his girlfriend had broken up with him and that he almost had not made it through the week alive. And I'm going to flunk him? I'd rather have him read *Josie's Dreams*.

I was finally free of my coterie of followers and entering Caroline Summers' office, an airy and amazingly well-appointed space. This room looked nothing like my own office, which was an untidy jumble of papers, books, and sterile nondescript furniture. Her desk was graced with a delicate lamp of twisted silver branches tipped with glowing bulbs, her stark black filing cabinet was softened with a turquoise table runner. The place was completely free of clutter.

The elegant decor matched Caroline herself, a cool, beautiful woman in her early forties. I'd always thought she would have looked perfectly in place on a modeling runway. She had halo-blond hair, always pulled back in a braid or chignon. Her pale face was absolutely perfect in shape and symmetry, and her eyes were so blue they appeared unreal. She wore cold, vibrant colors—purple, magenta, metallic teal. Even her voice had an icily gorgeous quality, like bronze cathedral chimes.

Not surprisingly, she was one of the most poised people I'd ever met. Nothing—from the scandal of the dean's affair with one of his students to the joint and bloody suicide of three English majors two years ago—had ever appeared to rock her off-balance. She dealt with everything calmly and efficiently, so I found it exceptionally easy to work with her, despite the fact that we clearly had stylistic differences.

"Hi, Caroline. Did you need me?" I asked, stepping inside.

She looked up from her monitor and smiled. The expression transformed her into a much warmer creature, though it still didn't bring her to my level of shaggy-dog friendliness. "Good afternoon, Taylor. Your class looked like it was having fun."

I laughed. "Well, I told them to write an end-of-civilization story starring their classmates, and the idea seemed to please them. I can't even hazard a guess as to what kinds of wild ideas they'll come up with, but at least they'll get a little practice throwing a few sentences together, and that can't hurt."

"I think it sounds like an excellent idea," she said, waving me to a seat. Her smile had already faded; she looked serious and stylish again. "I have an offer for you that you're free to turn down, but I think it's something you might be good at. It's a tutoring job for a sick boy who would like to get his high school equivalency diploma next fall."

I raised my eyebrows. "So he's a high school kid? I've never really taught anyone younger than a freshman."

She glanced at a printout—notes about the student, I presumed. "Actually, he's nineteen. I gather he's missed a fair amount of school over the past couple of years due to his medical condition. I was told he's doing fine on his own in math and science, but his father was looking for an English teacher. I was asked if I could recommend someone from my staff, and you're the first one I thought of."

I guess I couldn't keep the surprise from my face, because her smile came back, fainter and a bit ironic. "You have a reputation," she said, "of being able to deal well even with the students who are not particularly interested in receiving an education."

"So this kid is difficult?"

She spread her hands as if to indicate she had insufficient information. "I don't know much about him except that he's been sick for years, he's had spotty success with his schooling in the past, and his father wants him to earn a high school diploma. I didn't get many details about his personality except that he's 'inattentive' sometimes. Maybe he's got ADHD. Maybe he's disorderly. Maybe he's sullen and uncooperative because of his illness, whatever it is."

"They didn't tell you?"

She consulted her notes again. "Kyotenin degradation," she read, then looked up at me. "I don't have a clue what that is."

I shook my head. "Never heard of it. What else do you know? Who talked to you about this?"

"The boy's father came to the dean, who came to me. I admit I don't know much more. Just that his father wants him to get tutoring twice a week for the next four to six months, until he can take his high school equivalency test. He did imply that, if his son decided to attend college in the future, he might need continued tutoring past that point. He said this," she added, "because he seemed to think there might be some financial incentive to the teacher who accepted the job."

I tilted my head to one side. Her voice was carefully impersonal, but I read a little disdain in it for the father, flinging about offers of money rather than concentrating on the well-being of his son. Or maybe I was coloring her voice with my own instant disapproval.

"So how much is he offering?" I asked. "Just out of curiosity."

She read the figure from her paper. "Two thousand dollars for each two-hour session."

I sat forward in my chair, manufacturing a cough of astonishment. Let me put this in perspective. Last year, I earned $130,000 teaching at Sefton. This part-time salary would multiply into damn near half of what I made in the full year.

"Are you sure this kid isn't dreadful? Because that's a lot of money to pay for some run-of-the-mill tutoring."

"I told you. I don't know anything about him except what his father said." She watched me with those lake-blue eyes. "So are you interested?"

"Maybe. I'd have to meet the boy first. The money would be great, yeah, but it's not worth it if the kid's unteachable or violent or crazy. But otherwise—sure, I'd be glad to do it. I've got light days on Tuesdays and free days on Fridays, so it shouldn't be a problem to find the time. Where does he live, by the way? Here in Houston?"

"No, actually, he's in our part of the world," she said. Caroline was the only other teacher in Sefton's English department who commuted from the Chicago metropolitan area. "One of the wealthy northern suburbs."

"That would make sense, if his dad's throwing around that kind of money. But why come to Sefton? Why not look for someone at Northwestern?"

"I believe his father is an alumnus of Sefton and possibly even on the board of trustees. At any rate, he's been a longtime donor to the business college here."

"Really? Have I heard of him?"

"Oh, I think so," she said dryly. "We're talking about Duncan Phillips."

Now my eyes went wide and my breath evaporated from my throat. "Duncan Phillips? The defense guy? I read that he has tighter security at his house than they do at the White House."

"Possibly. I was told that our candidate would have to be willing to undergo a security review—which I think means something much more extensive than a few questions asked by an elderly house guard. Would a background check inconvenience you or your family?"

I smiled at the polite wording. "You mean, have I ever been arrested for drug-smuggling or larceny or sedition? No. Not sure I could vouch for Jason, though."

"Who?"

"My brother. No, I'm sure any of his misdemeanors would be minor ones. And I can't think my mom or dad would have any unexpected skeletons in their closets."

"So I can go ahead and tell the dean I've found a candidate? And you'll set up the interview with Duncan Phillips' people?"

"Sure. Just tell me who to call."

She flipped through the printout, frowned, and flipped through it again. "You know, I think there's another piece of this, and I left it at home. It's the gate code and the phone number and the name of the person you're supposed to ask for." She shook her head, looking irritated at herself. Me, I leave behind important papers all the time, but Caroline had probably done something so inconvenient only once or twice in her life. "It's in my briefcase on my desk at home. I know exactly where it is. Damn."

I shrugged. "No big deal. I can come in tomorrow and get it from you."

"No, they specifically asked that you get in touch by tomorrow morning. I'd text you the information but I'm not going home tonight." She looked up. "Tell you what. I'll just give you my door code, and you can get the paper from my condo."

I felt instant misgivings. I don't mind hanging out in Marika's house by myself, and any time I'm alone at Jason's, I feel perfectly free to ransack cabinets and cupboards, but Caroline was not someone with whom I felt an easy intimacy. "Oh—I don't know—" I demurred, but she was shaking her head and jotting something on a slip of paper.

"It'll be fine. I trust you to lock the door behind you and refrain from stealing my jewelry," she said, handing over the note.

I laughed when I saw the numbers written above the address. "One-one-two-four," I said. November 24. "That's my mom's birthday. I don't even need to write this down."

She smiled faintly. "Really? That's the number of years between me and my siblings. And the combination is easy to remember, so I use it for everything. I guess I shouldn't."

I shrugged. "I use the same code for everything, too. Charlotte Brontë's birthday. I figure it's not immediately obvious, and if I ever forget it, I can look it up."

"Excellent idea. Next time I need a passcode, I'll choose the first publication date for *Old Curiosity Shop*. Much more creative than family birthdates and ages."

"But, Caroline, I feel strange about going into your place—"

"I told you, it's fine. I don't mind. But come in Monday and tell me how the interview went."

"All right. Even if they decide I'm not the one they want, this ought to be a little adventure."

೭

After my second class of the day, much less fun than the first one, I headed to Houston's Bezos Terminal and then out to O'Hare. It was early afternoon, and unexpectedly sunny in Chicago—but, of course, cold. I shivered as I stepped out of the local gate in Caroline's neighborhood and hurried down the street.

Caroline lived in the gracious old suburb of Evanston, a university town that managed to have an old-world charm that superseded the boisterous energy of the college students. Its lovely tree-lined streets and attractive multistory houses anchored the residential districts, while the main commercial streets were lined with fashionable boutiques and pricey eateries that didn't make much accommodation for students on a budget. Caroline lived in a spacious red brick condo, in a building no doubt converted from apartments a century ago. My mother's birthday worked not only for the locked outer door, but for the keypad at her own threshold as well. It was dark inside, though a little light drifted in past the half-closed drapes. I glanced around.

The main room was quite large, a living room-cum-dining room decorated in the same glass, chrome, and icy colors as her office. One marble-topped sideboard in the main room seemed to feature a collection of gifts, since none of the items on it looked like things Caroline would have picked for herself: a cross-stitched dragonfly, a carved wooden horse, a small crystal globe on a gold tripod.

When I caught myself looking around a little too long, I shook my head and administered a mental scold. "The briefcase, the briefcase, the briefcase," I muttered, and headed toward the desk in the corner of the room. This held a laptop, a printer, a stack of neatly organized papers, a silver statue of some kind of Nordic goddess (not my time period), and a slim satchel of expensive leather.

Ugh. Even worse than walking unattended into someone's house was opening her purse or briefcase. I felt extremely invasive and ill-at-ease, so I just slid out the loose papers without looking inside. To my relief, the very top sheet was neatly printed with contact information for the Phillips household.

Nothing else here I needed. I stuffed the paper in my bag and retreated, locking the door behind me. I didn't know why I felt like such a guilty thief, but I was vastly relieved to be back on the street and heading to the gate. Another jump, another short walk, and I was home.

Of course, I still had to make my appointment.

I studied the notes I had received from Caroline's hand and the paper I had taken from her desk. Not much information here. I found it strange that I had been told to contact Phillips' household, not Phillips himself—but, I suppose, if you're the single wealthiest man in the state, and you meet daily with the president of this country and others, and you own manufacturing rights to the most sophisticated and deadly military planes developed in the past twenty years, you don't have much time to answer phone calls and emails yourself. Although it would seem to me that when the calls and messages concerned your son, you might find a few free minutes here and there.

I called and identified myself to the impersonal male voice on the other end of the line.

"Taylor Kendall? Very good. Be here at ten tomorrow morning. Do you have the gate code for the entry foyer?"

Gate code. Caroline had mentioned it, but my mind had sort of skimmed over it. I guess I had assumed she meant the nearest local teleport pad, but, no, Duncan Phillips had his own private teleport facility on the grounds of his own house. I reeled off the number I'd been given.

"Yes. Very good," he said again. "We will expect you in the morning. Bring some identification."

He disconnected. I was left standing with my eyes wide and my mouth open, wondering just exactly what I'd gotten myself into.

CHAPTER THREE

I SPENT ALL OF WEDNESDAY EVENING THINKING ABOUT THURSDAY morning. First, I called Marika ("Guess where I'm going tomorrow?"), then I texted Jason, leafing through my new copy of *Sociological Theory in Mid-Millennium Urban Centers* so I could send the message in code. "Been offered a new job. You're a security risk. Prepare for investigation."

Finally, I texted Domenic, Jason's best friend since childhood, to see what he knew about Kyotenin degradation. I'd tried an online search but apparently hadn't figured out how to spell it right, since I couldn't turn up any useful information. Anyway, Domenic—who is currently studying for a medical degree at the downtown campus of Northwestern—usually had an entertaining and informative perspective on any topic, so I was interested in getting his take.

About an hour later, as I was in the bathroom brushing my teeth, I heard the subtle *ding* of a reply. My EarFone transcriber recited Domenic's words in a light, unalarmed voice. "Kyotenin degradation. Gradual and fairly gruesome deterioration of the musculature system, usually starting at the lower extremities of the body and working its way higher. Most often begins with malfunction of the toes and feet, leads to failure of the leg muscles, travels upward to affect the bowels and lower organs, and eventually incapacitates the heart. Invariably fatal. No recorded cases of anyone living past the age of twenty-five. Hope you don't have it . . . nope, you're too old."

I stood there for a long time, staring at my horrified reflection in the mirror. Caroline had just said Duncan Phillips' son was sick. She hadn't mentioned that he was under a death sentence.

Did he know he was dying? How did that shape his days?

Theoretically, all of us know we're mortal, but secretly most of us don't believe it. When I was a teenager, the thought of death only crossed my mind when I tried to figure out how to stop my mother from worrying. What would it be like to be nineteen years old and have that grim reality as a constant companion?

What would I do if I knew I would be dead within the next five years?

I didn't think I would be trying to earn a high school English degree. I couldn't imagine Duncan Phillips' son would be too interested, either.

I almost wished I was not going.

In the morning, I put on a calf-length amethyst-colored dress and black suede boots instead of my usual trousers-and-sweater combination. I figured, as I was going to visit a rich man's house, I should put a little extra effort into my appearance. My most stylish coat, a short leather jacket, wasn't quite heavy enough to keep me warm as I hustled through the cool Chicago morning and stepped into my local teleport gate.

Even so, I stood there shivering for a moment before punching in the numbers for the Phillips house. Trying to nerve myself for what was awaiting me on the other side of the brief transmission. But I finally entered the code and pressed my thumb chip to the payment button, and I was on my way.

I materialized in a gatekeeper's booth at the end of a long, sweeping driveway that led to a grand mansion of red brick and dark wood. I had quick, immediate impressions of *lawn, trees,* and *fortress* before a wiry young security guard opened the booth door and motioned me out. He was an African American who looked to be about twenty-five years old and lean as a racing dog.

"Name and I.D.?" he asked, consulting a terminal.

"Taylor Kendall," I said, flashing my Sefton card.

"Who are you supposed to meet with?"

This had been in Caroline's papers. "Someone named Bram Cortez."

The guard nodded. "Get back in the booth," he said. "I'll send you up to the house."

I stepped inside the gate, shut my eyes, and opened them in another world. The interior teleport pad featured glass walls through which I could see much of the first story of the Phillips mansion. A long, open foyer unfolded for what seemed like acres of fabulously expensive carpeting and artlessly arranged occasional tables loaded up with statuary and silver. A huge, curving staircase spiraled up to some distant height; great archways admitted glimpses of larger, more elaborate rooms to my left and right. The scent of imported hyacinths permeated even through the teleport walls.

A man waited for me outside the glass door, standing so still that for a moment I almost believed he was part of the decor. Gathering my wits, I stepped outside and gave him a quick appraisal. He was tall, maybe an inch or so above six feet, with short-cropped dark hair starting to fleck with gray. He had strongly marked features wrapped in skin just a few shades darker than my own. A well-tended mustache drew attention to his stern mouth, and his dense brown eyes assessed me with a sort of inexorable politeness.

"Taylor Kendall?" he said, his voice completely dispassionate.

"Yes."

"I'm Bram Cortez." On the page, I'd read his first name as if it rhymed with *tram,* but he pronounced it *Brom,* much like the composer. "I'm director of security here. I need to ask you a few questions. Come with me."

I nodded and half-expected to be motioned back inside the teleport compartment; in this house, I would not be surprised to learn the inhabitants beamed from room to room. But, no, he turned his back and led me down the length of the foyer and into a long hall that opened off the back corner.

We eventually came to rest in a small, well-lit office that displayed absolutely no personality. Beige curtains at the window, a plain wooden desk empty of any object except a closed manila folder, a couple of straight-backed chairs, no books, no art, not even a stray coffee cup. I hoped this was one of those odd seldom-used areas that sat empty until a stranger like me appeared; I would hate to think anyone spent the majority of his day in such a depressing place.

I watched Cortez, and when he sat, I followed suit. He opened the folder and began leafing through the papers. I could not believe he had not already memorized their contents.

I studied him while he reviewed my records. My mind has an odd habit of offering up poetry at random moments, and Bram Cortez was tripping all my William Ernest Henley switches.

> Out of the night that covers me
> Black as the Pit from pole to pole
> I thank whatever gods may be
> For my unconquerable soul . . .

When he looked up, his face showed no expression, but his eyes held an unwavering intentness that made me want to squirm and manufacture confessions. "You came highly recommended by your dean and your department chair, as well as by your students, whose class evaluations were forwarded to us," he said in a level voice. "However, you realize that this is a household of strategic importance to national and international security, and that you must undergo some scrutiny before you are allowed to work here."

I nodded. "So I understood. I assume you've already checked out my nonexistent police record."

Either my words or my insouciant tone surprised him, though he instantly erased the expression. "I have. I have a few more questions."

"Go."

"Your father was a software developer and part-owner of an AI firm. To your knowledge, how much time did he spend in politically sensitive areas like China and Russia?"

"I know he went to both of them a couple of times when I was a kid, but that was at least twenty years ago."

"Did he ever discuss the details of those trips with you?"

"Not that I can remember."

"Any reason you can think of for his failure to talk about those travels?"

"Maybe they weren't very interesting. Knowing my dad, he never set foot outside of whatever hotel he stayed at."

"Did your mother accompany him on these trips? Did she mention visits to China or Russia?"

"The topics of 'China' and 'Russia' simply did not arise when I was growing up," I said in a flat, distinct voice. "Isn't there anything else you want to ask me about?"

He gave me a quick lancet look that made me feel he might be able to slice my heart out simply by desiring it, so I subsided a bit. He glanced at his notes. "Your brother Jason," he began. "He's currently enrolled in the University of Colorado at Denver and spends about ten hours a week writing for an online media service. How long has he held that job or a similar one?"

The questions went on and on, stupid questions, senseless questions, bearing no relation to my ability to teach or, as far as I could tell, hold an intelligent conversation.

"Your ex-husband, Daniel Faberly. He's a computer technician for a company that provides support to military contractors. Do you happen to know what level his security clearance is?"

"It used to be pretty low-level, but he may have earned something higher by now. I haven't asked."

"When is the last time you communicated with Daniel Faberly?"

"I don't know. Maybe a year ago."

"Phone records indicate that he called you on July 16th last year."

It was with some effort that I controlled my rising temper. "That sounds about right."

"That's hardly a year ago, Ms. Kendall."

"If I'd known the parameters of the investigation, Mr. Cortez, I might have brought my old calendar. As it is, I'm relying on memory, and I just can't remember."

"What did you and Daniel Faberly talk about on that occasion?"

"His mother had died and he wanted to tell me."

"You'd been close to his mother?"

"We got along."

"Did you attend the funeral?"

"It was in Maine."

"You teleport every day, Ms. Kendall. A trip to Maine would not have seemed out of the way if you'd wanted to put in an appearance."

I came to my feet, smiling tightly. Clearly, I had surprised him again, for he was a few seconds behind me and obviously annoyed that he had not anticipated my move.

"You know what?" I said. "I don't want the job."

"Excuse me?"

"I was told I might do some good, tutoring a dying boy, and I was willing to do it, but this is bullshit, and I'm not going to sit here and listen to it. So just show me to the nearest secure teleport gate and I'll beam out of your life forever."

I swear a faint flush spread over his face; if he hadn't been so unemotional, I'd have thought he was embarrassed. "Ms. Kendall. I'm sorry if you don't like the questions that have been asked, but this is a high-risk establishment—"

"Yeah, whatever. What exactly do you want to know? I've never been arrested for anything, I don't know a single national security secret, and if by some chance I was able to stumble upon poorly guarded military plans hidden somewhere in this goddamn mausoleum, I first wouldn't recognize them and second wouldn't have a clue who to sell them to, either in America or outside of it. I'm a good teacher, I like kids, and the last person I intentionally hurt was my ex-husband, who deserved it. If that's not enough for you, then I'm out of here. Let's not waste any more of our time."

Jason says it's fatal to get me mad, not because anyone fears the consequences of my wrath, but because it's impossible to shut me up. In the general run of things, I'm passably articulate, but when I'm furious, the sentences come singing out as if I'm channeling the phrases of a vengeful angel.

"Ms. Kendall. Please sit down," Bram Cortez said.

I looked at his stern face and dropped back into my chair without another word.

He took his own seat and remained quiet for a moment, seeming to think something over. I watched his face, which, despite my antagonism, I rather liked. It looked like it had been a mask, a wall, an impregnable shield for most of his life; it was opaque, it let out no stray, bright thoughts or skipping laughter. Yet I did not read brutality or indifference in its hard lines. There was nothing to see except bone and dark pearlescent skin.

Finally, he looked up. "When I was told you would be coming here for an interview, and I began the background checks, I was astonished to realize you were a woman," he said at last.

This caused my eyebrows to rise almost to my hairline. "I'm astonished in turn to learn of your amazement."

"We don't hire women in this household," he said bluntly.

I stared for a moment. "There's so many things wrong with that statement I don't even know where to begin."

"Everyone who works here is male," he said, his voice wintry. "Cooks, crew, security personnel, everyone. It hadn't occurred to me that a woman would be offered as a candidate."

He didn't explain *why* Duncan Phillips would only hire men, and I figured the reason would only make me mad, so I didn't ask. In any case, it didn't matter since I obviously wasn't going to get the job. "If I'm not a viable option, why am I even here?"

"Because your name was put forward by the dean at Sefton, and Duncan Phillips made it clear that the Sefton candidate would be his first choice unless that person turned out to be a security risk."

"Thus the interrogation."

"Yes, although two other candidates have also been recommended—both of them men—and they are being thoroughly vetted as well."

I took a deep breath and blew it out in this unattractive horsey manner that I immediately wished I could recall. "Well, I'm sure you've found something to disqualify me by now, so let's just wrap this up—"

"No."

"No what?"

"No, I haven't found anything. I'm guessing your brother is something of a hellion, but that's not really a crime. You remain Duncan Phillips' first choice, and I have no legitimate reason to eliminate you. I will share that conclusion with him when I meet with him later tonight."

I met his eyes, unable to keep the hostility out of my own. "And if he decides to offer me the job, do you think I'll really take it? After all this?"

"I don't know," he said. "But before you turn it down, I'd like to ask you two things."

I could hardly imagine what. "Sure."

"Would you be willing to meet Quentin? Duncan Phillips' son?"

By this point, I was pretty certain I'd never want to cross the threshold of this house again, but I was consumed with curiosity, so I said, "All right. What's the second thing?"

He looked directly at me and this time the scalpel-sharp eyes seemed dull with a passing pain. "How did you know he was dying?"

I took a quick sip of breath. I barely remembered making the comment while I was ranting in full spate. "My supervisor told me the name of his disease and I asked someone about it. Does he know?"

Cortez's face turned even more impassive. "His father doesn't discuss it with him, but he knows. I'm not sure that he lets himself think about it."

I don't know why I asked it. "Is he close to his father?"

I don't know why he answered. "No."

The word hung in the air between us for five or ten seconds. "What happened to his mother?"

"Died when Quentin was a boy."

The lack of detail instantly made me surmise the worst—suicide, accidental drug overdose, mysterious circumstances. "Does he have other family members?"

"An aunt. His mother's sister. Her son is about Quentin's age, and they're friends. But they moved to Australia a couple of years ago, and he's hardly seen them since."

His voice was cool and impersonal, but I thought, *He likes this kid.* Isn't that funny? I would have gone to court and sworn it that very minute. "Does he enjoy school? Will he want me—or anyone—coming in to tutor him?"

He shrugged. "I don't know that he enjoys school all that much. He likes having people around." His eyes rested on me for a moment, assessing, calculating. "He'd really like you."

Based on which particular set of my responses did Bram Cortez make that assumption? "Well, let's go see him," I said.

∽

I fell in love with Quentin Phillips at first sight.

Bram Cortez and I traversed football fields of well-decorated hallways on two different levels to come to the handsome wood door that guarded Quentin's room. Cortez's knock was followed by the invitation to enter, but I spent very little time looking around the room. All I could see was the frail, smiling boy sitting in his wheelchair, his silhouette backlit against the sunlight pouring in through triple windows.

"Bram! I've checkmated you. You weren't paying attention."

"There's no way you've checkmated me," Cortez retorted.

The chair skimmed closer with a smooth motorized hum, and Quentin came into clearer focus. His face was an aesthete's, bony and lean; his arms and legs, all the parts of his body I could see, were painfully thin. He wore a T-shirt and sweatpants that seemed far too big, either chosen to disguise his skeletal frame or purchased at some earlier date when they were a better fit. His smile blazed out from his face in a way that stopped my heart. I almost could not keep from reaching out to pat the tangled honey-brown curls.

"I did, though! I did!" Quentin insisted. "Let me show you. I—"

"Hold on a minute, buddy, let me introduce you to someone," Cortez interrupted.

Quentin swung his chair tentatively in my direction and gave me a sideways look. I realized he been watching me from the second I walked in, he just hadn't known what to make of me. "Hi," he said.

I waved at his T-shirt, sporting the dates of an ancient Fat Hippos concert tour. "No way you bought that shirt for yourself," I said with mock seriousness. "You weren't even alive during their reunion tour."

He laughed. "No, I stole it from Dennis."

"You stole it from Dennis?" Cortez exclaimed. "He doesn't know you have it?"

Quentin looked both guilty and extremely pleased with himself. "No."

"He'll drown you," Cortez said with conviction.

Quentin laughed again. "No, he won't. He'll make me give it back, maybe."

"He'll make you give it back for *sure*, and then he'll drown you."

"Do you even know who the Fat Hippos are?" I demanded.

"Sure, I have all their XCDs," he said. "Wanna hear one? Which one do you like best?"

"'Back at Firestone,'" I said. "But I hate whatever that song is on track six. You know—about the gooey girl."

I could tell by Cortez's quick look that he hadn't thought I'd be able to name an album title, let alone a deep cut. "How do you know the Fat Hippos?" the security chief asked in a polite voice. "You seem like a well-brought-up young woman."

I grinned. "My brother the hellion."

"Bram won't let me play the Fat Hippos or any of those guys when he's up here," Quentin offered. "He hates monster rock, but I think it's strat. You know, it gives me a rush."

I nodded. "I have to be in the mood for it. Usually when I'm cleaning house. Then I crank it up."

Quentin crowed with laughter, then glanced over at Cortez, the mischief and the questions chasing each other across his face.

Cortez hastily explained. "Ms. Kendall, this young man is Quentin Phillips. Quin, this is Taylor Kendall. She's interviewing for a chance to be your English teacher."

Now Quentin's mouth fell open. I interpreted the look as one of shocked delight. "Really? She might come here to teach me? But that would be so jazz!"

"She might not be so much fun once you get past questions of musical preferences," Cortez said drily.

I laughed and held out my hand. "Nonsense, I'm even more fun when I start talking about novel structure and iambic pentameter. Quentin, I'm glad to meet you."

He stretched out his hand enthusiastically, and my fingers closed on a collection of bones. His skin was hot and dry, and his grip was weak. I wanted to cry right there.

"Do you play chess?" he asked.

"Not very well. Even if you can't beat Bram Cortez, I bet you're better than I am."

"Maybe we can play a game sometime," he said. "When do you start?"

"I haven't been hired yet," I said.

The boy looked over at Cortez. "Don't I get a say in this?" he asked. "I'm the one who has to spend time with her."

"It's up to your dad," Cortez said.

Quentin looked instantly disappointed, which gave me some kind of idea about how much his father consulted his wishes. "Well, it's been very nice meeting you," he said to me earnestly. "And I hope I get a chance to see you again."

Cortez took a step closer and cuffed the boy, so gently, on the shoulder. "I'll come back before I leave tonight," he said. "Then I'll be looking at that chessboard."

Quentin smiled again. "Just you wait," he said.

~

In a few minutes, we were back in the interminable hallway and making our long journey toward the front entrance. "If I'm ever invited back here, I'm bringing food supplies in case I get lost," I said.

Cortez smiled. "It's not complicated, it's just big. You'd find your way around pretty quickly."

We traveled a moment in silence, then I said, "So what are the chances that Duncan Phillips would hire me?"

"Good, I think. As I said, he's favoring the Sefton candidate, and I haven't found a reason to disqualify you."

"I know you've been trying."

He glanced down at me just in time to catch my grin, and I thought he almost smiled back. "And Quin obviously liked you," he said. "Though Quin likes everyone who's kind to him, so that's not much of a recommendation."

"Gee, thanks."

"Would you take the job if it was offered?"

I took a few steps without answering. "After my interview with you," I said slowly, "probably not. But having met him—absolutely."

"Yeah," he said. "That's Quin."

We didn't say anything more until we arrived at the teleport gate, which Cortez actually opened for me, as if it were a real door and we were back in a different century. When I had materialized in the booth a couple of hours earlier, I hadn't noticed the keypad, set like an expensive wall decoration into a rosewood square. But now I not only saw the keypad, I realized it didn't include a payment button. So either all visitors to the Phillips mansion were assumed to have transit passes in their thumb chips, or the household itself bore the travel expenses of its guests. Maybe both.

"If I'm hired," I asked, "do I get to jump straight to the house, or do I have to go through the guard gate every time?"

"Straight here," he said. "You'll get your own code. And then, if you're ever dismissed or become a security risk for any reason, we just delete the acceptance from the terminal, so you can't beam back. Easier than changing the facility's code and giving out the new number to everyone who's still using it."

"The rich are different," I said.

"Not the rich," he said. "The paranoid."

I raised my eyebrows. Again, he gave that rare smile that rendered him almost human.

"I didn't say that," he added.

"Okay. So who will let me know if I'm hired?"

"I'll call you one way or the other. If you take the job, when would you be available?"

"Tuesday afternoons and Friday any time."

"You'd be free starting next week?"

"Yes."

"Good. I'll hope to see you then."

I couldn't think of anything else to say, so I just nodded and shut the door. He stood there and watched me as I keyed in my gate number, and in a matter of seconds, he disappeared from view.

I was back in my neighborhood and wondering if my life had just changed, and in how many ways.

CHAPTER FOUR

THE ONLY REAL SOCIAL ENGAGEMENT I HAD FOR THE WEEKEND WAS going to a play with Jason, Domenic, and Marika on Saturday night. It was a community theater production of "Rent" somewhere in Evanston, and some girl Domenic wanted to date had a small role, so he'd told her he would come and bring a few friends. I did not have high hopes for the quality of the production, and it had taken some persuading to convince Marika to come up from Atlanta to so she could attend, but I was still looking forward to an evening of great amusement.

Marika and Domenic and Jason and I have been our own little group since we were teenagers. Any time we're together, we start feeding off each other until a sort of manic energy builds and pretty much anything can happen. Less often, now that we're older and more sober, but the potential is still there.

We had made plans for everyone to gather at my apartment—where, Jason had informed me, a meal had better be ready. So I made a spicy chicken dish, threw together a spinach salad, and set a few trays of chocolate chip cookies in the hotbox. I'm not a particularly inventive cook, but I can put a simple meal together and be pretty sure it's edible.

Marika was the first to arrive, staggering through the door on the highest heels I had ever seen on any human being. The clunky black shoes were rimmed with winking rhinestones, a motif that was continued in a spiral pattern up her opaque black stockings. She wore a short black miniskirt and a tight-fitting lace blouse, all covered up, when she first walked in, by a long leather coat that reached to her ankles.

"How can it be this cold anywhere on the planet at this time of year?" she demanded, heading straight toward the decorative mirror hung on my living room wall. The mirror, a gift from Marika, had a silkscreened pattern of butterflies across it, which made it impossible to get an uninterrupted inspection of your face. However, it was good enough for Marika to peer into as she reapplied her wine-colored lipstick and fluffed up her hair.

It did not need fluffing. Her hair is this wild explosion of light brown curls that tumble to the small of her back and give her pale, narrow face an expression of perpetual surprise. People go wild for her hair. Strangers stop her on the street and ask who does her perms. I've seen small children reach out to stroke it from their vantage points in shopping carts or on their fathers' shoulders.

"It's cold in Chicago until July third, and then we have about eight days of summer, and it gets cold again," I said. "You know that, you grew up here."

"Yes, but I didn't choose to stay here for the rest of my natural life. God, there was such a creep at Olympic Terminal. I swear I thought he was going to follow me to Chicago. But I remembered the code for the downtown police station, and I was going to punch that in if I saw him anywhere near me at O'Hare."

"How do you know the code for the Chicago PD?"

She shrugged. In typical Marika fashion, she was moving restlessly around the apartment, picking up books, touching the lamp, adjusting pictures on the wall, glancing out the window. I don't think she is completely still even when she's sleeping. "Oh, that time Domenic and Jason got arrested for, what was it, disturbing the peace."

"That narrows it down a lot."

"When they were serenading that girl out in her front yard. You were gone, so they called me. I thought it might be handy to know the code, so I committed it to memory. Eight-six-four-four-seven."

Jason walked in without knocking. "Smells good. Hi, Mareek."

She clumped over on her awkward heels to give him a hug. Normally she's about an inch shorter than Jason, but the shoes made her tower over him. Didn't seem to bother either of them. "So who's this girl we're supposed to be impressing?" she asked. "Is this serious?"

Jason made a rude noise deep in his throat and waved a dismissive hand. "When is Domenic ever serious? I'm not sure he even knows her last name."

"Hey, Jason," I said, "what's the gate code for the Chicago police?"

"Eight-six-four-four-seven," he said promptly. He didn't ask why. "When are we going to eat? I'm starving."

"As soon as Domenic gets here. You can open the wine if you want."

He had just poured three glasses when Domenic strolled in. He, too, was dressed all in black, with a long trench coat that floated behind him like a superhero's cape, but it was hardly the most striking thing about him. He's tall and reedy, with long flowing black hair that frames an absolute angel's face and luscious rum-and-coffee-colored skin that reflects his mixed Irish, Japanese, and African heritage. His dark mystic's beauty always makes me think of some enigmatic stranger arrived in the night to avenge a terrible wrong.

"Who dresses you people?" Jason asked from across the room. Marika and Domenic put their arms around each other and posed briefly. Even when she was wearing such outrageous heels, the top of Marika's head just reached the level of Domenic's.

"At least we don't get our fashions off of lakerboy-dot-com," Domenic said in his intense melodic voice that gives even his most casual utterance an almost hypnotic force.

As always, Jason was wearing well-cut and well-pressed cotton pants and a white shirt. "At least I look like an ordinary human being," he retorted. "You two look like the bad guys in an old Western."

"Who cares?" Marika said. "I'm hungry. Let's eat."

The meal, of course, was fairly raucous, with four determined voices competitively raised in jokes, anecdotes and insults.

"So who's this girl we're going to meet, Domenic?" I asked.

"You're not going to meet her," he said. "Once the play is over, you will talk amongst yourselves while I make a brief visit backstage without you."

Marika said, "Why do you even want us to go with you if you're embarrassed to be seen with us in public?"

My brother toasted her with his wineglass. It, too, featured a butterfly motif, since it, too, was a gift from Marika. In a high school Spanish class, she had learned that the closest approximation to her name was *mariposa*, which translated to *butterfly*, and butterflies had been her personal emblem ever since. "How could someone dressed as you are embarrass anyone?" Jason said.

"You should be grateful to have a friend so fashionable."

I changed the subject. "Hey, Domenic," I said, "what's the gate code for the downtown police department?"

"Eight-six-four-four-seven."

"And a good thing you know it," Jason said, "since I think we're all about to be hauled down there."

"For which of our crimes?" Domenic asked.

Jason nodded at me. "Ask her."

"Oh yeah. The security check," I said. "Did anyone get in touch with you?"

"Not me," Jason said. "Called my boss and my faculty advisor. And apparently had done a pretty thorough search on me before they even made the calls. I realize privacy is an arcane concept, but I admit I was a little disturbed to find out how quickly Duncan Phillips can get access to my life when he wants."

"Duncan Phillips?" Domenic repeated. "Why is he interested in you?"

"I might be taking a job tutoring his son," I said. "But apparently there are all these high-risk hoops to jump through. So I knew he'd be checking out my friends and my family—sorry about that. And apparently he never hires women, so I don't know if I have a real shot at the job."

"Never hires women," Marika exclaimed, instantly fired up. "Okay, I've got a friend who's a lawyer, we're skipping the theater and heading right back to Atlanta—"

Domenic was staring at me. "His son," he said. "Is he the one with Kyo-tenin degradation?"

I nodded. The other two grew quickly quiet, sensing something serious in the air. "He's nineteen," I said, knowing Domenic would understand the time limit that implied. "I almost hope I don't get the job, you know? I'll get too attached to him."

"You get attached to all your students," Marika said. "So what?"

"He'll probably be dead in five years," Domenic said. "Less."

"Well, that's shitty," said Jason.

Domenic shrugged—not a gesture of indifference, I thought, but help-lessness. "We can cure some kinds of cancer. We can wipe out polio and bubonic plague and leprosy. And our bodies find new ways to turn against us. There will always be new diseases that prey on humankind. That's the way it works."

"I never heard of it before," Marika said.

"It's pretty rare, which is about the only good thing about it. It's resis-tant to every vaccine and antibiotic ever developed and hasn't responded to a single treatment they've tried. A few years ago, they thought muscle and organ donation from a healthy subject would slow it down or even stop it, but then it turned out the disease infected the new tissue, so they stopped the transplants. It's pretty gruesome."

"Well, I'm depressed," Jason said.

"I don't think you should take this job," Marika said.

"I will if they offer it to me."

"If you do, you can snoop around his mansion and sell information to all the gossip sites," she said. Celebrity watching was one of her passions; she could give me the romantic and financial scoop on any actor, model, or billionaire anywhere on the planet. "No one can ever find out much about his private life—like, no one ever knows who he's dating until the romance is over—so you could make a fortune if you could get a photo of him with a new girlfriend."

"This is just fascinating," Domenic said.

"What happened to his wife?" I asked. "Quentin's mother?"

"Well. That was very strange," Marika said. "She was only about thirty when she died—in her sleep, they said, of a heart valve malfunction. I read a couple of accounts that said she drank herself to death or overdosed on sleep-ing pills. A lot of people think she killed herself because she couldn't stand living with him, but she didn't want to divorce him because of the pre-nup."

"Can we talk about something else?" Jason demanded.

Domenic ostentatiously checked his watch. "No time. We're almost late as it is."

We were all simultaneously on our feet. None of them so much as glanced at the table where the dirty dishes sat in sticky splendor. "On our way," Jason said.

⁓

The musical was not quite as bad as I'd feared but worse than I'd hoped, and Domenic's new crush was a mediocre singer at best. About every third line, Marika would lean over to me and whisper, "What did he say? What did she say? I didn't catch it," while Jason was consumed with giggles induced by one poor girl's completely inaudible delivery.

Domenic sat, serenely enthralled, appearing to watch every scene with beatific attention, but I was suspicious. My guess was that he was wearing a pair of VR contact lenses and was streaming some kind of media through his EarFone instead of watching the performance.

When the last number had finally been performed, we joined the rest of the audience in a polite standing ovation. "Well, *that's* over," Marika said in relief.

"Let's get something to eat," Jason suggested.

"We ate barely two hours ago," I pointed out.

"I'm hungry again," he said.

"We have to wait till Domenic's made his impression on the girlfriend," Marika said scornfully.

"I meant, after that."

"Give me a minute," Domenic said, and strolled away from us to talk to the actress. She was pretty, in an insipid blonde way; it never failed to amaze me how someone as exotic as Domenic could be drawn to such ordinary women. Then again, perhaps that's why all his relationships failed. Then again, if you were as exotic as Domenic, perhaps all your relationships would fail, anyway.

"I could go for some dessert," Marika said.

"I was thinking pizza," Jason said.

"Pizza!" I exclaimed. "You just *ate!*"

"Okay, someplace with pizza and dessert," Marika said, turning toward the door. "Rush Street? Or stay in the 'burbs?"

"Let's go downtown," Jason said. He was grinning as he watched Domenic charm an attractive smile from the blonde girl. "Be there in a sec."

"What?" said Marika, but Jason had already left us to stride over toward Domenic and the actress. I could see that his sunny face had assumed an expression of pained fury.

"Oh! I see! That's why you wanted to *come to the theater*," Jason exclaimed in a voice loud enough to carry to the back balcony. "I suppose you don't think it doesn't *count* if it's a woman. I suppose you think it won't *matter* to me."

The blonde girl looked over in alarm, but Domenic never even glanced in Jason's direction.

"Oh dear God," Marika murmured.

I grabbed her arm. "Let's get out of here." I pulled her toward the door, through the press of audience members who were craning their necks to get a better glimpse of the drama unfolding off the stage. We could still hear Jason ranting about *cheating* and *heartbreak* as we slipped out into the cold Chicago night.

"I don't know why those two are even still on speaking terms," Marika observed, drawing her long coat more tightly around her body.

I couldn't help it. I was laughing. "Ready to leave them behind any time you are," I said cheerfully.

She shook her head. She didn't seem to think it was as funny as I did. "No, I hardly ever get to see them anymore. I miss them. Maybe they'll behave a little more normally at the restaurant."

I stared. "Domenic and Jason? I don't think so."

She shrugged, a half-smile on her face. "Well, okay. So I'll put up with it anyway."

She seemed a little pensive, a rare mood for the headlong and oblivious Marika. "So, anything going on? You talk to Christopher again?" Christopher was her recent very dull boyfriend whom she'd dumped about a month ago, though he'd called her every day to beg her to take him back. You'd think one of the four of us could stay in a stable relationship for longer than a few weeks. Well, okay, I'd been married to Danny for four years, but I didn't count that as a success, and the other three considered it such a lapse of judgment that they put me in the negative column when we were totaling up our days of romantic happiness.

She made a dismissive motion. "Ugh. Christopher. I don't know why I put up with him even as long as I did."

I enumerated the reasons. "Nice—kind of cute—didn't call you whore-slut every other day." This last was a reference to Axel, the boyfriend before Christopher, who had been darkly handsome and a complete and total asshole.

"I suppose. Nothing like variety."

"Well, you haven't heard from Axel, have you?"

"Yeah, actually, he called last week, thought we should go to dinner sometime."

"You didn't agree, did you?"

She shrugged. "No, but—you know—at least I felt something for him. Felt nothing for Chris. I mean, are those the choices? Nice boring guys you can't stand to be around, or jerks who make you feel alive?"

We'd had this conversation before. About six million times, I would guess. I was spared the necessity of answering when Jason and Domenic burst out the door together, laughing and arguing simultaneously. I smiled at her and shrugged.

"Maybe," I said. "Solve it some other time. C'mon, let's go find some chocolate."

I didn't get home until about two in the morning. I offered to let Marika stay over, since she didn't like teleporting alone late at night, but Jason said he'd escort her home. I figured it was unlikely he would abandon her at the teleport gate, as he would me, so I felt reasonably secure putting her in his hands. Domenic, who probably needed more watching than any of us, went on his way alone.

I'd already brushed my teeth and gotten ready for bed when I thought to retrieve my messages. Unlike Marika, who rarely turns off her EarFone because she can't bear to be out of the information loop even for thirty seconds, I'm notorious for shutting the system down for hours and then forgetting to check for notifications. Turned out that I'd missed two calls while I was out. Naturally, the first one was from my mother, wanting to know if I was alive or dead. The second one was from Bram Cortez.

"Duncan Phillips has decided that you would be the best candidate to tutor Quentin. Please report back to his house on Tuesday afternoon at three. If that time is inconvenient for you, let me know. Come to the public gate on Tuesday, and we'll set you up with a code for the rest of your period of employment." There was a moment's pause; I would have thought he'd hung up, but the line still sounded live. "Quentin is looking forward to seeing you again," he said, and then disconnected.

CHAPTER FIVE

I ARRIVED AT THE GUARD'S GATE AT THE PHILLIPS MANSION AT FIVE minutes before three and was whisked inside the grand house precisely on the hour. This time I was met by a small, dapper man who sounded like the person I had talked to the first time I called the house. He seemed completely unremarkable. His thinning gray hair was combed back severely from his austere face, which featured a prominent nose and rather colorless skin. He looked to be about sixty, though his expensive and timeless suit didn't give me any clues about his actual age.

"Ms. Kendall?" he asked as I stepped out of the booth.

"Yes. Taylor Kendall."

"I'm Francis Melroon, the house steward. If you need anything at all—refreshments, equipment, materials, room maintenance—please call for me."

"How do I do that?"

"There's an intercom system. Quentin can show you the receiver in his room." We took a few steps into the hallway, and he pointed to a small, unobtrusive box set into the wall. It appeared to be made of gray plastic and was lined with a series of black buttons. "This one is keyed to my EarFone. This one alerts the gate guard. This one alerts house security. This one alerts the kitchen. One of us should be able to help you with anything you need."

If I'd had to guess, I'd have said I could alert Bram Cortez more quickly by standing in the center of the room and screaming, since he seemed like the sort of person who would react instantly to the smallest hint of commotion. But I did not say so.

"Thank you," I said. "Mr. Cortez mentioned that I would get my own door code at some point? Who would I talk to about that?"

"That's security. I imagine Bram will speak to you about it today or Friday. Now let me take you to Quentin."

He led me down the long hallway to an elevator elegant enough to be situated in a five-star hotel, and we rode up to the third floor. Down another hall, passing numerous doors, which I tried to count so I could memorize the path for future reference. Though would they ever just let me roam here of my own free will? How did that work, anyway? At what point did a newcomer turn into trusted visitor or valued friend? I didn't figure I'd be around long enough to find out.

We walked into Quentin's sunny room to find the even sunnier boy awaiting us. "Hey, Francis, is she here?" I heard him demand the split second before he saw me. "Ms. Kendall!" he exclaimed. "Good to see you again!" He held out his hand—less for politeness' sake, I judged, than for the chance at human contact. I shook it with some enthusiasm.

"Call me Taylor," I said. "I'm going to call you Quentin."

"I'll leave you to your lessons," Francis said and withdrew.

I scarcely even heard the click of the door shutting as Quentin began pelting me with questions. "Were you in Houston today? Bram says you teleport all over. Was it hot there? Do you like Houston better than you like Chicago? Hey, where else have you been? I traveled a lot when I was a baby, but I don't really remember it. I've mostly been in Chicago ever since . . . Do you know what? I really did checkmate Bram the other day. I can show you the board. I haven't changed it since. You want to see?"

I laughed and held up both hands. "Whoa! Slow down. I'll answer anything you want, but you've got to ask one question at a time."

He grinned sheepishly and his nervous hands made the wheelchair swivel back and forth.

"Sorry. Dennis says I never shut up, but I do, and anyway, it's hard to talk when you're swimming."

I vaguely remembered that name from my previous visit. "Who's Dennis? The one who was going to drown you, right?"

He nodded. "He wouldn't really drown me. He's my physical therapist. He comes in most days and helps me exercise. Usually we swim, because it's really good exercise but it doesn't hurt so much."

Hurt so much? "I don't know much about your disease," I said. "So you'll have to speak up if it makes you tired or cranky or—or anything." *If it makes you grow sicker and weaker and eventually die.* No, I couldn't face that conversation yet. "So if—if your joints hurt and it's hard for you to concentrate sometimes, you'll have to let me know that."

"It's not my joints, it's my muscles, and really, there's not much pain," he said, as if eager to reassure me. "I just don't walk very well right now, is all."

"Can you walk a little bit? Or do you always stay in your chair?"

"Well, mostly I stay in my chair because it's easier," he said, wrinkling his nose. "Dennis says I should walk more because it would be good for me, but I don't always listen to Dennis. And the Kevvi braces take so long to put on that I only do it when I have a really good reason."

"The Kevvi braces?"

He nodded. "Yeah, they're kind of strat. I strap them on under my clothes and then attach a little clip to my head—if I wear a hat, no one can even see it—and the clip picks up my brain impulses and my leg muscle impulses, and the braces help me walk. The motion's a little jerky, and I'm a little afraid I might fall down, so I don't go out by myself when I have them on. But Bram or Dennis or Francis will take me out once in a while, and it's kind of fun."

"Maybe you and I could do that sometime," I said.

"Okay! Today?"

I laughed. "No, not today. Today I think you and I need to get to know each other."

"Sure. What do you want to know?"

I glanced around the room. It was actually the outer room of a suite, at least so I surmised; a closed door led to what I guessed was the bedroom and bathroom. This space was set up more for interaction. In addition to a comfortable-looking couch, there was a table piled with electronic toys and players, a formal desk, and a couple of padded chairs. And of course the wide, deep windows, admitting copious amounts of sunlight and giving onto a view of lawn, tree and gardens.

"What I want to know," I said, moving toward the desk while he followed, "is exactly how much you know. I have a few quick tests here that will help me figure out your reading level and so on, and then we can go from there."

His eyebrows drew down in a disappointed frown. Had he been younger, he would have pouted. Actually, it seemed to me he skewed much younger than nineteen. There was so much boyishness to him, so much artlessness. The nineteen- and twenty-year-olds I was used to dealing with were tougher, more assured, more laconic, more wary. I had to assume Quentin had spent much of his later life in semi-isolation, segregated from peers. He was surrounded by and cared for by adults, and while that could make a child develop quickly, it could keep a teenager from maturing as he should. At least, that was my guess.

"I don't want to fill out tests," he said. "Not right now. I want to talk. I'll fill out the tests after you're gone."

In every class I've taught, I've learned that there will be a contest of wills between me and at least some of my students. They may be the best, most dedicated kids in the class, but at some point they're going to want to do something their own way, and it won't be the right way. I've also learned that I have to establish control early, let the students know that I'm flexible, but only to a degree, and that, in fact, there is an adult who's in charge.

And then there are times to let them win.

"Compromise," I said. "Do the short ones while I'm here, do the longer ones when I'm gone."

"But—"

I lifted a finger. "I'm going to be here a lot, Quentin. You'll have plenty of time to talk to me. But I'm really here to help you learn. And I can't do that if you don't follow my instructions."

His face looked mutinous. "What kind of tests?"

I seated myself in one of the padded chairs and opened my briefcase. I had been shocked to learn that teachers who work at the online-only colleges sometimes don't even own briefcases. Most often, I have my students take tests and turn in reports electronically, but I always administer a few pop quizzes on paper. It makes people think differently. And when they erase words or cross out sentences, I get a clearer idea of how their minds work. I wanted to know how Quentin's mind worked.

"Vocabulary. Spelling. Grammar. The grammar test is a little tricky, and I'm also going to ask you to write an essay, so you can do those after I'm gone. But I'd like you to do the vocabulary and spelling tests while I wait."

He had reluctantly wheeled up beside me, his chair just fitting under a specially designed segment of the desk. No more protests, though; I could see this was someone not accustomed to getting his own way often enough that it would occur to him to throw a sustained tantrum. "And then we can talk?" he asked.

I laughed. "We'll talk about schoolwork, but we'll talk."

He took the papers and glanced at the columns of words marching across the pages. "What will you do while I'm taking the tests?"

I pulled out my tablet. "I'm going to catch up on my favorite magazine. Don't you worry about me."

"Are you going to time me?"

"Nope. But I am going to ask that you concentrate, and once you start, you only talk to me when you have a genuine question to ask."

"When do I start?"

"How about now?"

He nodded glumly and bent over the first page. I flicked on my screen, but I didn't actually read. Covertly, I watched Quentin studying the spelling words and choosing his answers. He didn't waste much time, which meant he was either a fairly good natural speller or he wasn't being as careful as I would wish. I'd know when I saw his answers. The vocabulary test took him a little more time. It offered multiple-choice responses, but some of the words were hard. As far as I was concerned, what this exam measured most was how much someone had read, because books were where words could be found—never open a book, never learn a new word in your life.

"All done?" I asked when he put the papers aside with a happy sigh.

"Yes. So what do you want to talk about?" he demanded.

I laughed. "Give me a minute. Let me look at your answers."

The results were mixed. He'd gotten every single word definition right, but missed a dozen or so spellings. "I'm guessing you listen to a lot of audiobooks," I said.

He nodded. "I like to read, but the e-readers hurt my eyes and the realbooks are too heavy for me to hold. I like to lie in bed when my—when I'm really tired, and listen."

I wondered if he'd been about to say *when my legs are hurting*, but this was a boy determined not to complain. "Does anybody ever read aloud to you?" I asked.

"My mom used to. When I was little. Sometimes Francis does." I put some high marks down on my mental scorecard next to Francis' name. "But I'll listen to the audiobooks whenever I feel like it, even in the middle of the night."

"What do you like to listen to?"

His eyes kindled. "Do you know Tom O'Leary?" I nodded. He was a prolific writer who churned out action/adventure books set everywhere from Alaska to Antarctica to outer space. "Oh, man, I love his books. And Dirk Cunningham. And do you know Ardel Hawke? I've read all of his." He paused, perhaps assessing the quality of my smile. "What? I guess you think those aren't very good books."

"On the contrary," I said. "I'm glad to hear you so enthusiastic. Some people don't enjoy any books at all. Just think what they're missing."

"I know they're not classics," he said defensively. "But they're fun."

"Reading should be fun," I said, stretching my legs out to find a more comfortable position. "Sometimes it's serious and should remind us of the frailties or heroics of the human condition, but most of the time it should be fun. When you're nineteen, anyway."

"My last teacher made me read *Break of Day*," he said. "I didn't think that was fun at all."

"Well, it's a dreadful book," I said.

He laughed. "What do you like to read?"

"Pretty much everything. Depends on my mood. Probably my favorite stuff is 19th-century literature, because I like all the detail of thought and emotion. Everything examined so closely, even the most casual expression or turn of the hand. In the 20th century, I guess my favorites are Fitzgerald and Thomas Wolfe. In the past forty years—oh, I'd have to say I like Deb Holland and Carrolton Grant." I grinned. "That is, when I'm in a literary mood. But I also like mysteries and romances, and I've probably read something by half the science fiction writers publishing today."

"You like science fiction?"

"Yeah, and I watch Vampire Nightly Network and sitcom reruns and those sappy movies about mothers reunited with their lost children," I said. "Love that kind of stuff."

"But you're a lit professor," he said.

I nodded. "Storytelling is storytelling. It might be well-done or badly done, but the purpose is the same. To keep you engaged, to introduce you to people you'll never meet, and take you places you might never go. It all has form and conflict and build-up and climax. You know, when those cave-dweller ancestors were sitting around the fire describing how Hunter Shooga killed the buffalo and saved the life of Hunter Goeba, those were stories. They were meant to terrify and inspire and entertain. They were meant to stress the value of courage and strength and creative thinking. Even the schmaltziest TV movie does the same thing. Reinforces cultural values while keeping you enthralled. I guess I don't see much difference."

"Wow," he said. "That's great. So I'm not going to have to read *Break of Day* again?"

"Wish I never had to," I grumbled. "But *you* sure won't. At least, not as long as I'm your teacher. You say you like Ardel Hawke? He writes Westerns, doesn't he?"

Quentin nodded. "They're great."

"Maybe I'll start you with some of the classic Westerns, then. You ever read *Shane? Lonesome Dove?*" He shook his head. "Anything by Ernest Hay-cox? *The Earthbreakers*, that's his masterpiece."

"None of my teachers ever gave me Westerns before."

I laughed. "Pretty much my goal is going to be to keep you reading, no matter what the books are. I mean, we aren't going to just read Westerns, but that'll be a start."

"My last teacher wanted me to study Shakespeare," he said with disgust. "And the sonnets."

I grinned. "Well, we're going to do poetry too. You might find you like it."

"I hate it."

"What's your favorite song?" I asked.

"Carolina Blue's 'Lady oh Lady,'" he said without hesitation.

"It's a poem," I said.

"It is not," he exclaimed. "They sing it!"

"'Morning came, I was dreaming like a child,'" I began quoting. "'Thought I'd wake up to your smiling face . . . Sunshine fell on me, so sweetly and so mild . . . Thought I was still inside that magic place . . .'"

"How do you know that song?" he said.

I smiled. "You know any of the feenday bands?" I asked. *Feenday rock* was the term someone had coined for the music being played at the turn of the century, the fin de siècle. I guess to distinguish it from so-called "classic rock" of an earlier era. Well, hell, every decade has had a label or two for the music it's created—from heavy metal to swoon croon to suicide blast. I could listen to most of it, though anything too far to either end of the hard or soft scale tended to grate on my nerves.

Quentin was nodding. "Sure. Couple of the stations play nothing but feenday stuff."

"You know Bruce Springsteen? A poet. Listen to some of his words. One of my lit professors used to compare him to Byron. And Gloriana, she's one of my favorite current singers. Writes like an angel. Talk about poetry."

I could tell that he was beginning to doubt my sanity. First Westerns, now popular music. He was willing to go with it, but I could see him wondering how long they'd let me remain as his tutor. "You're kind of weird," he said.

"So true. I don't think it'll hurt you any. Now. I want you to complete two assignments while I'm gone."

"What are they again?"

I handed him a piece of paper. "This one's a grammar test. You're going to go through these sentences and mark up anywhere there's been an incorrect word choice or bad use of punctuation. Use a pencil." I handed him a second sheet. "I also want you to write a five-hundred-word essay on one of these three subjects. You choose. Turn off the grammar and spellcheck functions on your computer so I can get a more realistic idea of your skills. And *don't* use an AI program to write it."

He glanced curiously at the essay topics. "My Favorite Activity," "The Best Summer of My Life," and "Dream Monsters." He pointed to the last one. "What does this mean?"

"What do you think it means? Something you dreamed about. Something you made up. Something really scary. Something that might be scary to someone else but isn't to you. I have to admit, the guys in my class pick that topic more often than the girls do, though one of the girls wrote a very creative essay about her little sister."

"I don't really write much," he said doubtfully.

"That's okay. I just want to see how you put sentences together. If it's easier, you can dictate it first."

He looked relieved. "Maybe I'll do that."

"Pretend you're telling a story to—to someone." I almost said *to your best friend*, but frankly I wasn't sure he had any friends at all. "To Francis or Dennis or Bram Cortez."

"Or you."

"Or me. Absolutely."

Before either of us had a chance to say anything else, I heard my EarFone chime. "Hang on a sec," I said to Quentin before I answered. "Hi, it's Taylor."

It was Marika. "You'll never guess who called."

"Axel," I guessed. "Listen, Mareek—"

"Yes! How'd you know?"

"It was obvious. Listen, I'm working."

"You're off on Tuesday afternoons."

"Tutoring, remember?"

A moment's silence. "Oh, my God! You're in Duncan Phillips' house right now, aren't you? Have you gotten any photos yet?"

I couldn't help grinning. Quentin was watching me with great interest, though I knew he couldn't hear Marika's side of the conversation, discreet and a little tinny in my ear. "No to the second question, but yes to the first. In fact, right now Quentin Phillips and I are discussing poetry and literature."

"Sorry! I guess I'm interrupting."

"Who is it?" Quentin asked.

"My best friend Marika," I answered him. "She's a lot of fun."

"Fun? That's how you describe me to people?"

"Would you like to talk to her?" I asked Quentin.

He looked intrigued. "Sure."

"Wait, what?" Marika squealed. "Tay, I don't know—"

But I was already digging for the aux in my briefcase so I could cast the call to the speaker. I wasn't worried. Marika could talk to anybody. "Transfer," I directed, and the aux panel clicked to life.

"Hey," said Marika. "Can everybody hear me?"

"Hi, Marika," Quentin said happily. "I'm Quentin. It's nice to meet you!"

"Well, I'm delighted meet *you*."

"So where do you live?"

"Atlanta."

"Do you like the Braves?" he asked. "Do you go to any games? I like the Cubs, but I don't like the White Sox, and I wish they'd been sold to New Mexico last year."

"New Mexico!" she exclaimed. Quentin had unwittingly hit on one of Marika's passions. "They should have been sold to Nova Scotia. Pitching like that, they deserve to have their butts frozen off."

"But if they go, I hope they leave Nathwell behind," Quentin said.

"You'll never keep Nathwell in Chicago," Marika said scornfully. "He's too good for either of your teams. He belongs with the Yankees or the Cardinals or a team that has a chance at the pennant. We could use him here in Atlanta."

"I like the Braves," Quentin said.

"Damn straight you do. Best team in baseball, even if they don't win as often as they deserve to."

I'm not a huge baseball fan myself. Jason, Domenic, Marika—they will sit for hours and debate the merits of pitchers and sluggers who have been dead for fifty years. They watch videos of old World Series games, and they do this virtual playoff thing where teams of different decades who never met in real life are matched up on the most artificial of cyberturf. What could be more boring? Well, except for the endless conversations about it. I let my mind wander a bit, and I only segued back into the present moment when I caught my name.

"Maybe Taylor can bring it to you if I buy it," Marika was saying.

"What?" I demanded. "What am I bringing you?"

"A Braves shirt," Quentin said. "Marika said she'd get me one."

"No problem," I said. "Okay, Mareek, I'm hanging up now. I'll call you when I get home." We disconnected.

Quentin was beaming. "You're right, she is fun."

"All my friends are."

"Maybe she'll call every time you're here."

I laughed. "No, because I'm going to tell her I'm not available when I'm tutoring. Though I don't feel like we've gotten a whole lot accomplished today. You should expect a little more structure in our next few classes."

"Is it time to go already? You just got here!"

"I've been here an hour."

"But you could stay a little longer. We could play chess."

"Not today," I said firmly. "I've had a long day already. I need to get home."

I knew I was right, but his expression of resigned disappointment was almost enough to make me kick off my shoes and reset the chess board. How could someone, a teenager, *anyone,* be so desperate for companionship that he didn't even want a total stranger to leave the room? I was going to be sucked into his life, I knew it. I would come earlier, stay later, bring him gifts, let him talk to all my friends. I would allow him to climb into my heart and snuggle down.

"But you'll be back on Friday?" he asked.

"Absolutely. And when I arrive, you're going to have done three things. You will have taken the grammar test and written the essay, and you will have copied down the lyrics of one of your favorite songs. It can be 'Lady oh Lady' if you want. It has to have at least twenty-four lines, and that doesn't include any repetition of the chorus. Can you do that?"

"Sure," he said.

"And then we'll talk about poetry." I stuffed his tests into my briefcase and came to my feet. I sort of felt like I was leaving my puppy behind at the pound. "I had fun, Quentin. I'm going to like tutoring you."

"I had fun, too, Taylor," he said, using my name for the first time and liking the way it felt on his tongue, because he smiled. "See you in a few days."

Nobody was waiting for me as I exited Quentin's room, but I was not surprised, after I'd taken a few steps, to find Francis Melroon falling in step beside me, appearing from some small room down the hall.

"And how did it go today, Ms. Kendall?" he asked, leading me back the way we'd come. I was pretty sure I'd have managed if he hadn't appeared to guide me. Not positive.

"Good," I said. "He's a likable kid."

He nodded. "The most likable," he said, and not another word until he ushered me inside the teleport gate. I hit the code for home and let the Phillips mansion disintegrate behind me.

CHAPTER SIX

ON FRIDAY, I MET DENNIS.

This memorable event occurred only after an hour's worth of the chatter, laughter, reluctance, and interest that I was pretty sure would form the pattern of the rest of my sessions with Quentin. He had taken the grammar test, as requested, but had not yet completed his essay on "Dream Monsters," though he assured me he was working on it. He had, however, printed out by hand the full set of lyrics to "Cranberry Girl."

"Good," I said, scanning the lines, with which I was only vaguely familiar. The group, Ocean of Negligence, featured lugubrious synthesizer music and a whiny female vocalist and rated low on my scale of tolerance. "Before we discuss content, let's look at structure. What's the first thing you notice about this poem?"

I held it out for Quentin to glance at again. His eyes drifted over the page and then he looked back at me.

"It rhymes?" he said tentatively.

"Exactly," I said, preparing to launch into my well-rehearsed introduction to poetic form. There are hundreds, thousands, *millions* of brilliant poems that flow beautifully into conversational free verse, and I know that for many of my students, these would be more instantly accessible than the formal examples I make them learn. But I like to start with the stanzas and the sonnets, the rhythms and the rules. I like to show students the bones and building blocks of poetry before they learn how to take those skeletons apart and reassemble them into something familiar and yet altogether different.

We began with rhyme scheme, which was pretty easy in the case of "Cranberry Girl," since Ocean of Negligence stuck to an unvarying a-b-a-b configuration. "A lot of poems will have more complex patterns," I warned. "Maybe every third line will rhyme, or the last line of every stanza will rhyme with all the other last lines. It gets very complicated. The challenge for poets is to say what they want to say, in language as beautiful as they can make it, and still stay within the pattern of the rhyme."

"It's kind of jazz when you put it like that."

"It's even more jazz when you learn about rhythm and meter," I said. I began to outline the differences between forms such as iambic pentameter and anapestic trimeter, but I could see his eyes starting to glaze over, so I cut short my usual lecture.

"The point is that the poet can choose how many beats every line will have, and how many syllables will be in every beat," I said. "It makes more sense when you're looking at an actual poem. Here's a simple one by a British poet called A.E. Housman. You listen while I read—I think you'll like it."

I knew it by heart, but I looked at my book anyway.

> *Oh, when I was in love with you*
> *Then I was clean and brave.*
> *And miles around, the wonder grew*
> *How well did I behave.*
>
> *And now the fancy passes by*
> *And nothing will remain.*
> *And miles around they'll say that I*
> *Am quite myself again.*

Quentin chuckled. "That's funny."

"See? I told you you'd like it. Now, let's deconstruct it."

Quentin successfully identified the rhyme scheme (a-b-a-b) and the rhythm (iambic), but he got a little tripped up over the fact that the poet had deliberately alternated between tetrameter and trimeter lines. "How can he keep it all straight?" he demanded.

"Well, it takes work. But once you get a beat going in your head, it's easier than you think."

"Doesn't sound very easy," he muttered.

I ignored this. "Not only is a poet concerned with rhyme and rhythm, of course, he wants to use words to convey an image. Do you know what a metaphor is?"

He nodded. "It's when you compare one thing to something else."

"Exactly. So here's is a poem by Essex Bounty called 'Your Heart.' But all the way through, the narrator acts as though he's speaking about a jewel. He never mentions a human being at all. See what you think."

> *Guards at the gate, but I slip past*
> *With diversionary tactics.*
> *Barbed-wire fence, but I clear it fast*
> *With daring acrobatics.*

Dogs are calmed with a friendly pat
After my hands are scented.
Threshold stripped of a trip-wire trap,
Alarm box circumvented.

Dark inside—not safe as it seems.
I duck the electric eye.
Carefully step over crisscrossed beams,
Catching me ankle-high.

I finally come to the last sealed door
And grope for my bag of tools,
My heart (long accustomed to being poor)
Pounding like any fool's.

What if I breach the shadowed vault
To find the jeweled lure
Counterfeit—or webbed with fault—
Or stolen—or secure?

Worse, tell me, what if the legends lie?
No ruby of brooding glamour
Ever was chipped from some secret mine?
Quick, my file and hammer—

His eyes were sparkling when I was done. "That's strat!" he declared. "He's like a bank robber."

"Right. But what's he stealing?"

Quentin considered. "A heart? I don't get it."

"Some people are very closed. Kind of cold. You meet them, and you think maybe they don't have any emotions at all. But you know they do, because everyone does."

"Like my dad," he said, and nodded.

I was stopped short. "Your dad is—he's not a warm guy?" I absolutely did not know what to say.

He shrugged—or, more truly, hunched his shoulders up as if to ward off something. A memory, a blow. "Not really," he said. "Anyway. Go on."

My voice felt a little strained. "So, say a guy meets this girl, and he falls in love with her, but she doesn't act like she loves him back. But he thinks maybe she does, she's just not used to showing her emotions. So he tries different ways to sneak past her defenses."

"The barbed wire and the dog."

I nodded. "But once he breaks in, he's not sure what he'll actually find. What do you think he's worried about?" And I repeated the last two stanzas line by line, while Quentin correctly interpreted the imagery.

"Or maybe she doesn't have a heart at all!" he exclaimed triumphantly when I recited the final words. "All that work for nothing!"

"Very good! So he manages to convey all his hopes and fears without once describing the girl he's in love with, or even telling you exactly how he's trying to get through to her."

"Yeah. Pretty jazzy," he nodded. "Say it again."

"I'll print it out for you."

"I wouldn't mind poems so much, I guess, if they were all like that."

"I think I'll be able to find a couple more that you'll appreciate. In fact, I've got a book of Housman's poems at home. I'll bring it in for you. You'll like a lot of those."

The rest of the lesson didn't go quite as smoothly. Quentin was restless and unable to concentrate. I went back to rock lyrics, but even those didn't hold his attention. But I didn't give in to his requests to play chess, check the internet for baseball trades, call Marika, or learn a GameWhiz program he wanted to show me. I have to admit, I was feeling exhausted by the time our hour drew to a close.

"Now, next week," I began, when there was a knock on the door. I'd scarcely even glanced in that direction before Quentin had spun around.

"Come in! Come in!" he invited.

In walked a handsome, compact man with short-cropped curly hair, soulful black eyes, and the kind of deeply tanned skin that I associated with a Mediterranean heritage. His thin tight shirt showed off his admirable muscles, and even his three steps into the room were accomplished with a swagger.

"Hey there, Q," he said. "How's it going?"

If Quentin had been a puppy, he would have frisked. "Hi, Dennis! You're early! Does that mean you'll stay late? I'm feeling really good today, I think I could swim for even longer than an hour."

"Swimming and weights today," he said. "Need to build your upper-body strength." He nodded toward me. "Who's your girlfriend?"

Quentin laughed. "She's not my girlfriend, she's my teacher."

"Does she have a name?"

I came to my feet and stepped toward him with my hand outstretched. "Hi. I'm Taylor Kendall. I'm Quentin's English teacher. You must be Dennis. I've heard your name mentioned once or twice."

He brought my hand to his heart in an exaggerated gesture of delight.

"Simply thrilled to meet you at last. I've heard nothing but Taylor-this and Taylor-that for the past week. I was getting all prepared to resent you, because I'm used to having Quin's affection all to myself."

"I think he has enough to spare," I said dryly.

He laughed. "But you! You look nothing at all like I imagined. You know, dowdy and just a little *off*. But I can see you've opened a fashion magazine or two in your life."

I was dressed in black jeans and a floaty green silk shirt embroidered in bright colors. It was equally possible that he was being sarcastic or sincere. "Well, you don't look like the type who would drown people," I retorted.

He raised his eyebrows and looked from me to Quentin and back again. "Drown people? Who said I would?"

"I never said you had drowned anybody," Quentin protested.

"I think that's what Mr. Cortez predicted when he found Quentin wearing one of your shirts."

Dennis dropped my hand and grabbed Quentin in a headlock before I had even completed my sentence. "My Fat Hippos shirt! Gregory gave that to me. I should throw you out the window."

Quentin was squealing and squirming, and his wheelchair was skipping wildly from side to side, but he was clearly having a great time. Me, I was noting the mention of "Gregory" and wondering if the name denoted a friend, brother, or lover. Dennis seemed like the type to flirt outrageously and harmlessly with anyone who came his way—man, woman, baby, dog—and that was a characteristic I'd noted more often in shasta men than hetero ones.

"So, what do you think? Out the window or off the top of the roof? I know, I'll roll you down to the lake and push you in."

"Dennis! Let me go! I'll give it back!"

"Maybe I'll lock you in your father's hologallery. That seems like a suitable punishment. You'd have nightmares for a week."

"Hologallery?" I repeated.

Dennis rolled his expressive eyes. He still hadn't released Quentin, but he'd swung the boy around so that he stood behind him with both arms locked around Quentin's throat. Quentin's hands were wrapped around his wrists, and he had his head twisted back as far as he could to look up at Dennis.

"Quentin's dad has a hologallery of past girlfriends. It's so utterly gruesome. Ask the little monster to show it to you sometime, but pick a day when his dad's not home."

"Hey, let's go now," Quentin said. "He's out of town."

"I don't think so," I said. "I think it's time for you to go exercise away some of your energy."

"Nothing like water sports to restore the internal balance between mind and body," Dennis said in a pious tone.

"Seems a little cold to swim," I observed.

"Indoor pool, but surely an English teacher would be smart enough to figure that out?" Dennis said.

I couldn't help laughing. I liked him instantly. Of course, insults and threats are my love languages, so the banter was nothing new to me. But mostly I liked his easy, friendly, relaxed interaction with Quentin. It was rapidly becoming clear to me that anyone who seemed fond of Quentin would earn huge points in my book, and Dennis scored high.

"Hey, Taylor, why don't you come swim with us?" Quentin invited, pulling away from Dennis and coming closer to me. "I just do laps lots of the time, there's plenty of room."

"Thanks, but I've got hundreds of things to do at home."

"Some other time, then," Dennis said.

"You bet," I said, not meaning it. When Quentin came close enough, I patted him on the head. Most nineteen-year-olds would jerk away from such a patronizing gesture, but he liked it; he smiled up at me. "See you next week, kid. Tuesday."

He was a little less reluctant to see me go now that Dennis was on hand, and he merely waved me toward the door.

I stepped outside and found Bram Cortez waiting for me.

"Hello," I said. "I guess you're today's escort detail."

He smiled slightly, but enough to give his stern features a pleasant cast. "We don't want you to get lost."

"You don't want me wandering through the mansion picking up small *objets d'art*," I said, strolling forward. He fell in step beside me. We headed, not for the elevator, but for the elaborate stairway that spiraled down to the ground floor.

"Oh, that wouldn't trouble me so much," he said, completely deadpan. "Our security cameras would register the theft, and we would be able to bring you to the attention of the authorities almost immediately."

I grinned. "Yeah, I've been thinking you were the type of guy to set up monitors in every room. Does somebody just sit there and watch the camera feeds all day?"

He glanced down at me. At five-foot-eight, I'm taller than the average woman, and I was only a few inches shorter than he was, but there was an air of latent menace about him that made him seem bigger. "How thoughtful of you to concern yourself with our security measures," he said. "We do spot checks of the cameras as they run. We also keep the recordings for a year before discarding them."

"Good to know," I said.

We descended half a flight without speaking. "How's Quentin doing?" he asked after a while. He didn't seem like the type to be bothered by silence, so

I assumed he was genuinely interested.

"I don't really know yet. I've only had him a couple of hours. I think he wants to learn—no, I don't think he cares about learning," I corrected myself. "I think he wants to please me. He doesn't know me very well, obviously, but he likes me to be here. And he thinks if he does what I want, I'll come back. So he tries to do what I want, but he gets distracted easily, and sometimes I find it hard to make him concentrate. And frankly," I added, "he seems a lot younger to me than nineteen."

Cortez nodded. "Yes. I don't know if that's because the disease has slowed down some of his emotional development. Or if it's because the disease has made him so helpless that the rest of us treat him like a child. Or if it's because he's had so little interaction with kids his own age that he doesn't know how to behave." He shrugged. "Or if he learned a long time ago that a childlike manner would disarm and secure the people he needed to have around him to survive."

I gave him one quick look. We had just entered the foyer, and this conversation was about to abruptly end. "Interesting assessment," I said. "It seems to be working on me, at any rate. I find myself very partisan, and I've only known him a few days."

"Wait till you've known him a couple of years."

I started to say, "But I'm only going to tutor him a few months," but of course, that wasn't the point. "Well, I'm glad to see that he seems to have won some allies," I said.

He smiled and pulled back the teleport door for me. "Everyone in the household."

"How long before I'm a trusted enough member of the household to get my own door code?" I asked.

"Just what I was about to mention," he said coolly. "If you have one in mind, you can tell me now, and I'll make sure it's in place before you come back. Six digits."

"Great," I said. "Zero-four-two-one-one-six."

He nodded, apparently committing it to memory; I would have needed to write it down if I didn't know it already. "Excellent," he said. "We'll expect you at the front door on Tuesday."

"So long," I said, letting him shut the door while I keyed in my street code. "See you next week."

If he replied, I didn't hear him, because I was already thirty miles away.

∽

The weekend was relatively quiet, giving me a chance to catch up on my housecleaning, my laundry, and my viewing of the Vampire Nightly Network. I jumped down to Atlanta Saturday night so Marika and I could see a movie. She hates the three-D surround-sound total body experience of the LucaPlexes, so we went to an old-fashioned theater showing a retrospective of 1980s classics. After singing along with "Footloose," we stopped for pizza, then swung by her house so I could pick up the Braves shirt she'd bought for Quentin. I promised I'd have him write her a thank-you note as his next essay assignment.

On Sunday, I joined Jason and my mom for brunch. I found them in the living room, putting together a puzzle under my father's radioactive gaze. Not an activity that appealed to me, so I headed to the kitchen to cook the meal on my mother's inconvenient and old-fashioned appliances. After we'd eaten, Jason and I headed out into the chilly sunshine, already making tentative plans for the following weekend

"How are your tutoring sessions going with Quentin Phillips?" he asked.

"Good. The household is a little odd, and I find it really strange that I've never so much as laid eyes on Duncan Phillips. I mean, if I were a parent, I'd want to meet my son's tutor and make sure she was doing a decent job. But I'm not sure he cares."

"That makes him sound like a real prick."

"Yeah, I have a feeling I wouldn't like him." I pulled my jacket tighter and walked a little faster. "But I sure do like his son."

⁓

The next week sort of galloped by. I'd assigned short papers for all of my Sefton classes, so I spent most of my evenings reading and correcting them. The range of ability among my students never ceased to amaze me. Devante Ross, who couldn't get a noun and verb to agree if he took them to marital counseling, wrote with such humor and style that I hated to take points off for grammar (but I did). Evan not only put together poetic, though bleak, sentences about the cycle of life, he also embedded quaint, delicate pencil sketches into his electronic files. They were often my favorite parts of any assignment.

It was during this week of intensive grading that I also read Quentin's first paper, which he had given me in hard copy on Friday afternoon. I hadn't read it until I got home that night, since he wouldn't be quiet long enough for me to even skim the pages, so I gave up trying. Instead, we dissected another rock poem, this one by the suicide blast group called Aspirations of Kudzu, for as long as I could hold his attention. Which was until Dennis arrived and I conceded defeat.

That night I read his essay, and then I turned off the light and stood at the window and cried.

Dream Monsters
by Quentin Calcott Phillips

It takes me a long time to fall asleep. I keep thinking about things. Sometimes I turn on the radio and listen to baseball games. I like the Chicago Cubs and the Atlanta Braves the best, but when they are playing each other, I am always wanting for the Cubs to win.

When I do fall asleep, sometimes I dream that I am playing baseball. I want to be the shortstop because then I can make those great plays that save a run. I can jump so high in the air that none of the opposing players can hit a home run out of the park, the ball always goes into my glove instead. Everyone in the stadium cheers. Sometimes they chant my name over and over, fifty thousand people at once, "Quen-tin! Quen-tin!" It sounds like they are saying "engine" over and over again, but I know it's my name.

In my dream, I can run faster than any other player, even faster than the ones who are the fastest. My legs look blurry to anyone who is watching. I do not hit the ball so well, but my teammates don't mind because, once I get on base, I can steal on any pitch. I can steal home on a suicide squeeze. I can steal first base on three strikes. I have never been thrown out stealing.

In my dream, I am running the bases just for fun while the grounds crew is cutting the grass. In my stadium, we have real grass not that artificial turf stuff that is so terrible. I am running very fast, but I'm not paying attention, and the guy who is cutting the grass is not paying attention either. Suddenly I trip over something, and I fall down, and the guy on the lawn mower runs right over my legs. I yell at him to stop, so he stops, but the lawn mower is still on my legs and it is cutting them to pieces. "Get off! Get off!" I yell, but he can't hear me because the motor is so loud. I see him put his hand to his ear, trying to hear me, but I cannot shout any louder than the motor, and he does not turn the motor off. And so my legs are all chewed up.

I know it is a dream, because in real life I'm not a baseball player, so I'm happy when I wake up. But even when I wake up, my legs are all chewed up and I cannot walk in them or run in them or even catch a fly ball. And I know my dream monster is real.

I know this essay is supposed to be longer but this is all I can think of.

How was I supposed to grade a paper like that?

I called Domenic, and he met me for dinner, just the two of us. We went to a small Italian restaurant where the maitre d' knew him by name and the waitress flirted with him the whole time we were there. He talked most of the night, in idle and mellifluous tones, and I just listened, letting myself be soothed by his presence and his voice. I never once mentioned that I was sad, but obviously he knew something was wrong; he was taking care of me, in his Domenic way, just existing, just being beautiful and kind. When the meal was over, he walked me to my teleport gate, kissed my cheek before I stepped inside, and stood there and watched me until I disappeared.

The gesture was more comforting than I could say.

CHAPTER SEVEN

MONDAY WAS A DAY OF HEARTACHES.

It started early on, in class, when Evan Stodley sat motionless and glassy-eyed at the back of the room. I saw Nancy Ortega and a couple of the other girls give him looks of concern while we discussed *Rage of Man,* but he didn't look over at them or up at me. I kept my eye on him while class proceeded, and I let myself move casually around the room the whole hour, making points, gesturing, calling on students. When the bell rang, I was standing right in front of Evan, and I gestured at him to stay in his chair.

"Wednesday," I said. "Have the book finished. *Everyone* have the book finished. That means you, Devante."

"Hey, I only have a hundred pages to go."

"Good thing you're such a fast reader. See you all in a couple days." Evan made no move to get up as the other kids filed out, and once the room was empty, I seated myself at the desk across the aisle.

"So what's wrong?" I asked.

He hunched his shoulders, still not looking at me. "I—I didn't have much to say, I guess. I—haven't read the assignment."

"And I wish you had, but that's not what I'm concerned with right now. Clearly, you're upset about something."

He made a gesture as indeterminate as the shrug and gave no other answer.

"I know you and some girl broke up a couple weeks ago," I said. "Is that it? Are you seeing her again?"

"It's not her fault," he said swiftly. "She told me—she was very clear. I just—see, I have these feelings, and they're no good any more, and I have to get rid of them, but I can't, I don't know how."

Boy, I've been there. "Sure would be a lot easier if it was like a water faucet, wouldn't it?" I said. "Turn the emotion off and on. Not the way it works, though. Unfortunately."

"Everybody says—time—it takes time—but I don't think there's enough time. I don't think I can go through another week like this, you know? Another *day.* I mean, maybe I'll feel better a year from now, but how do I get through the year? So I—" He stopped and shrugged again. He had lifted his hands as if to run them through his hair, but they were shaking so badly that he returned them to the desk, tightly laced together so their trembling was not so obvious.

"So you?" I prompted. "So you've been thinking about doing something to yourself? Hurting yourself, maybe?"

"I wouldn't want her to know," he said earnestly. "I wouldn't want her to think it was her fault. That would be a terrible thing to do to someone, leave them behind with that kind of guilt. If it looked like an accident, maybe, you know, something to do with a car—"

If I'd had any doubts, I was now pretty sure this was way beyond my level of expertise. "Lots of ways to kill yourself, Evan," I said evenly. "And none of them are good." For the life of me, I couldn't keep the little Dorothy Parker jingle from circling through my head: *Guns aren't lawful, Nooses give, Gas smells awful, You might as well live.* But that wasn't the tone I was going for here. "You're twenty years old. You have every imaginable fabulous experience still waiting for you. Love with women you don't know how to dream up—friendship with the most unexpected people—explorations of places it wouldn't occur to you at this minute to go see. You kill yourself, none of that comes true."

"I can't think that far ahead," he whispered. "I can't see it."

I couldn't remember if Evan had family nearby or if he commuted in from a long distance, as I did. Even if he had family, that didn't mean anybody was paying attention to him. "Who have you talked to about this, Evan?" I asked. "Your roommate? Your mom or dad? Anyone?"

"Umm—" He rubbed his face with his shaking fingers then quickly replaced his hand on the desk. "Nancy, a little. She's the one who made me come to class. She said it would make me feel better."

I was grateful for that; she had clearly meant to turn the problem over to me. "Well, she was right," I said. "One of the best things to do for depression is distract yourself, did you know that? Someone told me that once when I was depressed. Sometimes something as stupid as a TV show or a phone call is all it takes to snap the mood, just enough to help you think a little straighter."

He glanced at me quickly, sideways. "You were depressed?"

I smiled. "Everyone gets down now and then. Everybody in the world. The trick is to recognize when your situation is really serious and you can't handle it on your own. Then you ask for help."

He gave me another swift look. "You're going to call somebody, aren't you? Tell them about me."

I nodded. "Yeah. Or I'll walk over with you to the mental health clinic. It's just across from Dorsett Hall."

He shook his head. "I can't make it that far," he whispered, and suddenly crumpled forward over his desk, resting his forehead on his hands.

I jumped up and gave him an awkward hug. You can't really get your arms around someone curled over a desk, and anyway, I'm not supposed to touch my students. But the hell with that. "It's okay," I murmured. "Evan, it's okay."

It took the mental health team about fifteen minutes to arrive after I called. I had been a little worried that they would arrive like pest-control professionals, brisk, efficient, and cold, but I relaxed when I saw them. The woman was petite and kind-looking, older than I was by maybe a decade. The man was burly enough to manhandle Evan out the door, but the expression on his face was of a gentle sweetness that instantly made me trust him.

"Hi, Evan," the woman said, crouching down next to him. "I think maybe you should come talk to us for a while."

It was another five or ten minutes before they had Evan calm and agreeing to walk on his own power to the electric cart they had waiting outside. I offered to come with them, but the woman seemed to think they'd do better without my help and Evan seemed willing to put himself almost bonelessly in their hands. I accompanied them to the outside door anyway, feeling helpless and stupid, and wishing I knew magic words. Spells for sanity and serenity, love potions, healing charms. All I could do was promise to call Nancy and let her know where he was, and then promise to check on him myself.

Once they'd left, I headed down to Caroline's well-decorated office to tell her that a student was in trouble. She looked up rather blank-faced when I entered, and for a moment I had the impression she didn't recognize me.

"Oh. Taylor," she said, seeming to shake herself out of an abstraction. "What's wrong?"

"One of my students is having an emotional meltdown, and I had to call the health center to come get him," I said. "Is there something else I'm supposed to do? Notify his parents? Notify the dean?"

She motioned to a chair and I took a seat. "The clinic should get in touch with his parents," she said. "I don't think we need to notify the dean unless he ends up dropping out. What's wrong, did you find out?"

"He's obviously suicidal, and the cause seems to be a breakup with his girlfriend. I don't know. He's sort of a frail kid anyway. I wish there was something more I could do."

"I'm sure you've done the best thing you could for him," she said, but her voice was a little muffled. She had slumped back in her chair once I announced the cause of Evan's troubles, and, like him, she seemed more interested in the patterns on her desk than the expressions on my face. "In fact, it's probably no accident he chose to talk to you. You have a sort of—aura of safety about you. Makes people think they can confide in you."

I was stunned, not so much by the comment as by the realization that Caroline herself was about to make a confidence. This extraordinarily self-possessed woman was looking, now that I took the time to examine her, like she'd spent the whole night sitting up drinking whiskey and contemplating the evils of the world.

"Caroline," I said quietly, "is something wrong?"

She seemed to consider. "Yes, actually," she said in a precise voice. "I don't need suicide intervention, but I just—it's been a hard week."

I had read somewhere that the way to get people to tell you things was not to ask questions but to share your own experiences so that they felt comfortable replying in kind. Part of me did not exactly want to hear Caroline's secrets—she was my boss, we had never been close, and this felt weird—but the part of me that is instantly roused to sympathy when a stranger at the teleport station is crying was the part of me that took over now.

"I sure know about hard weeks," I said. "Hard years, too."

She glanced up. "When you got divorced, how long did it take you to get over it? How did you get through?"

I hadn't even known Caroline was aware of my personal history. "The divorce wasn't the worst part," I said. "The worst part was the year before the divorce, when everything was going wrong. When I would lie there next to Danny every single night and think, 'What am I going to do? How can we stay together? But how can I leave him?' I couldn't envision the conversation in which I told him I was walking out. I couldn't envision packing my clothes and going through the furniture and parceling out the books. I knew I would get better once we made the break, but I didn't know how to make the break."

She leaned forward, her perfect features intense. Today, her pale hair was pulled so tightly back from her face that it seemed her cheekbones hurt. Or maybe the pain that showed around her eyes was rooted in another cause. "But how did you know you would get better?" she demanded. "How could you be sure of that? Didn't you ever think, 'This man will leave me, and I will be quietly but irrevocably unhappy for the rest of my life'?"

"Not really," I said honestly. "But things had made me sad before. High school breakups, my dad's death. Events that were horrible at the time, but that I lived through anyway. I did know—" I gestured; how could I explain? "It would take a long time. Longer than I wanted, maybe. It's like breaking your arm. It's not going to heal overnight, no matter how unhappy you are that your bone is broken. But it will heal."

"So how do you get through the time that it takes to heal? How do you endure it?"

Evan's question exactly. "Well, me, I kept really busy. I would make plans for weeks in advance. Not a Monday rolled by that I didn't know exactly what I was doing Friday and Saturday night. I joined a reading group that met every other Wednesday, so those were a couple of days I didn't have to worry about. And I took some night classes, so there were a few more hours that were taken care of. I saw movies with friends. Had dinner with my family. It's not so hard to keep yourself busy if you make it your life's work."

"It sounds exhausting."

I laughed. "Well, it is. But the more you wear out your body, the more you distract your mind. And the more you hypnotize your heart."

"Didn't you want to get even with him?" she asked.

"With Danny? For what?"

"For hurting you. Didn't you want to hurt him back?"

I noticed she hadn't asked what went wrong with the marriage. She was assuming Danny had been the one at fault; she didn't seem to realize that I could have been equally to blame. Clearly, in her own situation (which I was hoping not to delve into too deeply, to be honest), she perceived herself as the victim of some scheming and unscrupulous man. Or woman. With Caroline, I wouldn't have taken any bets.

"No, I can't say I wanted to hurt him," I said slowly. "But I can't say I really wanted him to be happy, either. I wouldn't have minded if he went bankrupt or caught some nasty disease or got dumped by the next girl he fell in love with. But I didn't want to be the agent of destruction. I just wanted my own hurting to stop."

"So, how long?" she asked next. "Before you were better."

"For me, three months is about the time I spend just enduring. Just getting through the days. Takes me another six months or so to have intermittent good days sprinkled in among the bad ones. Another three months where I feel good more often than I feel lousy. And then, one day, about a year after everything falls apart, I find myself laughing at something someone has said, and looking forward to some little thing that's coming up in the next twenty-four hours, and thinking, 'You know, I have a pretty good life.' And then, at that moment, I realize I'm cured. I'm over it. No more pain."

"A year?" she said. "That's all?"

"Well, at the time, a year seems like a pretty long proposition," I said. "But it goes by faster than you think."

"Actually, it sounds like a pretty short time to me," she said. "I was thinking in terms of decades. Lifetimes."

"I guess you haven't had too many bouts with despair."

She shook her head. "No. Nothing like this, anyway. But you make me feel a little more hopeful."

I couldn't think of anything I'd said that could be remotely construed as comforting, except for the promise of a time limit. But I said, "As far as I can tell, the only benefit of suffering—I mean, the single, barest, most poverty-stricken reason to be grateful for it—is that at some point it gives you a chance to help somebody else through the same kind of pain. Other than that? Not profitable. It doesn't build character, no matter what anyone tells you. It doesn't make you smarter, kinder, more patient, anything. It just lets you tell someone else, 'Hey, I was there, and I survived.'"

She gave me a tentative smile, the first one I'd seen this afternoon. "And you seem to have survived quite intact."

I smiled back. "You know," I said, "I have a pretty good life."

⤜⤛

Marika called while I was on my way to Bezos Terminal. She was crying. I supposed I should just expect everyone I spoke to this day to be in tears.

"What's wrong?" I demanded.

"I know I shouldn't have, but Axel called, and I said I'd go to lunch with him—just as friends, you know—but then he started flirting. And I really wanted—Taylor, I just wanted to jump up and run around the edge of the table and kiss him, so that made me mad, so then I was hostile—"

"You were in a public place, I take it?"

"Yes, and I—he said something, I don't remember what, and I threw my water in his face, and then he started shouting—"

I couldn't help a grin, which, fortunately, she couldn't see. "So I guess you didn't stay at the restaurant much longer."

"No, he just stormed off, and I had to pay the bill, and I felt like such an idiot the whole time. And I just—I'm so miserable. Could you come spend the night and cheer me up? This isn't how I thought my life would work out, you know? I'm thirty-four years old. I thought I'd be married and have kids by now, I thought I'd be happy. Instead, all I do is match up with abusive ex-boyfriends and do stupid things. And then—"

She continued on in this vein while I thought rapidly. It was close to five by now. I could get to Marika's within an hour, but the time zone change meant I wouldn't arrive until seven. We were close enough to the same size that we were able wear each other's clothes, but there were certain items that just weren't shareable.

"I can spend the night," I said, "but we have to shop first. I need makeup and a toothbrush and underwear. And maybe an outfit."

"Shopping would be fun," she said, her voice sounding a little cheerier. "And maybe dinner."

"Great," I said. "See you in about an hour."

⤜⤛

Marika and I were out until almost midnight, talking over the disappointments of life and finishing off a bottle of wine before returning to her opulent house and tumbling into bedrooms on opposite ends of the second-story hallway.

I was only slightly hung over in the morning, so I was out the door with a minimum of groaning. Back to Olympic Terminal, back to Houston, and on to a light day at the campus. It was livelier than usual during my office hours, since about half of the students in my lit class dropped by to ask about Evan or give me updates. Nancy Ortega and her girlfriend, Simone, had gone to visit him at the clinic, where he'd been admitted. Nancy filled me in on his family history, which was none too savory, and expressed a belief that his mother and father would be of no help in this crisis.

"But we'll be his family," she said with calm self-assurance. "Devante rents a house with a couple other guys, and they've got an extra room. We're going to move Evan there as soon as he gets out so we can keep an eye on him."

I wasn't sure that living with Devante Ross would aid anyone in the recovery of his sanity, but I applauded the spirit behind the decision. "You wonder sometimes how anyone makes it to adulthood, don't you?" I mused aloud.

Nancy stood to go. "But so many people do," she said, "so we know it must be possible. See you tomorrow, Ms. Kendall."

I must admit, I was feeling just a wee bit worn down by the time I headed up to Chicago for my hour with Quentin Phillips. Not a good state in which to brace that eager and energetic young man.

"Hey, Taylor! Do you know what? I've joined an online chess club, and I won my first three games. Bram says I need to move up to the next higher level, but I don't want to. I like winning. Did you see Marika? Did she give you my Braves shirt? She texted me, she said she bought it already. Did you watch the Cubs game last night? Two-run homer in the ninth inning, won the game. Man, I wish I had been there."

"Oh—hell—the shirt," I said, dropping my briefcase on the desk and taking a seat. "It's still at my apartment. Sorry, Quentin. I couldn't get it because I wasn't home last night."

"And then I—you weren't home last night?" he repeated, his eyes widening. "Where—never mind."

I smiled. "I was at Marika's, in fact. I went over after work, and we stayed up too late talking, so I decided I'd just spend the night. But the shirt's at my place, not hers, so I didn't get a chance to bring it. Sorry. I'll remember on Friday."

"Maybe you forgot my homework, too," he said hopefully.

"Maybe I did. Maybe we'll have to come up with some creative class ideas."

"You could read to me," he suggested.

"Actually, you know, not a bad idea. Let's read."

So I picked up one of the Haycox Westerns that I had remembered to bring last Friday, and we started at chapter one. Amazing that such a restless boy could sit so quietly. Was it the power of words or the power of an adult's attention? I made him do some of the work at first, having him read five pages to every ten of mine, though it was obvious it was much more effort for him to read than to listen. Eventually, I just took the book back and spent the rest of the hour with it in my hands.

"That was fun," he said, when we finally stopped. "Let's do that Friday, too."

"No, Friday I'm going to remember all your assignments and I'll make you work like a dog," I said with mock sternness. "In fact, time for an assignment now. I want you to write a note to Marika."

"I texted her yesterday!"

"Right. This is going to be an essay, only you're going to write it to Marika, so it doesn't have to be formal. But I'm going to grade on originality and creativity and proper sentence structure."

He did not look entirely pleased. "What am I going to write her about?"

"You can pick the topic. You can give her the play-by-play on a baseball game. You can tell her about a typical day of your life—you know, which tutors come in, what kind of physical therapy you do with Dennis. You can describe all the people who live or work at your father's house, a few paragraphs about me, a few about Dennis, a few about Bram Cortez. But I want you to pick a theme and stick to it."

"How many words?"

"A thousand."

"Due Friday?"

"I think you can manage that." I gestured at *The Earthbreakers*, lying open on his desk. "And in your free time you can go on and read ahead. I won't mind. I know it by heart."

I had just closed my briefcase when there was a knock on the door, and Bram Cortez entered.

"Hey, Quin," he said. He nodded at me. "Ms. Kendall."

I gave him a look of exaggerated irritation. "Oh, please. Only my students call me Ms. anything."

Quentin laughed. "Even I call her Taylor."

"I never like to be too familiar until invited," Cortez said gravely.

"Well, consider yourself invited. What can we do for you, Quentin and I?"

"Actually, I came to tell you the teleport system's down," he said.

"Down here at the house, or down-down, all over the city?"

He didn't even crack a smile. "Down-down."

"Great. I wonder how I'm going to get home?"

"You'll have to spend the night!" Quentin exclaimed. "We've got tons of guest rooms."

"Actually, I was coming to offer Ms. Kendall—" Bram Cortez stopped dramatically and gave me a deliberate look. "Offer *Taylor* a ride home. I have a car," he added.

"It's a jazz car," Quentin admiringly. "A vintage Mustang in perfect condition."

"Really?" I said, eying the security officer. "I would have expected you to have something less—flashy. More armored, maybe."

Again, not a glimmer of a smile. "Like a HumVee-49?" he suggested. "That's my corporate car."

"Bulletproof," Quentin interjected. "For when he takes my dad to important meetings."

"I was kidding," I said.

"Ah," Cortez said. "In any case, the Mustang is at your disposal."

"No! I want her to stay!" Quentin pleaded.

I couldn't help glancing at Bram Cortez, who was thinking exactly what I was thinking. *This is not a house where I would be welcome to spend the night.* "Gotta go, Quentin," I said gently. "I'll be back on Friday. And—hey, tell you what. If Mr. Cortez takes me home, he can pick up the Braves shirt and bring it back for you."

Too late I realized my slip of the tongue. "Bram," Quentin said.

"What?"

"Yes, please call me Bram," Cortez said civilly. "Since I'm to call you Taylor."

He didn't exude the chatty sort of bonhomie that would make me comfortable addressing him by his first name. I mean, he was no Dennis. He wasn't even Francis. But it was rather a trap of my own making. "Well," I said. "Bram. I'm grateful for the offer. What kind of name is Bram, anyway? Family name, maybe?"

"It's short for Abramo," he said. "I'm named after my father's grandfather. And my sister Elena was named after our great-grandmother."

I love glimpses into family life and would have liked to pursue the topic. *Are you close to your sister? Is your father domineering and purposeful, or romantic and sweet? How does your mother fit into the family?* With someone else I might have asked the questions, but Bram Cortez didn't seem like the type who would dish about family dynamics with someone he barely knew.

"Well, Abramo, I'd love a ride home, if it wouldn't inconvenience you too much," I said. At the same time, I was thinking, *What will we talk about in the car?* It had to be a good forty-five minutes to my apartment. Maybe longer. "But doesn't somebody have to stay here and, I don't know, monitor the monitors?"

"I have a round-the-clock staff of guards on premises," Cortez said. "I think I can leave for a couple of hours."

Couple of hours. He was estimating even longer than I was. "Well, then. Great.

"Thanks. Quentin, I'll see you in a few days. Don't forget to write your essay."

"Bye, Taylor. See you Friday."

CHAPTER EIGHT

I FOLLOWED THE SECURITY GUARD OUT QUENTIN'S DOOR, THROUGH the hallway and down the miles of stairway. We accomplished this entire trip in silence. As we reached the ground floor, I headed automatically toward the foyer, but Cortez (I would never be able to call him Bram) turned in the opposite direction. "This way," he said, and led me down a wide hallway toward the back of the mansion.

I tried not to stare too obviously, though I had not been to this part of the house before and I knew Marika would want details. We walked past what had to be the formal dining room, huge and elegant and decorated in cream and gold. The chandelier itself was as big as Quentin in his wheelchair and at least as fragile, decorated with coins of cut glass that glistened even in the low light of a shuttered room. Most of the other doors we passed were closed. Eventually we turned down a broad, well-lit stairway, and exited onto an asphalt-covered area that was about as big as a city block. It was ringed by six separate garages housing what I guessed was a fleet of powerful and very expensive automobiles. A few sports models—which might have been owned by the staff or been part of Duncan Phillips' less valuable collection—were parked in out-of-the-way places between the garages.

I've never understood the American male's fascination with cars. As far as I was concerned, Henry Ford had sat down and fashioned the Model T simply as a way to transport humans from one point on the map to another, and the invention had caught on because it was a fantastic improvement over the horse and buggy. Successive improvements to transportation systems—light rail, airplanes, and teleport—had superseded automobiles, at least in my opinion. I just couldn't understand why anyone would want to maintain, insure, or drive a vehicle.

Intellectually I knew there must be women who were fascinated by cars, but the only people I knew who absolutely loved them were men. Jason and Domenic could talk cars all day, describing make, model, manufacturer, specs, speed, fuel requirements, comparative advantages to those fuel requirements, fatality rate—you name it. They attended auto shows for the new models and checked out museums of the antiques.

Jason had never owned one, never having had the requisite money for the purchase or the maintenance, but for a while Domenic had kept a beat-up champagne-colored old Akisa. Whenever we had gone anywhere within the greater metropolitan Chicago area, he had insisted on driving us there, which meant we all had to teleport to his apartment, wait while he fetched it from some off-site garage, fight over which lucky person got the front seat and which two unfortunates got crowded into the back, and then take a long, slow, tortuous drive through a city of three million people. Even though only a fraction of those residents also owned cars, that was enough to clog the roads with traffic any time night or day. And God forbid there would ever be anything like convenient parking near our destinations, so the whole exercise had to be played out in reverse. Finally, Marika and I refused to participate in the drives; we just met Jason and Domenic at whatever bar or restaurant we had chosen for the night.

Once I asked Domenic, "Why do you want a car, anyway?"

He said, "Why do guys want anything? To impress girls."

Marika snorted. "I can't speak for all females, but I have to think that a high percentage of the women on this earth don't give a rat's ass about riding in some tumbledown contraption that you want to describe in great mechanical detail as you try to make it to a wedding or some event that really matters to her, only no way will you be on time because you're stuck in some mile-long traffic jam on Lake Shore Drive and the car's about to overheat anyway. You want to impress a girl? You take her to a nice restaurant and buy some expensive wine. But leave the auto behind."

I think it was about a month later that Domenic sold the car.

I had to admit, though, Bram Cortez's vintage Mustang was a lot more impressive than Domenic's lousy Akisa. For one thing, it had probably cost five times as much. For another, the silver-gray machine was a sleek but whimsical little number with curvy lines here and pointy accents there. I was sure Bram Cortez would have been able to rattle off the correct terminology—fins, fenders, spoilers—but I didn't really want to hear it.

"Looks nice," I said politely.

"You ever ride in one of these?" he asked, palming the outer keypad to unlock the doors.

"A Mustang? Or a car?"

He grinned. "Mustang," he said. "I assume you've been in a car."

"Not often."

"Climb in."

I slid onto the satiny gray leather seat and strapped myself in. A decade or so ago, as car safety became a mania with manufacturers, 360-degree airbags had become standard features on most models. Upon impact (so I was assured by Jason and Domenic), the passengers of a car would be instantly surrounded by a protective cocoon. However, the receptacles for these airbags often took up so much interior space that there wasn't much room to put your feet, rest your elbow, or raise your head. At least, that had been the case in Domenic's Akisa. There was so much space in this front seat that I wondered if Bram Cortez had had the safety devices removed.

"How long have you had this car?" I asked.

"About five years," he said, starting the engine. It purred to life and we were in motion while I was still waiting for the jolt and shudder I had come to expect from the Akisa. "I wanted one twenty years ago, but I was in the army then, and cars weren't part of our travel allowance."

I leaned back against the seat. Well, hell, maybe Domenic was right. A good car just might impress a girl. "You were in the army? That seems to jibe."

"With my personality, you mean?"

"What I've seen of it. How long were you in the service?"

"Ten years. That's back when we were seeing some action along the Chinese border. Lot of skirmishing, but nothing ever conclusive because—" He shrugged. "War in the 21st century is just too dangerous. You can't pull out your ultimate weapons or you'll end the world. So it's all drones and IEDs and one city bombed to hell, but you can't ever just annihilate the enemy or you'll annihilate yourself, too."

While he spoke, we traveled slowly down a long, cloistered drive protected by marching ranks of bareheaded trees. As we passed a black wrought-iron gate, Cortez waved to the guard, then pulled out onto a wide, empty road. I realized we had to be even farther out in the northwestern suburbs than I had thought.

"But all those raids and roadside bombs cause a lot of deaths," he continued. "After a while, it just seemed stupid."

"So what did you do after you left the army?"

"Became a cop."

"That also fits."

He kept his eyes on the road, but a faint smile touched his lips. "Are you saying I'm predictable?"

"Oh no. I don't know you well enough to predict a thing. But, you know, soldier—cop—security guy. Kind of a common theme. Where were you working? Chicago?"

"Not at first. I was in Boston, in Denver, then L.A. Then I came here."

I looked over at him. "The Hot Zones."

He nodded, still watching the road. A few cars had started passing us, and someone had come up behind us at a pretty rapid speed, whipping by before I'd even been aware the car was approaching. "Yeah. Seemed like a good idea at the time. Sort of like war in its way. A lot of battle strategizing. 'This is what this gang might do, here's how we can block that.' Life-and-death stuff."

He was silent a moment. "Lot of boys die young in the zones," he finally went on. "They're the ones starting the wars, they're the ones running the gangs. Juntas, that's what we called them when I was on the force. Used to be a word they used for paramilitary groups in Central America who ran drugs and attempted coups. Now that's the word we're using to describe kids who're dead before they're twenty. I saw more people die on the South Side than I saw die the whole time I was in the army."

Did you ever kill anybody? I wanted to ask, but I wasn't comfortable making the inquiry. For him, at least as far as I could tell, this conversation was a rare run at intimacy, and I didn't want to jinx it by asking stupid questions. "Is it really as bad as they say?" I asked instead.

"Worse. People living in—squalor's not a good enough word for it. Tearing down old brick buildings to build these hodge-podge shacks to live in. In some places, the city water and sewer lines still work, and in some places they don't. No one who lives there knows how to fix the broken pipes and no one from the city will come in. So there's whole neighborhoods where people live, but they have to cart their water in from somewhere else. The weird thing is, they've got all sorts of power—batteries and generators and old solar reflectors—so you'll be in some godless dump of a building that smells like blood and urine, and some kid'll be sitting on the floor of this bombed-out building, playing games on the latest-model laptop. I saw that more times than I could tell you."

I spread my hands. "You have to wonder—how does anyone survive? Where do they get food? How do they eat? You'd think the Hot Zones would eventually disappear because everyone would be dead."

"Plenty of people in the Hot Zones hold jobs. They earn enough to buy food, but not enough to move out. And there are a lot of charities that set up food banks on the rim of the zones."

"I used to work in one."

For the first time since we'd gotten in the car, he looked over at me. "You did?"

"When I was in college, I belonged to a service sorority. Some of the girls volunteered at health clinics, some tutored kids and adults. I joined the food kitchens. Worked there once a month for three years." I felt a wave of the old sadness wash over me. "I knew it was important work, but I could never tell how much good I was doing. There just seemed to be so much need and not enough resources to fill it."

He nodded. "I used to ask myself, how can we fix this problem? I could never figure out the answer. There were days I just wanted to go into the South Side and torch the whole place, burn it right to the ground, and whoever survived, survived. Other days I wanted to go door to door, handing out bread and hundred-dollar bills. I don't think either course of action would have changed a thing."

"So how long were you a cop?"

"Eight years."

"What made you quit?"

"Almost getting killed. Me and the three guys I was with got ambushed. Two of them died. Two of us got out alive."

I waited a beat to see if he would offer any more details. "The strange thing," he said after a moment, "was that it had happened before. I'd seen other guys go down, and I'd be shaken up—we all would be—but I'd go back the next day anyway. I was convinced, for a while at least, that the job I was doing was worth the risk. We were losing men, but we were saving lives. I was in a war, and even if I wasn't winning, I was making a stand. That's what I used to think, anyway."

"What changed your mind?"

"I don't know. The pointlessness of it, maybe. We might be able to wipe out the Hot Zones—somehow, some way—but not by patrolling the streets and taking out one felon at a time. Nothing I did, walking those streets with my gun in my hand, was going to change the equation. If there was no reason for me to risk my life, I wanted to stop risking my life. So I got out."

"And then what? You came to work for Duncan Phillips?"

"Not right away. I took some high-risk security jobs, did some political work, got some training to catch up on my technology. Didn't start working for Phillips until three years ago."

He signaled and took a ramp from the street to an elevated highway. Instantly, we were engulfed by cars, all moving extremely rapidly and with no apparent respect for the laws of physics that said no two entities can occupy the same space. If someone wanted to be in our lane, they just came right over, heedless of our existence and our speed. Cortez grew quiet as he negotiated a few lanes to get to some more advantageous alleyway of death. Why one such lane would be preferable to another was a mystery to me, but I trusted that he knew what he was doing.

I concentrated on doing my math. Say he had joined the army when he was twenty-one. Ten years there, eight on the police force, a couple years to knock around, three years with Duncan Phillips . . . "So you're about forty-four?" I asked aloud. Not really meaning to.

He looked amused. "Forty-five this summer."

I could feel myself blushing. "I just—well, I couldn't tell by looking. Not that it matters."

"So when do I get to start asking you questions?" he said.

I laughed. "What could there possibly be for you to ask? You've already got a complete dossier on me."

"I can think of a few things I'd like to know."

"Let's finish with you first. So. Duncan Phillips. How'd you get this gig?

Do you like it? What's he like, anyway? I still haven't met him."

"He's a bastard," Cortez said calmly. "I can't stand him."

I absorbed that for a moment in total silence.

"When I first started working for him, I didn't care," he went on. "Hell, I've set up security for presidential candidates that I wouldn't vote for to run a carnival, let alone the country. I don't have to like a guy to try to keep him alive, right? And the money was good. And the job was a whole lot easier than the one I'd just left. And I thought I'd take a little time to figure out what else I might want to do with my life. So, no problem that I didn't like him. He wasn't paying me to like him."

"What changed?"

He gave an infinitesimal shrug. "I got to know him."

"Why do you stay?"

For the second time since we'd gotten in the car, he glanced at me. "Quentin. That's why anyone stays."

"Dennis—Francis—they don't like Duncan Phillips either?"

Cortez actually snorted. "Oh, no."

"What's he done that's so awful?"

Cortez was silent a moment, watching the road. We were still in the suburbs, green lawns and substantial trees visible from the highway, but the buildings were crowding closer together as we drew near the city limits. "Name it," he said at last. "But I don't want to talk about Duncan Phillips."

"Okay, we can talk about you some more."

He actually laughed. I didn't think I'd heard that sound before. "There's not much to tell."

"Marital status?"

"Divorced. Twice."

"How long were you married?"

"Seven years the first time. Two years the second time."

"What went wrong?"

"A lot of things. Hard to pinpoint. But both marriages failed."

"There are all kinds of failures," I pointed out. "Failure of love, failure of communication, failure of tolerance."

"Failure of hope, maybe," he said thoughtfully. A car swerved suddenly into his path but he maneuvered around it, completely unruffled. Someone behind us honked furiously, and horns sounded in response all around. None of this seemed to faze him. "I think they both gave up on me, figured I'd never change."

"No one ever does change."

"I have," he answered.

Traffic came to a complete halt for a full minute, then slowly started inching forward again. "But I didn't change in time for them," he went on. "What went wrong? Right woman, wrong time. Wrong woman, wrong time. For me, it was always the wrong time. I was too busy being super soldier or super cop, patrolling the Chinese border or bashing in heads in the Hot Zone. Thought I was the toughest guy around. I liked being married, the few hours of the day I remembered I was married, but neither of my ex-wives liked it so much, and I didn't worry about it a lot when they left. I went on being Mr. Macho, leading all the raids, throwing the first punches, shooting off the first bullets.

"Then one day it dawned on me. I might know more about hand-to-hand combat than any guy on the force, but hardly a soul on this earth loved me. My sister, maybe, but nobody else. Doesn't matter how many medals you have, how many creeps you bring to justice, how many wars you stop or start—doesn't matter if you save the world—if you die and no one's at your grave crying, your life has not been worth living."

I was absolutely stunned by this speech. That anyone would make it—that Bram Cortez had made it—that he had made it to *me*. To have gone from being a man who could embrace that life to a man who could reject it was a stark testimony to the truth of his earlier statement. Indeed, he had changed.

"I can't imagine that," I said softly. "If I were to die tomorrow, I can think of at least fifty people who'd come to my funeral, and probably half of them would be sobbing. My family—my friends—my students—my former students—my co-workers. I mean, there's never been a time in my life I wasn't connected to other people by pretty significant emotional bonds."

"That's because you've figured out what's important."

"No! Every day I wrestle with that. What have I done this day, this year, ever in my life, that has mattered? I haven't cured disease or saved the poor or even had much luck getting my students to reliably improve their use of apostrophes. I don't know that I've ever made a valuable contribution to the world. But I've never felt alone in it, either."

"I think that's the key," he said. "That's what I'm working on."

Ahead of us, in the extreme right-hand lane, two cars came together with a percussive thud followed by a musical tinkling of glass. Cortez looked over, seeming to assess the damage and the degree of danger to the victims. The drivers, both of them young men, had already leapt from their cars and begun a heated verbal exchange. Neither seemed to be suffering so much as a sprained rib. Cortez returned his attention to the road, and we drove slowly on.

"So what about *your* marriage?" he asked. "To Daniel Faberly. Which lasted four years and a few months. What went wrong there?"

Funny how talk about my divorce seemed to be a recurring theme this week. Still, it was only fair that I answer the question; he had fielded so many of mine.

"At the time, it seemed very layered and complicated," I said. "I would have hourlong conversations with friends about the precise level of insult in some offhand comment Danny had made. I could tell you why he didn't respect me or exactly how to interpret some gesture he made over dinner. But mostly I think we went into the marriage with different expectations. I thought we'd grow and mature and work toward common goals—like owning a house and having kids and getting to know our neighbors. I don't know. Mundane stuff, I guess. I thought we'd meld together as a couple.

"Danny thought he needed to stake out his territory as an individual, which meant he had to challenge me at every turn. I mean, sometimes, it seemed like he was trying to thwart me over the simplest things, like getting dinner on the table before nine at night. I was saving money to buy a dining room set. He took the money and bought a new computer. We needed the computer. We could live without the dining room table. But—I don't know that I can explain. We never wanted the same things. And it seemed like he deliberately subverted my dreams. And I felt like I was always fighting to define myself and keep my dreams at an equal weight with his."

I shrugged and stared out the window at the slow-moving cars. "Marriage is a power struggle, some of the time. Maybe a good marriage isn't. But unless your goals are always in complete agreement—and how could they possibly be, between two individuals?—someone's going to lose on every divergent issue. And I think it's important that you take turns winning. But I also think it's important that you don't spend all your time drawing battle lines. Some of the time, it should be fun."

I glanced over at him and caught him grinning. "The fun is the best part," he agreed.

I laughed and stretched my feet out till they touched a rounded plastic compartment. The housing for the protective airbag, perhaps. "Though you sound like a jerk when you say, 'I'm leaving this guy because it's not fun.' Or 'because it's too difficult.' And I fretted for a long time about whether I was making the right decision. Was I trying hard enough to make the marriage work? Should I give in more often? If I loved Danny, wouldn't I want him to be happy, wouldn't I want to give him things, let him have his way? I thought I was letting go too soon." I smiled. "Of course, my brother and my friends thought I had held on too long, but they were partisan."

"Do you ever want to see him? Danny?"

"Nope. I talked to him last year when his mother died, but I haven't heard from him since. He's in California now, I think. Every once in a while, I run into one of his friends, who tells me how well he's doing. Married again, someone more submissive, I hope, and working at some great job. Good luck to him." I glanced over. "How about you? In touch with your ex-wives?"

"Marilee calls now and then. My first wife. She's got a good heart—she cares about everybody—she couldn't wish bad luck on anyone except maybe some baby-killer. I think she likes me better these days, because she sees some softening in me. Actually, we're sort of friends, and it's nice."

"Maybe she'd come crying to your graveside."

A flicker of a smile. "Maybe. But not Ellen. She was too unhappy and too mad when she left. I think she just wants to forget she ever knew me and move on with her life."

"Best to honor that, then."

"Oh, I do."

"I'm sure I'd be civil if Danny called again," I said thoughtfully. "I used to play this game with myself. Say Danny called in the middle of the night, in the middle of some tragedy. He needed to borrow ten thousand dollars, or he was violently ill and needed someone to come save his life. Something like that. What would I do? Give him the money? Go take care of him? Save his life?"

"And?"

I laughed. "Some days I would and some days I wouldn't. I think—no matter who it was—if someone I knew and had had any affection for ever called me and needed something desperately, and I could supply it, I'd give it to him. One-time emergency deal. But I don't think I'd let that person back into my life on a permanent basis. That's what I think."

"Interesting game," he commented. "I'd do anything for Marilee. Ellen wouldn't call, so it's not even an issue. Couple of my ex-cop buddies—yeah, I'd go bail them out, if I could. Can't imagine that too many of them would think to call me if they suddenly needed help."

"That's as sad as saying no one would come to your grave."

"I know."

We drove on a few minutes in silence. Crept on, more like. We were absolutely locked in traffic, bumper-to-bumper cars in all lanes on both directions of the freeway. It was the Lake Michigan of automobiles. You were sure there had to be a far shore free of tire tracks, but you could not visualize it from where you sat.

"This would drive me crazy," I said at last. "Being stuck in traffic like this. How can you stand it?"

"I don't come into the city that much."

"Where do you live?"

"Palatine. Not all that far from Quentin's. You still run into traffic, but nothing like this."

"Well, sorry to bring you into these hellish conditions."

"I don't mind," he said. "I like the city."

Another silence. It seemed Cortez's confidences were over, and for the life of me I couldn't think of any interesting new topics to introduce. My eyes wandered over the dashboard screens, crowded with LED indicators, and my attention was caught by a heads-up stereo display.

"What do you usually listen to in the car?" I asked. "No, let me guess. Audiobooks about financial investments or historical battles from World War II."

He smiled slightly. "I do like nonfiction books," he admitted, "but I'm more apt to listen to history than money tips. Good guess, though."

"How about music?"

"There's a few things there. Check them out. Put something on if you want."

I tapped the buttons so the readout came up. He had a good selection of feenday bands, one or two more contemporary swoon croon albums, and a few albums by groups I'd never heard of. I went with the mellow ancient rock of Santana and we both listened in contented wordlessness for the next twenty minutes or so.

I'd decided I shouldn't distract him with any more nosy questions since, impossible as it was to believe, traffic had gotten denser and drivers had become more reckless. The speed would pick up for a few miles, then suddenly everyone in front of us would come to a screeching halt, for some impediment that we never discovered. We were very close to the city now and the towering brick and glass buildings were throwing their shadows across the glutted highway. There were streets in Chicago, I swear, that had never felt the kiss of sunlight. That's how close and crowded and high those buildings were.

"Do you happen to know the best exit for your neighborhood?" Cortez asked.

"Um—not really. I live right off Diversey."

He nodded. "I know your address. I've been spying on you, remember? I'm just not sure of the best way to get there."

"Teleport code is five-six-seven-two-one," I said helpfully. "Nearest stop to my apartment."

"Never mind," he said, and I saw him key my address into a dashboard screen. "Is there street parking in your neighborhood?"

"Um, I guess? But you can just drop me off."

"I have to come in and get Quentin's shirt."

I could just run up and fetch it for you and run back down, I wanted to say, but of course he could figure that out for himself. He probably wanted to come up and check out my apartment, make sure I wasn't harboring revolutionaries or building bombs in my spare time.

"Great," I said. "I'll give you a beer."

"I'm on duty."

"Really? Don't you have, what was it, a dozen men covering for you back at the Phillips mansion?"

"Not quite that many. I'm not officially off until six."

"Probably be six before you get back, but it's up to you," I said. "Wouldn't want to waste my beer."

He grinned and concentrated on negotiating back toward the exit lane on the right. I honestly couldn't have told him if this was the way to my apartment or not. I read an essay once that said the invention of the teleport had turned us into a population of geographical idiots. Not only could we not differentiate the countries on the globe, we couldn't provide a reliable map of our own cities. True in my case, I must say. Actually, I'm probably better with a world map than a local one. I know that the lake's to the east, Evanston is to the north, Atlanta is to the south, and Houston is *way* to the south, but I couldn't really reckon miles and I absolutely could not draw a map to scale. There were neighborhoods not three miles from my apartment that I had never been in. Back in the days when people drove, or walked, or took buses from point to point, they physically had to cover every mile they traveled, so they developed a familiarity with their closest landmarks. But I skipped straight from the teleport gate to the other side of the city, and I couldn't tell you what lay in between.

But there was no need to worry—the onboard navigator took us directly to my building. "Hey, this is my street!" I exclaimed.

"And, look, parking right down the block," he said. "Probably the only time a space has opened up in the past ten years."

A few minutes later, we were stepping into my apartment. I hadn't been expecting company, so I hadn't exactly cleaned the place up, and I gave one quick look around as I tossed my purse to the table. Only a few dishes in the sink, only a few bills on the dining room table, a few more pairs of shoes than strictly necessary strewn around the living room. It could have been worse.

"Of course, the question is, Where did I put Quentin's shirt?" I asked aloud. "I thought I left it in here so it would be visible enough for me to remember it. Hmmm . . ."

My apartment is not large. The kitchen, dining room and living room all open off each other to form one big space. Most walls are lined with bookcases. The living room features, in addition, a jaunty selection of furniture, some second-hand, some left over from my marriage: a big red couch, a puffy brown chair, a rocker, some wooden stools, and an entertainment center. The dining room holds a table, mismatched chairs, a glassed-in cabinet that used to belong to my grandmother, and more bookcases.

There are also various boxes and piles in the corners—clothes, papers, books, things I haven't gotten around to sorting or putting away. The kitchen is too small to require furniture or accommodate boxes.

Cortez was looking around with great interest, and I wondered what would first grab his attention. He zeroed in on the item that most people noticed right away: a half-size bronze sculpture of a naked girl, sprouting stained-glass angel wings from her back.

"What's this?" he asked, walking closer to examine it.

"Butterfly Woman. A gift from my friend Marika."

"I like it," he said. "She looks happy."

"It's my very favorite thing that I own."

"What about this?" he said, pointing to a small furry bat—fake, I mean—hanging upside down from one of the bookshelves.

I grimaced. "A gift from my friend Domenic. He decided that if Marika was going to give me butterflies, he would give me bats. But that was the only one he gave me, and then he got tired of it."

Cortez's eye had been caught by a volume lying open beneath the bat. "This seems like a strange book. *Sociological Theory in Mid-Millennium Urban Centers.*"

"That's from my brother Jason."

"Have you read the whole thing?"

"Oh, no." I didn't bother to explain. I glanced around the room again. "Well, hell. I don't think it's in here. Must be in the bedroom."

Uninvited, Cortez followed me to the bedroom, no doubt to see what other strange objects I had lying about in there. First thing he saw, of course, was the water bottle hooked over the headboard of the bed. Well, it's not just a water bottle—it's more like a supersize canteen, with a long, snaking plastic straw that curls down to just above the pillow.

Cortez pointed. "What's that? Or will it embarrass me?"

"No, of course not. It's a water container. Jason rigged it up for me. I get thirsty in the night."

"Sure, but a nice tasteful mug of water—"

I flung myself on the bed, arms outstretched. "I hate getting up in the middle of the night. I don't even like to lift my head from the pillow. Once I wake up, I can't fall back asleep. So Jason made me this—spigot. See, you can lie here, and guide the straw to your mouth, and take a drink of water—" I demonstrated. "Without moving an inch."

He was regarding me quizzically. "Doesn't it drip all over your face at night?"

"No, there's a little valve or something that keeps the water inside until you suck on it." I sat up. I could tell I was flushing. "Would you like to try it?"

"I don't think so, thank you very much."

I came quickly to my feet. "So where would I have put the T-shirt? Not in the dresser, since I wasn't going to keep it. In the closet? Does that make sense?"

He pointed to a stack of boxes next to the dresser. Was this really the reason he'd wanted to come up, so he could catalog all my idiosyncrasies? "What's in the boxes?"

"New shoes I haven't worn yet," I said, my voice muffled because my head was in the closet.

He did a silent mental count, I guess, because next he said, "Nine pairs?"

I pulled my head back out. "I don't like new shoes. I actually have a phobia about them. I'm afraid they'll hurt my feet. So I'll buy them and then not put them on for, oh, six months. By which time the shoes they're replacing will have literally fallen to pieces on my feet. And then I have to wear them."

"That seems a little extreme."

"I know. I'm not good with new things. I usually wear the same two pairs of earrings every day. I don't change my hairstyle much. I don't rearrange the furniture. I like things the way they are."

"Do you like new people?"

"Almost always." He didn't say anything, so I added, "I know. It doesn't make sense."

"I was thinking," he said, "it's better to like new people than new products."

And which do you prefer? I wanted to ask, but I didn't. "Where the hell is that shirt?" I demanded.

"In a bag under the couch," he said. "Or at least something is."

I gave him a look of great irritation and hurried back into the other room. Sure enough, there it was, almost invisible under the frayed red skirt of the sofa. He had sharp eyes, Bram Cortez, though a rather devious manner. Would not have expected that of him.

"Here," I said, formally handing him the bag. "I hope he likes it."

"He will. Quentin likes every gift."

A moment's silence. "You can still stay and have a beer," I said.

He shook his head. "No, I need to get back. I have to check on Quentin before I leave for the day, and go over reports with the guys on duty. But it's been interesting," he said, without a change in his voice.

I smiled. "Very. Why were you so talkative?"

"I'm always talkative," he said, and headed for the door. "You just haven't been around that much."

And he smiled at me from the threshold—gave me a real smile, not that faint look of amusement that I had seen on his face before. I know my own expression must have been one of sheer astonishment, because he laughed out loud, shook his head, and walked out, closing the door behind him.

I thought, *Friday will not come soon enough.*

CHAPTER NINE

But Friday brought no sign of Bram Cortez. First I read and corrected Quentin's letter to Marika, then we turned back to the poems of A.E. Housman, dissecting them for meter and meaning. *When I was one-and-twenty, I heard a wise man say, "Give crowns and pounds and rubies but not your heart away . . ."*

"I like it," Quentin said, "but it's too cynical."

"How so?"

"Basically, the poem says you're stupid to fall in love. Right? And that seems pretty cynical. I mean, some people fall in love and are happy together."

"I'd like to think so," I replied. "I can't say that I know too many people who are happily married, however."

"Dennis is happy," he argued. "With Gregory. And my aunt and uncle have been married for thirty years, and they seem happy."

"And my mom and dad were together almost that long," I said. "I suppose the real lesson would be, 'Choose wisely,' not 'Never try at all.'"

Quentin was silent a moment, brooding. The early April sun streamed in through the window, ecstatic and golden, filling his hair and his rough boy's cheek with leonine shadows. "I don't think I'm ever going to be married," he said at last. "Probably won't even meet a girl to fall in love with."

He never talked about his doomed future, so my heart squeezed down a little. Was he ready to discuss it now? "Why do you think that?" I asked.

He gestured. "Well, I practically never leave the house! Where would I meet somebody? Unless Francis started bringing in his nieces."

No; today was not the day he'd talk about it. "Well, let's see. The weather's getting better. We could start taking some excursions. I know—on the first nice day, you'll put on those funny-sounding braces you told me about, and we'll walk down to the beach. We might not meet any girls, but it would be fun, don't you think?"

"That would be jazz," he said, excited. "Ultrajazz."

"Good. We'll plan it."

His attention started to wander after that, as I expected; I never did get more than twenty or thirty solid minutes of concentration from Quentin. He would be distracted by the sight of a bird playing just outside the window, or the chime of a text on his EarFone, or a thought he had while in the middle of a completely different sentence. It was hard for me to keep up and just as hard for me to hold on to my patience.

"You know what?" he asked suddenly, a propos of nothing at all.

"I have no idea."

"My dad has the biggest gun collection in the Midwest."

"Is that right?" I cared nothing about guns. In fact, I was pretty sure gun ownership was strictly regulated within city limits, if not forbidden outright, due to gun-control laws passed after much controversy some years ago. But perhaps we were far enough out in the suburbs that the laws didn't apply here. Or perhaps such laws never applied to someone as wealthy and powerful as Duncan Phillips.

He nodded. "Yeah, you want to see them?"

"You mean they're not in a vault somewhere?"

"Oh, no. They're all in his study on the second floor."

"I'm not really that interested in guns, Quentin."

"Yeah, but these are stratojestic," he said pleadingly. "You've got to see them."

I was tempted. Since my first visit here four weeks ago, I'd seen very little of the Phillips mansion—the front foyer, a few hallways, Quentin's room, the stairs to the back garage. Marika endlessly hounded me for more details and could not believe I had not been offered more chances to look around the estate.

"Your dad probably wouldn't want me gawking at his private collection," I said.

"No, he wouldn't mind! He likes to show off his guns." He pointed himself toward the door. "Come on. Before Francis or Bram gets here."

"What?" If we were hiding our activities from the steward and the security officer, I had even worse misgivings. But Quentin was already out the door, and in any case I was about to be left alone in the house. I snatched up my purse and ran after him.

We took the elevator down a single floor, and the doors opened onto a completely unfamiliar vista. Where the third-story hall was pleasant and airy, the second level of the mansion was extravagantly ornate. I stepped out into a hallway that was twice as high as the one we'd just left. The walls were covered with gold-flocked blue paper, the ceiling was delineated by dental crown moulding, and the plush navy carpet was so thick it muffled every footfall.

"Gosh," I said, wide-eyed as a yokel, "spend any money decorating this part of the house?"

Quentin grinned and pointed. "My dad's private suites are down there. I never go there. There's one of the offices where he meets people. There's the hologallery—hey, we could go there instead."

Hologallery? I dimly remembered Dennis making some comment about the creepiness of this place. "Is that where he keeps portraits of his old girlfriends?"

"Yeah, you wanna go see?"

"Umm—maybe some other time. In fact, I'm thinking we probably shouldn't be here at all—"

But he had flicked the forward switch on his chair and was skimming over the blue carpet well ahead of me. "No, really, no one will mind. The study's right down here."

We passed a few closed doors and then entered a room on the far end of the hall. I supposed the dark velvet curtains and the heavy, baroque furniture were supposed to give it the clubby look of a rich man's den, but the high ceilings and wide proportions made the room seem anything but cozy to me. That, and the array of weapons covering the walls.

I pirouetted with my mouth hanging open. When Quentin had referred to a gun collection, I had expected a few glass-enclosed cases of antique muskets, maybe a service weapon or two. But Duncan Phillips seemed to have gathered the entire chronicle of American firearms into this one room, and laid them out, item by item, in rows that reached from the chair rail at the mid-point of the wall almost to the ceiling.

"A lot of these are historical," Quentin said. "See, there's a flintlock musket from the American Revolution. And there's a Colt revolver from the Wild West. And there's a Tommy gun that belonged to Al Capone."

He made a quarter-turn and pointed at a different wall. "There's a Glock 9mm, and there's one of the early stun guns—but it doesn't work. And there's the prototype laser gun that the soldiers used in the China wars. And this is a Trellin-X modern laser, but it's been outlawed, so you won't find one like it except if you hang out with mercenaries or revolutionaries."

"Who taught you so much about guns? Bram Cortez?"

"Dennis."

"Dennis? Likes guns?"

"Sure. He and Bram go down to the range and practice together sometimes. Dennis says Bram's better than he is with a projectile weapon, but that he's better with a laser. He comes in here with me all the time and tells me stories about each of the models."

As he spoke, he reached up to take a tiny, elegant weapon from its mount on the wall. It was smaller than the palm of my hand, encased in silver-colored steel or some other alloy, and looked to weigh about as much as a light bulb.

"Quentin! Put that back!"

He looked over at me with the devil in his eyes. "Why? I won't hurt anything."

"What if it's loaded?"

"Of course it's loaded," he said scornfully. "They're all loaded." He held the delicate little piece up to his eye and sighted down its tiny barrel. Fortunately, he was aiming at the window, not me.

I felt faint. I glanced around the room again, imagining all sorts of natural disasters knocking the guns to the floor, causing them to fire their bullets and their infrared beams at any hapless visitor who had the bad luck to be standing there. "They're all loaded?" I repeated stupidly. "How dangerous is that?"

Quentin turned to look at me, the gun still held up to his eye. "It's only dangerous if someone doesn't know what he's doing," he said.

I made my voice as cold as I could. "Put. That. Back. Right this minute."

He lowered it from his eye, but presented it to me like an offering. "Why don't you try it?" he said. "Just hold it a minute to get the feel of it. You'll like it. Dennis says this is a lady's weapon. I think my dad's last girlfriend gave it to him."

"I don't want to hold it—"

"Just for a sec," he wheedled.

He scooted closer, hand still outstretched. The gun lay in his palm, harmless as a napping kitten. Even I could tell which part was the barrel and where the dangerous trigger fit into the grip. "Fine," I said under my breath, and picked it up as gingerly as possible.

"No, you're not holding it right," Quentin said. "You have to—"

I marched straight over to the wall where it had been displayed. "Here? Is this where it goes?" I hung it from the nearly invisible pegs inserted into the wall. "Like that?"

"Taylor, you didn't even—hey, why don't you try the Glock instead?"

"You touch another of these guns while I'm in the room, and I'm walking out of this house and never coming back," I said, enunciating each word with absolute clarity.

"Oh, Taylor, don't be mad," he said, rolling over and placing a hand on my arm. I was shaking; I'm sure he could feel it. "I know how to handle a weapon. I wouldn't have hurt you!"

"Guns are little death machines," I said in a quiet voice. "I'm sure Dennis and Bram think they're fun, but don't you know why guns were invented? To kill people. They're not toys, Quentin. If you're going to handle one, don't do it around me. Do it around someone who knows how to use one. Or don't do it at all."

"Okay, okay, we won't come back here," he said in a pacifying voice. "Let's just leave right now, okay? Come on, Taylor."

And he headed out the door as I followed close behind. I saw him glance at some of the other closed rooms as we made our way back to the elevator, and I was pretty sure that he wanted us to explore the taxidermy lab or the torture chamber or some other equally gruesome spot, but that he had realized this would be it for me today.

"You want to go back up and play chess?" he asked when the elevator door yawned open.

I had yet to play chess with him, and he asked every day. As soon as he played a single game with me, he would lose interest; I figured the excitement of the unknown would be worth more to him than the tedium of the reality. Besides, I'd reached my limit this afternoon.

"I don't think so," I said. "I'm just going home."

"I'll ride down to the lobby with you."

"Okay." I stepped in beside him and he chattered happily for the next minute about some online friend he'd made. We hadn't gone two feet down the marble foyer before Francis appeared from nowhere.

"Quentin. Ms. Kendall. I was looking for you to escort you out," he said with his usual regal calm.

"I was just showing her some of the house," Quentin said.

"I hope that's all right," I added quickly.

Francis nodded. "Perfectly fine, as long as someone's with you. We wouldn't want you to get lost."

I tousled Quentin's hair. "See ya next week, kid. Be good."

"Bye, Taylor! Bye!"

I stepped into the teleport gate and disappeared. The minute I was back on my own street, I was already calling Marika.

I passed a quiet weekend and was pleased when Monday and Tuesday were relatively serene, both at home and at Sefton. Nancy told me Evan was out of the health clinic, though he wasn't in class, and she promised to give him the reading assignment for the week. Caroline called the most boring staff meeting imaginable to discuss new requirements for pass/fail courses and updated procedures for students wanting to drop or add classes after the posted deadline. I was not the only one yawning before the hour was over.

And then it was back to Chicago and Duncan Phillips' house, where once again I did not see Bram Cortez.

Quentin was in high spirits, which meant hard to teach, so I resorted to the strategy I sometimes use in unruly classes. "Pop quiz!" I announced, after the first fifteen minutes were utterly wasted. "Quick! The more answers you get right in the shortest period of time, the higher your score. Who wrote *Romeo and Juliet*?"

Anything rapid-fire had an intrinsic appeal for Quentin. His eyes lit with excitement, and he yelled, "Shakespeare!"

"What's the name of the main character in *Game of Thrones*?"

"Jon Snow."

"Who killed the navigator in *Dream of Nortook*?"

He thought a moment. "Wes Drachney."

I had to think even faster than he did and tailor my questions to the books I knew he had read, so this was actually more tiring for me than for Quentin. I kept it up as long as I could, and he only missed three questions. By the end of the session, I was exhausted, and he was as energized as a street kid on amphetamines.

"Hey, that was fun," he bubbled as I subsided into my chair and tried to catch my breath. "Do I pass? Do I get an A?"

"You passed brilliantly. A-plus."

"Ask me some more questions."

"I can't think of any," I replied honestly. "I'll put together another quiz for next week—how's that? Only this time you have to do some research on your own."

"Why? What kind of quiz?"

"You have to read—let's see, one book—before next Tuesday. That gives you a week. I'll have a quiz ready for you and we'll see how much you absorbed."

"I might need more than a week."

"The Friday after that? That would be ten days."

"Maybe. What book? Is it long?"

"I'll give you a choice."

We spent the rest of the hour compiling a list of possible novels, with me giving him a little background on each one. He ultimately decided on *Ticket to Terrazone*, Devante Ross' favorite book, which suited me just fine. I figured I'd give Devante the chance to earn extra credit by having him write the quiz. Win-win.

"How come I never get to ask you questions?" Quentin wanted to know.

"You ask me questions constantly."

"Yeah, but I mean, like on a test."

"You want to make up a quiz for me? That's terrific. What's it going to be on?"

He considered. "Aspirations of Kudzu. Their second release."

"I don't know their stuff very well."

He raised his eyebrows in a supercilious expression that I had never seen him wear before. "Well, you've got ten days to learn it, then, don't you?"

I couldn't help smiling. "Okay. Friday and Tuesday, we'll do our regular lessons. Then *next* Friday, I quiz you, you quiz me. I expect a real test, though. At least twenty questions written out in advance."

"I can do that," he said. "That'll be fun."

Probably I should have had him test me on the collected works of a respectable poet instead. Billy Collins and Mary Oliver, for instance, are pretty accessible for someone trying to sift through the lines on their own—or maybe I could have tried him on Louise Bogan if I wanted to make sure he was reading verses with a clear entry point but a more formal structure. Certainly he wouldn't learn as much from "You're my sweet fantasy, my one reality" as he would from any of those three or a hundred others. Then again, I was pretty sure he'd make it through a dozen song lyrics, when he might give up after a single traditional poem.

I wondered, every once in a while, what Duncan Phillips might think of my unorthodox style of teaching.

I was putting everything back in my briefcase when there was a knock on the door a moment before it was pushed open. I turned quickly, but Dennis was the only one who strolled through. He was dressed in a white poet's shirt and tight-fitting black jeans, both enhancing his soulful Mediterranean good looks. His dark curly hair looked freshly combed, and his face was deeply tanned. The picture of health and beauty.

"Hey, pet. Hi, sweetie" was his greeting. "Class all over?"

I covered my disappointment with a smile. "Who's pet and who's sweetie?" I wanted to know.

"You can be either. Both." He waved an indifferent hand. "I express my affection for the universe at large." Dennis approached Quentin and ruffled his hair with idle fondness. "So how did learning go today?"

"It was great," Quentin said enthusiastically. "I get to make up a test for Taylor."

Dennis smiled at me. "Isn't that like Quin helping me learn to swim?"

"You know what they say," I replied. "Best way to learn something is to teach it."

"Then I should be teaching marital bliss," Dennis said.

I glanced at Quentin, who had already slipped out from under Dennis' casual hand and was at his computer, looking something up. "Troubles at home?" I asked.

He hunched a shoulder, smiled slightly, and changed the subject. "I understand you went cruising through the gun exhibit the other day."

I couldn't suppress a shudder. "And I understand you're the expert who's explained all the models to our young friend here."

"One of my many manly traits. A love for weaponry," he said. "I could teach you to shoot, if you'd care to learn."

"I don't think so," I answered. "The only reason I was glad to see the room was so I could tell my friend Marika about it. She lives for tidbits of gossip on Duncan Phillips, and so far I haven't been able to supply very many."

"Was she impressed?"

"No! She was annoyed. She thought I should have been begging for admission to the hologallery instead."

Quentin looked up from his monitor. "Hey, yeah! Let's go!"

Dennis rolled his eyes. "I can't stand the place. But you really should see it at least once, if you haven't. Otherwise, you simply haven't had the complete Phillips Mansion Decadence Tour."

Quentin had joined the two of us where we stood just inside the doorway. "C'mon, Dennis, take us to the hologallery," he pleaded. "I know Taylor really wants to see it."

"I don't," I protested. "Marika wants me to see it."

Dennis shrugged. "Reason enough."

"Anyway, Dennis has to take us," Quentin informed me. "He knows how to break the code."

"He what?" I demanded. "You mean, security code?" The full implication suddenly became plain. "You mean, the door's locked and we're not supposed to go in, and only Dennis knows how to break in?"

"Don't be modest," Dennis said to Quentin. "I taught you how to do it, too."

Quentin looked abashed. "I tried the other day and I didn't get it right. Bram came down and asked what I was doing."

"Wait," I said. "Hold on. What exactly is required for us to get into this room?"

Dennis looked at me with a smile so mischievous that for a moment he reminded me of my brother. "Duncan Phillips doesn't care to have people know the room exists. Door's locked, and it's monitored by one of Bram Cortez's security cameras. You've got to turn off the camera, then break into the room. Simple, really."

So many things wrong with that explanation it was hard to know where to begin. "But if the cameras suddenly go down, won't that instantly alert Cortez and the other security personnel that someone's messing around with the system? Won't they come looking for us? And wouldn't that be embarrassing?"

"Glitches happen all the time with the monitors. If we cut the camera in just the right spot and we only stay in the room in a few minutes—" Dennis shrugged again. "I think we can be in and out before anyone comes investigating. Don't you?"

See, this was my problem. I had no interest in the hologallery. I didn't care if I never had a chance to satisfy Marika's raging curiosity about the room. But a challenge to my ability to defeat the system—that I found hard to resist. This was my brother's legacy to me, that I would ruin my good name just to prove that I wasn't afraid to try something stupid.

"And if we get caught?" I said.

"So you've come to Bram's attention," Dennis drawled. "Is that so very bad?"

I felt myself blush, and I wanted to kill him. Fortunately, the always impatient Quentin was already tired of talking. "Can I cut the camera, Dennis?" he asked, sending his chair in little jerky motions to the left and then the right. "Can I? I think I know what I did wrong. I want you to show me, but I want to do it. Can I?"

Dennis turned from me to get the door for Quentin. "You bet. You have the necessary tools?"

Quentin held up a keyring of small screwdrivers, thin metal wires, and infrared beam blockers. "All ready."

Dennis paused to give me a limpid look. "Birthday present from me last year," he explained. He followed Quentin into the hall. "Let's go, buddy."

I couldn't help but follow.

We took the elevator down to the second floor and were once more enveloped in its plush navy luxury. I thought I knew which door led to the hologallery, but Quentin and Dennis made their way casually past it, so I trucked along behind them, keeping what I hoped was an innocent expression on my face. In case anyone happened upon us in the hall.

A moment later, the two of them came to a stop and Dennis nodded at Quentin. He hitched himself closer to the wall, aimed one of the beam blockers at an inconspicuous plastic square set right above the baseboard, and then began using one of the slim screwdrivers to pry the cover loose.

"Why this particular outlet?" I asked Dennis in a low voice.

He pointed toward a spot on the crown moulding back down the hallway. "Camera in the wall right there, faces the elevator doors. No camera trained on us here."

"And once the feed is cut, how much time will we have before someone notices?"

Dennis grinned. "Kind of depends on who's on duty. And if anyone's monitoring the cameras at the moment—which often, during the day, they're not. If it's Bram, we have about three minutes before he figures out where we are. If it's one of his baby cops, lots longer."

"Bram Cortez seems fairly efficient," I said.

"Entirely."

"Dennis!" came Quentin's excited whisper. "This is the part I messed up last time. Help me."

Dennis leaned over and began giving him calm, detailed instructions. I watched (you never know when you might need to disable a security system) but couldn't really figure out which key turned off what mechanism. Even I, however, could tell when the steady green standby light blinked off. "Camera's down," Dennis said. "Door."

Quentin shot his chair down the hall and had the door opened before Dennis and I had taken the ten paces needed to get there. "Good job," Dennis approved. "You make me proud."

I had no comment to offer, either praising or criticizing Quentin's grasp of lock-picking techniques, because I had stepped across the threshold and could only stare.

The hologallery was a high-ceilinged room about three times as long as it was wide. I assumed there was hidden track lighting, which had sprung on as soon as we entered, but the room gave the impression of existing in almost total darkness, velvety and lush. This then created the setting for the artwork on display. Each separate piece created its own light, or seemed to.

I took a few involuntary steps forward and felt my mouth fall open. Marching down the narrow length of the gallery was a parade of women sculpted in light. They were irregularly placed, but there appeared to be three rows of women with twelve or fifteen figures in each row—thirty or forty sculptures in all. Every woman was semi-nude, and each had been meticulously recreated in an amazingly three-dimensional form, so that a visitor could instantly perceive the variety in the form, height, voluptuousness, and skin texture of Duncan Phillips' mistresses.

And each sculpture appeared, Pygmalion-like, to have been brought to life by its creator, for each one moved. This one bent to retrieve some object fallen to the floor, this one turned her head as if to glance at someone over her shoulder. Another folded and unfolded her fringed shawl across her chest— first concealing, then revealing, her small, delicate breasts. Another lifted her leg in a sexy chorus-line kick, then flung back her head as if to laugh.

Every single woman wore a mask or a scarf or a hat that covered her face in such a way that her features were wholly obscured.

I took a few slow steps deeper into the gallery, my mind reeling, my mouth still gaping. Here, a hooded woman brought both hands to her mouth, kissed them, then tossed that kiss out to an unseen watcher. Beyond her, another glowing statue offered a small opalescent apple to her incandescent sisters, then brought it back to cradle it against her cheek; her eyes peered out knowingly from a winking, feathered mask. A third woman put her hands to her veil as though to lift it, then instead tightened its folds around her face and gazed out with shadowed, hollow eyes.

I turned to look back at my companions. Quentin was near the doorway, perhaps studying some lock combination that I had not noticed upon my entrance. He seemed to have very little interest in his father's array of radiant lovers. Dennis was right behind me, watching me with a faint smile.

"I think I'm going to be sick," I said.

"Extraordinary, isn't it?"

I gestured at the shifting, posturing herd of discarded lovers. "How does he—why would they—I mean, do they pose for him? Do they know they're going to be put in this—this zoo?"

"Well, as you might guess, I've never actually been there when he asked them to model for him," Dennis said, and even his suavity seemed a bit shaken by the mercilessly sybaritic exhibit. "But what I suppose is that he asks the women to pose, and they think it's romantic or something. They don't realize he's just going to add them to this electronic harem. They think it's unique and exciting."

"You can't see their faces," I said.

He nodded. "That's what I find most disturbing, too. Like he's obliterated their individuality. They're merely bodies to be counted up."

"How much time does he spend in here? Does he bring other people here? Marika says this room has been whispered of for years but that no one's ever seen it."

Dennis spread his hands. "Again, not questions I can answer from experience. I've never been invited here. I have to think some of his cronies have had a chance to walk down the line and get their jollies. But maybe it's just all for him."

"I think I'm going to throw up."

"Well, not in here," he said. "Let's go."

But I turned back to get one more look, still not quite believing what I was seeing. Here, a dancer pirouetted, one hand above her head; there, a girl appeared to be painting her fingernails with golden polish. But I noticed an odd thing (though what could count as odd in this setting was hard to fathom). Each mistress had been decorated with an identical gem, a round plum-sized crystal that she wore on a chain around her neck, or on a belt around her waist, or in a tiara tucked into the veil that wrapped her head.

"They all have the same jewelry," I said. "Does he make them pose with that, too?"

Dennis glanced over at the statuary and back at me. "Parting gift," he said. "Flawless opal shaped like a sphere. They don't seem to know it's a good-bye present, though—legend has it each woman is delighted to receive it. Then the portrait, then the dump. You could hardly get more romantic."

"I *am* going to be sick."

"Well," he said, "at least now you know. If you ever start dating Duncan Phillips, be prepared to run when he starts showering you with the really big jewels."

I gave him a look of unspeakable revulsion, but before I could come up with a suitably crushing reply, Quentin came gliding over. "What do you think, Taylor?" he asked. "Pretty weird, huh?"

You're nineteen, and your father keeps a gallery of life-sized holographic mistresses in his house. Exactly what kind of neurosis is that going to give rise to in later life? Except, of course, Quentin wasn't going to have much of a later life. I couldn't keep myself from reaching out to ruffle his hair.

"Pretty weird," I agreed in a casual voice. "What do you think about it?"

He wrinkled his nose and looked briefly over at the gesturing sculptures of light. "Well, I like looking at naked women," he said, "but it's not as much fun once they've been your dad's girlfriends."

I choked back a laugh. "Yeah, that is kind of the gross part," I said. "Now if they were lingerie models, or something—"

He laughed. "Yeah! That would be pretty jazz!"

"So, if all of us have had our fill—" Dennis said, letting the sentence trail off with a questioning lilt.

"I'm out of here," I said and headed straight for the door without looking back. The others followed, and Dennis locked the door behind us.

"Now, you," Dennis said, pointing to Quentin and the little box on the wall. "Turn the cameras back on, and we have safely completed our little exercise in B and E 101."

I watched Quentin carefully do his burgling in reverse, wondering why he never was quite so meticulous with any of the projects he completed for me. Maybe it was the lawlessness that appealed to him; perhaps if I asked him to plagiarize, he would attack the assignment with zest.

"How many cameras are there in the house?" I asked Dennis. "Every hallway? Every room? Is there a camera in Quentin's suite? Do they watch me teaching?"

He grinned. "And would there be something wrong with that? Are you doing anything inappropriate?"

I slugged him on the arm exactly as I would have slugged Jason or Domenic. "No, it's just—you know—someone watching me all the time. Yuck. I don't like it."

"As far as I know, there are only cameras in the public areas. The whole first floor. All the hallways. The office where Phillips meets with business associates. I don't think there are cameras in the bedrooms and private living areas." He grinned. "Although—Duncan Phillips—a camera in the bedroom might be just the toy he likes best."

I flicked a warning look at Quentin, who had just joined us. "All done," he said breathlessly.

Dennis looked at his watch. "Good timing," he approved. "Good job all around. Now it's time to go work out."

"And it's time for me to go," I said. "I must say, a most educational afternoon."

Dennis leaned forward to kiss me on the cheek. He'd never done it before, but it seemed entirely natural. "See you next week," he said. "Don't get lost on your way to the door."

But no chance of that. Francis met me as soon as the elevator doors opened, making me wonder how unobserved our escapade had really been, and escorted me to the teleport pad. I wasn't rude to him, but I have to say, this was one day when I was more than eager to get free of the Phillips mansion and all its inhabitants.

CHAPTER TEN

THE FRIDAY SESSION WITH QUENTIN PASSED RELATIVELY SMOOTHLY.
He was more focused than usual, so we got a fair amount of work done. Or maybe he was so attentive because neither Bram nor Dennis made an appearance, so he didn't have anyone else to distract him. I confess I felt oddly deflated when I went home. I chalked it up to the little headache that had built up over the course of the day.

The weekend itself held only one highlight—meeting Jason and Domenic in Atlanta to go to an afternoon Braves game with Marika. The day was warm, and once the game was over, the row of teleport booths outside the stadium was swarmed with sweaty fans looking to go home.

"Come on," Marika said. "Let's find a different gate."

She led us a few blocks away to a wide, paved plaza in front of a towering mirrored skyscraper where a single portal stood deserted in the afternoon sunlight. "Hardly anyone uses this one on the weekends," she said with satisfaction.

Before she could open the door, we saw a grungy teenaged boy flicker into life behind the smoky glass, then disappear. Marika snatched her hand back with a yelp, but the guys were laughing.

"Oh, it's been forever since I played round robin," Jason said.

"Don't even think about it," Marika warned.

"I did it once in twenty jumps," Domenic claimed.

"I don't believe you," Jason said.

Marika rolled her eyes at me, but I was grinning. In the big cities, all the teleport booths have big red NEXT buttons that fling commuters to the nearest available gate, which could be anywhere in the city. These were all installed after some poor young man was trapped in one of the gates as a sudden violent fire broke out and swept toward him. He was either unfamiliar with his destination code or paralyzed by fear—at any rate, he didn't manage to punch in the numbers that would whisk him away, and he quickly burned to death.

Because the NEXT function is a safety feature, it's free. You don't need a transit pass or even a thumb chip to activate it; you just hit the button. Of course, you have no idea where you'll end up, but the theory is you'll be somewhere safe where you can gather your wits and proceed to your desired neighborhood.

Naturally, about five minutes after the NEXT buttons were installed, restless teenagers invented a new game. They would start out at one terminal and see how many jumps it took them to get back to their original spot. I can't tell you the number of times I've stood waiting for my turn at a gate and seen a ghostly face materialize behind the glass then vanish into darkness.

"Let's try it," Domenic said. "Twenty jumps each. See where we end up."

"I'm ending up at home," Marika said, stepping inside the booth. "I'll see you when you get there."

I wavered for a moment, half-ready to embrace the adventure. I'd played round robin once—with Jason and Domenic, of course—and I'd found it exhilarating but unnerving. Too many Chicago neighborhoods where I didn't want to linger for even a few seconds, too much adrenaline spiking through my body. Too many times of feeling myself dissolve and reassemble in too short a time. I shook my head and followed Marika straight back to her place. A couple of hours later, I was home.

The rest of the weekend I spent cleaning the apartment, checking in with my mom, shopping online, and listening to Aspirations of Kudzu. I had five more days to prep, but I wasn't sure what the first part of the week would hold, and I wanted to be prepared.

Monday afternoon, Devante Ross stayed after class and helped me prepare a quiz about *Ticket to Terrazone*. Thirty questions, about half of them obvious and half of them obscure, and I awarded Devante the extra ten points he needed to make an A-.

"You're the bestest teacher ever," he said solemnly.

"That would mean more if you were the bestest student," I retorted.

His face lit with its customary grin, and he hoisted his books. "You're going to miss me when school's out for the summer," he threatened as he left.

I sighed. Unfortunately, it was true.

Tuesday morning in Houston it rained so hard that they had to close some of the streets for flooding. Even in mid-April, the temperature had started to climb noticeably, and on short walks between campus buildings, the sultry humidity wrapped itself around you like a suffocating parasite, desperate and inescapable. Attendance on campus was sparse, so I spent my office hours guiltily reading fiction.

Tuesday afternoon, I met Duncan Phillips.

It had seemed strange to me that I had spent so much time in this man's house, received payment deposits directly from his bank, and was having what seemed to be a marked effect on his son, and had never yet met him. Certainly, I would have been investigating anyone who walked across my threshold twice a week to mold the mind of my child. I would have asked for references before I had someone come in and water my plants in my absence. But Duncan Phillips didn't seem to be that sort of father.

At any rate, the impression I had formed of him, both through observation of his household and the comments let fall by Dennis, Quentin, and Bram Cortez, had led me to think I wasn't missing out on much by failing to make his acquaintance. So, after the first couple of weeks, I had started to come to the mansion without thinking much about its owner one way or the other.

My mistake, as it happened.

The time with Quentin had gone unexpectedly well. He was tired, which slowed down his capacity to think of diversions, and so it was with some docility that he listened to my explanation of subjective and objective pronouns. It was only toward the end of the hour that he started to get restless, and look out the window, and make quick, involuntary movements in the direction of his computer.

"And I'm assuming you've made some progress reading *Ticket to Terrazone*?" I asked, raising my voice to catch his attention.

"Yeah, it's great," he said, with some of his usual liveliness. "Hey, I know where there's lots of realbooks. My dad has a library, there's got to be a million books in there."

"Well, I'm sure it's an impressive collection, though a million seems like a high number—"

"No, it is! It's a million! You could ask Francis. Some of them are worth a lot of money, too. You want to ask Francis?"

"No, really, it doesn't matter to me if—"

"I know! Let's go look. You can count for yourself."

"I hardly think, if your dad really has a million books, that I could count them in an afternoon."

"Well, let's go look anyway," he said, pointing himself toward the door. "You like books, right? You'll love this."

"Quentin, I don't know that I should keep exploring your dad's house whenever you get bored," I protested, though, I admit, somewhat weakly. Marika had been fascinated and delighted by my description of the hologallery—and not nearly as repelled as I had been, but then, she hadn't actually seen it—and commanded me to make use of any such additional opportunities that arose. Surely she would encourage me to accept Quentin's offer.

"Yeah, but anyone can go into the library!" he countered. "It's not like we need to break in or anything. You'll like it. Let's go."

No surprise that I followed him out the door, down the hall, into the elevator, and down to the main floor. I expected Francis to appear and guide me majestically to the teleport pad, but he was apparently busy elsewhere. Quentin and I proceeded with only a hint of stealthiness down the main hall, then through a ponderous double door that opened onto a vision of splendor.

Floor-to-ceiling bookcases in a room whose ceiling had to be twenty feet high. Each bookshelf was made of some rich rare wood, darkly lambent in the half-shuttered light, and each shelf was completely filled with hardbacks. I glanced from case to case, picking out the matching bindings of a dozen collections, though most of the volumes seemed to be singular, of varying heights and widths and covers. I wondered if there was some system to their organization—19th-century novels here, examinations of the Vietnam War there, travelogues in the middle aisles—and assumed there had to be. Otherwise, you could get lost for days, trying to hunt down *Sociological Theory in Mid-Millennium Urban Centers* but getting seduced by Ann Radcliffe and Anne Tyler and Anne Sexton along the way.

I didn't think there were really a million books here, but there sure were a lot.

"See? You like it, don't you?" Quentin demanded. "I knew you would. I bet you could find any book ever published in the world here."

I didn't bother trying to correct this truly outrageous claim. "Yes, I like it a lot," I agreed. "I've always wanted my own library of physical books. With nice cozy chairs to sit on while I browsed through my collection. I'd probably walk in some days and not come out for a week."

"You'd starve, though."

"No, I wouldn't," I said loftily. "My soul would be nourished by literature."

"Yeah, but you—hey, Taylor! I just thought of something." He spun his chair in a circle and headed toward the door. "Wait here."

"Where are you going?" I asked in alarm.

"I'll be right back. Stay here!" he called and disappeared.

I was tempted to run after him, because I did not like the idea of being un-chaperoned in Duncan Phillips' house, but I was also tempted to stay and start reading. As is so often the case, my less virtuous nature triumphed. I strolled forward and began randomly scanning titles on one of the middle shelves.

This appeared to be the history section, because it contained massive books dedicated to dissecting the World Wars, as well as a few smaller volumes on Korea, the Ukraine war, and the recent Chinese Revolution. I stepped a few shelves over to find myself segueing into biography, which seemed to be heavily weighted toward warmongers and other predominantly male world leaders. Where were the cases holding Margaret Atwood, Maya Angelou, and May Sarton? I moved on.

Quentin had been gone maybe fifteen minutes and I had finally drifted into fiction when the door opened behind me. "Next time you complain about not liking a book I've assigned to you, we'll come down here," I said without looking at him. "You'd have to find *something* you liked on these shelves."

"No doubt," said a deep male voice that was definitely not Quentin's. I spun around. "But I don't believe you're in a position to assign any task to me."

I stared at him and could not think of a single thing to say.

The newcomer was medium-tall, dark-haired, and handsome in a polished way that made his perfectly cut hair and his exquisitely fitting suit seem part of a calculated presentation. His eyes, dark gray and unwaveringly fixed on me, gave no hint of emotion—irritation, amusement, fury, interest. I had seen his face a hundred times, a thousand, in online magazines and television newscasts, so I recognized him instantly. But the digital images never conveyed the sheer physical impact of his presence, wary, feral, and infinitely engaged.

He waited for me to speak.

"I'm—hello, I'm Taylor Kendall, I didn't know—" I stammered. "I'm sorry."

He didn't move, just continued to survey me. "Taylor Kendall," he repeated. "I don't know anyone by that name."

I was sure my cheeks were flushing; my whole body was flushing. I could feel the heat rise along my stomach and my armpits and my throat. "I'm teaching your son," I said. "English. I'm from Sefton University."

"Ah." He took one step into the room, precise, almost robotic. He still watched me without appearing to blink. "And how long have you been on my payroll?"

I had to think quickly. "About—just over six weeks now."

"How often are you in my house, looking about my rooms?"

Now I could feel the bright red color in my cheeks, and all I could think about was that illicit foray into his living erotica collection. "I come twice a week to tutor Quentin, but usually we're just—I mean, I go to his suite and we stay there—"

"Until today."

Until last week, actually. "He knows I love books. He thought I'd enjoy seeing your collection. He told me it was—he said anyone could come in here, I assumed it was a public room."

He took another two steps forward, and I felt a moment's mad panic. I mean, what could he do to me, what would he even consider doing to me, here in an accessible room of his own house with his servants and his son likely to burst in at any moment? But there was such an aura of danger in his unnerving stare, in his tense and coiled body, that I truly felt a stab of fear. Maybe it was just guilt, but I didn't think so.

"Why are you so nervous, Taylor Kendall?" he asked softly.

"I'm—you caught me off-guard, walking in unexpectedly—and you don't seem all that pleased to find me here, to tell the truth—"

My inane words caused him to smile, a lethal little smile, and I really did back up a pace, as unobtrusively as possible. "Of course I'm pleased," he said, in the voice of a panther purring. Did panthers purr? More to the point, did they purr right before they pounced on dinner and devoured it?

"It's not every day I find attractive young women lurking among the 20th-century classics. It seems like something of a reward for enduring a rather troubling morning."

I couldn't say a word.

He came closer at a more relaxed, natural pace, walking toward me like a man and not a predator. "So what do you think of my collection, Taylor Kendall? If you're a Sefton University English professor, I'd assume you'd have some love of literature."

I gestured at the bookshelf behind me, using the movement to cover up two more steps away from him. "Well, I was mired in history for a while, so I've just made my way to fiction, but I have to say this is the most complete collection I've ever seen outside of a university," I said. Talking about books gave me back a shadow of my usual coherence. "And you've got real depth in your early-20th-century female authors. I mean, I'd expect the whole Virginia Woolf canon, but you've also got the complete works of Elizabeth Bowen, and everything by Gertrude Stein, and Edna St. Vincent Millay's poems and—"

"I'm not particularly interested in women's writing," he interrupted.

I fell silent.

"I'm more interested in women," he said.

I stared at him as I imagine the mouse gapes at the hawk.

"So tell me a little about yourself, Taylor Kendall," he said. He came closer, and this time I resisted the urge to back away. What would happen if I ran for the door? Would he chase me? Would he laugh? Would he forbid me to ever cross his threshold again? Did I want to cross it? Would I die of mortification and unease even as we spoke? "Where do you live? Are you married? What kinds of things do you like?"

"I live—here in Chicago," I said, stammering again. Babbling, actually. "Teach in Houston, of course. I like to travel—I—um—I teleport almost every day, so I'm in lots of different cities, Atlanta, Denver, you know, places like that, sometimes I go over to London or Berlin, but not so often—"

"You're nervous again."

"Well, you know—I guess—a little."

He smiled. I could tell that he thought it was a warm smile, the kind that attracted or maybe melted the women he usually talked to, but it didn't reassure me at all. "So you like to travel," he prompted. "Do you travel alone? With a friend? Somebody special?"

"I'm divorced," I said baldly.

He nodded. "I'm sure the man's a fool."

"Most men are," I said before I could stop myself.

His smile widened; he laughed softly. "I agree with you there," he said. "For different reasons, I suspect. And you don't have anyone else in your life right now? Boyfriend—steady guy—lover?"

The door blew open, and Bram Cortez stalked in.

"Mr. Phillips," he said, not looking at me. "The Mercedes has been brought around."

Duncan Phillips did not turn his head to regard his security chief. "Give me just a moment," he said.

Bram looked at his watch. "I thought you were supposed to be there in twenty minutes. You could teleport, I suppose."

Now Phillips pivoted on one very expensively shod foot, his face again set and emotionless. "No, I need to bring some delicate items with me," he said. "The car is better."

He turned toward the door without looking at me again. Any other man, having started even such a bizarre flirtation with any other woman, would have faced her again, smiled, apologized, intimated that he would like to see her in the future, the sooner the better. Not Duncan Phillips. I saw his perfectly set shoulders rise in a tiny shrug and his hands come up to touch his collar and his tie. Then he strode forward like a Buckingham Palace guard, not glancing at anything around him, nodded to Cortez as he passed, and left the room.

I found myself staring at the security chief, who was staring right back at me. Glaring, more like. His face looked stark with shock, and he appeared to be trying to force some reasonable expression back onto his features through an overlay of fury.

"What in God's name are you doing here all by yourself?" he demanded at last.

I spread my hands. "I came here with Quentin. He wanted me to see the books. He said he'd be right back."

"You're not ever supposed to roam this house alone."

"I know that. I know that visitors are always escorted from room to room, and you're afraid I'll get lost or steal something or take photographs to feed to the tabloids, but it just happened, it's not my fault—"

"That's not why you're not allowed here unescorted," he said deliberately. He jerked his head at the door through which Duncan Phillips had disappeared. "He's why. And the rule only applies to women."

I felt myself go cold bone by bone. "He—but—are you saying that a woman isn't safe in—it's daylight, it's a public room, it's—you mean, has something happened here?"

"Yes," he said brusquely, and let it go at that.

I began shivering with an uncontrollable chill. I'd never fainted in my life, so I didn't know what it felt like to have a swoon coming on, but at the moment, total unthinking unconsciousness had a certain broad appeal. "Then can I just say how glad I am that Duncan Phillips had an appointment somewhere else and that you came to find him?"

Cortez looked at me like I was the stupidest person on the planet, and I felt myself blushing again, for completely different reasons. Heat, cold, heat; my body was revolving too rapidly through its own seasons. "You were watching," I said in a low voice. "On the camera. You saw him come in and find me." A beat. "You rescued me."

"I happened to look at the monitor when he walked in," Cortez said curtly. "Some other day I might not have been paying attention."

"I don't know—what can I say?—this is—" I put my hands to my cheeks, and felt my fingers shaking. "Thank you, though."

"You'd better leave," he said.

I dropped my hands. So much for sympathy. "I'm on my way even as we speak."

But before I could take a step forward, the door swung open again, this time to admit Quentin and Francis. "Hey, Bram!" the boy said happily. "I was showing Taylor the library."

Cortez turned smoothly to face Quentin, though I thought I saw a quick, significant glance pass between the two men. "Hey, Quin. What were you showing her?"

"The books," Quentin replied. "Well, I had to go up to my room because I thought I left one of my dad's first editions there, but I couldn't find it, and then my cousin called, but I knew Taylor would find anything she wanted by herself. Pretty jazz, huh, Taylor?"

"Spectacular," I said as enthusiastically as I could.

Quentin came closer. "So what did you find? See something you'd like to take home? It's okay, people borrow books from the library all the time. There's no charge or anything."

"Taylor needs to get going," Cortez said.

Quentin was instantly dismayed. "Not yet! Just a few more minutes! You can help me pick out my next book—you always say everyone should always have their next book in mind—"

I smiled tightly. "I think you can find what you need on your own, buddy."

"Well, okay," he said grumpily. "But I'll see you Friday."

Involuntarily, I looked over at Bram Cortez. Because, you know, for a moment I wasn't sure that I would be allowed back at the mansion, and I had not even remotely settled the question of whether or not I wanted to return. The guard had his eyes fixed on me; his face gave nothing away. But he gave one short, sharp nod.

"Of course you will," I said. "Now, do you and Francis want to accompany me to the door?"

Because, the hell with it. If Cortez was going to be all tough and hostile, I wasn't going to look to have a moment alone with him at the telepad, eager to express my thanks again and hoping he would tell me he'd raced down the hallways in a desperate attempt to save my life or my virtue.

"Sure," said Quentin, and the three of us made an odd little party as we slipped out the door and down the hall. Quentin talked happily for our whole brief journey, and Francis from time to time nodded or smiled. He was the one who held the door for me as I stepped into the teleport chamber, and he gave me a look that seemed filled with knowledge and rue.

"Have a safe journey home, Ms. Kendall," he said. "We look forward to seeing you again in a few days."

But as the system whisked me away, I still was unsettled enough to think I might never return.

⟨⟩

"Of course you can't go back there," was Marika's pronouncement. "What a dog. You should call the cops."

"Oh, I can just imagine how that conversation would go," I said. I was feeling much better, having soaked in an ultra-hot bath, drunk a bottle and a half of beer, changed into my footie pajamas (still chilly enough at night to justify wearing them), and curled up on the couch to call Mareek. "'Well, officer, he didn't touch me, and he didn't threaten me, and I have no reason at all to think he meant me harm except for a few ominous words let fall by the household staff, and my own sense of great unease.'"

"Okay, but you can't go back there. You're in danger."

I was silent for a moment.

"Tay? You hear me? You can't go back."

"There's Quentin," I said at last.

"Right, but Quentin's got a houseful of *male* bodyguards who will keep him company, and his rich supercreep daddy can afford to hire any number of other tutors, so it's not like he exactly needs you."

"He does need me. You haven't spent any time with him, you don't know how vulnerable he is. He's so childlike. He's so sweet. I want to sweep him up in my arms and rock him to sleep. I want to hold him like a little baby and just say over and over again, 'It's all right. It's going to be all right.' And, of course, it's *not* going to be all right. Not for Quentin. I just have to be there for him as long as he needs me." I took a deep breath, speaking out loud the decision I had made without even knowing it. "So I'm going back Friday."

"You can't ever be alone there. Not for a minute."

"I know that. I'll make sure Francis or Dennis or even Quentin is with me whenever I'm in the halls."

"Or Bram Cortez," Marika said.

There was a moment's profound silence. Honestly, I'd said very little about the man. What was there to say? I'd told Marika about our drive home, and our conversation about ex-spouses, and she'd asked me a few questions and then seemed to lose interest. But that's the thing about Marika. Bloodhound. Can't throw her off a scent.

"Sure," I said cautiously. "If he's around."

"So was he watching you?" she demanded. "On the monitor? Do you think he watches you while you're tutoring Quentin?"

"Dennis says there aren't cameras in the private rooms."

"Bet he does."

"Why would he?"

"He likes you."

"Oh, you can't possibly infer that from—"

"You like him."

I was silent.

"What's he look like again?" she asked.

"Ordinary."

"Specifics, please."

"You know. He's tall. Dark hair, going a little gray, cut really short. A small mustache. That kind of skin that has a dark undertone even when it's fairly pale. Muscular. And he has a sort of—readiness—about him. I can't explain. As if you could burst through the door shooting double-barreled shotguns, and he wouldn't be caught by surprise, and he'd knock you to the floor before you had time to turn your weapons his way."

"Oh yeah," she said dryly, "you like him."

Well, okay, it was true, but I couldn't figure it out. "Here's the thing," I said. "He's not my type. He's a loner. He's an island. You couldn't—I mean, even assuming it went that far and you wanted to pursue a relationship with the guy—you couldn't *have* a relationship with the guy. He doesn't connect."

"That's why he likes you," she said softly. "'Cause you can connect with anybody."

CHAPTER ELEVEN

FRIDAY ROLLED AROUND WITHOUT ANY INTERESTING INCIDENTS TO distinguish the intervening days. I didn't let myself think about it too much once it was time to whoosh on over to the Phillips palace. I just gathered my books, stepped into the teleport booth, and let myself be flung across time and space back into the lion's den.

Which seemed to be empty of lions. Francis met me at the gate, Quentin greeted me ecstatically at his door, and the whole hour passed with an unalarming ordinariness that made the last of my frayed nerves reknit and stop complaining. Quentin and I took each other's quizzes, both of us scoring high marks though I did just a bit better percentagewise, and we laughed even more than usual. I have to say, it was one of our better sessions.

As the hour drew to a close, there was a knock on the door, and Bram Cortez stepped inside, Dennis at his heels.

"Hi, guys!" Quentin exclaimed. He had an inexhaustible supply of enthusiasm for the arrival of new guests. "What are you both doing here?"

"I've come to take you down to the pool," Dennis said, "and I imagine our own very dangerous house cop has come to walk Taylor down to the teleport gate." From Dennis' quick look in my direction, I guessed that someone had told him the story of my encounter earlier in the week, but now, of course, was not the time to discuss it.

Cortez didn't crack a smile. He said to Quentin, "Unless you'd rather I took you to the pool and Dennis took Ms. Kendall to the door."

"Taylor," Quentin corrected. "You're supposed to call her—"

"Taylor," Cortez amended. "Dennis could take Taylor to the door."

"I have a better idea," Dennis said. "Let's all go to the pool."

"Oh, yeah! We could play tag—or keepaway! I've got this big inflatable ball and we—or dodge ball! That would be fun, and we could pick teams—"

"I'm on duty," Cortez said stiffly.

"'Bout twenty guys here covering the place," Dennis said. "I think you could be spared. Besides, you'd still be on the premises to fight off any intruders who happened to make it past the forcefield."

My eyebrows lifted. "There's a forcefield?"

"Shock wall," Cortez said briefly.

"That does make me feel secure."

"So let's go play," Dennis said.

"Love to," I said insincerely, "but I don't have a suit."

"Mr. Phillips keeps a selection of unworn bathing suits in the women's locker room, for guests who arrive with just such a deficit," Dennis informed me.

My mouth fell open. Because he said it so triumphantly, or because I was sure it was true, I couldn't tell.

"A similar selection exists for the men," Dennis added. "But I happen to know Bram keeps his own suit here in his own locker, because he exercises in the pool almost every day."

"Well, I guess we've covered all the bases," Cortez said. "Let's go swim."

Quentin cheered and headed out the door. The men hung back to allow me to go next, so I numbly followed. I had no interest at all in stripping down and parading my partially clad, imperfect body before the eyes of my student, his shasta friend, and the unreadable Bram Cortez. Okay, it didn't bother me so much to be semi-nude in front of Quentin and Dennis, though of the three, Dennis was the most likely to make comments that were pointed and embarrassing. But I felt shivery and odd to think about taking off most of my clothes before Bram Cortez. There was no denying it, and no real reason to examine it closely.

Isn't it strange? Can't count the number of times I've worn skimpy suits to the Evanston or Oak Street beaches and paraded without shame before thousands of strangers. But gather together a few people with whom I have some history, even an acquaintanceship, and suddenly I feel like a bathing suit is immodest, exhibitionist, and entirely too intimate.

But here I was, headed to the locker room to try on one of the "unworn" outfits. All I needed now was for Duncan Phillips to decide to come in for a quick swim, and my day would be complete.

Once we were on the ground floor, the scent of chlorine led us to the pool room, which was not visible from any of the hallways. "Shoes off," Dennis said from behind me, so we strolled barefoot into the tiled room, Quentin rolling along behind us. And a lovely place it was, too, with a high skylight above and walls formed completely of glass overlooking the struggling spring garden. The pool was Olympic-sized and jewel-blue, and an intricate pattern of turquoise-and-white ceramic squares decorated the flooring all around its perimeter.

"Girls' room," Dennis said, pointing to a door. "We'll be out in five minutes."

The three of them turned toward another door, and I headed in the direction indicated. Where to find this pristine swimming apparel? I looked in a few of the empty lockers before thinking to try what looked like a closet, and sure enough, there were about four shelves of neatly folded bathing suits laid out for me to choose from. Sizes weren't immediately apparent, so I picked them up one at a time and held them up to my chest, trying to gauge the fit. There were a few two-piece options, but forget that; I was looking for maximum coverage.

Eventually, I settled on a textured forest green racer that, when I tried it on, was comfortable enough but cut much lower than I liked and for a woman with a more ample bosom. The minute I jumped in the water, the straps could very well slide off my shoulders and down my arms. I was *not* going to risk that mortification. I pulled a hair ribbon from my purse and reached awkwardly over my shoulders to thread it through the straps. Once I'd tied a knot, I wriggled my arms experimentally and was happy to find the suit seemed much more secure.

When I stepped back out into the sunlit pool area, I found all three men already splashing around. Not only did Quentin have a simply humongous inflated ball, but there were a few smaller toys available as well, including noodles, rafts, and inner tubes. In fact, Quentin was floating in the middle of a bright emerald donut that was equipped with a squirting device that seemed to draw water up from the pool itself, and he was furiously spraying his two companions. They were circling him, calling out strategy to each other, clearly bent on dumping him over headfirst. I had a moment's anxiety for Quentin, so clearly overmatched, but his vivid face was a study in sheer unalloyed devil-driven joy, and I could not help but smile as I watched.

Then I looked around for a weapon.

A second armed inner tube, this one a fluorescent orange, had been placed most invitingly on the side of the pool. Moving quickly, I tossed it in the water, slid inside it feet-first, and paddled over to the warriors, all the while desperately pumping the trigger to prime it. I made it to the field of combat just as the first satisfying jet of water gushed from the barrel, right into Dennis' face.

"Tay-ughlog-uh" was Dennis' greeting, since he spotted me a split second before I made my partisanship known.

"Quentin!" I shouted. "You and me against the bullies!"

"Bram's right behind you!" Quentin shouted back, and the hostilities were on.

A big wave of water splashed over me from behind, so I spun as quickly as I could and fired off another round. Dennis, meanwhile, had reared from the water and landed with both arms pushing down on Quentin's inner tube, trying to force it below the surface. He was behind Quentin, rendering Quentin's gun useless, so I shot a few squirts into his face and effectively drove him off. Suddenly my world started whirling out of control, as Cortez took my raft and spun it in three rough circles. Water in my face, up my nose, burning down my throat. I couldn't stop laughing.

This went on for about half an hour, an absolute madhouse soaking frenzy of a fight. It ended when Cortez swam up behind Quentin, grabbed him in a headlock, and dragged him from the safety of his inner tube. I'd already been dumped from mine. Dennis had flung it back to the tile flooring, then proceeded to pelt me with walls of water that he created by driving the flat of his hand into the pool.

"Wait—wait—stop," I cried, whipping my head from side to side, trying to see what was happening. "Quentin—he's out of his inner tube—can he—*stop that!*—can he swim? Is he okay?"

"He's fine. Better in water than on land," Dennis replied, continuing to splash me but with much less force. "Anyway, you know Bram would never let him drown."

Treading water with both feet and one hand, I put up my free hand to push my soaking hair behind my ears. Never mind feeling insecure about my body; now I had to fret about how dreadful I looked with my sodden hair streaming down my back and my mascara no doubt running in rivulets down my face. "At this moment, I'm thinking not only would Bram Cortez let Quentin drown, he'd push him underwater and hold him there. You would, too."

Dennis gave me a lazy smile. While I was pretty much aware of the effort it was taking to keep my head above water, he looked completely at ease, a creature in his natural element, like a swan or a seal. "You loved it," he said. "By the way, nice touch with the ribbon tied around your shoulder straps. I've always admired your sense of fashion, but this—"

"Go to hell," I said amiably.

Quentin and Bram Cortez swam over. Dennis was right, Quentin seemed quite comfortable in the water, moving rapidly, pain-free. His long spindly body floated like a birch branch. For a moment, my heart contracted. He was so thin. He was a pale skeletal shadow of a boy.

But he was laughing.

"Hey, Taylor, good job!" he called, giving me a friendly splash as he got close enough. "But I think we need someone else on our side. These guys are too big."

"Let's get Francis next time," I said demurely. All three of them laughed at that. "Or maybe I'll bring a ringer. Marika. How's that?"

"That sounds great!" was Quentin's predictable response.

Dennis turned toward the open middle of the pool. "C'mon, Q, time for us to do some work."

Quentin's eyes, stricken and pleading, were immediately upon Bram Cortez and me. "Don't go," he begged. "Stay awhile, and we can play some more games when we're done."

"I don't know if I—" I began.

"Okay," Bram Cortez said.

"Okay," I echoed.

Happy then, Quentin swam after Dennis. I watched for a few minutes, as Dennis led him through a series of exercises. Sometimes he gripped Quentin's arms or shoulders, holding him steady in the water; sometimes he would support the boy from the torso, requiring him to work his arms or legs. I couldn't catch all the instructions or all the banter, but the light, noncommittal syllables skipped back to us over the water, teasing, kind, encouraging. From time to time, Quentin would look up at Dennis, pleased at a compliment or laughing at a joke, and the bond between them was so evident it gave me a shiver.

Or maybe I was just cold. "I need to get a towel and be out of the water for a bit," I said to Bram Cortez.

He nodded in the direction of a white wicker hamper. "Towels are over there. I'll fetch some."

He swam to the other side of the pool and climbed out with quick, economical grace. I hadn't had much chance to notice while we were all roughhousing, but he had the sort of body I would have expected: taut, well-muscled, marred in a few places by old scars that still looked angry. This, obviously, was someone who considered his body a weapon and cared for it as thoroughly as he would care for his gun or his sword or any other piece of combat equipment. He would not hesitate to use it, and he expected it to perform whenever he demanded. I imagined that he had never been betrayed by a slow reflex or a strained muscle, just as he never would have been caught unprepared with his laser uncharged or his revolver clip empty.

Still, for a weapon, it was a rather attractive one.

I hoisted myself to the side of the pool, hoping I didn't look as ungainly as I felt, and once out of the water was instantly aware of the full weight and drag of my body. I sat at the tiled edge, dangling my feet in the water, and continued to watch Dennis work with Quentin.

Cortez draped a huge white bath towel around my shoulders and sat next to me at the pool's edge. "Are you cold?" he asked.

I wrapped myself in the towel's fluffy warmth. "A little. Thank you. But that was fun."

He smiled. "Yeah, every once in a while I come down and swim with them. Seems to make Quentin happy."

I sighed. "Yes, but—constant, unvarying, twenty-four-hour-a-day attention is what would really make Quentin happy. I try to play with him a little every day, too—I don't really give him a full hour of teaching, as I know I should—but I can't structure the entire day around making Quentin happy. Sometimes I want to, I really do, but—it would take my whole life."

He nodded thoughtfully. "I've felt that way a few times myself. I think,

'Oh, I should do this for Quentin, or I should do that for Quentin,' and then I think, 'You can't build your life around this boy.' And you can see Dennis feels that way. And Francis. And you have to ask yourself—why does he need so much attention from outsiders? And then you remember, oh yeah, because his dad's a class-A bastard."

The words were delivered in a calm, unaccented voice, but nonetheless they made me jump. "He's not on my list of favorite people at the moment," I said.

Cortez gave me a quick sideways look, as if assessing damage, but he did not refer to the incident from three days ago. "Duncan Phillips has done a lot of things that would make a reasonable man hate him," he said, still in that conversational tone. "But he really only had to do one thing—this one thing—to put himself beyond the pale as far as I'm concerned."

"I hope you're going to tell me what it was."

He nodded. He was looking out at the water, watching Dennis and Quentin. I had the sense that, if the slightest thing went wrong, if Quentin slipped for a moment from Dennis' hands and dropped his head below the water, Cortez would leap in and swim over to save him before I had even drawn breath to scream.

"A couple years ago, there was some medical breakthrough in the studies of Kyotenin degradation. Or so they thought. Organ donation would slow down the process of deterioration, or even stop it altogether. Bunch of test cases in hospitals all over the world—they even had a program here down at Northwestern's hospital in the city. Quentin's doctor asked Duncan Phillips if he'd participate, since the most likely donors were the parents or siblings of the patients."

I felt much colder than I had when I first climbed out of the pool. "He said no," I guessed.

Bram Cortez nodded. "He said no. He didn't even have himself tested to see if he was a close enough match. He wasn't willing to donate a kidney or a lung or part of a liver or even, as far as I could tell, a pint of his own blood to try and save his son's life."

Cortez was silent a moment. "Dennis and Francis and I got tested, of course, but none of us was even the same blood type. Not that it would have done any good—for a program like that, Quentin would have needed his guardian's permission, and clearly his dad wasn't going to give it."

"That damn legal majority act," I exploded. About five years ago, there had been a challenge to the controversial law that made minors dependent on a parent or guardian until the age of twenty-one or a successful bid for emancipation, but it had failed. "If I could tell you the number of times I've seen it screw up the lives of my students—"

He nodded. "Stupidest law ever passed."

"Do you know if Quentin ever considered suing for emancipation?"

"His aunt suggested it at the time. But Duncan Phillips made it clear he would fight the action in court—and since he could afford the best lawyers in the country, he undoubtedly would have won."

"Why would he bother? Since he clearly doesn't care much about Quentin's well-being, why wouldn't he just set him free?"

"Didn't you know? Kids who get emancipated are awarded a percentage of their parents' money, if their families are wealthy enough. Quentin would have walked away with twenty million or so. His dad wasn't about to let that happen." He was still watching the swimmers, so he didn't catch my expression of mingled fury and horror. "Anyway, so that's the real reason Quentin's aunt isn't around much anymore."

"How could any parent be so cruel?" I whispered.

"Quentin never talks about it," he said, "but he knows he's going to die. He knows he's probably going to die in the next five or six years. He knows that I'll be here till that day. I've told him so. What he doesn't know is, the day he dies, I'm waiting for Duncan Phillips to come home, and then I'm going to kill the man with my bare hands."

Now he looked over at me. His eyes were so black that nothing reflected back from them, not the sun bouncing through the glass walls, not the light rippling off the pool, not my face, so close to his. He seemed as calm as if he had just ordered a sandwich and as sincere as if he'd just declared his belief in God.

"I don't think you should say things like that," I said at last.

He lifted his shoulders in a small shrug and didn't add anything else. He continued watching me, and I watched him right back.

An arcing spray of water cut across both our faces and made us look quickly back to the pool. Dennis had swum over silently while we were discussing murder.

"You look so serious," he said.

"Talking about Duncan Phillips," Cortez said.

"That is enough to turn the brightest day gloomy," Dennis agreed. "So let's talk about happier things."

I glanced out at the pool to see Quentin swimming laps. Part of the exercise program, I assumed; otherwise, he would not willingly have let three other people hold a conversation in which he was not included.

Cortez nodded out toward the water. "How'd he do today?"

"Not bad. It was good we took some of the edge off by playing around beforehand—made it easier for him to concentrate. I think he's losing some strength in his legs, though. I need to watch him. I'm not sure how much longer he'll be able to swim like that unassisted." He too looked out to where the lone figure patiently made its way up and down the crystal blue aisles.

"What happens if he can't swim anymore?" I asked. "I mean, isn't that practically the only exercise he gets?"

"He'll still swim. I'll just get him a chest belt that will keep him afloat while he works his arms. And maybe I'll get him some ankle floaters, too. As long as he's moving at all, I'll keep him working out in the water."

"This is making me so sad," I said.

Dennis reached up a wet hand to pat me on the shoulder. "It makes us all sad, sweetie. But it's made us all better people—kinder, more tolerant, able to make friends with others whom we normally would have despised."

I smiled, because I could tell he was trying to cheer me up, change the subject, and bait Bram Cortez all at the same time. "What, you mean like you and Mr. Cortez here?"

"That's exactly what he means," Cortez growled. "You think I normally hang around with shasta freaks like this guy?"

I hadn't thought about it before, so I took a long, lingering look at him. "If I had to guess," I said slowly, "I'd say that at one point in your life that's really how you felt. But I don't think you do now, and I don't think it's because of Quentin."

Dennis gave me a moo-cow look of earnestness, clearly fabricated for the occasion. "It's because he's learned to grow and change as a person," he said.

"It's because it's too much trouble to hate people who are unfamiliar," Cortez said. "I don't even think 'Live and let live' anymore. I think, 'Huh. That guy's different. Wonder what he knows that I don't know?'" He jerked a thumb at Dennis. "Of course, in his case, he doesn't know squat that I don't know, so it's kind of a waste of time."

"Don't let him fool you," Dennis confided to me. "We're best buddies. We even go out drinking sometimes."

"Really?" I said, not sure if I should believe this or not. "What do you talk about?"

"Cars," they said at the same time.

"Cars! You couldn't come with anything more boring!"

"See," said Dennis, "this is why men and women will never be friends."

"Well, I wouldn't want to be friends with anyone who didn't have a better topic of conversation than that."

"We could talk fashion instead," he drawled. "Though I'm not certain it's your strong suit."

"I admire your own Eurotrash getup," I replied. "I can just picture you lounging on the beach, attracting no little share of attention."

Cortez laughed out loud. Dennis grinned. "You know, Taylor, my sweet," he began, and then paused as if struck by a new thought. "That's such a formal name, isn't it? What do they call you?"

"What does who call me?"

"Your friends. Your family. You must have nicknames."

"Tay, usually."

"Do you have a brother?"

I looked at him with misgiving. "Why?"

"Do you?"

Cortez answered. "Yes, she does."

"What does he call you?" Dennis asked.

I regarded him with complete disbelief. "Now why would I tell you that? That'd be like painting a target on my back and going down to the gun range."

"If I was your brother, I'd call you Tay-Tay," Dennis decided. He practiced a few times. "'Hi, Tay-Tay! C'mere, Tay-Tay.' Oh yeah, that is definitely it."

I couldn't help laughing. "You're dead on. Though sometimes he calls me Tay-Kay. You know, K for Kendall."

"Tay-Tay is better," Cortez observed.

I gave him a look of irritation, but before I could speak, Dennis asked, "What's your middle name?"

"Why would you want to know that?"

Dennis spread his hands in the water, a look of complete innocence on his face. "Just asking! I thought it might be useful to know."

"Well, I'm not telling you any useful facts about me," I said sullenly.

"Anastasia," Cortez supplied.

Again, I gave him a fuming look, but Dennis appeared delighted. "Taylor Anastasia Kendall!" he exclaimed. "But that changes everything! That's so feminine—so romantic! It gives me a whole new picture of you."

I was still glowering at Cortez. "What, did you just memorize the entire file on me?"

"Pretty much."

"When's her birthday?" Dennis asked.

"June 20," Cortez answered. "Couple months away."

Dennis looked over at me. "He likes you," he said. "I can tell."

"This is so unfair," I said.

"I like you, too," Dennis said. "But it's different."

Quentin came splashing over just then, churning up as much water as possible with the windmill motion of his hands. "Hi, guys," he said a little breathlessly. "I've done my laps. Can we play some more?"

"That's what we've been waiting for," Cortez said, and slid back into the pool. Feeling a little misused, I considered refusing, but it was, after all, what we'd been waiting for. So I cannonballed in, sending water everywhere, and the fight was on once more.

We played for another half hour or so, splashing, dunking, yelling, laughing. I had never seen Quentin look so alive or happy. On the other hand, he was a frail kid, and I wondered how long he could keep this up, even in the supportive medium of the water. Not to worry; both Dennis and Cortez were keeping their eyes on him, and the minute that I began to think Quentin looked a little tired, Dennis called off the games.

"Time to get you out and dry, young man," Dennis said.

"No! Just a few more minutes! I—"

"Out," Cortez ordered, and after a few more protests, Quentin submitted. We all swam a little wearily to the side of the pool, and I saw Cortez make a stirrup of his hands to boost Quentin from the water. Dennis was already out, towel ready, and he wrapped Quentin up and practically carried him to the wheelchair. Hard enough on me to leave the water and become responsible for all my own weight again; I imagined it must be ten times harder for Quentin.

"This was fun," I said, toweling my hair.

Cortez looked over. "We'll have to do it again sometime," he said in a polite voice.

"Hey, yeah! How about Tuesday?" Quentin suggested.

"Maybe not that soon," I said, smiling at him. "But soon."

Dennis glanced at me. "Next time, bring your own suit," he said softly.

I was still laughing as I disappeared back into the women's locker room. Actually, I was still laughing a half hour later when I got home.

I wasn't laughing quite so much that night when Jason called to inform me that we were going to some community theater performance Saturday night. Apparently, Domenic's soon-to-be-ex new girlfriend had a small role in a musical production of the life of Barack Obama, and they'd all decided I should make them dinner before we set out.

I groused about it, but I secretly rather enjoyed myself as I cleaned the apartment, ordered groceries, and made the meal. Marika arrived first, tumbling into the room with her usual explosion of energy. Tonight, she was dressed in some layered red dress dripping with sequined balls, and her lipstick and fingernail polish were the exact same shade. Her wild hair was tied up in a knot on the top of her head, but it still came spilling down in its normal abandoned curls. Her spike heels were at least four inches high.

"How do you think you're going to walk anywhere in those?" I demanded.

"Where are we walking? Down the street to the teleport gate. I'll be fine. I like your dress."

Mine was more sedate, a tightly fitting bodice of purple set into a flaring black skirt that came to my ankles. I figured I was too dressed up for community theater, but anything I put on would seem tame in comparison to whatever Marika had chosen, so I'd added a rhinestone belt and glittering silver shoes. The guys, when they arrived, wore their usual outfits, Domenic in flowing black and Jason in khakis and a buttoned-down shirt.

"Who raised this boy?" I asked. "Who taught him how to dress?"

"When we're running from the crime scene, I'm not the one they're going to be able to identify just by describing my clothes," he replied.

Over the meal, we covered the usual topics—music, gossip, insults, and former lovers. I thought Jason would stalk from the room when Marika mentioned that Axel had called again.

"Hey, man, as long as she knows it's stupid, she can do whatever she wants," Domenic said. He looked at Marika. "You do know it's stupid?"

She waved her hand in his direction. "Like I'm going to take advice from someone who can't stay in a relationship longer than a month."

I passed around the bread basket and tried to change the subject. "I say, let's have a moratorium on discussions of our love lives," I suggested.

Marika looked over at Jason. "She's seeing someone."

"I am not seeing someone! Why would you say that?"

Jason sat up, all alert, like a watchdog who'd just caught the promising sound of breaking glass. "Are you dating Duncan Phillips? Am I about to become the brother-in-law of a very wealthy man?"

I gave Marika a quick guilty glance. "I haven't told him."

"Told me what?"

I shrugged. "I did actually meet Duncan Phillips the other day. I was alone in his library and he came in and he—I couldn't tell if he wanted to beat me up or take me down right there in the house."

"Some men confuse sex and violence," Domenic said.

Jason looked grim. "So—what—he threatened you? You were afraid?"

"A little," I admitted.

"I told her not to go back," Marika said self-righteously. "But, oh no, our Taylor, she had to hurry right back three days later."

"But nothing happened there in the library?" Jason asked.

Marika answered before I could. "No, because her new boyfriend came rushing in to save her."

"Marika, will you stop saying that?"

"Who? What boyfriend?"

"She's referring to the security chief at the Phillips house. We've met a few times. He gave me a ride home the other day. He came into the library before anything happened—if anything would have happened, which I have to doubt."

Domenic was nodding. "Knight in shining armor. That's a nice touch. No wonder you like him."

"I think Marika's right," Jason said. "I don't think you should go back."

"Well, I'm certainly going to be careful," I said. "But I don't think anyone has to be worried."

"So, Duncan Phillips," Domenic said. "What's his deal? He's sounding worse all the time." He ticked items off on his fingers. "A complete bastard to his only son. Widower of a woman who died under mysterious circumstances. Famous for his ex-lovers. Infamous for a holographic gallery of his discarded mistresses—"

"Which I kind of like, may I say," Jason interrupted.

Marika snorted. "You are so perverted."

"Sounds to me like Duncan Phillips is the one who's perverted," Domenic observed. "Can't believe no one's up and murdered him."

I thought back to my poolside conversation with Bram Cortez. No surprise that Domenic had plucked that thought out of the air; he was, after all, completely fey. I said, "My guess is that it's just a matter of time."

CHAPTER TWELVE

THE NEXT TWO WEEKS WENT BY QUICKLY AND EASILY. MY STUDENTS in Houston were cramming for exams, so I held a couple of intensive review classes that nobody wanted to skip.

My student in Chicago had become susceptible to bribery, so I knew that if I promised to swim with him afterward, he would behave well during the actual tutoring sessions. Once Bram Cortez joined us and once he did not. I told myself that the aquatic interludes were equally fun on both days.

I passed one weekend shopping in Atlanta and one weekend hiking through the mountains near Denver—where it was actually colder than it was in Chicago. Marika said she had not thought such a thing was possible.

The following week was sultry in Houston and downright gorgeous in Chicago. "We can't stay inside on this beautiful day," I told Quentin. "We have to go outside. We have to go to the beach. Where are those Kevin braces you told me about?"

His face lit up. "Do you mean it? Do we have to study when we go to the lake?"

"Oh, we'll be working," I assured him. "You just wait and see. Where are your Kevin things?"

"Kevvi braces," he said. "I think Bram has them."

Better and better. "Then let's call him."

A few minutes later, Cortez was inside the room with Quentin, and I was out in the hall, not allowed to watch the apparently intimate process of attaching the device. I'd called Francis to ask him to either delay Dennis' arrival or tell him where we were going so he could join us, but Francis said Dennis had taken the day off anyway. Perfect. No reason to hurry back for anyone.

The door flew open and Quentin walked out. I felt a moment's disorientation at seeing him out of his wheelchair. For one thing, he was much taller than I had realized, still thin as a stick but somehow older-looking, more mature, now that I saw him stretched to his full height. For another, the braces were an imperfect invention, and he moved with a slightly jerky motion, slow and halting, as if he wasn't certain where the floor was. But he looked so delighted that I couldn't dwell on this, and I couldn't help but give him a hug.

"Let me see them," I demanded. He hiked up his pants to display tiny black wires spiraling up his legs, then turned his head so I could see a similar spider's web of connectors tapping into the base of his skull. "Wow. Weird," I said. "Does it hurt?"

"Nope," he said. "I'm a little dizzy, but if I hold on to you or Bram—and it always gets better—"

Bram was instantly at his side, wrapping an arm around Quentin's shoulder. "You know the rules," he said. "The minute you get tired, you tell me. Because if you overdo it, you'll get sick, and I won't take you back out again."

"I know, I remember," Quentin said. "Let's go!"

Francis was at the teleport station with a duffle bag full of beach items he had collected—a couple of blankets, some water bottles, an assortment of food, and a Frisbee.

"You're amazing," I said to him. "You want to come with?"

"I don't believe so," he answered with a smile. "But thank you all the same."

The next problem, of course, was logistical. Teleport systems had one great flaw, in that they could not instantaneously transmit two adult individuals. Most booths could handle one large and one small body—a parent and a child, or an adult and a pet—and "family-friendly" stations were set up to accommodate groups at the more heavily traveled destinations. In addition, all booths contained a FOLO key that ensured that anyone who hit the same button would end up in the same place. But it still wasn't ideal, and most people who wanted to travel in packs had to regroup after they'd relocated.

"I want to go first," Quentin said right away.

Cortez didn't even hesitate. "No. Taylor goes first."

"But Bram—"

"Ladies always do," Cortez said.

This shut Quentin up. It made me a touch indignant, but I made no protest. I didn't have much appreciation for chivalry, but I did have deep admiration for any argument that would let you get your way with Quentin. I picked up the duffle bag and stepped into the chamber.

"See you there," I said and fizzed on over to Oak Street Beach.

This particular stretch of shoreline, one of the few accessible public areas snuggled up to Lake Michigan, is always crowded. First day of spring when it's really too cold to sunbathe, middle of summer when the alewives are rotting in the tide, late September when winter is hovering balefully just across the waves—the beach is always a mob scene. Because, in Chicago, if you wait for perfect weather to go down and play in the sand, you'll never get a chance to do it.

Anyway, there's something mesmerizing about the water. When I was in high school, I used to study on the lakefill built just to the east of the North-western campus in Evanston. Bring a blanket and a sack lunch, find a big boulder that no one else had claimed, and plop down for the afternoon. Half the time I spent just watching the water, the gentle encroach and retreat of the waves, the endless varieties of blue over blue as the sky changed color and the water changed color while the sun made its lazy journey to nightfall. The lake is so big that you can't see to the other shore. You can imagine it's an ocean; you can imagine it's the end of the world. There is something majestic about it, something both calm and infinitely dangerous.

And, apparently, half the population of Chicago agreed with me and had turned out this afternoon to bask in the same sense of wonder. Sure, any of these people could hop on over to Tahiti at any point in the year to enjoy the surf and the sun, but it takes time and effort to gather your things and lumber through international teleport terminals to spend an hour lolling on the beach. But if you live in Skokie or Mount Prospect, you can wink on over to Lake Michigan with five minutes of prep and spend your whole day at the water's edge.

I barely had time to step from the teleport pad, glance at the people arrayed on the sand, and settle the strap of the bag more securely over my shoulder before Quentin came stumbling out of the gate. Oak Street Beach is a popular enough destination that there are three portals lined up right in a row, but Quentin emerged through the same one that had carried me.

"Wow! That's superjazz," was his first enthusiastic comment. I put out a hand to steady him, and he took it with complete unselfconsciousness.

"Haven't you teleported before?" I asked.

"Yeah, but not for months and months. It's just—suddenly you're some-place else and you can't even feel it."

I supposed that for someone whose transit even through the relatively restricted confines of his house was something to be accomplished only with great effort, the marvel of teleportation must seem even more miraculous than it did to me.

"Well, I'm glad you're here," I said, smiling at him, and then Bram Cortez materialized beside us.

"How you doing, Quin?" he asked. I was still physically attached to Quentin, my hand in his, but apparently I was invisible. "Did that shake any of your braces loose? You still feeling okay?"

"I'm great, Bram! This is so stratospheric."

"You let me know the minute you feel tired—or sick—or funny."

"You bet. Hey, can we go sit over there? We can watch them play vol-leyball."

Indeed, some enterprising young men and women, stripped down to way too few clothes for this early in the season, had stretched a net across the sand, and they were energetically knocking a white ball back and forth. To me, it looked too cold and too exhausting to be fun, but they were all clearly having a grand time.

"Not too close," Cortez said. "I don't want a ball hitting you in the face. Come on. Over here."

And just like that, he detached Quentin's hand from mine, wrapped it around his own waist, and led the boy away. I followed, loaded down like a mule, and thinking, *Two women left him, and it wasn't even because he was spending more time with the kids than he was with them. Amazing.*

But secretly, I have to admit, I was a little dazzled. I knew he adored Quentin, but I'd never seen him demonstrate quite this level of care. It was attractive. It was sexy. It just would have been a little more sexy if I'd felt part of the circle.

In a few minutes, we were situated on a blanket and looking through the bundle of goodies Francis had packed.

"Hey, look, cookies," I said. "And candy bars. And soda." I looked up, grinning. "We are gonna be so sick by the time we get home."

"Can we go swimming?" Quentin asked.

"No," said Cortez.

"Why not? I won't be cold."

"The water's a lot colder than the air is right now," Cortez responded. "So, yeah, you'd be freezing. Anyway, you can't get the braces wet, you know that."

"Anyway, you're supposed to be working," I told him. "Remember? This is a study hour. We've just had a change of venue."

"I thought maybe you'd forget," Quentin said.

"Damn unlikely," I replied.

He giggled, flashed a look at Cortez to see if I'd be rebuked for swearing, and took a bite of his cookie. "I didn't bring any books," he said.

"We don't need books. We're going to talk about a couple of poems that I know by heart. So you just get yourself comfortable."

Quentin squirmed a little where he sat and pulled his sweater tighter around his shoulders. Cortez stretched out next to him and threw his arm over his eyes to block out the sun.

"I wasn't talking to you," I said.

I could see his smile, partially shaded by the angle of his arm. "I don't have to study," he said. "I can get as comfortable as I like."

"Did you know there are poems about almost everything on the planet?" I asked Quentin in a very schoolmarmy tone of voice. "There's even a poem about your friend Bram here."

"There is?" Quentin demanded. "I don't believe you!"

"Well, it's not exactly about him," I conceded. "But it's about someone named Cortez."

"I want to hear it," he said.

First, I gave him a little background on Keats, and the Romantics in general. Shelley and Byron are far more interesting stories, but I glossed over them because Quentin was a very young nineteen. Sex and booze and poetry; debauchery hadn't really changed that much over the centuries.

Then I launched into a declamation of "On First Looking Into Chapman's Homer." I have to confess here that I always hurry through the first octet, because I find it labored and somewhat boring; all the good lines come at the end. But they are very good lines, describing that great magical sense of discovery:

> Then felt I like some watcher of the skies
> When a new planet swims into his ken;
> Or like stout Cortez when with eagle eyes
> He stared at the Pacific—and all his men
> Looked at each other with a wild surmise—
> Silent, upon a peak in Darien.

Maybe it didn't register with Quentin exactly the way I'd hoped, though. "Stout Cortez," he repeated and tried to smother a laugh.

Cortez grunted. "Scrawny Quentin," he replied without taking his arm off his eyes or making any other sign of sentience.

"Well, let's move on," I said. Now I turned to Shelley and "Ozymandias," because if any sonnet can be said to be popular with my students, this is it. Maybe they like the moral in the poem, the lesson that time erodes even the most sublime arrogance. Maybe they just groove on the theme of destruction. In my opinion, it's one of the most vivid pictures painted in poetry, of the great, monstrous, sneering sculpture toppled to the ground:

> And on the pedestal these words appear:
> "My name is Ozymandias, king of kings:
> Look on my works, ye Mighty, and despair!"
> Nothing beside remains. Round the decay
> Of that colossal work, boundless and bare,
> The lone and level sands stretch far away.

"I like that," Quentin said. "Say it again."

So I repeated the poem, then I recited "Chapman's Homer" again. We talked about rhyme scheme and the structure of the Petrarchan sonnet, and how the lines with the most impact were, in each case, the final lines—and how, in each case, they were composed of simple words, declarative sentences, descriptive phrases that conjured a sense of vastness and awe.

Quentin stretched his hand out to indicate the beach around us. "The lone and level sands stretch far away," he intoned.

"I wish they were lone," I said. "But that's the idea."

Quentin poked at stout Cortez, who gave every evidence of having fallen asleep. "Hey, Bram, do you know any poems? Taylor knows lots."

Cortez stirred, but merely dropped one arm and lifted the other to shield his face. "A wonderful bird is the pelican," he said sleepily. "His bill can hold more than his belly can. He can take in his beak enough fish for a week, though I'm damned if I see how the hellhecan."

Quentin shouted with laughter at this, though I grimaced. "Just my luck, that will be the poem he remembers from today's session," I said severely. "You have, with one limerick, undone all my hard work."

Now Cortez rolled to his stomach and pushed himself up on his elbows. He was smiling. "Are you guys done?"

Quentin glanced at me. "I think so."

"Oh yes," I said.

"Good. Let's play Frisbee."

There wasn't much room on our corner of the beach to play a running game, and I wouldn't have thought Quentin was up to it anyway, but naturally I underestimated the lengths to which Bram Cortez would go to make everything all right for Quentin. He staked out a small triangle for us near the edge of our blanket, then proceeded to throw the Frisbee with amazing gentleness and accuracy right in Quentin's direction. We must have played for an hour; Cortez never once missed. Quentin never had to leap or stoop for the plastic toy, which came twirling right into his outstretched hands.

I, on the other hand, had to catch Quentin's wildly uneven passes, so I was running and jumping all over the place, tripping on other people's discarded backpacks, skinning my knees as I dove into the sand. I was comforted by the fact that my own throws were not much better, and Bram Cortez had to leap just as high and run just as furiously to catch some of my more ill-considered tosses. He never missed one, though. Never dropped one. Is that the ease of the natural athlete or the tutored physical ability of a man trained to kill another man with his bare hands? Either way, he was impressive to watch.

The exertion tired us all out, and we dropped to the beach exhausted but happy. Cortez quizzed Quentin for five minutes about his state of well-being. "How are your legs? Does anything hurt? How about your lungs? Any trouble breathing?" After Quentin's first few reassuring responses, my attention wandered.

"Hey! There's an ice cream truck!" I exclaimed. "Anybody want ice cream? My treat."

Everyone, it turned out, wanted ice cream, not just the three of us. I waited in line about fifteen minutes before I was able to return with my treasures, cones for them and a Dreamsicle for me. We ate in contented silence, then the two of them dropped down to the blanket for a nap. After Cortez again asked Quentin how he was feeling, nobody spoke for about half an hour. I really think both of them fell asleep.

Not me. I sat up and watched the pageant before me. The volleyball game—or another one in the long round of the tournament—was still in progress. One pretty redheaded girl seemed to be the most popular player of the event, and in between serves her male teammates clustered around her with a flirtatious attention. I spared a moment to hope she was good-natured as well as beautiful. A few feet from our blanket, on the side away from the volleyball game, a young mother was helping her toddler learn to walk in the sand. He kept turning up his face to give her a toothless smile of such delight that even I would have bent over him for another backbreaking hour to help him navigate the unfamiliar terrain, and I've never been a sucker for babies the way Marika is.

But mostly I watched the lake, the endlessly fascinating, endlessly changing, briefest imaginable sculptures of waves poised upon the water. How many centuries had the tides crashed and receded just like this, before there were human eyes to watch and wonder? When we were all dead, starved off our planet or blasted off by our own apocalyptic weapons, how long would the water ceaselessly, indifferently, continue to pound out its own rhythmic heartbeat, diastolic, systolic, ebb and flow? I don't spend much time pondering the great cycles of the universe, but an afternoon at the beach gives me a shivering sense of eternity and reminds me how insignificant a span my own lifetime is in comparison.

I glanced down at the men to find Cortez awake and watching me. "You look so serious," he said. "What are you thinking about?"

"A poem."

He grunted. "Why am I not surprised?"

Quentin stirred. It seemed entirely natural that he would waken at the first sound of voices. "What poem?" he asked.

I gestured at the water. "'Dover Beach.' There's a line—someone's watching the ocean—and he talks about how the waves 'bring the eternal note of sadness in.' I think of that every time I'm near the water."

"I don't feel sad," Quentin said.

"That's good."

"How do you know so much poetry?" Cortez asked. "I mean—it seems to be in your head the way other people have memories in their heads. Like it's always there."

"It pretty much *is* always there," I admitted. "And they *are* memories. Little stray thoughts organized as gorgeous rhymes."

"Did you learn them in school?" Quentin asked.

"Some. Some I found on my own, just reading anthologies. And some," I sat up straighter, launching into casual-lecture mode, "like 'Dover Beach,' in fact, I learned through unusual channels. Like science fiction."

"I guess you'll explain that," Cortez said.

"I read Ray Bradbury's *Fahrenheit 451* when I was a teenager. That's the temperature at which paper burns, and in this story, banned books are being burned to keep people from reading them. Anyway, at some point in the book, all these refugees are sitting around a fire. And they get up, one by one, and recite some famous piece of literature that they have memorized. And in this way, they plan to make sure that, even if all the great works are destroyed, these passages will be passed on to the next generation. Someone recites 'Dover Beach.'

"Well, I just fell in love with it, and I memorized it the next day. Then I memorized a dozen other poems that seemed important to me—things by Robert Frost and Emily Dickinson and Sharon Olds. If someone bans the *Norton Anthology of Poetry,* I'm ready. They're not going to burn down the libraries without a fight from me."

I could tell Quentin liked this idea. "Maybe I should memorize a poem," he said.

"Maybe you should," I answered. "Is there one you really like?"

He debated. "Something by A.E. Housman."

"Good choice. You think about it during the week. We'll pick one, and then I'll give you some time to memorize it, and then I'll test you on it one day."

"But what if I forget it?" he asked. "I mean, you know, after you test me. What if I forget a month later, and they burn all the books?"

I hid my smile. You can't make fun of the very motivation you've used. "You have to practice it on a regular basis," I said solemnly. "Maybe the first Monday of every month you recite it again, or write it out. That way you'll always remember."

"Okay," he said happily. "Bram can learn one too."

I didn't even glance at Cortez. "Excellent idea," I said. "Then we'll have a lot of good poems around our little fire."

Quentin leaned back on the blanket and closed his eyes. "Dennis too," he said drowsily. "And maybe Francis."

For a moment, I thought he was drifting off to sleep again, maybe to dream in rhyme and meter. Then suddenly Cortez lunged to his knees and started shaking Quentin by the shoulder.

"Quin? Are you okay, buddy? Quentin, are you all right? Can you hear me?"

Panic strung all my veins to wire. "What's wrong? What's happened?"

Cortez slapped a hand to his right ear, activating his EarFone. "Rush Pres," he barked out, then scooped Quentin up in his arms. Rush Presbyterian was one of biggest hospitals in the Chicago area. As soon as someone answered,

Cortez started firing off orders. "Tell Dr. Hammond or someone in the exotic diseases department that I'm bringing Quentin Phillips in. Emergency," he snapped. "Prepare an adrenaline injection, prepare for possible transfusion. I'll be there in five minutes."

And he started running toward the line of teleport gates with the boy in his arms. He was barefoot, as was Quentin; their shoes and some of their clothes were back on the blanket. I scrambled after them.

"Bram! What's wrong with him? What should I do? Do you have to notify his father if he needs medical treatment?"

He didn't even look back at me. "I'm authorized to sign anything. Call Francis. He'll know what to do."

"But I—"

It was pointless. Even with Quentin in his arms, he was running so fast I couldn't keep up. I jogged to a stop and stared after him. No surprise that the cluster of people waiting at the teleport gates fell back to allow him instant access to one of the portals. He was still talking—to the hospital, to the people at the gate, to Quentin, I couldn't tell—and he seemed both completely in command and absolutely cool. He placed Quentin with infinite gentleness inside the small cubicle and punched in the codes—including, I knew because I had done it myself, the delay code that would allow him to retreat and close the door before the transmission began.

The look on his face as he watched Quentin disappear through the glass made me want to stumble toward him across the sand and put my arms around him to offer comfort.

But he only stood that way, desolate and afraid, for about five seconds. Then he pushed his own way into the portal, closed the door, and vanished.

I turned back to our rumpled blanket on the sand, gathering up the candy bar wrappers, the soda cans, the discarded shirts and shoes. Then I plopped myself down in the middle of the blanket and called Francis.

"It's Taylor," I said. "Cortez has taken Quentin to Rush Presbyterian. I think you should tell his dad."

"Certainly," he said, in his calm, reassuring voice. "Can you tell me exactly what happened?"

"Everything was fine," I said, feeling my body start to tremble. Aftershock, maybe. "We worked a little, we played Frisbee—but it wasn't like Quentin was running around too much, we tried to make sure he didn't get overtired—and then we ate some cookies. And some ice cream. I don't know, Francis, maybe he had too much sugar. Is that a problem for him? But Cortez was watching him so closely, I don't think he would have let him eat something that—anyway, then he just sort of sank back on the blanket and wouldn't talk—"

"Sometimes exertion brings on these spells," Francis said. "He'll probably be just fine. They'll know what to do for him at the hospital."

"I feel so dreadful," I said. "I'm the one who said we should come out to the lake, and then he was walking, which he doesn't usually do, and I know it tired him out, but he—"

"It's not your fault, Taylor," Francis said. Since he always called me Ms. Kendall, his use of my name gave me a small, brief rush of warmth. "It's the fault of the Kyotenin degradation. And his father."

I hadn't expected the sudden, quiet, almost deadly venom—from Francis, of all people—while I was sitting in this happy, sunny place miles away. "His father?" I repeated stupidly. I didn't really think he'd elaborate.

But. "For not getting Quentin the treatment that could have slowed down the degeneration," Francis replied instantly.

"The organ donation? I understand that didn't have the beneficial effects they hoped."

"There were other treatments he refused," Francis said coldly.

I put a hand over my eyes. I was having a little trouble coping with the unreality of the place, the event, and the conversation. "Yeah. I think he has a lot to answer for," I said. "But I guess you have to tell him anyway. Is there anything else I can do?"

"No, Taylor. Thank you for calling."

We disconnected. I looked around again, at the sand, the water, the parade of people. The volleyball game continued uninterrupted, and the mother of the toddler now was rocking him to sleep in her arms. No one seemed to have noticed our quick little moment of trauma. No one else seemed terrified, or lost, or even uncertain. How was it possible that one great event could have so little consequence to anyone but me?

I stuffed the extra shoes and shirts down into the bag, resolving to wash the clothes at my own place so I could return them, clean and fresh, to their respective owners. Then I stood, brushed sand off my pants, shook out the blanket, and draped it over my shoulders. No reason to go back to the mansion now, so I trudged to the teleport pad and headed straight home.

Dennis met me at Rush Pres that evening. "Goddammit" had been his reaction a few hours earlier when I called him. "He's been doing so well lately."

"I just wanted to let you know," I said. "I thought about going down to the hospital, but I don't want to get in the way."

"Well, I'm going," he said. "When do you want to meet?"

"And where," I added. "Because I've never been there."

"Wait for me at the teleport gate," he instructed. "Eight sharp."

He was there before me, even though I was early. He looked like he'd spent the day getting a haircut and crying. His face had an exposed, vulnerable look, and his eyes were squinched up tightly as if against an internal pain. I couldn't stop myself from placing a hand on his arm.

"Dennis," I said urgently. "Are you all right?"

He smiled tightly and dropped a kiss on the top of my head. "Oh, this was just what I needed to take my mind off my own troubles," he said lightly. "Really. I mean it."

"If you want to talk about it—"

"Got plenty of people to pour my heart out to, sweetie. But thanks for the offer. We're here for Q."

I glanced around. Like Oak Street Beach, Rush Pres boasted a row of three teleport terminals at the main entrance. Beyond them, the hospital opened up into a huge, echoing space, all white corridors and chrome fixtures and that pervasive, unsettling smell of chemical intervention. "I don't even know where to go. Bram said something about the exotic diseases department? Dr. Hamilton?"

"Hammond," Dennis said confidently. He took my hand and led me down the hallway. "Been here lots of times, sweetie. I know exactly where I'm going."

"Bram said he was authorized to get Quentin medical treatment. Are you, too?"

Dennis nodded. "And Francis."

"Does his dad do *anything* for him?"

"Not that I've ever noticed," Dennis said bitterly. "Encouraged him to die, maybe."

I glanced at him. His open, handsome face was still clenched, still angry. Was this because of a fight with Gregory, or was this because of his fear for Quentin? "Francis mentioned something," I said hesitantly. "About Duncan Phillips not agreeing to some treatment."

Dennis nodded. We had reached a hallway of elevators, and he pushed a button for going up. "Several treatments, in fact. Some pretty dangerous, some not so much. No to all."

"So then—I mean, he must be on some kind of—drugs, or—I mean, he's getting physical therapy, I assumed—"

"He sees the doctor once a week. Bram or Francis or I take him. Gets an injection, gets his responses tested. Routine stuff. But he's not on the gene therapy program. He didn't participate in the organ transplant project. Both of those failed, didn't help the kids at all, so, okay, maybe no harm done. Well, jury's still out on gene therapy, but it doesn't look promising. There was a new drug about a year ago, pretty risky, but we knew a few patients who started taking it. So far, no results. Duncan Phillips wouldn't even consider it. Wouldn't even look at the data. Just said no."

The elevator *pinged!* and the doors slid open to reveal an empty, sterile cubicle. We stepped inside. I said, "Maybe he just doesn't want to endanger Quentin. Or maybe he doesn't want to raise Quentin's hopes and then see them destroyed—"

Dennis looked at me with dead hatred in his eyes. "He doesn't care if Quentin lives or dies," he said and dropped my hand.

We made the rest of the journey in silence, up the elevator, down the corridors, stopping at a nurse's station to explain our mission. I had to fill out a visitor's form; Dennis, apparently, was a familiar face. The nurse shot a scan gun at both of us to check for fever and infections, then waved us down the hall.

We turned two more corners before we came upon Bram Cortez sitting on a molded plastic chair outside a closed door. He had a tablet in his hand and appeared to be staring at its screen without absorbing anything it showed him. He was wearing shoes and a different shirt, so either Francis had dropped off a change of clothes for him or he'd found time to swing by his own place in the past few hours. He glanced up when he heard our footfalls, and I thought I saw a look of relief or pleasure cross his face. He rose to his feet.

"How's he doing?" Dennis asked.

"Sleeping now. The epi woke him up, and he was responsive—a little slow, but within tolerances. Could move his extremities, remembered all the relevant data, wasn't having trouble breathing. Hammond seemed to think he'd be fine, but wants to keep him here a day or two."

"Can we see him?" I asked.

"When he wakes up. Should be another hour or so."

Dennis looked at his watch. "Then let's go eat something."

Cortez gestured at the door. "I don't want to leave him."

"Have you eaten?" I asked pointedly. "Since the ice cream cone?"

"No."

Dennis took my hand again. "We'll bring something back for you," he said.

About fifteen minutes later, the three of us were seated in a circle of uncomfortable plastic chairs, consuming sandwiches from the hospital cafeteria and sharing a large bag of chips. No one seemed very hungry.

"So what happened?" I asked. "Francis said that exertion sometimes brings on these—spells."

Cortez nodded. "And too much excitement seems to feed into it."

I spread my hands. "But then, when I said I was taking him out, why didn't you say no? If you knew this would happen—"

Cortez looked at me, his dark eyes sad and compassionate. "It doesn't always happen. It's a roulette game. And can we tell that boy he can never leave the house? Never go play on the beach? What kind of life is that? He had a good day, Taylor. He loves being with you. He'll remember the poems and the Frisbee game and the ice cream cone longer than he'll remember one more goddamn visit to the hospital. He's been here so many times, the trips all run together in his head. Coming here is worth it to him to have a day like that. He'd tell you that himself."

"Besides," Dennis added softly, "he has to exercise. If he just sits there in that chair, he'll die even sooner. That's why he works out with me. That's why this wasn't, really, bad for him. Keep him confined, and you hasten his death."

"I just feel so responsible," I said. "No matter what you say."

Dennis put his arm around me and kissed me on the cheek. "We all do," he said. "Welcome to a very exclusive club."

I leaned against him briefly to soak up a moment's comfort, then straightened up in my narrow chair. "So are you guys going to stay here all night?"

"I might," Cortez said. He jerked his chin at Dennis. "You shouldn't. You look like shit."

"Remind me to give you my assessment of your physical beauty at some time when I have more energy."

"Dennis is having personal problems," I said. "But he won't talk about them."

He flicked my cheek with his finger. "But I'll confide in Abramo once you're gone, Tay-Tay."

I giggled; I couldn't help it. "Unfortunately, I can't stay too long. I've got to be in Houston tomorrow morning. But I want to at least be here when he wakes up."

"Dennis can take you home afterward," Cortez said.

I shot him an irritated look. "Who are you, my mother? I think I can find my own way back, even at midnight."

Dennis had an expression of unholy amusement on his face. "I think, Señor Cortez, if it's that important to you that Taylor get home safely, you should escort her yourself. I'll stay with the patient until you return."

"No one has to—"

"All right," Cortez said.

I threw my hands in the air. "*Worse* than my mother."

Dennis was rifling through his pockets. "I don't suppose anyone brought a deck of cards? We could play strip poker."

Cortez held out his tablet. "Got some gaming apps, if you want to play something."

"I thought, something the three of us could all enjoy together?" Dennis said.

Cortez was absolutely deadpan. "Taylor could recite some of her favorite poems and the two of us could analyze the rhyme structure."

"Now, that *is* an attractive program," Dennis approved. "However, my hearing—I'm having a little trouble with my ears—"

"You can both go to hell," I said.

"That's a promising start to a poem," Dennis said.

"If you think—" I began, but Cortez threw a hand in the air and tilted his head toward the door. His ears were quicker than mine, because I didn't hear anything, but when he jumped up and opened the door, we could all see Quentin sitting up in bed. Instantly, we rushed in to crowd around him.

"How you doing, buddy?" Cortez wanted to know.

"Are you mad?" Quentin asked immediately.

Cortez shook his head and reached out to pat him on the shoulder. "Not even a little bit. You can't help it you got sick."

"Well, if I'd been there, you wouldn't have gotten sick," Dennis said huffily. "I would have made sure you sat very quietly and didn't run around playing Frisbee and buying ice cream for everyone on the beach."

Quentin giggled. I said, "I know! I kept saying, 'Now, Bram, let the poor child sit still for a few minutes,' but oh no, Mr. Cortez here just had to keep egging you on—"

Quentin giggled again and flashed a quick look at Cortez to see how he was taking the abuse. Cortez was smiling. Quentin said, "Well, it wasn't all Bram's fault. I did kind of want to run around and have fun. But it was jazz, wasn't it, Taylor?"

I leaned over to kiss him on the forehead. "Superjazz," I said. "Maybe we could go back tomorrow."

Everyone laughed at that, and we spent a few more minutes in raillery and nonsense. It was obvious Quentin was too weak to talk long, so I wasn't surprised when Cortez hustled us out of the room before we'd been there a quarter of an hour.

"I'm going to take Taylor home," he said to Quentin. "But Dennis will stay with you while I'm gone, okay? You all right with that?"

"Sure."

"Go," Dennis said, settling himself into a chair next to the bed. "I won't leave until you finally get back."

I cast him a doubtful look. "You make it sound like that might take a while."

The look he gave me in return was wicked. "What could possibly keep him?"

I wanted to hit him, but I contented myself with casting him a fulminating glance. In a few minutes, Cortez and I were out the door and walking down the antiseptic hallways.

"You really don't have to—" I began.

"I know."

"I constantly come home late at night without an escort."

"Not such a good idea, maybe."

"I'm thirty-four years old and I—"

"Soon to be thirty-five."

"And I can take care of myself."

He hit the elevator button before I could even do that small task. "None of us really can take care of ourselves all of the time," he observed.

And that silenced me for the long walk to the row of teleport gates and the brief moment of transmission. We entered two different booths at the same time, but since there was only one portal on my street, I materialized a few moments before he did. Once he stepped out beside me, we strolled wordlessly down the quiet streets of my neighborhood. It was close to ten o'clock and few people were out. Many houses and apartments had already gone completely dark as the responsible members of society lulled themselves to sleep in preparation for the next day of bustling productivity. The warm afternoon air had chilled to a more normal Chicago frost. Our footsteps sounded loud, significant, almost ominous on the deserted sidewalk. If we had been in a movie, we would have been fighting for our lives sometime in the next few frames.

"So you think he'll be in the hospital a few more days?" I asked, finally breaking the silence as we moved within sight of my building.

He nodded. "Don't be planning on a lesson on Friday."

"No, of course not. But can I go see him then? Or tomorrow?"

"Sure. He'd like that."

"Will he be home by Tuesday?"

"That's what I'd expect. I'll keep you posted."

At the front doorway to my building, I keyed in the security code, but Cortez made no move to walk away. "Are you coming up with me?" I asked.

"Have to make sure you get home safely."

"Are you coming in?"

"Just long enough to make certain there are no murderers lurking in the closets."

"There have never been murderers in the closets."

"Always a first time."

And sure enough, he followed me into the apartment, went straight to the hall closet, peered inside, and then headed to the bedroom, where I did not follow him. I had gone to the refrigerator to open a beer.

"All clear," he said when he rejoined me.

I gestured with my bottle. "Want one?"

He took it from my hand. "Just a sip."

I watched as he put his mouth to the rim and closed his eyes, taking a long, heartfelt swallow. Then he opened his eyes, smiled, and handed the bottle back. "I have more," I said dryly. "You could have your own."

He shook his head, still smiling. "I have to get back. Or Dennis will start rumors."

"Mustn't have that."

"So you'll come by the hospital on Friday?" he asked.

"Maybe sooner."

"I'll let you know if they send him home earlier."

"All right."

He headed for the door and I moved behind him, ready to lock up as soon as he left. On the threshold, he turned back to look at me. "It wasn't your fault," he said. "It wasn't mine, either, though it feels like it. Quentin's sick. We can't change that."

"I can't stand knowing that."

"I know," he said. "I can't either. If it makes it any easier, Quentin adores you. You've brightened his life more than I think you realize."

"Yeah," I said. "I guess it helps."

"All of our lives," he said. And he bent down and kissed me. At first, all I could taste was the beer, on my mouth, on his; or maybe the heady, intoxicating sensation came from somewhere else entirely. He put one hand up to my cheek, and the heat of his skin altered my pores. His mouth on mine felt like fate, like change. I closed my eyes and kissed him back.

We did not touch except for lip to lip, hand to cheek. He was the one to draw away, and he looked down at me solemnly for a moment. I could read strong emotion in his eyes, but not the exact printed text. What was he thinking? What were my own eyes conveying to him?

A moment of that serious, quiet appraisal—then, astonishingly, he smiled. "Don't tell Dennis," he said and sauntered out the door, shutting it behind him.

I hadn't even set the lock before I was phoning Marika.

CHAPTER THIRTEEN

AS MY ENGLISH LIT CLASS ENDED ON WEDNESDAY, DUNCAN PHILLIPS came calling.

It had been a whirlwind hour, because it was the last review session before Friday, when students would take the nationwide exams that would determine whether or not they actually would move up to the next level. My own finals would be administered two weeks later, and those would determine their letter grades. Sefton would not award degrees to students who couldn't earn passing grades from a teacher, no matter how well they did on the national finals. Some students cared about this, some did not. As with everything.

I spent most of the hour quizzing them on vocabulary words, since a huge part of the standardized test was based on identifying synonyms, antonyms, and "wrong word combinations." I divided them into teams and gave extra points for rapidity, so there was a great deal of hilarity by the end of the afternoon. Even Evan Stodley was laughing. Devante Ross, who was so much smarter than he liked to let on, only missed three words. Nancy Ortega didn't miss any. I was so proud of them all that I almost wanted to cry.

It was while Devante was trying to define semi-recumbent ("It's, say, when you're lying down, but maybe not all the way down") that a movement at the doorway caught my eye. Standing there was a cluster of people who had arrived quietly enough not to be heard over the chatter and laughter in the room. Caroline Summers, looking tense; the dean behind her, looking even more tense; and Duncan Phillips.

"Game over! We win!" Devante crowed just as the ending bell shrilled down the hall.

"By one lousy point!" Dave Zirster yelled back. "And you didn't win that point—you cheated—"

"We didn't cheat! We had the answer just as time ran out."

"Yeah, but you—"

I forced my attention back to the class. "That's enough, I think," I said. "You did a great job. I want to wish each of you good luck on your test Friday. Anyone who wants to come to my office Thursday for individual coaching, just let me know. See you on Monday!"

By this time, all of them had noticed the visitors in the doorway. Naturally, they knew who Caroline and the dean were, and some of them also recognized Duncan Phillips. Devante shot me a look so stern and speculative that I wondered what he knew about the billionaire. That kid was not only smart, he was intuitive; I was sure he'd go on to be a world leader. I gave him a smile and nodded. *It's all right.* He shrugged and followed the others out of the room.

Caroline, the dean, and Duncan Phillips came in. "Ms. Kendall," the dean said in his nervous, fussy voice. "I'm aware you know Duncan Phillips, one of Sefton's greatest benefactors."

"Yes, we've met. I tutor his son. How is Quentin, Mr. Phillips?"

"Doing very well," Duncan Phillips answered pleasantly. He did not appear quite as feral in this setting as he had when he had trapped me in his own home, but there was still a balled-up intensity to him that gave him an electric presence. He looked appraisingly around the room, as if he was considering purchasing it for his portfolio, and then turned his watchful gray eyes on me. "I enjoyed your class. What part of it I was privileged to see."

"Yes, Mr. Phillips has expressed an interest in observing some of our teachers in action in a typical setting," the dean bleated. He was such a small, thin, colorless man that on an ordinary day he was easy to overlook. In Duncan Phillips' shadow, he seemed practically invisible.

I glanced at Caroline, who looked just as furious as I felt. I was pretty sure this had not been her idea. "Hardly a typical day," I said. "Usually I'm covering new material, not going over vocabulary words, but I'm helping them prep for the national tests on Friday."

"Sefton has a good record on the national exams," Phillips said in his sinister, purring voice. "I know. I've seen the percentages."

"We have an excellent graduation rate as well," Caroline said icily. "Both results are rooted in the same cause: We have superb teachers."

If the dean was invisible to me, Caroline was invisible to Duncan Phillips. He said, "How would you describe your teaching style, Ms. Kendall? What makes it innovative?"

"I try to engage the students, getting them to interact with me and each other," I said. I glanced at Caroline. "That's the whole Sefton philosophy. That's why we don't offer online programs—we want the personal interaction."

"Mr. Phillips is considering increasing his endowment to Sefton," the dean said. As if this would encourage me to add more nuance and detail to my answer.

All I said was, "That would be jazz, as his son says. Superjazz."

I thought I saw Caroline hide a smile.

Duncan Phillips leaned against my desk, taking a half-seated posture while the rest of us disposed ourselves awkwardly around him. "What is the most valuable thing you think your students take away with them when they leave?" he asked.

"You mean when they leave Sefton?" I asked.

"No. *Your* students. When they leave *your* classroom."

I was growing increasingly uncomfortable at the level of personal interest he was exhibiting, but I tried not to show it. "I would like to think that what they take away from Sefton is a well-rounded education. What *my* students learn, I hope, is a love of reading. An ability to analyze a story or a poem for its technical skill, as well as to enjoy it for its beauty and its heart. I hope they also take away some basic understanding of grammar and punctuation. What I have seen them leave with is deep friendships with their classmates. All of that seems equally valuable."

The dean suddenly touched his hand to his ear and murmured a hello, moving away to hold a conversation in more privacy. Caroline took advantage of the distraction to speak up.

"Other teachers in the English department have goals that are similar to Taylor's. For instance, Harold Fogarty teaches drama, everything from Shakespeare to Lorelei Hart. He says an appreciation of theater gives students an understanding of life."

She might not have spoken at all, so completely did Duncan Phillips ignore her. "If you were to have additional funding for your classroom," he asked me, "how would you direct the money?"

"We've said for years that we'd like to establish a physical library of the minor authors who are sometimes only available in e-books. We'd like better production studios so we could create high-quality recordings of lectures and class presentations. And I know a couple of schools have started experimenting with holographic technology so a professor or a guest speaker can essentially beam in from another location." The minute I said it, I wished I hadn't. The memory of his own holographic technology surfaced irrepressibly in my mind.

He waved my answer away. "No," he said. "If *you* had the extra funds for *your* classroom."

That was too particular to miss. I heard Caroline's breath hiss softly in. I said flatly, "If someone donated money to my classroom, I'd hand it over to the department head. Caroline, how would you use a special endowment?"

Before she could answer, the dean rejoined us, looking a little shaken. "That was Meyers. He—well, there's a little crisis. I've got to get over to Gorgon Hall. Mr. Phillips, I'm sure I leave you in capable hands with these two women." And he said a few more fluttery words and was gone.

Duncan Phillips glanced once around the room and smiled at me. "Maybe we could finish our conversation somewhere else," he said. "Over coffee somewhere, perhaps?"

"I can't," I said. "I'm late as it is." I picked up my briefcase and slung the long strap over my shoulder. "'Bye, Caroline."

"I'll see Mr. Phillips out," she said faintly, no doubt annoyed at my defection. But I couldn't get out of the room, or the building, fast enough. I didn't look back once to see if they followed. I just hurried as quickly as I could to the nearest teleport gate and hurled myself to the first city I could think of where Duncan Phillips neither lived nor, as far as I knew, had friends.

Atlanta.

❧

I didn't make it to the hospital on Thursday, since students dropped by my office continually from nine in the morning to nearly six at night. I did call Quentin a couple of times, and he sounded so cheerful that I started to relax.

Friday, I arrived at the hospital around three in the afternoon, bearing cookies I'd baked myself and a new hardcover by Ardel Hawke. I found Quentin and Bram Cortez playing chess while Francis gave Quentin sotto voce advice. Nonetheless, the home team appeared to be losing.

"Chocolate chip cookies! I didn't know you could bake," Quentin observed, stuffing two in his mouth in rapid succession.

"Is that an insult? Why couldn't I bake?"

"You're a teacher. All you do is read."

"Well, I eat, too."

"These are excellent," Francis said, sampling one. "Better than mine."

"Your cookies are great, Francis," Quentin said loyally. Then he looked at me. "But these are supergreat, Taylor."

Bram Cortez was on his third one before he offered a comment. "Almost makes a man want to get sick if this will be his reward," he said.

I risked a glance at him. Once you've kissed a man and he's walked out your door, you're not always sure what you'll say the next time you see him in front of half the people you know in common. But he looked completely at ease, happy enough to see me but not so ecstatic he couldn't keep his blushes down.

I tried to match his nonchalance. "If you ever end up in the hospital, I promise I'll make you cookies."

"This day's getting better all the time."

Quentin was restless. "Hey, Taylor, you want to play a game of chess with me once I beat Bram?"

I glanced at the board. "Doesn't look to me like you're going to beat him any time soon. Anyway, I brought you another diversion." I handed him the book.

"Strato!" he exclaimed. "I can read it tonight."

"Why wait?" Bram asked. "Kick us out and start it now."

We all laughed and moved on to new topics. I settled myself into a chair next to Francis, who leaned over and began to quiz me on my favorite recipes, so we debated the merits of hotboxing and conventional baking. When Quentin seemed sufficiently absorbed in his game with Bram, I quietly inquired about his condition, which Francis assured me was improving.

"He'll probably be home tomorrow."

"Has his father been by to see him?"

Francis shrugged. "Not that I've heard."

I glanced at the players, who did not seem to be paying attention to our conversation. "He dropped by to see me," I said.

Bram Cortez's eyes lifted quickly to my face, though Quentin hadn't seemed to catch my words. Cortez didn't say anything, though. Francis asked, "Dropped by to see you where?"

"Sefton. Came to my class with the dean and the department head. Talking about how he was going to make an endowment to the school. But it was pretty clear he was there to see me. I can't tell you how creepy it was."

"You need to start being careful," Bram said.

Quentin exclaimed, "I am being careful! You can't checkmate me."

"I guess I do," I said.

"I'll be at the door Tuesday when you arrive," Francis promised.

I smiled at him. "I was counting on it."

I stayed a little more than an hour, and when I stood to go, Cortez came to his feet. Quentin was instantly alarmed. "Don't go, Bram! One more chess game! Or we could play a video game—"

Cortez smiled at him. "I've been here almost four hours, bud. I've got to get back to work."

"I can stay a while longer," Francis said.

"Okay," Quentin said, instantly reassured. "Hey, you want to play chess?"

Cortez and I walked out the door and down the hallways, not speaking. The hospital was busier at four in the afternoon than it had been late at night. Human nurses bustled between rooms and the robo-techs wheeled quickly by, chattering to themselves. Every few minutes an intercom announcement paged a doctor whose name was unintelligible, and from every desk and doorway came intermittent squeaks, blips, and chimes. The light was a washed-out white that gave an alien feel to every face and surface, and the permeating smell was both clinical and chemical. Nothing quite like a hospital. You can't ever pretend you're not there.

Cortez broke the silence when we reached the teleport gates. "I've had my last eight or ten meals here, and none of them have been very good," he said. "Want to get something to eat? Or even just some coffee?"

"I'll have you know I turned down coffee with Duncan Phillips a couple days ago," I said grandly.

He smiled. "I'd like to think you'd rather have it with me."

"I'd rather have coffee with almost anyone but Duncan Phillips," I said, "but I'd like to go with you."

"Any suggestions?"

"It's actually warm out," I said. "Let's go to Ozone."

And so we did. Ozone is one of the trendy downtown eateries that prides itself on its international menu. The owner makes a point of teleporting in delicacies from around the world on an hourly basis. So you can eat sushi obtained this morning from Japan or salmon freshly caught off the Alaskan coast. Marika always orders croissants from Paris, while Domenic prefers the Argentinian beef. Jason and I go for the freshly roasted Brazilian coffee. I have to admit that I don't really care about all this up-to-the-minute authenticity, and that all coffee pretty much tastes the same to me. What I like about Ozone, at least in the spring, is its outdoor terrace, which is ringed by heat lamps. You can sit outside on a 60-degree day, feeling the breeze swoop in off the lake, and still not freeze to death. I count this as a real advantage.

We got a table right by a heater, too, which made me even happier. Cortez ordered a meal, but I just got salsa and chips and then, because it was Friday afternoon and I couldn't tell if this was a date or not but I was feeling in a celebratory mood, a margarita. At that point, Cortez asked the waitress for a beer.

Once she departed, he glanced around the patio, assessing the clientele, noting the people who were present and, perhaps, what kind of threat they offered. I saw his eyes go more than once to three young men sitting at a table set up closest to the sidewalk. They wore clothes at the extreme edge of youth fashion, and they were laughing too loudly for a Friday afternoon. If they were old enough to drink alcohol, I'd be surprised.

He didn't comment on them, though. "So," he said instead, "Phillips came to scope you out at Sefton."

"That's the way I read it. Made me a little nervous."

"You've got to start being careful."

"I heard you the first time."

"So far, he hasn't been the type to track someone to her home," he said seriously. "He tends to work more in public venues. His house. Parties at other people's houses. Hotels. If a woman later says he took advantage of her, he can say, 'Why didn't you scream?' So far, it's a strategy that's worked for him."

"Are you trying to scare me?"

"Yes."

"Good work. I'm scared. Are you telling me not to come back?"

"No. I'm trying to underscore what you already know. Don't walk around that house alone."

"Wouldn't even cross my mind."

Our drinks arrived. I took a small, delicious sip of that sublime salty-citrus combination. Used to be, I could down enough margaritas to crack my lips and leave my tongue sore. These days, one round of tequila will do me in, so I savor the single pleasure.

Cortez nodded at my lime-colored drink. "You know that stuff will rot your stomach."

"Beer will make you fat," I retorted. "Pick your poison."

"You talk tough," he said. "But you're not so wild. You hardly even drink, according to the vast amount of research I've collected on you."

"It seems completely unfair that you know so much about me and I know so little about you."

He was laughing. "What do you want to know?"

"When's your birthday? What's your middle name?"

"August 6th. Bonifacio."

"What?"

"Bonifacio. Boniface. He's a saint."

"That is—an unusual name."

"Maybe for laker girls and their friends. Pretty common in my set."

"You would have been teased a lot at my high school," I admitted. "Does Dennis know?"

He grinned. "I don't think so, but go ahead and tell him if you want. In fact, why don't you text him right now?"

I laughed back. I could feel the tequila hitting me, and I hadn't had half my drink. "I like Dennis. He relaxes me."

"I would think he'd put you on edge. He can't sit still or shut up—so neither can anyone else when he's nearby."

"I know. I like that. He supplies his own energy, so he doesn't require any from me. My friend Marika is like that, too." I took another sip of the margarita. "Hey, I'll have to introduce them. They'd love each other."

"I don't think I require any energy from anyone," he said.

I smothered a smile. He sounded almost miffed. "You," I said, "you're the one who makes me nervous."

"Why?"

"Because you're so watchful. Because you pay attention to every little thing. It puts me on guard."

"That's not my intention."

"Oh, I'm getting over it. I'm hardly tense at all anymore when you're in the room."

He smiled. "I guess that's progress."

Our food arrived right about then, and we lost a couple of minutes arranging our plates to our satisfaction. I covered my whole plate with a layer of chips and slowly drizzled salsa evenly over each one. I might have to ask for a second cup of salsa, or maybe some guacamole.

Bram took a bite and then looked over again at the table of teenagers. The three had now been augmented by a fourth, and a fifth one stood on the sidewalk, leaning over the heat-lamp barrier, laughing loudly at someone's joke.

"Why are they bugging you?" I asked.

"They're wearing junta colors."

"Yeah, but—here in such a public place—"

He shrugged. "I'm sure the manager's already alerted the cops. I hope."

"Can you try to just enjoy your meal?"

"I will. I am."

We ate a few minutes in silence, and then began talking idly. About Quentin, of course, and then I mentioned some of my students, and then he said he'd been thinking about taking some classes.

"Really? In what?"

He shrugged. "Art appreciation? Piano? I don't know. Something completely different from everything I've ever done in my life."

"Strato," I said, meaning it sincerely though my tone was flippant. "I never even thought about taking classes in—I don't know—weapons usage. Teleport maintenance. Things completely outside my experience."

"Or I've thought maybe I could teach something."

"Not piano, though."

"Weapons usage," he said with a grin. "Tactical maneuvering. Except that puts me right back in the world I left."

"Have you given any thought," I said slowly, "to what you'll do when—after Quentin—when you leave Duncan Phillips' house?"

He nodded. "Thought about it. Haven't come up with anything. I can get a security job almost anywhere. But I don't know if that's what I want to keep doing."

"Of course, the great difficulty in switching careers mid-life is financing the new one."

"I could afford to take a few years off. I've got plenty saved," he said. "If you were really inquiring into my financial status."

I could feel myself turning red. "No! I was just—it's expensive to go back to school, and without an income—you're a jerk."

He was laughing. "'Cause if you were really looking to follow the money, there's someone a lot wealthier than me who seems a little interested."

"I can't believe you'd even joke about it."

"I wouldn't except that you—"

A woman shrieked, and then the whole world exploded into hyperfast motion. Bram had leapt to his feet and was racing across the patio, dodging tables and knocking aside waiters, before I had even identified the source of the commotion. I heard more screams—shouts from another direction—the sounds of crashing glass and china—and quiet, deadly ricochet noises that even I knew came from a handheld weapon. Bram was tangling with the four junta members sitting on our side of the wall; the fifth one seemingly had fled. Two of the boys were already out of commission, writhing and moaning on the brick of the patio. The other two were attacking Bram with fists and knives and maybe other weapons I couldn't see through the melee. A blonde woman standing near the fight scene was screaming hysterically, while a frantic dark-haired man tried to calm her down. A few feet over from them, another woman lay motionless on the ground, a long bloody gash running across the front of her yellow dress, her arm outstretched as if to reach for something that had been snatched away.

I was on my feet, not remembering when I'd jumped up, staring around in paralyzed horror. The third junta kid had been knocked to his knees by a blow from Bram's hand, and the fourth one was locked in a wrestler's grip that looked likely to snap his neck. Restaurant workers were circling around the combatants, shouting out words of encouragement or warning, but no one came close enough to help subdue the rowdies. Not that any help appeared to be needed.

I was still in shock, still staring, when three police cars wailed up, lights strobing across the sidewalk and sirens snarling down. Now there was even more mayhem, half of the officers rounding up the junta teens, half of them barking orders at the restaurant staff. Bram stood bracketed by two tough-looking older officers bristling with weaponry and attitude, and calmly related his version of the events. I saw a smear of blood across his shirt, but he looked relatively unscathed.

Abruptly my legs buckled, and I sat down with a thump. I drained the last watery drops of my margarita, then finished off Bram's beer. Two paramedics appeared from nowhere, no ambulance in sight, so I assumed they'd teleported over. They knelt on either side of the fallen woman and began covering her with gauze and tubes.

Our shaken waitress came by our table a few minutes later. "Are you—would you—can I get you anything else?" she stammered. Her hands were trembling on her tray and her face looked ashen, but she was desperately trying to keep herself together.

"What happened?" I asked. "Did you see?"

She glanced over to where Bram was still talking to the police officers, who were nodding and pointing at something down the street. The junta kid who'd run away, maybe. "One of those boys—he grabbed that woman's purse—and she tried to hold onto it. But he had a knife and he—I hope she's all right. She's bleeding so much."

"I guess I'd like another margarita," I said. "And another beer."

She was still gazing at Bram and the cops. "That man there. He just rushed over and knocked the kid away from her. I mean, one punch and the kid fell down. He's like a superhero or something."

"Yeah," I said dryly. "He's an ex-cop. He's my date."

Now she looked back at me, wide-eyed and amazed. I couldn't tell if she admired my choice in men or feared for me. "He must be something," was all she said.

"I know," I replied, "I'm still trying to figure out what."

She had returned with our drinks, and I'd downed half of the second margarita, before Bram came back to the table. The rest of Ozone's patrons had either doubled their drink orders, like me, or hurriedly paid their bills and departed. The restaurant manager was moving between tables, stopping to express regret to each customer, offer a trip to the hospital, a free meal, whatever it took to ensure this dreadful experience did not give them a lingering distaste for Ozone. The cops were interviewing the people who'd been sitting closest to the scene of violence. The woman who'd been sliced open had been carried away at some point when I wasn't looking.

I saw Bram shake hands with two of the officers, nod to a third, and make his way back to our table much more slowly than he'd left it. He was watching me the whole time, and his eyes were still fixed on me as he dropped into his seat.

I gestured at the bottle. "I got you another beer."

He picked it up and took a long swallow. "I hope it's on the house."

"I would think the whole meal would be. Although I guess it's not really the management's fault."

He glanced around once, still watchful, still assessing. Didn't he ever just stop? "In a way it is," he said. "Trendy place like this draws lots of attention. Draws all sorts of people. They're known for not turning anyone away, but then they should have their own security on staff. They do at night. They should during the day."

"What happened to that woman?"

"I think she'll be okay. Paramedics got here pretty fast."

The restaurant manager made his way to our table. He was small and round, with thinning black hair that was probably dyed. He was wearing a tuxedo that, on better days, probably looked tidier than it did at the moment. He was smiling brightly, but there was a thin film of sweat across his face, and I figured it wasn't from the heat lamp.

"Good afternoon, friends, I am so sorry for the events of the afternoon—"

Bram looked at him without saying a word. The manager gasped, recognizing him as the avenging angel who had kept a terrifying situation from becoming disastrous. "Sir!" he exclaimed. He had a faint accent, maybe French, maybe Greek, and a certain volubility with his hands. "How can I thank you—you have done us such a great service—your quickness to act, your great fierceness—"

Bram brushed aside his raptures. "Let it go. How is the young woman? My friend was just asking."

"The doctors seemed most hopeful as they took her away. But you, sir! Where would we be without your quick thinking? Absolutely you shall not pay for this meal! What are you drinking? I shall have another round brought out to you immediately. I shall—"

"No more for me," I said quickly.

"Me either," Bram said.

"Then you shall have a certificate for a free meal upon your return. No! You shall never pay again any time you come to Ozone!"

I thought I could read the expression on Bram's face, which said he was never coming back here, so this offer was a pretty good deal for the manager. "Thank you," I said. "But you don't have to do anything special for us."

Ten minutes of thanks, protestations, and gift certificates later, he had finally departed from our table and we could go back to our interrupted meal. I had lost all interest in the salsa and chips, and Bram just picked at the remaining items on his plate. However, we were making pretty good progress on our second round of drinks.

"Good thing I don't have to do anything tomorrow morning," I observed. "Because I'm going to wake up with a hangover."

He smiled with a seeming effort. "From two margaritas?"

"You said it yourself. I'm not much of a drinker."

He pushed his plate aside and looked at me seriously. "I don't know why," he said, "but I think you're mad at me."

I scrunched up my eyebrows and tilted my head, as if I was considering an interesting puzzle someone had presented to me. "I don't think mad is the right word," I said at last.

"Disturbed."

"Maybe."

He shrugged. "I was a cop. You know that. I'm a security guard. You know that, too. What I do best is stop people from hurting other people. You shouldn't be surprised."

I nodded. "I don't think what's bothering me is that you can do it," I said slowly. "It's that you like to."

"Aaaahh," he said, and took a drink of his beer.

"And that you look for opportunities to do it."

"I don't have to look. The opportunities are always there."

"Maybe."

"And would you rather have had me sit here, knowing I could save a woman's life, and just watch? Do nothing?"

"No."

"Then? What do you want from me?"

"I'm still assimilating," I said. "This isn't how we played when I was growing up."

"This isn't playing."

After that, there wasn't a whole lot more to say. We finished our drinks, and Bram left money on the table despite our free status, a gesture I liked. We walked silently to the teleport gate and then paused a moment before opening the portal door.

"Take you home?" he asked. I could not tell from his neutral tone if he wanted me to accept or reject the offer.

I smiled and gestured at the sky, where dusk was gathering its muscles but had not yet sprung for the kill. "Still daylight," I said. "I think I'm perfectly safe."

"Will we see you Tuesday? I'm sure Quentin will be home by then."

"I expect so. I can't imagine anything would keep me."

He looked down at me a moment, the expression on his face hard to read. As if it wasn't always hard to read. At the moment, he wore a small smile, a rather sad expression, and seemed full of words he could not form. "You don't understand how much it hurts me," he said at last, "to not be able to protect Quentin. Because that's what I know how to do. And I can't help him at all."

"So you're looking for fights," I said.

"Maybe."

"And someone you can save."

"I suppose."

I nodded. "Give him a hug for me," I said, and stepped into the teleport gate before he had a chance to reply. After I'd coded in my stop, I turned to watch him, and then I hit the transmit button. His face dissolved, and I was at my own gate, and for the first time in my life I didn't like teleporting. It created farewells that were far too abrupt.

⌒

The weekend went quickly, particularly since I spent most of Saturday regretting the second margarita and trying various painkillers in an attempt to dissipate my nagging headache. Jason came in Saturday night to hang out at Mom's, so I went over for dinner.

Sunday wasn't much livelier. I talked to Marika, finished grading some late papers, watched VNN for three hours straight, and was actually looking forward to going back to work the next day when my EarFone sounded late in the evening.

"Taylor," I said chirpily, happy for any distraction.

"Ms. Kendall. It's Devante." His voice was raw and hoarse, and I would not have recognized it if he had not identified himself. I felt dread close me in a cold vise.

"Devante. What's wrong?"

"It's—Evan's killed himself, Ms. Kendall. Here at the house. I don't know what to do."

CHAPTER FOURTEEN

BY MIDNIGHT, EVERYTHING HAD BEEN MORE OR LESS SETTLED. I HAD packed an overnight bag and gone straight to Devante's place, though I did pause to phone Caroline, who said she'd take care of the other necessary calls. The cops were at Devante's house when I arrived. So were about twenty students, a few neighbors, and some adults I took to be parents. Devante was still talking to the police, his big athlete's body looking wasted and small, as if all his bones and tissue had compacted down. One of his roommates, a normally arrogant in-your-face troublemaker, was sitting on a dilapidated couch with his arm around a sobbing girl. The smell of pizza wafted in from the direction of the kitchen.

"Oh, Ms. Kendall!" a voice cried, and in a few moments I was surrounded by a group of frantic students. Nancy Ortega, her girlfriend Simone, and most of the other kids from my comp class. Some were crying; some, like Devante, were just stunned and shrunken. My heart breaking for all of them, I looked around for someplace we could sit and talk.

This turned out to be the dining room. Devante and his buddies roomed in a large, rundown old house in Montrose, the hip-scary address of Houston, and they hadn't done much to decorate it in the conventional sense. So this room offered no ordinary dining table; instead, a collection of TV trays and inflatable chairs and throw pillows served as the furniture. The room also held the entertainment hub, which featured an attendant array of speakers so huge and so numerous that I was surprised the students hadn't all gone deaf.

I lowered myself into a translucent plastic armchair and they all disposed themselves around me. "Tell me exactly what happened," I demanded.

Nancy, who had been weeping when I arrived, had gained some self-control, though she seemed unwilling to move more than a foot or two away from me. "We thought Evan had been doing better. We all went out Friday night after the exam. He thought he'd done well on it. You know, so it wasn't like he was worried about flunking out or anything—"

"What about his classes? He was a little behind in my course—how was he doing with his other teachers?"

"They all knew," said Simone. "You know, that he was depressed. They were all giving him wasting room."

Wasting room. One of those strange phrases you hear around campus and never know exactly how to define. "What about his parents?" I asked.

Nancy and Simone exchanged glances. "They used to be kind of tough on him, but once he spent time in the clinic, they pretty much backed off," Nancy said. "I don't think—that wasn't it."

"And the ex-girlfriend?"

"He never talked about her anymore," Simone said. "We all thought he was okay about her."

Did it really matter what had set him off? What had pushed him beyond his level of endurance, what had broken his heart? "So what happened? What did he do to himself?"

The girls started crying. Dave Zirster said flatly, "Climbed in the shower and cut his wrists. And turned on the water so all the blood would wash away. Devante found him, but he was already—all the hot water was gone, he was just there in the cold shower, and he was dead."

I took a deep breath and let it out slowly. "Okay," I said. "I feel just as bad as you do, so I don't know anything to say to make it any better. But let's talk about it as long as you want."

Which was until midnight, and even then, I think some of them would have stayed longer, going over the same few details again. All of us thinking, *What signals did I miss, what words could I have said that I failed to say, how could I have altered events?* The truth is, you rarely get a chance to save another life, and to miss your chance, to blow it so spectacularly, cuts you deep.

I began feeling a little more sympathetic toward Bram Cortez and his heroics. Saving one life might have made it a little easier to lose another.

"It's late—everyone go home now," I insisted. "And those of you who consider this home, you go to bed. And you get some sleep."

"Don't leave," Simone said. "I mean—can you come back early tomorrow morning? I don't—tomorrow afternoon seems so far away."

"I'm spending the night at the teacher's dorm," I said. This was a utilitarian collection of studio apartments set aside for the use of commuting teachers who got trapped on campus, or visiting professors who did not want the trouble of hunting for lodging for eight weeks, or seminar speakers who would be in town overnight. I'd only made use of it half-a-dozen times, but I had to admit it was handy. "I'll be here bright and early. Want to go out to breakfast?"

About ten of them agreed, so we planned where and when to meet. I figured I'd be paying for everyone, so the inexpensive pancake house sounded pretty good to me. I shouldered my bag, said my farewells, and headed toward the door.

Nancy stopped me with a hand on my arm. "Ms. Kendall?"

I turned. "Yes?"

"My final paper. I'm going to write it on Evan."

I nodded. "Absolutely. Any of you can. Essay—journal entry—it's pretty much freeform, you know."

"Poem," she said.

❧

The next forty-eight hours were, as I'd expected, dreadful, full of anguish and questions. Sorrow is bad enough without the what-ifs to complicate it. I had a couple of the mental health clinic's grief counselors at class Monday afternoon, but the students didn't want them there, so I let them go and led the discussions myself. Feeling woefully inadequate to the task.

But then, there is no easy way to dissipate sadness. It follows you and chases you and corners you in dark alleys until, one day when you least expect it, it grows tired of the sport and finds new prey. Emily Dickinson said it better, of course, in a slightly different context.

> As imperceptibly as Grief
> The Summer lapsed away—
> Too imperceptible at last
> To seem like Perfidy—

But we were a long way from that point.

The campus memorial service had been arranged for Tuesday afternoon, which obviously meant I would not make my appointment with Quentin. I called Francis Monday night to explain the situation. He expressed his condolences and asked if he could tell Quentin I would be there Friday as usual.

"That's my plan," I said. "How's he doing? Is he home?"

"Yes. He doesn't seem to have suffered any lasting ill effects from the collapse."

"I'm so glad. I'll see you all in a few days."

I didn't attempt to contact anyone else in the house.

The service was held in Sefton's small, plain, nondenominational chapel. It had been organized by the students and featured mainly commentaries by Evan's contemporaries. I had been invited to speak, but once I learned I had been the only teacher so honored, I declined. I thought it should be a chance for the students to express themselves, and for me and the other teachers to listen.

Dave Zirster opened the service, introduced each of the other speakers, and generally kept everything moving, and I thought he did a splendid job. About a dozen students spoke, some reciting tales of Evan's sweetness, others describing a favor he'd done for them or an act of kindness they'd observed. Devante told a funny story about a trip to a bowling alley and a disastrous bout with peanuts that had everyone laughing and crying simultaneously. I mentally applauded him for the tale and the strength it took to tell it.

Nancy Ortega recited her poem in a quiet, firm voice, and the entire audience was in tears by the time she had finished. Everyone except Nancy. She gave us all a look of contained intensity. "Evan Stodley," she said. "We will not forget him."

She was the last one scheduled to speak, but all my students were turning in their seats to look at me, clearly expecting me to take my turn, despite my earlier decision. So I did, though I had nothing prepared and nothing in mind to say.

"I've never had to do this before," I said, looking out at the sea of upturned faces. "Attend a funeral service for a student. If I'd practiced something to read, I probably would have picked a poem. The one that keeps coming to my mind is 'Prayer to Persephone,' by Edna St. Vincent Millay. In it, she talks about a young girl who has just died, and who therefore will be going on to the underworld—which, for those of you who don't know your mythology, was ruled over half the time by Persephone, the reluctant wife of Hades.

"And so she tells Persephone about this girl, who will be 'a little lonely child lost in Hell.' And the last few lines of the poem have always seemed so comforting to me as she asks the goddess to care for the girl." I spoke the final words in a quiet voice.

"Persephone,
Take her head upon your knee:
Say to her, 'My dear, my dear,
It is not so dreadful here.'"

I paused briefly. "I don't think it can be dreadful where Evan has gone. And death is a place we all will eventually go, and I do not think it will be dreadful for any of us. But what I want to say to you today is this. Don't follow him there a day sooner than you have to. Hold on to your lives. Love your lives. Live them to the fullest. Realize what a gift every single day is. And never forget to love the people around you the best that you can for as long as you can. And don't let it take a death to learn that lesson."

I had nothing else to say. I stood there a moment, as if waiting for the inevitable questions from my class, then I quirked my hands up in a gesture of helplessness. As I stepped down from the podium, Dave Zirster moved forward and said, "Let's all join in on the first verse of 'Amazing

Grace,'" and the hymn began. I was not the only one who found it impossible to sing.

⤬

Quentin still looked pale three days later when I arrived—pale and, somehow, shadowy, as if he had taken one step closer to Persephone's dark and haunted realm. He was sitting in his chair, though, which was a decided improvement over lying in the hospital bed, and he was chattering like a convocation of crows when I first arrived.

"Hey, Taylor! Did you hear that Dennis moved? He and Gregory got a bigger place together, and someday he's going to let me come see it. You know what? Bram says I didn't get sick because I was outside at the lake and he says we can go back sometime, when you feel like it. But he said maybe we should drive and not teleport, he thinks it might be easier on me, but I like to teleport—"

More in this vein for the first thirty minutes of my visit. I tried to respond lightly and in kind—and I also tried to catch his wandering attention and get him to buckle down to a lesson—but I didn't have much luck with either endeavor. I was surprised, then, when Quentin's voice came to an abrupt halt, and he leaned forward to get a good look at me.

"Taylor," he said, "you seem so sad."

The unexpected sympathy made me want to cry again, and I had been crying too much over the past week. "I am sad."

"Why? Did something bad happen? Francis just said you had an emergency at Sefton."

Which is what I had asked him to say, but now I couldn't think of any way to keep the truth from Quentin. "One of my students died over the weekend. And I miss him."

"Was there an accident? Was he sick?"

I shook my head. "No accident. I guess he was sick—not like you are—sick in his heart. Depressed. I thought he was better, but he killed himself." I shrugged slightly. "I didn't want to tell you because—"

"Because you don't want me to think about young men dying," he said. "I know."

I looked at him. "You never talk about it."

He glanced out the window then back at me. "I think about it, though. I wonder what it's like. I try not to be afraid, but sometimes I am afraid."

"We all are."

"Sometimes I think, well, maybe it's better."

"Better?" I choked on the word. "Why would—"

"You know. Like the poem. I've been trying to memorize it, but it's pretty long."

For a moment I didn't know what he meant, but then I remembered how much he had immersed himself in Housman, and how I had hoped he never came across "To an Athlete Dying Young."

I recited softly, "'Smart lad, to slip betimes away from fields where glory does not stay . . .'"

He nodded. "'Now you will not swell the rout of lads that wore their honours out . . .'"

"But, Quentin, that's a poem that rationalizes grief. He's not really happy the boy died. It's not really better. No one believes that."

"Yeah, I know, but I—" He shrugged. "And, really and truly, Taylor, I wouldn't mind so much. It's just that—I think about all the things I haven't done. Places I haven't seen. Things I don't know. I've never even a kissed a girl. You know. What's that like? I've never had—well. And, you know, I'll be dead in three or four years. And I don't feel like I've lived. And that bothers me."

"Oh, Quentin," I said. "Oh, honey." And I crossed the room and knelt beside him and put my arms around his painfully thin shoulders. And though I was the one trying to comfort him, I was also the one crying. In the end it was Quentin who said those magical, meaningless words, "It's all right"—although I, like anyone who has ever heard them, did not believe him.

⁕

When I got home that night, I called Domenic. "Are you free for dinner? I have a question that I'm reasonably sure you can answer."

"Sure. Meet me someplace?"

"I'll cook if you want to come over."

He arrived about twenty minutes later, a wine bottle in hand. "I hear you've had a rough week," he said and kissed me on the cheek.

"I think I should stop forming attachments."

"That's been my modus operandi," he said. "What did you make? It smells good."

I lit candles and poured wine and we sat down to dinner. Pasta and garlic bread and a fruit salad. "If you were trying to find a hooker to sleep with a nineteen-year-old boy," I asked, "where would you start?"

Being Domenic, he did not strangle on his wine, or cough into his baked penne, or stare at me and demand, "Are you insane?" He took a contemplative sip from his glass and then began to pull apart his bread.

"Well, I wouldn't go to a hooker," he said. "Not a professional, I mean. Your best bet is probably one of the campus zydeco girls."

"The what girls?"

He gave me that angelic smile. "Zydeco girls. They've got the rhythm but they don't give you the blues. Cynics will tell you it's the most successful work-study program at colleges across the country."

"I think I need more details."

"Students who need extra money to get through college hook up with other students who have more disposable income. I said zydeco girls, but of course both men and women participate. There are a lot of rules about consent and condoms and payment methods, and it's all pretty transactional. The schools don't officially sanction it, of course, but everybody knows about it."

"*I* didn't know about it," I said. "I wonder if any of my kids down at Sefton—huh. I don't think I want to know."

"It's not a big deal," he said. "It's just what some kids do."

"Part of me is horrified," I said primly. "And part of me says this is exactly what I need. How do I find one of them?"

"Usually a few bars where they hang out. You can go to one of them."

"I'd think there'd be online forums or specialized dating apps."

"Sure, of course there are. But it's always been such a local, hands-on sort of venture, if you know what I mean, that a lot of times people just show up at one of the meeting spots when they feel like making a connection. You might post a notice in one of the forums, say you'll be at such-and-such a place on Saturday afternoon, and set up interviews."

"What sort of place? Where should I suggest?"

He grinned. "Well, if you're trolling for Loyola girls, there's a pizza parlor not far from the old L stop. Northwestern girls, there's a hotel bar that gets a lot of traffic. U of Chicago—"

"How do you know all this?" I interrupted.

He opened his eyes wide, all innocence and charm. "People confide in me."

"I mean, you've had girls hanging all over you your whole life. I can't believe you ever had to hire anyone."

"For many people," he said carefully, "the attraction is the lack of emotional commitment."

"Oh, well, then. You're the ideal zydeco boy."

"I've committed to a lot of things in my life," he said, unruffled. "My career. My family. My friends. I've always been available any time *you* needed something, for instance."

"That's true," I said. "It would just be good to see you settle down with someone nice and be happy."

His eyes glittered in the candlelight. "You first."

⌒

Three days later I was sitting in the bar of an upscale Evanston hotel, interviewing pretty young college girls with questionable morals. Every once in a while, when I realized exactly what I was doing, I was so dumbstruck that I couldn't speak rationally for a few minutes.

Fortunately, my companions—all Northwestern students—were self-assured, articulate, and gracious enough to handle the conversational load on their own. Still, the topic was not designed to make any of us seem like intellectuals.

"I'm looking for an easy-going young woman who'd be willing to spend some time with a nineteen-year-old boy who has some health problems" was my opening pitch. I'd included the same basic information in the message I'd posted to the zydeco forum, so I figured I had already weeded out anyone who was repulsed by illness or disability. Still, as I have learned in my years as a teacher, it never hurts to repeat the salient points.

The first four girls were all acceptable—different from each other in looks, attitude, and charm, but acceptable. But Elise was a little too cool, a little too elegant for unsophisticated Quentin. Arcadia was too sympathetic, too inclined to say "that poor boy" when I related details of his situation. Emma was too clinical, wanting to know how often she would be expected to offer sex and if I paid by the hour or the act. Margot was too disengaged.

The fifth woman I interviewed did not at first seem to be a promising candidate. She slid into the booth across from me as nonchalantly as if she were meeting her best friend and gave me a casual "hi." She had short straight blonde hair, cut raggedly around her face and adorned, in odd places, with beads and gold thread and tiny dragonflies. Her clothes were colorful, tight, and revealing. She wore almost no makeup, so her fine translucent skin impressed me with its natural glow, but she had taken to extremes one recent beauty trend that I absolutely could not fathom. She had had rows of diamonds inset into each of her cheeks, tracing a sparkling arc down the curve of bone, and she had accented her extremely blue eyes with sapphires at the outside corners of both lids. A few of my Sefton students had taken up this fashion as well, but mostly they confined themselves to an onyx beauty mark next to one eye or a ruby set at the corner of their lips. These were surgically implanted, mind you—permanent and, at least at the installation stage, painful. I could not help but wonder if this girl's jewels were real.

"Hello," I responded cautiously. "I'm Taylor Kendall."

"I'm Bordeaux."

Of course you are, I thought. It's the name du jour for all the young girls coming into my classes. I had had three of them last year and four the year before. A few years ago, it had been Colette. In my day, the popular name was Azolay; Marika and I once counted twelve in our senior class alone.

"Nice to meet you," I said. "As you know, I'm looking for a friendly young girl to be a companion to a nineteen-year-old boy who has some health problems."

On top of everything else, she was chewing gum. "What kinds of problems?"

"He's got a degenerative muscle disease that causes him pain and requires him to use a wheelchair most of the time."

"Really? What is it?"

She was the first candidate to ask for more details about the illness itself. "It's called Kyotenin degradation."

To my astonishment, she nodded. "Yeah, I knew a guy in high school who had it. He died last year. It was really sad."

"I think it's pretty rare" was all I could think to say.

She leaned her elbows on the table with complete unselfconsciousness. She had rose-and-thorn designs tattooed around each wrist, and rubies were inset into a few of the petals. "He tried some of these really rad cures, but nothing worked. They had this big drive at the high school to see if anyone had a matching blood type so they could do some organ reconstruction, so we all went in to be tested. I donated blood and tissue for about three years, but it didn't do any good."

Every word she said just made me want to goggle at her—and I absolutely hate the word *goggle*. "That was pretty generous of you," I said.

"Well, you know. He was a nice guy. And you'd like to think if you were dying of some weird muscle thing, people would try to help you out. I used to go hang out with him till he got so sick he didn't remember me."

"How old was he when he died?"

She blew a bubble and popped it. "Twenty-one."

"Quentin's nineteen. I guess I said that already."

She nodded. "What's he like? Robbie was a little goofy, you know, like a big kid. Like his brain didn't grow as fast as everyone else's did. I always figured it was because of the disease. But he was smart. He read all the time and he would help me with my math homework and he always beat me at chess."

I could feel myself smiling. "You play chess?"

"Oh yeah. All the smart guys love chess, so I figured I better learn it if I was going to be at the big purple-and-white." She gave an exaggerated headshake when she named the Northwestern colors, and it was pretty clear that she was awed by neither the school's reputation nor its current crop of students. "I'm not too good at it, but that doesn't seem to matter."

"Quentin's never slept with a girl," I said. "And he doesn't know I'm hiring someone. I'm going to tell him you're a student of mine who needs a little extra tutoring. I'm his English teacher, by the way."

"Jazz," she said, nodding.

"And if he likes you and you get along and you want to see more of each other, great. In fact, that's what I'm hoping for. But if that's not the way it works, I don't want you to force anything. I'll pay for your time regardless. I just want him to have—" I gestured inconclusively. "Some normalcy, I guess."

"Yeah," she said, brushing a hand across her sparkling cheek to push back a wayward lock of beaded hair, "don't we all want that."

I was planning to offer her the job anyway, but the complete sincerity with which she made that absolutely ludicrous reply won my heart. Of course, it's always risky to play matchmaker, but I had to believe I had found the perfect girl for Quentin.

"I usually go over on Tuesdays and Fridays," I said. "When can you start?"

"Tomorrow's Tuesday," she said. "That works for me."

CHAPTER FIFTEEN

I HADN'T FIGURED OUT HOW I WOULD BREAK THE NEWS TO ANYONE at the Phillips household that I was bringing in a new pupil, so I decided not to give any advance warning. Tuesday afternoon, Bordeaux and I teleported over to the main outer gate, one right after the other, so I could introduce her to the security guard and explain that she came in under my aegis. As I expected, he immediately dialed the main house to get permission, so when Bordeaux and I made the next short leap to the foyer, both Francis and Bram Cortez were waiting for us.

"Hi," I said, as casual as Bordeaux herself. "I didn't get a chance to call ahead. This is Bordeaux, a Northwestern student that I've been tutoring. It occurred to me that it might be beneficial for both her and Quentin if they could study together some of the time, so I thought I'd introduce them. That's all right, isn't it? I don't think Quentin will mind."

Francis was shaking the young lady's hand and giving her his own name with his usual flawless civility. Cortez was frowning at me, but his look was speculative, not furious. It was clear that, within seconds of laying eyes on Bordeaux, he had formed a pretty accurate idea of who she was and why I had brought her. I had not seen him since the incident at Ozone, and a lot had happened since then. This was probably not the only thing he'd want to ask me about if we ever had five minutes alone together.

"We'll need to do a security check, of course," he said slowly. "But I imagine Quentin will be delighted to meet her."

I turned to make formal introductions. "This is Bram Cortez, the head security officer here. You'll see him at the most unexpected times, so watch your step whenever you're on the premises."

"Hey there," she said and shook his hand. She didn't seem too impressed. But then, she hadn't seemed too impressed when I told her, eventually, who her true employer was. Her exact words had been, "He's kind of a big fat prick, isn't he? Hope I don't run into him."

I had had to forcibly restrain myself from switching on my EarFone and repeating this to Marika instantly.

"Hello, Bordeaux," Cortez said gravely. "Glad to meet you."

Cortez disappeared right after that, presumably to begin investigations into her past, but Francis led us to the elevator and down the hall to Quentin's room. As soon as Francis had left us at the closed door, Bordeaux looked over at me with a grin.

"Well, he was sure eating you up with his eyes," she said.

"What? Who?"

"That Bram person. You guys got a thing?"

I gave that sort of laughing gasp you can't suppress when a verbal punch hits you right in the stomach. This outspoken young woman didn't miss a damn thing. "You know—good question," I said. "I'll tell you when I figure it out myself."

Quentin spun around from his computer as Bordeaux and I walked in. "Hey, Taylor, did you know—oh." His mouth actually snapped shut, and he sat back in his chair. "Hello?"

I made the introductions. "Hi, Quentin," Bordeaux said with careless charm. "Great view you have. Look at those trees." She moved over to the window and began to play with the blinds.

Quentin was glancing between the two of us with a look I had never seen on his face before. Anxiety, that was part of it, and—I frowned a moment, trying to analyze his expression. And jealousy?

"You have other students that you tutor?" was all he said.

"One or two," I said sort of dumbly. "I just took on Bordeaux."

"And she's going to be here every week? Every time you come?"

"Well, maybe not every single time. We'll see how it goes. But I thought you might enjoy having a friend in class."

"She's not my friend," he muttered.

I was shocked. I had not expected this reaction at all. Quentin loved to be around people. His happiness increased exponentially every time someone new walked into the room. Except—and of course I had not thought of this before—he had been the only non-adult and the de facto center of our collective universe. I was guessing here that he wanted all my attention, did not want to divide it with a stranger.

Perhaps I had just made a terrible mistake.

Bordeaux turned from the window at that moment, an easy smile on her face. The sunlight caught the diamonds in her cheeks, the sapphires at her eyes, the scattered glitter in her hair. "Hey, it'll be fun," she said with relaxed assurance. "Just wait and see."

∽

Indeed, Quentin started to melt before our first hour was over. How could he not? Bordeaux was a little ball of happy-go-lucky sunshine that just beamed warmth and contentment into the room. She settled herself on the couch and listened to our first lesson, tossing out comments when appropriate and asking questions when she missed something. When I made a quick reference to *Break of Day*, she interrupted right away.

"No—wait—Quentin, did you absolutely hate that book? I mean, have you ever in your life read anything so abysmally dreary?"

"I only read part of it," he admitted. "Taylor said I didn't have to finish it."

"God, you are so lucky! My lit teacher made us read the whole thing and write papers, and this one girl, she started crying in class and she had to be sent away for an emotional breakdown. Because of a book. I mean, aren't there enough other things in life to cry about?"

"I liked *Josie's Dreams*, though," he offered.

"Yeah! Superjazz, although I thought maybe a little way-too-much when the granddaughter went all loop-di-lune at the end."

He laughed. "What else did you read for class?"

She rattled off a list of titles, most of them considered classics of the first part of the century. "And my roommate? She was skimming chapters and getting AI programs to write her papers, but I read every book. I mean, if you're going to go to college, you may as well try to learn. Otherwise, what's the point?"

"Did you study poetry?" He glanced at me, where I sat mute and invisible, hoping they would begin to connect. "Taylor makes me read poems. I didn't think I'd like them, but I do."

"Oh, yeah. I did a whole class on women poets. Sylvia Plath and Nikki Giovanni and Joy Harjo. I loved it."

I was curious. "Did you cover any of the earlier women poets? Emily Dickinson or Elizabeth Barrett Browning, maybe?"

"We did two days on Dickinson but I don't remember Elizabeth Barrett Browning. Is she any good?"

"Is she—okay, I know you guys were having a nice little chat, but I just can't let that go. You sit right back and get comfortable."

Grinning, Bordeaux wriggled back on the sofa, then opened the tiny purse she kept on a long strap over her shoulder. "Hey, Quentin, you want some gum?"

Quentin's eyes widened with a wicked glee. If I'd had to guess, I'd say that at some point in his life, this pleasure had been forbidden to him, maybe when he was a boy and got sticky stuff smeared all over the carpet. "Sure. What flavor?"

"Oh, this'll melt your mouth off. It's called Chernobyl Cherry, and I. Just. Love. It."

I waited until they had unwrapped their gum—thought to offer me some, which I declined—and seemed to be capable of paying a reasonable amount of attention again. Then I launched into lecture mode.

"Elizabeth Barrett was a well-known British lady poet of the mid-1800s. She came from a large family, lots of brothers and sisters, but she was pretty sickly. In fact, for years and years she believed that if she ever exercised or even got any fresh air, her mysterious ailments would worsen and she would die. So she basically stayed in her house, lying on a couch all day. All she did was talk to her brothers and sisters, and write letters to her millions of friends, and publish poetry.

"Robert Browning was about six years younger than she was—he was also a poet, but by the time he was in his early thirties, he hadn't published much, and what he did publish was murky and hard to understand. Anyway, he read one of her poems and sent her this amazing letter, saying something like, 'Miss Barrett, I love your poems with all my heart, and I love you too!'"

Bordeaux arched her eyebrows. "That's kind of intense."

"She thought so, too. But she wrote him back, and he wrote her again, and for the next couple of years they corresponded practically every day. He started visiting her, and they would still write letters on the days they'd visited. Their collected letters take up two whole volumes.

"Well. Of course they fell in love. Robert wanted to get married, but Elizabeth's dad was creepy and bizarre, and he refused to allow any of his children to marry. One or two of them eloped, and he never spoke to them again. Elizabeth couldn't bear the idea of leaving her family—plus, of course, she believed she was on the verge of dying. But the interesting thing was, Robert kept asking questions about her health, and it turned out she didn't really have an identifiable disease—she'd just been languishing because everyone thought she was frail. So, as he encouraged her, she started taking carriage rides, and going for walks in the park, and gradually regaining some of her strength. Pretty miraculous when you think about it."

"So what happened? Did she die?" Quentin asked.

"After a long courtship, they eventually did elope. They went to live in Italy, where the climate was much kinder to Elizabeth's constitution, and they had a son. I believe they never spent another night apart until Elizabeth's death fifteen years later."

"So she did die," Quentin said.

"Yeah, but fifteen years—not too wasted," Bordeaux said. "I'd take fifteen years of happiness after thirty-some years of being cooped up in a house with a crazy dad."

"I'd take it after nineteen years," Quentin murmured. I cast him a quick worried glance, but he smiled; it had been a joke. Of sorts.

"Anyway," I resumed. "Elizabeth wrote this long cycle of sonnets about how much she loved Robert. One of them is pretty famous. 'How do I love thee? Let me count the ways.'"

"Oh yeah, I like that poem," Bordeaux said. "Maybe I'd like all of them."

"Mmm, maybe. A lot of them are rather maudlin, but some are absolutely lovely. In fact, one of my favorites is the first poem in the cycle, which starts out very dark and forlorn as she talks about her life so far and all her 'melancholy years.' And then she senses some great shadowy shape moving behind her, and it grabs her by the hair and pulls her backward. And the poem goes:

> *"And a voice said in mastery, while I strove—*
> *'Guess now who holds thee?'—'Death,' I said. But there,*
> *The silver answer rang—'Not Death, but Love.'"*

I stopped and smiled at them. Neither seemed quite as moved as I always was by this triumphant surprise ending. "Not death, but love," I repeated. "It's such a hopeful concept, especially for someone who wasn't exactly noted for her upbeat attitude."

"It's very nice," Bordeaux said politely.

I grinned. "Well, hey, read all of them, or don't read any of them, but I just wanted to share that gem with you."

"Is that your favorite poem, Taylor?" Quentin asked.

"Oh, no. I only like Barrett Browning in bits and patches."

"So what is your favorite poem?"

"Depends on my mood. On the top of the list is one by another Victorian lady poet." They looked only marginally interested, but that was good enough for me, so I plunged on.

"Christina Rossetti. Now she had a lot of sorrow in her life, and spent years taking care of sick aunts and dying parents, and she wrote all these gloomy verses about how you shouldn't plant rose bushes at her grave after she died because she wouldn't be able to see the flowers anyway. And she fell in love with a nice guy, but they ended up not getting married because of religious differences. So. A lot of heartbreak. Anyway, she wrote this one unexpectedly exuberant poem that I've always loved. Especially the last two lines:

> *"My heart is like a singing bird*
> *Whose nest is in a water'd shoot;*
> *My heart is like an apple-tree*
> *Whose boughs are bent with thick-set fruit;*
>
> *My heart is like a rainbow shell*
> *That paddles in the halcyon sea:*
> *My heart is gladder than all these*
> *Because my love is come to me.*

Raise me a dais of silk and down;
Hang it with vair and purple dyes;
Carve it in doves and pomegranates,
And peacocks with a hundred eyes;

Work it in gold and silver grapes,
In leaves and silver fleurs-de-lys;
Because the birthday of my life
Is come, my love is come to me."

"Yeah," Bordeaux agreed. "Those last two lines are marbro."

I had no idea what marbro meant, but assumed it was along the lines of jazz and strat. "You'll notice," I said, "that many poets reserve their best images and most beautiful words for the last two or three lines of any poem. It's like the spire on a church. It's what the whole structure was built for."

"What's vair?" Quentin asked.

I looked over at him and started laughing. "I had that very question, so I looked it up once. It's squirrel fur. Popular in medieval times as an ornamental trim."

"Squirrel?" Quentin repeated, wrinkling his nose. "Wouldn't you pick fox or mink if you were going for ornamental?"

Bordeaux was grinning. "Kind of makes the poem a little less wonderful, doesn't it?" She puffed out her cheeks in what I assumed was an attempt to look like a squirrel. Quentin fell into a helpless fit of giggles.

"Well, I still like the last two lines," I said.

"Is class always this much fun here?" Bordeaux asked.

Quentin recovered enough to say, "Every day."

"Then I'm coming back for sure."

Quentin looked quickly between us. "Of course you are! Taylor said you would! We're going to study together."

By which I gathered that, in the course of the hour, he had overcome his jealousy and admitted her to his never-exclusive circle of friends. "She might not come every single day," I said. "Sometimes you and I might have more intensive work to do. But I think it will be good for both of you to study together."

Bordeaux smiled. "Suits me."

I stood, because the hour was over, and Bordeaux bounced to her feet as well. But instead of turning toward the door, she headed for the chess set that always waited hopefully on Quentin's computer table.

"You like chess?" she asked him.

His eyes lit. "Yeah! Bram plays with me sometimes, and Taylor says she will, but she never does. I have some online opponents, but it's more fun in person."

She tossed back her short hair, and her beads clicked together. "I'll play with you."

"Right now?"

"Sure. I don't have to be anywhere for—" She glanced at the wristwatch strapped over the thorn tattoo. "About four more hours." She smiled. "Now, I know some people can take a month to play a chess game, but I would think we could manage a game in four hours."

"Stratospheric!" he exclaimed. "Bye, Taylor! See you Friday!"

I couldn't help smiling, but as I moved toward the door, I made a final admonition to Quentin. "When Bordeaux gets ready to leave, be sure Francis or Bram is around to escort her back to the foyer. Okay? I don't want her to get lost in the house."

He nodded without looking at me, so intent was he on studying the board for his first move, but Bordeaux gave me a slow, considering examination. "I won't steal anything," she said.

I shook my head. "Trust me," I said, "that's not it."

She thought about it a moment longer, then nodded; I knew I would have to tell her the truth. Nobody's toy, this girl. And, charming and relaxed though she could be, confident about her own worth. I liked her better with every passing minute.

"See you guys in a few days," I said and left. I didn't think they noticed when the door closed behind me and Francis and I walked down to the foyer without her.

CHAPTER SIXTEEN

BORDEAUX MET ME AT MY PLACE FRIDAY AFTERNOON SO WE COULD travel up to Quentin's together. Today she had blue beads knotted throughout her blonde hair, although they didn't seem to have been chosen to coordinate with her shirt, a bright orange, or the flower-print Capri-cut pants she wore to finish her ensemble. Still, there was something fresh and fetching about her. Made me want to go out and buy my own hair beads.

"I just wanted to let you know," I said, "why you can't go wandering alone at the Phillips house."

She was moving through my apartment, inspecting things, laying a light finger on the items that intrigued her most. She came to a full stop before the statue of the butterfly girl.

"That is dimensionally marbro," she said in such an admiring voice I was certain it had to be a compliment. "That is jazz without cessation."

"A friend gave it to me. Listen, Bordeaux, you need to be careful when you're at Quentin's house. You don't want to be alone there if his dad is anywhere around."

She turned to look at me, her blue eyes narrowed but not shocked. "What would he do to me?"

I spread my hands. "I was alone in the library with him, and I was terrified. He didn't touch me, but he seemed like he might—do anything. You want to make sure Francis or Bram Cortez is present to escort you any time you're walking through that house."

"I know how to defend myself," she said. Her hand went to the little purse she carried over her shoulder. It was so small that I had assumed it only had room for gum and a tube of lipstick. But her gesture made me think she carried a weapon of some sort, a knife or some tiny stun-gun designed for the woman traveling alone at night.

"My point," I said, "is that you shouldn't have to. Just make sure you have company when you're walking the halls."

"What does Quentin think about all this?"

I ushered her out the door. "I never asked him."

We teleported one at a time to the outer gate and then the inner foyer. Francis was waiting and walked beside us in his usual stately fashion. When we reached Quentin's room, I motioned Bordeaux to go on in ahead of me, and I stayed behind.

"I'm thinking Bordeaux might be coming here even more often than I do," I said with a smile.

Francis nodded. "Which would be perfectly acceptable to me."

"Maybe she should get her own code for the foyer gate."

He looked regretful. "I'm sure that would be much more convenient for her, but I'm afraid I can't comply."

"Why?"

He seemed to be choosing his words carefully. "The only one who can authorize an individual new door code is Mr. Phillips himself. And since I don't believe he's aware of Miss Bordeaux's presence here—and I am not entirely sure he needs to have it brought to his attention—I cannot see an easy way to get Miss Bordeaux her own code."

"I see," I said and thought for a moment. "Hypothetically speaking," I went on, in phrases just as careful as his, "would one person be able to lend another person his or her individual door code?"

"In theory, that would be possible. But the system keeps track of who has arrived and when they've left. If, say, Dennis lent his code to one of his friends—who perhaps wanted to come over for an afternoon swim—and then Dennis attempted to teleport over and join him, the foyer door would reject Dennis' transfer. He would be automatically rerouted to the front security entrance, and then, I'm afraid, the guards would be called and everyone would know how he had tried to circumvent the system. At that point, things wouldn't look so good for Dennis."

"So if Dennis ever lent his code to a friend, Dennis had better be sure he didn't come over when his friend was here."

Francis nodded. "Exactly. I am glad you understand."

Which, of course, was not Francis' way of endorsing my idea of giving Bordeaux my gate code, but he had certainly explained how I could do it if I wanted to. I thanked him and went in to join the others, and within five minutes had given Bordeaux my code. She seemed to understand perfectly that she could never use it on Tuesday or Friday afternoons when I would also be arriving, but I found myself hoping that she would use it very often on other days.

Today's session went even more smoothly than Tuesday's, since both my students had read the assigned homework. I was a little startled to learn, halfway through the hour, that they'd read the chapter together.

"Oh. So you've come here since Tuesday," I said blankly to Bordeaux. She must have arrived the way ordinary visitors did, teleporting to the outer gate first before a guard got the okay to send her on to the house.

"Oh, yeah. It's practically the only way I can really concentrate," she said nonchalantly. "I have to find a study buddy. And Quentin's the only one in this class." She grinned at him. "I figure I'll come this weekend, too. Supposed to be beautiful out. We can get a blanket and study out in the yard. Francis said he'd bring us sandwiches when we got hungry."

"Well, then," I said briskly. "Let me make sure I assign lots of homework so that you have plenty to keep you busy."

The rest of the hour went fast, and once again I was the only one to leave when the metaphorical bell rang. Francis was waiting for me in the hallway, though part of me had hoped to see Bram there instead.

"Miss Bordeaux is staying late again?" he inquired.

"If you think that's all right."

"I think it's splendid."

"Good. So do I."

The weekend was quiet, enlivened only by phone calls, trash TV, and Sunday brunch at my mother's. Monday I spent at Sefton in a series of staff meetings Caroline called to discuss recalibrating the graduation requirements for a liberal arts degree.

Tuesday I had hoped to spend my afternoon session at the Phillips mansion working outdoors, to prove I could be just as free-spirited and fun as Bordeaux, but a chilly wind blowing off the lake made the ideas of "spring" and "Chicago" seem incompatible. So we stayed indoors and spent the hour deconstructing classic science fiction short stories like Isaac Asimov's "Nightfall" and Ted Chiang's "Story of Your Life."

"You coming or staying, Bordeaux?" I asked as I got ready to leave.

"Oh, I've gotta stay," she said lazily. "I still haven't beaten Quentin at chess. I'm going to, though. It's my lucky day."

"Good luck, then," I said, smiling, and stepped out of the room. To find Bram Cortez leaning against the wall, waiting for me.

"Hi," I said, shutting the door.

He nodded toward the room. "She's going to stay a little longer?"

"She is. But I have to get away. All the teenage energy is wearing me down."

He smiled. "I'm here to offer you a ride, if you'd like it."

"Oooh, a car ride? That's a special treat for a girl."

"Special and rare. Accept or reject."

"Accept, thank you."

We didn't talk much more as we threaded our way through the mansion. Only after we were settled into the leather luxury of the silver Mustang did the conversation began in earnest.

"I haven't seen you since I brought my new student in," I said as we drove down the tree-lined streets. "But you haven't said a word about her. Does that mean you approve?"

He glanced at me. "Once I checked her out, I thoroughly approved. I wish her grade-point average was a little better, but as a hired professional girlfriend for Quentin, she seems about perfect."

"She is perfect," I said. "I hope Quentin likes her. So far, he seems to."

"Quentin likes everybody. No fear."

"Then I'm a happy girl."

He kept his eyes on the road. "You've had a bad time of it lately," he said. "I heard about your student at Sefton. I'm sorry."

I shook my head. "I keep asking myself—what else should I have done? What signs did I miss? I know his friends were paying attention. And, at the end, none of us helped him."

He signaled and pulled onto a highway ramp. "Been times in my life," he said, "when I've thought no one could ever help anyone. I could tell that someone I knew was hurt—I knew I was hurt—and no one could figure out how to reach a hand over to the next guy. I had this picture in my head, all these bodies kneeling on the ground, hunched over, their hands over their heads. Just one big desert landscape dotted with these dark sad people who were close enough to touch and yet separated from each other by miles of—grief, I suppose."

"That's pretty bleak," I said. "You still feel that way?"

"Some days. But mostly not."

"More often right after you got divorced," I guessed.

He glanced at me. "Yeah, I suppose."

"After I first left Danny," I said, "I had this sense of panic. All the time, in the pit of my stomach. 'I'll never find anyone to love me again.' And I had this sense of time running out. Every day that would go by—another day without love. And the panic would intensify. And I just wanted to rush out—meet somebody on the street—fall in love right away—and have that happy delirium again. I thought nothing else would dissipate the fear."

"So did you?"

"What, rush right back out into romance? No. Dated a few guys, but nothing ever turned serious."

"And what about the panic?"

I laughed. "Strangely enough, it dissipated on its own, to be replaced by an easy contentment at the shape my life has taken. Not that I wouldn't like to be married again—or at least fall in love. I just think I'll be more leisurely about it when the next chance comes."

"So you won't be inviting a guy to spend the night any time soon, but a kiss in the doorway is okay."

His voice was absolutely uninflected. I stared over at him and felt the blood rise, vein by vein, to the top of my head. My mouth opened, but at first no words would drop out. Finally I said, "To pick an example completely at random, yes."

"Good. Just checking."

At the exact same moment, we both started laughing.

"Is this one of those days," I said, "that you would say no if I invited you in for a beer?"

"Gotta get back," he said. "But I wouldn't say no on Friday. In fact, if you were interested in going to dinner on Friday evening, I wouldn't say no to that either."

"Now, wait," I said. "Would that be a date? I mean, advance planning, that sounds like a date to me."

He was grinning. "I don't think people over forty are allowed to use the term 'date.' Maybe we should call it a social engagement."

I crossed my arms. "I won't go unless you admit it's a date."

"Fine," he said quickly. "We're dating."

I opened my mouth to parse the differences between *one date* and *dating*, but then I decided I didn't want to wade in waters so muddy. "You're sort of a tricky guy," I said instead.

"You're not the first to think so."

"And probably not the last."

He gave me a quick, appraising look. "You never know."

All too soon, or so it seemed to me, we were pulling up in front of my apartment. He kept the car idling, obviously not intending to come up this time. I paused with my fingers on the door handle. "I'll be seeing you Friday, then," I said.

He seemed amused, as if he knew he had knocked me off balance, but knew also that I didn't mind at all. "Get some beads for your hair," he suggested. "Maybe some gold string."

"I was going to go with some jewel insets."

He reached over and touched the corner of my mouth. "Ruby," he said. "Right there."

"You think it'll make the boys like me better?"

"Guarantee it. You'll get lots of dates then."

I laughed and opened the door. "Maybe you don't know it, but sometimes I take the stupidest dares."

"Counting on it," he said. He was still laughing when I shut the door—appeared to be still laughing as he drove away. I, feeling dizzy and girlish, made my way unsteadily up the walk and up the stairs.

My heart is like a singing bird...

❧

Wednesday I said goodbye to my students at Sefton in the last class of the semester. It wasn't really a class, in that no subjects were actually taught, but—to me, anyway—it seemed like the most important hour of the past four months. I handed out grades and returned final papers and told them how much I had enjoyed teaching them. We talked about Evan, and the memorial service, and their summer plans, and the grades they'd gotten on their standardized tests. (All of them had passed, several of them with exceptionally good marks. Nancy, in fact, had gotten one of the highest scores in Texas.) We talked about the classes they planned to take next year, and I was gratified to see how pleased many of them were to learn that I would be teaching a sophomore comp class in the fall.

"Well, there's an easy A," Devante said loudly.

"I don't think I want you in another one of my classes," I said. "I think it's full already."

"Are you teaching summer school?" asked one of the girls who had struggled most of the semester but pulled out a solid B at the end.

"No," I said. "Are you taking a class?"

She nodded glumly. "Yeah. I need another English credit."

I shrugged. "Hey, you've got my email address. If you need a little help some afternoon, just let me know, and I can meet you here."

"Good, because Dr. Fullerton just doesn't understand my papers," she said.

I wanted to say, *Well, it's a learned skill*, because it was, but that was obviously the wrong response. "Glad to help," I said. "And I'd be glad to hear from any of you, any time—with good news or bad. And anyone who doesn't take my class next year, I hope you'll drop by my office now and then and let me know how you're doing." I glanced over at my favorite student. "Not you, Devante."

He smiled broadly. "Hey, I'm in the class. You're not getting rid of me that easy."

The time passed too quickly. I wanted to silence the alarm when it signaled the end of the hour. I rose and stood by the door so I could shake each student's hand as he or she walked out. "Goodbye—have a good summer—it was great having you—goodbye—"

Nancy and Simone gave me quick embraces and promised to come by from time to time in the fall. Devante gave me a bone-crushing hug that practically lifted me off the floor, tall as I am. "I'll be around," he said and sauntered out. I stood in the middle of the empty room and tried not to cry.

This happens to me every year.

CHAPTER SEVENTEEN

THINGS WERE A LOT CHEERIER IN ATLANTA AS MARIKA AND I SAT IN her house Thursday morning, planning a shopping trip. She wanted to know in detail what Bram and I were planning for our date, was it just dinner, or would we go hear music afterward or perhaps see a movie? Maybe we'd go dancing? "Because all of that factors in," she explained.

"I don't know. I don't know if we're going someplace fancy or someplace traditional or someplace trendy—although, this being Bram, I would rule out the really marbro."

"The what? What does that mean?"

"I don't know. I was hoping you would."

She waved an impatient hand; too many other things to worry about. "If I'm guessing right, all you've ever worn around this guy are your dumpy let's-just-throw-some-clothes-on outfits so that you feel comfortable. So we might want to spice it up with bright colors just for a change."

"Dumpy! My clothes are fine—"

"Sure, if you're going to walk the dog."

"Well, excuse me if I don't dress like a zydeco girl every time I walk out the door—"

"A what? Who have you been talking to?"

"That one came from Domenic."

She waved this away, too. "Whatever. I'm thinking red."

"Sure, I like red, but an elegant cut. Oh, and I need one of those jewel insets," I added, laying my finger at the corner of my mouth. "A ruby."

I said it just to make her jump, but she frowned and tilted her head to one side. "You know, your face is so austere that I think it would add just the right touch."

"I was kidding."

"You can buy temporary ones. They last a week."

My eyes opened wide. "Really? Then I gotta get one."

She jumped up. "Me, too. Let's go."

My suspicion was that Bordeaux had acquired both her tattoos and her insets at a backroom parlor next to a drug paraphernalia shop a few blocks from campus, but of course that was not the kind of establishment I would enter under Marika's care. The Peachtree Promenade was an upscale shopping and commercial district that catered to the very wealthy and the ultra fashionable. Discreet doors opened onto face-and-body spas, hair removal clinics, cosmetic enhancement emporiums, personal trainer gymnasiums, hair salons, haute couturiers, and other establishments I could not even name. More prominently located were boutiques, galleries, shoe stores, and tailors' shops where most of the hardcore buying took place—and the cafés, ice cream parlors, and fern-filled restaurants where shoppers could recruit their strength for a few more hours in the determined pursuit of beauty.

"Are you sure I can afford anything here?" I asked Marika as we stepped from the ivy-covered teleport booth onto the well-maintained sidewalks that snaked through the promenade.

"You're working for Duncan Phillips. You can afford whatever you want."

We started by looking at clothes. I exaggerate only slightly when I say we must have considered five hundred dresses before we found the perfect one. It was closely fitted on top and full-skirted on the bottom, made from a moire silk in haughty crimson. We accessorized it with a black silk shawl and shiny black heels, even though I complained that I didn't want new shoes. The next stop was a nail salon so I could get a manicure in a polish that matched the dress. Marika insisted I get a pedicure as well, "just in case you end up taking your shoes off." I felt the heat rise to my cheeks, but I meekly did as she commanded.

After a light lunch, we made our final stop at the Jewels to You salon, where a handsome young man discussed all our options at self-enhancement through precious stones. By the time he was done with his spiel, I was almost tempted to throw caution to the winds and go for the real gems permanently grafted on, but we stuck with our original plan and opted for temporary adornments.

Once we were settled into adjacent chairs, our "body technician" explained what type of glue he was about to use, how long it would hold, how we could dissolve the adhesive earlier if we wished, and what discount we would receive if we returned within a month either for a new temporary bond or a more permanent one.

As Bram had suggested, I selected a small, brilliantly faceted ruby and had it set a quarter of an inch from the left corner of my mouth. Marika chose a yellow topaz to go at the edge of her right eye. Once the jewels were applied, we had to sit in our chairs for thirty minutes without speaking. I'd have thought that would be a challenge for Marika, generally so restless, but she remained absolutely motionless for the requisite period of time. She can sacrifice anything, even conversation, for the sake of fashion.

We were both delighted with our results, however. We stood before the mirror for a good fifteen minutes, uttering exclamations of delight and turning our heads from side to side to better view our enhancements.

"You know, I might actually have to come back and have this done permanently," Marika said.

"Live with it a week first," I advised. "You might not like it as much as you do right now."

"I think I will."

"Yeah, I think I will too."

We capped off the decadence of the day by stopping for rich chocolate desserts at a fancy patisserie. By this time, it was late afternoon and I was worn out. After promising to call Marika as soon as I got in Friday night ("or Saturday morning," she added), I left her at the teleport gate and zoomed on over to Olympic Stadium. A couple more quick jumps, and I was home. It could not have been a better day.

⌒

I was still delighted, but somewhat embarrassed, the following day when I had to start facing friends and family members with my new beauty mark in place. The little ruby seemed garish as a spotlight, and my investment in it silly and out of character.

Francis said nothing when he greeted me at the door, though I was convinced he was mentally shaking his head at my lapse of taste. I pretended I didn't notice. "Bordeaux said she was arriving separately," I told him, "so you can just bring her up when she gets here."

"She's already in Quentin's room," he said.

"Oh. Well. Good. We can get started right away, then."

But Bordeaux, unlike Francis, could not refrain from making an immediate comment on my bright new accessory. "Hey, look who's setting fashion trends," she said, coming close to get a good look. "Spicy job, Taylor. Looks great with your skin color."

I put a hand self-consciously to my face. "It's temporary," I said quickly. "Just for fun."

"Yeah, that's how I started," she said. "But once you've paid good money for a real diamond, you start thinking, 'And I'm just gonna paste this on? I don't think so.' I started sleeping a lot better once I had the grafts."

"I want to live with it a while before I make a decision like that," I said.

"I think it looks very nice, Taylor," Quentin said politely.

When Dennis arrived as the hour drew to a close, he was even more enthusiastic.

"Aren't you the raving beauty?" he said, drawing me over to the window to admire the jewel in sunlight. "Aren't you just the most fashionable girl ever? Who would have expected it of our staid Ms. Kendall?"

"It's just temporary."

"Isn't that how Bordeaux started?" he asked.

I turned away from the window. "Oh—you've met her already?"

Bordeaux nodded. "Hi, Dennis."

"Yes, we've all fallen madly in love with her in the past two weeks," he replied. "Francis said, 'Now we mustn't forget that our first loyalty to any woman should go to Taylor,' and Bram said, 'Taylor who?'"

"I'm glad to see you're back in your usual high spirits," I said, ignoring a tiny stab of jealousy. It had been fun being the only girl in this all-male household. "Last time I saw you, you were a little down."

"All is well again, sweetie, but thanks for noticing." Always one to avoid talking about his personal life, Dennis turned immediately to the room at large. "Who wants to swim? Bordeaux, are you staying?"

"You bet."

"Taylor?"

"Can't," I said. "I've got plans tonight, so I've got to get home and change clothes."

"What kind of plans?" Dennis asked, his face so innocent that I realized he knew exactly what my plans were. Bram didn't seem like the type to gossip about the women in his life, so I had to assume he had asked Dennis for a list of possible restaurants, and Dennis had guessed the rest.

"Dinner with a friend," I said, my face just as guileless as his. "I sure hope we have a good time."

Bordeaux looked over, intuitive enough to sense something in the air, but Quentin was completely oblivious. "Okay, well, see you Tuesday, Taylor," he said. "And I really do like your ruby. It makes you look marbro."

"And so young," Dennis murmured, ushering me to the door.

Francis was waiting when we stepped into the hallway, and he escorted me to the portal when the others headed for the pool. He waited until they were out of earshot to say, "Bram regrets that he can't drive you home, as he had hoped, but says he will fulfill his other obligations to you as detailed."

I bit my lip, but the smile came anyway. "I can't believe that's exactly how he phrased it."

Francis was having trouble keeping his own smile in check. "I understand, some evening engagement," he said. "He mentioned a time frame of seven o'clock."

So much for keeping secrets in this house. "Where are we going, do you know that, too?"

"I believe Dennis was able to supply some advice on that subject, if you were wanting some advance information. I rarely dine out, so my recommendations in this instance would have been virtually useless."

We had reached the gate by this time, and I turned to give him a warm smile. "We trust you on so many other points that this is hardly something to hold against you."

He inclined his head majestically in thanks. "And while we are exchanging compliments, may I say the jewel inset is quite lovely."

"It's temporary."

"Nonetheless. I hope you have a wonderful time tonight, jewels and all."

I waited until I had been beamed back to my neighborhood, but then I started laughing so hard I didn't think I would stop by seven o'clock.

∽

I was so nervous by 6:45 that I could neither sit still nor continue primping, so I paced restlessly through the apartment. Marika called four times while I was getting ready, so I finally warned her that I was deactivating my EarFone and wouldn't turn it on again until Saturday. I don't know if she believed me or not, but I did turn it off, and subsequently calmed down.

When the doorbell sounded, my heart leapt up so painfully that for a moment I couldn't breathe. What was this all about? It wasn't like I was going on a blind date. This was a guy I knew and liked, which was why I was spending the evening with him in the first place. I took a deep breath, smoothed down my drifting skirt, and answered the door.

Bram stood there, dressed all in black and looking darkly handsome. He had gotten a recent haircut, which emphasized the starkness of his bones, and even his thin, strict mustache looked freshly trimmed. But there was nothing severe about the smile on his face or the approval in his eyes.

"Even better than I hoped," he said. "You look beautiful."

"Thank you. You look rather dashing yourself."

"Dennis helped me dress."

"And why exactly did you tell everyone in the house that we had plans tonight?"

He grinned. "I didn't. I asked Dennis for some recommendations, and he said, 'Oh, good, you're finally going out with Taylor.' And then he turned to Francis and said, 'Did you hear? Bram and Taylor have a date.'"

"And you said, 'What makes you think it's Taylor?'"

"I did. And he said, 'Because she's the only woman you've even spoken to in ten years.' Which isn't true," Bram added, "but at this point there didn't seem to be any reason to correct him. I hope you don't mind."

I turned my hands palm-up. "They're like brothers. I try not to give Dennis any ammunition, but other than that—of course I don't mind."

"Anyway, if you don't like the restaurant, you can blame Dennis."

"Where are we going?"

He smiled. "Secret. Are you ready?"

I grabbed the black shawl and draped it over my shoulders. This being

Chicago, even in June, I'd probably freeze before the night was over, but I wasn't about to ruin the ensemble with a jacket. "Ready."

I was surprised, once we stepped outside, to find that his Mustang was nowhere in sight. He set off at a brisk walk in the direction of the teleport door. "Not so fast," I said. "I'm not used to heels."

"But you look good in them."

"Thank you again."

There was no line at the neighborhood gate, and Bram stepped back to let me go first. "And I code for?" I asked.

"O'Hare."

I raised my eyebrows. "A foreign destination?"

"Oh, no. It's domestic. See you there."

A few minutes later, we had regrouped at the teleport terminal and were strolling around the big hub. I loved O'Hare on a weekend night. During the day, it was crammed with business travelers rushing to conferences and sales appointments; on weekend days, it was filled with vacationers wearing brightly colored shirts and ragged cotton shorts, heading off to fun-filled locations. But on Friday and Saturday nights, coming to O'Hare was like sauntering through Times Square. The older women were dressed in black gowns and ropes of diamonds, the younger women wore form-fitting gauzy dresses and crystal jewels around their throats. The men wore black tuxedos and brightly starched white shirts, or neat suits and shiny loafers. Where were they going? The New York Metropolitan Opera? The Berlin Orchestra? The Moscow Ballet? London's West End? It was such a pageantry of excess and opulence, of arrogance and wealth, but it appealed to me in a fairytale way.

And now I too was one of the beautiful people about to be whisked away to an exotic location with an attractive man.

"I would make you cover your eyes, but that doesn't seem practical," Bram said. "Here we are."

Here was the city gate for Lahaina. I felt my face go childlike with wonder. "We're going to Hawaii for dinner! Oh, Bram, how delightful!"

"Have you ever been there?"

"On a couple of day trips with Marika. We loved it."

"Good. We have reservations in about twenty minutes, so I hope this line moves quickly."

There were maybe thirty people ahead of us, most dressed more casually than we were, and one or two balancing surfboards against their hips, but indeed the line moved rapidly. Again, Bram allowed me to go first, though he insisted on paying for my trip with his thumb-chip pressed against the sensor, and merely said, "Wait for me there."

Lahaina International isn't much to wax ecstatic over. It's a small, very white, very crowded teleport terminal always crammed with more people than it was designed to hold. Not the best introduction to the relaxed and magical world of Hawaii, I always thought. Within seconds, Bram appeared beside me, then guided me to the local gate that I assumed Dennis had specified. Another quick jump, and I was stepping from the portal into the dazzling sunshine and jostling crowds of Front Street.

I closed my eyes and took a deep breath of that scented air, full of ocean and orchids and coconut oil. I guessed it was about 2:30 in the afternoon here, though my stomach still said, "Eat dinner! Eat dinner now!" I wondered if Bram had thought about the time difference when he made the reservations.

By his look of astonishment when he stepped out of the gate, I realized he hadn't. I couldn't keep myself from giggling, though I tried to muffle the sound with one corner of my black shawl. A sheepish smile came to his own face.

"I guess our dinner reservations are in about five hours. What was I thinking?"

"This is too funny," I said. "The exact same thing happened to Marika and me the first time we came here. We wanted to get an early start, so we teleported over at eight in the morning. From Atlanta. So there was a six-hour time difference. It was two in the morning here."

He moved into the constant stream of human traffic, and I fell in step beside him. "What did you do?"

"Well, of course, every bar on Front Street was still open, so we had a couple beers. Then we found a tour bus going up to Haleakala to see the sunrise, so we bought tickets and rode on up. It ended up being a great day by the time it was all done."

"So do you feel like killing five hours till dinner, or do you want to go back to Chicago?"

"Oh, I want to stay!" I exclaimed. "But I'm starving. Let's say I buy you lunch, and then we just walk around for a while, or take a tour, and then we go for dinner."

"You realize it will be three in the morning before we get home."

I gave him a challenging look. "And you don't think you can stay awake that long? You're not that old."

He reached for my arm to pull me out of the way of a couple of tourists who were each pushing baby strollers. Then his fingers slid down my bare skin and he caught my hand in his. "I'm just looking out for your welfare. Don't want your mom to worry."

I smiled. "Let's get lunch."

We ended up at an outdoor café that featured a soup and salad bar, and I went back about five times to get another plateful of fruit. Bram watched in amazement as I bit into my sixth or seventh slice of fresh pineapple.

"You're going to have acid burns all over the roof of your mouth," he said.

"People are always amazed at how much pineapple I can eat," I said. "And strawberries. That's what I'd live on if I could."

"I gotta have meat."

"Well, protein's important too."

We didn't linger at the meal, and soon we were cruising down Front Street again. We didn't find much except tacky little tourist shops selling ships made of seashells and sand dollars painted with ocean scenes. So much of Lahaina is relatively new, since the city had to be rebuilt after devastating wildfires some years back. The bright paint and shiny surfaces make an odd contrast to the air of ancient mystery that hangs over the rest of the islands. I could sense Bram getting restless.

"Want to go to the beach?" he asked.

So we teleported over to Waikiki. I stripped off my new shoes and stuffed them into a plastic bag that I begged from a merchant selling seashell jewelry. Hand-in-hand again, we walked on the fine sand at the edge of the restless ocean. The crimson skirt drifted just above the waves and swirled around my calves; the fitted bodice lay cool against my skin. My hand seemed small and slight in Bram's. I loved the feeling.

"Let's bring Quentin here someday," I said.

"Not a bad idea. Have to make sure it's a time when he's pretty healthy, though."

"They have doctors here. We could plan ahead. He'd love it."

"Maybe come for a few days. Get a hotel room so he'd have a place to rest when he was feeling tired."

"Bring Dennis," I said with a smile. "And Francis."

"Bordeaux," he added.

I raised my eyebrows. "Did she come over *every* day these past two weeks?"

He nodded. "She takes her job seriously." He glanced at me. "But she seems to genuinely like him. It's only been a couple of weeks, but she's slipped right into the routine of the household, and she seems to have developed that sense of protectiveness for Quentin that we all get. I saw her in the pool with him. She watched him the whole time, like she was ready to go catch him if he slipped underwater, even though Dennis was right there." He shrugged. "You can fake affection all kinds of ways, but you can't really fake worry. I think she cares about him."

My little nugget of jealousy melted away. One more soldier in the Guerre de Quentin. "Then yes. We'll bring her when we come back."

The sun-filled hours slipped exquisitely by. I felt like I was appearing in a film montage of a happy couple falling in love—the walk on the beach, the scenic boat ride, the pause at the florist's stall for us to buy matching leis. I was sunburned and starving by the time the dinner hour rolled around, but I was also giddy with a sort of satiated delight. *My heart is like a rainbow shell/ That paddles in the halcyon sea . . .*

"What a perfect day," I observed as, back on Front Street, we walked through the gathering dusk toward our dinner destination.

"Not over yet," he replied, and turned me inside.

We were escorted upstairs to a table that overlooked the ocean. There were no windows—there was no wall—it was just us and a roomful of diners on a hardwood floor elevated above the street. Oh, and a leaf-thatched roof overhead, its green pointed edges making a sharp serration where the ceiling met the open air. The setting sun threw gaudy orange stripes across the rippling sea, and fishing boats moved shadowy as sharks off into the graying distance.

"Perfect," I breathed.

"Romantic," Bram said. "Just what Dennis promised."

Our waiter was a tall, lanky, long-haired blonde dressed in black cotton and sporting braided leather bracelets around his knobby wrists. He had an easy smile that made me smile right back, and he pulled up a chair to join us at the table.

"We don't have printed menus," he explained, "but I can tell you what's available tonight. What do you think you're in the mood for?"

"I don't think I want seafood," I said.

"I had a burger at lunch," Bram added.

"Let's talk about pasta," our waiter said.

Bram ended up with lobster, while I chose the recommended risotto primavera, and it was wonderful. The salad was superb. The wine was excellent. The key lime pie at the end of the meal was divine.

"This is the best meal I have ever had in my life," I said to Bram. "I never want to eat anywhere else as long as I live."

He smiled. "We'll have to make nightly visits here when we come back with the whole gang."

"I can't wait that long."

"Then you and I can come back next week."

I shot him a quick look and said nothing.

"That is, if you're willing to commit to another date," he added. "But this one seems to have gone pretty well."

"Best date ever," I said. "Let's come back."

It was almost ten, Hawaii time, when we'd had our last bites of key lime pie and Bram had figured a tip for the waiter. Despite my best efforts, I could not smother my yawns.

"I warned you," he said, coming to his feet and reaching for my hand. "Way past your bedtime."

"The sun makes you sleepy, too," I protested, stumbling beside him and yawning again. "And the food—and the wine—but I am really, really tired."

"You'll be home in no time," he said, leading the way back to the local gate.

A few jarring moments leaving Lahaina International, a few weary minutes trudging through O'Hare—more deserted than I had ever seen it—and then suddenly we were in my neighborhood, moving down its silent streets. After the sunshine and warmth of Maui, Chicago was shockingly cold. I pulled my inadequate shawl more tightly around my shoulders.

"Sorry," I said when I yawned again.

"Almost there."

I was grateful for the toasty warmth I felt the instant we entered my apartment. I was certain I should invite Bram to stay awhile, but I knew I could not remain awake long enough to put together a coherent sentence. He had come just two steps inside, so he did not appear to plan on lingering.

"Want me to check for assailants in the closets?"

"I appreciate the thought, but I'm fine. Bram, it was a wonderful day. Evening. Outing."

"I thought so, too."

I came close enough to rest my hands on his arms. "And something to look forward to next week," I added. I had kicked off my heels the minute I walked in, so I had to rise to my tiptoes to kiss him goodbye. He tasted like chardonnay and sunshine.

"Goodnight, Abramo," I whispered.

"Goodnight, Tay-Tay," he whispered back. He kissed me again and slipped out the door.

I was in bed and asleep, no doubt, before he had even made it back to the teleport gate.

CHAPTER EIGHTEEN

JASON CALLED AT NINE A.M. I STILL HAD MY EARFONE DEACTIVATED, but Jason has the emergency override code, so I knew who it was before I even answered.

"Do you know what time it is?" I demanded without opening my eyes.

"Yeah, do you?" came Jason's voice. "I tried calling you till about two in the morning. What's your alibi?"

I was too tired to play this game. "Um—I was rescuing kittens that some-one had thrown in the Chicago River."

"That is so lame. How was your date?"

I turned on my side and snuggled deeper under the covers. I felt as if my body had been partially dismantled during the night and bits of my bones and muscles had not yet been snapped back in place. "How do you know about my date?"

"Marika told me. She said you were supposed to text her when you got in. She was worried when she didn't hear from you, so I said I'd call."

I yawned noisily. Begin the new day as you ended the old one. "When did you talk to Marika?"

"Well, we just got off the phone right now. But we went to the ballgame last night, which is when she told me about your evening plans."

"You went to the ballgame with Mareek? Here?"

"Nope. Atlanta."

I yawned again. "Domenic go, too?"

"Nope. Just us."

"Who won?"

"Braves, five to three. What are you doing tonight? I'm spending the weekend at Mom's, if you want to hang out."

"Sounds good. Nice quiet evening is what I need right now. See you later."

"Call me when you wake up."

I managed to fall back asleep and didn't actually get up until about one in the afternoon. When I turned the phone back on, I found that Marika had left me three voicemails and six texts.

"Good, you're finally awake!" she exclaimed when I called. "Tell me, tell me, what happened?"

SHARON SHINN

"We went to Hawaii."

"Hawaii! That is so romant—wait. You went to Hawaii when? I thought he was picking you up at seven."

I started giggling. "You got it."

She snorted with laughter. "Kind of an uncool way to start the date. But that's good, then you get to see how he handles setbacks."

"He was chagrined but game. We had lunch, then we walked on the beach, then we went for a sailboat ride—my whole body is completely encrusted in salt, I have to take a shower—and *then* to dinner. The food was incredible. But it was past three when we got in."

"So did he spend the night?"

"Marika!"

"Well, did he?"

"No. He kissed me goodnight. He said we'd go back to Hawaii next week. He did not stay over. It wasn't an option."

"It's always an option. But you have plans for next week already? That's good, that shows he's definitely interested."

"That shows he has no other social life, but yeah, it's good."

"And you had fun? You like him?"

"I had fun," I repeated quietly. "I like him."

❧

Dinner at Mom's Saturday night was less exotic but more relaxed. Of course, I had to endure Jason's mockery about my new facial adornment ("Hey, Tay, looks like you got a big ol' zit there right by your mouth"), but my mother told me it was pretty. After the meal, we played Scrabble for a couple of hours. I'm such a word person, you'd think I'd be a whiz at Scrabble, but Jason and my mom are both such cutthroat competitors that I lose about ninety percent of the time. I had to be satisfied with small victories like playing *equinox* on a double word.

"What would you like to do for your birthday, Tay?" Mom asked after she won the third consecutive game. "I was thinking of having your Aunt Jennifer and your cousin Azolay over for dinner. And you can invite Marika and Domenic if you like."

Jason gave me a smile of unholy amusement. Domenic absolutely hates Azolay. "That would be fun," he said in dulcet tones. "Let's do that."

Conveniently enough, my birthday fell on a Saturday night two weeks from now, so it was simple to make plans. Jason and I promised to issue the invitations to our friends. "This will be great," I said. "Something to look forward to."

❧

The following two weeks went by at a languorous, indolent pace. I love having summers off, though I'm often teaching summer school or tutoring private students. This year, all I had were my sessions with Quentin, so I filled the rest of my days with hedonism. I read, watched movies, hung out at Marika's, had late dinners with Domenic, and went to ballgames with Jason. He had paused his studies for the summer and had returned to Chicago for the season, moving in with our mom. She was in heaven, making him full breakfasts every morning and feast-day dinners every night. I joined them every couple of days and wondered how long it would take me to put on ten pounds.

I enjoyed having him around, though, available to me in two minutes instead of the hour or so it took for him to come in from Colorado if we decided to get together on the spur of the moment. Teleport between cities is instantaneous, of course, but you have to factor in the time it takes to walk to your local booth, wait in line, make your way through O'Hare or Olympic, find the gate to your destination, and finally end up where you want to be. I've never managed it in less than forty-five minutes.

But there was another reason I liked knowing that he was staying at our mother's house. There's something about geographical proximity. You can feel it when someone is ten miles away versus a thousand. The gravitational pull is stronger. The connection is tighter. The resonance hums along your bones.

The true highlight of those two weeks was the second trip to Maui with Bram. If anything, this was more fun than the first visit. I was a little more at ease—still excited, still wanting to appear to my best advantage, but relieved of that bubbling sense of nervousness that had dogged me like a chaperone on our first outing.

"We could go to Hawaii every Friday," he suggested as we stood just inside the doorway of my darkened apartment, arms wrapped around each other for physical support as much as affection. This time it was four a.m. I had closed my eyes and was resting my forehead against his chest, and I thought it very likely that I would fall asleep standing up.

"No," I said drowsily. "It makes us too tired to think about doing anything else."

I could feel the laugh rumble behind his ribs. "What else might we be thinking of doing?"

I blushed and looked up. "That isn't what I—I mean, I'm not even coherent at this hour—"

He kissed me quickly. "We can think of some other place to have dinner," he said. "Only not next Friday. I have to go out of town for the weekend. My sister Laney is having a party and she wants me to come down early."

"That's sweet," I said, and then yawned right in his face. "Sorry."

He laughed again. "But the next week. For sure."

"For sure," I said, and kissed him again.

⤳

Tuesday of the week before my birthday, Bordeaux arranged a picnic lunch out on the broad lawn of the mansion. She had Quentin strapped into his Kevvi braces before I even arrived, and she informed me that she had already asked Francis to pack us a lunch.

"And one of Bram's security guys will carry it out to the pond for us," she said, shaking back her short shaggy hair and giving me her trademark smile, "but we won't let him stay."

Moving slowly to accommodate Quentin's halting pace, our little caravan traveled down the elevator, out the back hallways and across the emerald expanse of grass to the ornamental lake situated about an acre from the house. Bordeaux and the guard spread out the blanket and unpacked the goodies while I insisted Quentin lean on me for support, even though he said this made him look like a heezling. But soon enough we had dismissed the guard, dropped to the ground, and started sipping our bottled water. All three of us were smiling.

"Great idea," I said. "Doesn't seem like schoolwork."

"We'll write essays about our trip to the pond," Bordeaux said. "Descriptive passages about the greenery we see around us."

"Descriptive passages that engage all five senses," I amended. "Sight, sound, smell, texture, taste."

"I can do that," Bordeaux said. And I had no doubt she would; she did all the work I assigned Quentin, and she finished it with such flair that I often wished she really was one of my students.

"You might have to help me a little," Quentin said to her. He was sitting with his skinny legs straight in front of him and his arms behind him to prop up his body. I thought at any minute he might collapse from the unaccustomed strain.

She gave him an affectionate smile. "Don't I always?" She studied him for a moment, the tension of his wrists and the hunch of his shoulders, and she easily, casually scooted over so she was sitting behind him, spoon fashion. One of her legs went on either side of his; she wrapped her arms around his stomach and pulled him back to lie against her chest. He did so with a small sigh of contentment, closing his eyes and allowing his head to rest against her collarbone. She tilted her head just enough to look down at him, at his innocent, peaceful face, and she brushed the top of his head with her mouth.

They've slept together, I realized. *Already. She's managed it.* Managed to win his trust, managed to break down his fear and his awkwardness, managed to teach him that simplest and most complicated act—hell, managed to get into the house in stealth or at least maintain some privacy during her acknowledged visits there. I had liked her before; I adored her now.

She looked up and caught me watching her. She didn't smile. She didn't nod or give me a thumb's-up or in any way acknowledge that she had achieved my goal, but I was sure she knew what I was thinking, what I had deduced. And then she closed her eyes and rested her cheek against Quentin's tousled hair, and I thought, *She loves him.* And I thought, *Sometimes the world is not such a dreadful place.*

⁓

Friday, Bordeaux had to attend a special lecture at Northwestern, so I had Quentin to myself.

"Just you and me, buddy," I said as I stepped inside the room. "Think you can stand it?"

"Oh, I'm seeing Bordeaux tonight," he said. "You'll miss her, but I won't."

"I meant," I said dryly, "could you stand being alone with me? I was hoping you would say you'd love the special one-on-one time with me, that you'd missed our private talks, but I see I think too highly of myself."

He laughed. "How can I have missed you?" he said callously. "You're here all the time. Now if you went away for a while, I'd miss you."

"Well, I just might! I'll take a month's vacation and see how you like that. You'd be forgetting your rhyme schemes in no time."

"Yes, Taylor, but I wouldn't forget *you,*" he said in a shamelessly moony voice. I had to laugh again.

"Did you write your excursion essay like you were supposed to?"

"Yep. It's all ready for you."

"For your next assignment, I want to you to write a poem."

"I can't write a poem! A poem about what?"

"I was going to leave the choice of topic up to you, but since you're being so mean to me, I'm going to make you write it about me."

He grinned. "I'm not being mean to you. Anyway, I can't write a poem about you. Or anyone."

"Sure you can. The easiest way to learn how to write a poem is to steal somebody else's."

"Isn't there a word for that? Like plagiarism?"

"Not if it's just for practice, just to get the sense of the rhythm and the rhyme scheme."

"Give me an example."

"Okay. You like Housman. How about . . . '*Oh, when I was in love with you/Then I was clean and brave/And miles around the wonder grew/How well did I behave . . .'* You remember that?"

"Uh-huh."

"So if you're going to write about me, you change a few words. Like . . . *'Oh, when you were so mad at me/Then I was scared and shy/And I hung my head—'*" I paused and groped for a rhyme. "*'So shaggily—'*"

"*'And asked myself, why, why?'*"Quentin shouted before I could think of a last line.

"Excellent!" I said, clapping. "You see how it's done? The real verses just give you a template."

"I might be able to do that."

"Well, for sure you can, 'cause you're gonna."

He giggled. Quentin liked nothing so much as when I used poor grammar. "You want to practice on a couple more examples while I'm here?" I asked. He nodded, so we broke out the Norton's and tried a few more substitutions. I warned him that, for his actual assignment, he'd have to pick a poem we hadn't even looked at today. "And Bordeaux can't write it," I added. He laughed again.

By this time, he actually seemed intrigued by the idea—and it was the first thing he talked about when Bram and Dennis strolled in together as the hour snapped to a close.

"Guess what, you guys? I have to write a poem! About Taylor!"

They both looked suitably impressed, though now, with a fresh audience, the assignment seemed narcissistic instead of educational. "Really, a poem about Taylor," Dennis said in a silky voice that instantly made me wary. "I could do that, I think."

"Don't," I said. "Don't even start."

"And so could Bram," Dennis added.

I felt my face go hot. "I thought you were supposed to be at your sister's," I said to Bram.

"Going over this afternoon. Right after you leave, in fact."

"There once was a woman named Taylor," Dennis began. "Who was looking for love with a sailor—"

"Can't you stop him?" I begged Bram.

He shrugged. "Usually not."

"She was *so* fond of stripes—and criminal types—"

"Has he been practicing?" Quentin asked.

"That she settled instead for a jailor."

Could have been worse, I suppose. "You," I said to Quentin, "can on no account write a limerick as your poem to me."

"Maybe we should all write birthday poems for Taylor," Bram said.

"Hey, that's right!" Dennis exclaimed. "Your birthday's coming up, isn't it?"

"Tomorrow," Bram said.

"I didn't get you a present!" Quentin wailed. "I would have!"

"Your poem will be your present."

"But I won't see you until next week!"

"Email it to me tomorrow. That will be perfect."

"We'll all email our poems to you," Dennis said.

I glared at him. "No, Quentin is the only one I want to complete this assignment."

"Well, I'm going to send you a poem," Dennis said. "I suppose if Bram doesn't like you as much as Quin and I do, he doesn't have to write you a poem. Or send you any birthday remembrance at all."

I gathered up my purse and my briefcase. "I'm leaving," I said. "Bram, have fun with your family. Quentin, you know what you're supposed to do. Dennis—" I paused at the doorway. "I'll get back to you."

I could hear them all laughing as I stepped into the hall to meet Francis. "I'll probably never understand men," I observed.

"No?" he said sympathetically. "Well, probably more useful to turn your energies elsewhere, then."

"Just what I was thinking."

CHAPTER NINETEEN

I WOKE UP SATURDAY MORNING AND THOUGHT, *I'M THIRTY-FIVE years old.* It sounded horribly ancient, cronelike, an age so advanced it was bereft of any possibility of romance or glamour. Strange how thirty-four had not sounded quite so dreary. It's the benchmark numerals that really bring home the accelerating pace of the world.

I flipped to my side, bringing down the spigot from my water cache to take a sip. It was my birthday, I could lie in bed an extra hour if I wanted to, contemplating the ravages of time or perhaps, as my mood improved, more happy topics. I smiled. I could never forget a line from an execrable poem that one of my students had turned in years ago: *Graceless as a grizzly, time lurches on.* It was an image that still recurred to me on days that did indeed seem heavy-footed and inexorable. What's the Noel Coward line about the potency of cheap song lyrics? Even when they're bad, if they're apt, they stick in your head.

When I finally got up, I took it easy. I luxuriated in a long shower with scented soap, ate two bowls of strawberries for breakfast, and talked to Marika for an idle half hour.

"You're coming to my mom's tonight, right?"

"Absolutely. Didn't you say Azolay's going to be there? *And* Domenic?"

"Oh yeah."

"Wouldn't miss it."

It was noon before I bothered to check my email messages and found a handful of birthday greetings awaiting me. I went through them in the order received.

Domenic's was a straightforward happy birthday message with the notation that he hadn't had time to buy a present. I have never yet gotten a birthday or Christmas gift from Domenic within six months of the holiday. Jason's was encrypted, so I had to search the apartment for about fifteen minutes before I found the damn sociology book and could do the decoding. *God, you're old. I bought you a sturdy cane down on Rush Street, with a skull's head on the grip. Reminded me of you.*

Marika wonders why I tell her she's lucky to have no brothers.

Three colleagues from the Sefton English department had also sent me birthday greetings, as had Caroline. My cousin Azolay sent one of her bright little notes saying how much she was looking forward to seeing me tonight. I like Azolay, mostly, but a little of her goes a long way.

The next message was from Dennis, and I opened it with some trepidation. It featured a colorful graphic of a bunch of roses and came accompanied by a verse:

> *Roses are red*
> *(I want to alert you all)*
> *Except when they're dead*
> *Or paper, or virtual.*

He'd spaced down a few lines and added, "And you thought it would be something embarrassing, didn't you? Love you, sweetie. Mmmmwah (big fat kiss). Dennis"

I was still smiling when I opened the next message, which happened to be from Quentin. He had sent me the poem I had assigned as homework, preceding it with a note. "Dear Taylor: I hope you like this, though it doesn't really seem like a present to me. And I hope you have a really wonderful, superjazz, marbro birthday. And Bordeaux did NOT help me write this (but she told me it was good). Love, Quentin." The poem was based on Housman's "When I was one-and-twenty."

> *When I was barely nineteen*
> *A woman came to teach.*
> *She said, "I'll show you poems—*
> *'Your Heart' and 'Dover Beach.'"*
>
> *She said, "I'll read you stories*
> *Your young man's heart will touch."*
> *Now I am almost twenty,*
> *And I have learned so much!*

I can't describe how much this moved me. I put a hand to my mouth, as if to hold back a small cry of pain, and I read it again. A third time. *Stupid woman,* I thought fiercely, *you're going to cry.* But I was five-and-thirty, and I had a right to be foolishly emotional.

The doorbell rang a little after one in the afternoon, and when I opened the door, I could barely see the face of a delivery person behind the wall of red roses he carried. "Looking for Taylor Kendall," he called through the foliage.

"That's me," I said, and then thought about amending my reply to the more correct *That is I,* and then thought, *Don't be ridiculous,* and then opened the door as wide as it would go.

"Come on in. Wow. That's—wow. That's a lot of roses."

He brushed past me, leaving a light scent and a velvet sensation against my skin. The only surface big enough to hold the vase was the dining room table, so he carefully set it down there and gave me instructions on care and watering. "Yes, fine, thanks a lot," I said, trying not to sound too impatient but really wanting him to leave so I could read the attached card. Finally, after what seemed like an hour, he was out the door. I practically tore the card from its little white envelope and devoured the handwritten words:

> *I sent thee late a rosy wreath*
> *Not so much honoring thee*
> *As giving it a hope, that there*
> *It could not withered be.*
> *And thou thereon didst only breathe*
> *And sent'st it back to me,*
> *Since when it grows and smells, I swear,*
> *Not of itself, but thee.*

And in the corner of the card, below the verse, the confident, legible signature of a man who wants to make it perfectly plain that he knows who he is, likes who is, and expects you to respect who he is: *Bram.*

I stared at the card, stared at the roses, stared at the card again. Where in the world had he come across the Ben Jonson stanza (which I much preferred to the opening octet)? I would not have believed it would have occurred to him to send me flowers, let alone such a lavish display; and if he had ever before this day opened a book of poetry, I would be astonished to learn it.

I bent over the massed roses till my face touched the petals, closed my eyes and inhaled. Exhaled. *Thou thereon didst only breathe and sent'st it back to me* . . . Reached into the bouquet at random and snapped off one of the tightly coiled scarlet buds. Touched my mouth to the petals and breathed again. Looked around the apartment for a sturdy envelope and wondered if Francis would be willing to give me Bram's address.

If you count Jason as one of the guests, I was the second one to arrive at my mother's, where the air was loaded with the irresistible scent of Traditional Dinner: roast and onions and baking potatoes and a cherry pie set out to cool.

"I'm too hungry to wait," I said. "Let's eat now."

"I made a pie and a cake," my mother said, "since there will be seven of us. Do you think that's enough? I can send Jason out for ice cream."

Jason was busy blowing up black balloons and distributing them around the house. He had tied one to the arm of my father's chair, through the winking gold haze of the hologram; the ribbon appeared to be attached to the image's wrist in a display of maudlin celebration. I had to admit, having viewed Duncan Phillips' much more sinister collection of radiant portraits, my father's glowing figure seemed fairly benevolent these days.

"I can't go," Jason said. "I've got to put up the streamers."

"There will be plenty of dessert," I said. "Jason, I don't think we need black streamers. The balloons are enough."

"I bought'em," he said. "I'm putting'em up."

"Why don't you open your presents now, before the others get here?" my mother suggested, handing me a small square package and a large flat one. Her gift was a gold and opal charm for my slide bracelet; Jason's was a book called *Name That Vampire.* "These are both great!" I exclaimed. "I love them!"

"What did you get from your boyfriend?" he asked.

I was blushing. "I don't have a boyfriend."

"Jason told me you've been seeing this nice man who works for Duncan Phillips," my mom said.

I shot Jason a killing look, but responded casually. "We've had dinner together a couple of times. No big deal."

"So what'd he get you?" Jason demanded.

"Roses," I said defiantly.

"Well, isn't that lovely," my mother said.

"How many?" Jason asked. "If it was anything less than a dozen, don't even waste your time with the heezling."

"I didn't count," I said frostily. Thirty roses. Now twenty-nine.

The doorbell rang, and Mareek stepped in alongside Azolay. My cousin is a lean, ultrachic, ultra-energetic blonde who speaks in exclamatory sentences and doesn't seem to have any clue how inappropriate most of her comments are. Or maybe she does, and that's why she says them in her sugar-sweet don't-I-love-you voice. "Look who I ran into at the teleport gate," Marika said in an uninflected voice.

"I almost didn't recognize her! I just adore her hair! Marika, promise me you'll never cut it. I know people think that curls are so unfashionable— straight, straight, straight, that's what all the style magazines say—but on you, they look outstanding."

"Thanks, Azolay. You give me back my confidence."

"It smells divine in here!" were the next words from my cousin's mouth. "The past three nights, I've been out with people who've insisted on going to the most expensive restaurants. French crepes here, special creme sauce there. And I said to myself, 'When I go to Taylor's party, I'll have a nice simple meal.' I'm looking forward to it!"

"Domenic here yet?" Marika asked.

"Oh, no."

"Too bad."

"Bram sent Taylor roses," Jason said.

"What? When? You didn't call me?"

"It's not that big a deal—"

"How many? What color?"

"Do you two have such dull lives that you have to live vicariously through me?"

"I do," Jason said.

"You know I do," Marika added.

"Quentin sent me a poem," I offered.

Marika looked at Jason. "We'll have to go home with her and see for ourselves."

"Just what I was thinking," he answered.

Azolay, after a quick trip to the kitchen to offer more disguised insults, came tripping over to us again. "Taylor! I brought you a card! I hope you're having the best birthday ever!"

"Well, thanks, Azolay."

"And here. I brought you a present," Marika said baldly. Azolay made all of us rude.

First, I admired Azolay's absolutely generic card, then I opened Marika's present, a small box with about five yards of curled lavender ribbon exploding from the top. Inside, a tiny ruby sat pristinely on a bed of white cotton. "Another inset!" I said in delight. "Jazz without cessation."

"For when you get the nerve to go back," she explained.

"Bordeaux will be so proud of me," I said, picking it up carefully and holding it to the light.

"You're not actually going to have it grafted on, are you?" Azolay demanded. "I mean, seriously, Tay. You know what kind of women wear jewel insets."

Marika brushed her hand across her cheek. She still hadn't gone for the permanent installation, but she'd had the temporary topaz reapplied already, and I was betting her next trip back would be for surgery. "Trashy women," Marika said. "Don't I just know it."

"Now, Marika, you know I didn't mean—"

"Hey, no problem," Marika said. "Just the kind of women I like."

Before anyone had to think of a reply to that, the doorbell rang again, and my aunt Jennifer arrived. Jennifer was much like Azolay, only a little less so. Where Azolay was blonde, Jennifer was graying, and she didn't have Azolay's relentless energy. Something to be thankful for.

Domenic was right behind her. "Happy birthday, old thing," he said, kissing me on the top of the head.

A few minutes later, we were all settled around the dining room table, where Jason and Marika had gone to some trouble to make sure Domenic and Azolay were seated side by side.

"Domenic!" Azolay exclaimed. "It's been years since I've seen you, but I don't believe you've changed a bit."

"Thank you," he said, reaching for the platter of roast.

"I remember, a few years ago, the high school kids in my neighborhood were doing that black-on-black style, just like you've got on today, and I thought, 'That look is just too severe to be attractive.' But you've managed to pull it off for a long time now, haven't you?"

Jason was chewing vigorously and watching the action, just like a man eating popcorn at the movie theatre. Marika was staring at her plate, trying to hide her smile. Neither of the older women appeared to notice.

Domenic, of course, showed her no reaction. "I guess I'm not one to follow fads," he said. It was a subtle dig at her own ensemble, a prairie-style dress in a small floral print.

"I have a style consultant," Azolay began.

"Really? I wouldn't have thought so," Domenic said.

"Oh, thank you. It looks so effortless, you know, but I always appreciate her guidance. Maybe it's time you dropped that bad-boy look and tried a more mature style. I'm sure Genevieve would be glad to give you some pointers if you'd like to consult with her."

"I'd be glad to receive pointers from anyone named Genevieve," Domenic said.

Marika dissolved into giggles and even Jason had to glance away. Azolay appeared bewildered. Aunt Jennifer said, "Well, Domenic, nice to see you again. You look just like you did when you kids were in high school. You, too, Marika. Only Taylor really looks her age of the whole bunch of you."

"Thank you," I said, toasting her with my glass of iced tea. "My birthday is now complete."

That was the way the entire the meal went, with Azolay and Domenic sparring, Aunt Jennifer chiming in with the casual cut, and my mother offering everyone more roast, more green beans, more pie. We had left the table and were milling about between the living room, dining room, and kitchen when Domenic broke free of his nemesis and found a chance to talk to me alone.

"I told you I didn't have a present," he began.

"Truthfully, I didn't expect one."

"But I do. Of sorts. Information. They're starting a new experimental program at Northwestern General to look into Kyotenin degradation."

"Really? What kind of program?"

"Based on a very small one at Johns Hopkins that's had some phenomenal results. Not in curing the disease but in slowing it down. Stabilizing it. It's radical because it involves cloning, and the ban hasn't been lifted all that long. I don't have all the details 'cause I just heard about it yesterday, but I knew you'd want to know."

"Yeah, but—apparently Duncan Phillips hasn't let Quentin go for any kind of experimental treatment in the past few years. This probably won't change his mind."

"Lot of parents won't do the experimental programs. They're risky, and people die in trials. But this one's had a high rate of demonstrable success. That might make him more open to the idea."

I doubted it, but I was getting excited on Quentin's behalf anyway. "So these kids in the Johns Hopkins program—they're living past twenty-five? They're retaining their motor functions?"

"Two of the subjects just turned thirty. Both of them are still in wheelchairs but have retained almost full usage of their arms and upper torsos, with some limited movement in their legs. And they both report a noticeable lessening of their habitual pain. Three of the other participants aren't as mobile, but they're still functioning and breathing on their own. And they're twenty-seven and twenty-eight. It's unprecedented."

"Oh, Domenic, this would be so wonderful. You haven't met Quentin but he's such a great kid—I just can't stand the thought—I've got to think of what to say to his dad. There has to be a way to convince him."

We talked a while longer, Domenic giving me what information he had, until Jason and Marika joined us.

"This is a great party," Jason enthused. "Tay-Kay, I think you should get older every day."

"I heard Azolay invite you down for some event," Marika said to Domenic. "Are you going to go?"

"I told her I was always busy. And she said, 'Busy doing what?' and I said, 'Selling illegally harvested organs.' So now I think she's telling her mom that I should be arrested."

"So you're really busy forever?" Marika asked. "Because I wanted you all to come over Thursday night."

"This Thursday?" Jason asked. "I can make it. Why?"

"I'm having a party," she said mournfully.

Domenic laughed. "You don't seem too excited about it."

"I'm not. I got suckered into it. It's a going-away party for Erika Sosher. You remember her, she was in all my classes in high school and we roomed together for one semester in college."

"Vaguely," Domenic said.

"Anyway, she's moving to Paris or Marseilles or something. We're not especially good friends anymore, but I'd already said I'd come to the party if Jodie held it, and then Jodie couldn't hold it, and—anyway, now I'm hosting a party Thursday night."

"Who else is going to be there that we know?" Jason asked.

She recited a list of people who had grown up in our neighborhood or attended high school with us. Most of them, like us, would be commuting in for the occasion. Half-a-dozen of them I would actually enjoy seeing again.

"Sure, I'll come," Domenic said.

"Me, too," I said.

Marika frowned at me. "Well, of course *you're* coming. You have to help me clean and decorate and get the food together. I can't do this without you."

"What if I already had plans?"

"Oh, please. You're on summer break and you're just tutoring twice a week. You've got nothing but free time, and I need you."

I shrugged helplessly. "I'll be there."

Azolay descended on us in a little blonde whirlwind. "You guys, I just had the best idea! Let's all get together next weekend! We can meet at my house. I'll cook. Saturday or Sunday, either day is fine with me."

"I can't," I said. "I'm going out of town."

"Working," Marika said.

"I need to help mom clear out the basement," Jason said.

"Don't want to," Domenic said.

Azolay threw her hands in the air. "Honestly! The four of you make it so hard to stay friends! I guess I won't see any of you again till Jason's birthday." And as she swirled away again, we all looked at each other in pure horror.

"Jason," Domenic said solemnly, "you have to be a man about this. Kill yourself now."

After Azolay and Aunt Jennifer had left, and after the rest of us had helped Mom with the dishes, Marika and Jason and Domenic and I went to a movie. Then the three of them came back to my apartment to count roses, and notice that there were only twenty-nine, and ask about that, and formulate theories about what the number could signify or whether the florist had accidentally miscounted. I handed out beers and said nothing, even after the guys had gone away and it was just Mareek and me. We stayed up talking until almost two a.m., discussing the menu for Thursday as well as our clothing options, and then I settled her on the couch and sought my own bed.

It had been a good day, start to finish. Perhaps thirty-five would be a pretty good age after all.

CHAPTER TWENTY

MONDAY, I SPENT A FEW HOURS AT NORTHWESTERN GENERAL, MEET-ing the Kyotenin degradation specialists and gathering information about the new cloning program. The doctors seemed mystified to learn that I was not the relative of a child suffering from the syndrome, but they were perfectly willing to give me the specifics I wanted.

Tuesday, I teleported to the Phillips mansion about a half hour before I was expected, but I still did not manage to catch Francis unprepared. He was at the gate in five seconds, inclining his head in his courtly way and observing, "You're early today. Quentin and Miss Bordeaux are somewhere in the house with Bram. Doing what, I'm not entirely sure."

"I need to speak with Mr. Phillips, Francis. Is he here?"

This, unlike my premature arrival, did catch the steward off-guard. "Mr. Phillips? You need to talk with him?"

"Urgently. Is he here?"

"Something I could help you with, perhaps? Or Bram?"

"It's about a medical program for Quentin. I need to talk to his dad."

"It won't do any good."

"It might. Let me talk to him."

Five minutes later, Francis had ushered me to what I could only think of as the weapons room, though I'm sure Duncan Phillips considered it a study. For the third time in my life, I came face-to-face with this strange, feral, intense man. He was sitting behind a massive mahogany desk that was littered with papers and envelopes, though most of his attention seemed to be focused on the laptop computer open on the desk.

"Mr. Phillips, Ms. Kendall would like a few minutes with you," Francis said in an impassive voice.

Duncan Phillips slowly rotated his chair in my direction, though for a moment his eyes remained fixed on the screen, so his body turned my way before his head did. When he did wrench his attention from the computer, at first he wore a blank expression, as if he were still contemplating news from another country or another century, and I was not interesting enough to fo-cus him on this time or place.

"Ms. Kendall?" he repeated as if the words signified nothing to him, not even a name.

"Taylor Kendall," I said. I had stopped just inside the door and wasn't sure exactly how close I wanted to get to the man. "Quentin's English tutor."

Recognition remodeled his face. He smiled and leaned forward across his desk, suddenly fully engaged. "Ms. Kendall," he said. "Of course. I remember you. Francis, you may go."

Francis looked straight at me. "I'll be just outside the door," he said and stepped from the room.

I was, for the moment, alone with Duncan Phillips.

"I wanted to talk to you because—"

"Are your classes at Sefton done for the semester?" he interrupted. "Or do you teach some kind of summer courses?"

"All done."

"So you've got a lot of free time on your hands these days."

An apprehension about how he might ask me to spend that time led me to fabricate an instant lie. "Well, I've taken a summer job, and I've been spending a lot of evenings with my family, so I scarcely have any free time at all."

"None?" he said, coming to his feet and slinking around the side of the desk. I remembered the first time I'd met him, when I thought he seemed pantherlike. The metaphor still held. He perched on the front of the desk, but not as if he was settled there; he appeared to be poised to spring at a moment's notice. He watched me with those unblinking eyes. "That's unfortunate for you."

"Yes—well—I'll be fine," I stammered. "But I wanted to talk to you, to tell you about a new medical program I've heard of. For patients with Kyotenin degradation."

"I've seen all the studies on the disease, and there are no programs worth investigating," he said flatly.

I couldn't help myself; in my excitement, I took a step deeper into the room. "Yes, but this is a new one at Northwestern General, based on a cloning program at Johns Hopkins that's had real results. They're taking a group of candidates—"

"Ms. Kendall, this is not interesting to me."

"A group of candidates in their late teens and early twenties," I persisted. "Kids who've already degenerated to a noticeable degree. At Johns Hopkins they were able to arrest the progress of the disease—"

"These studies mean nothing."

"Arrest it to such a degree that no more damage was done. The subjects lived three to five years longer than the most optimistic projections, with no additional damage—"

"I have no intention of enrolling my son in any of these medical trials."

"But this one's different. It's already had results. And there are no outside organ or blood donations required, just self-cloning—"

"Ms. Kendall," Duncan Phillips said, and his voice was so icy that it cooled even my burning enthusiasm. "I am registering Quentin for no programs. I am taking him to no new doctors. I am investing in no new research. I am done with him."

Done with him? Done with Quentin? "But if you don't try this program, he could die."

"I don't care if he dies," Duncan Phillips said. "I wish he hadn't lived this long."

I stared at him and couldn't think of a single thing to say.

"My wife wanted more children, after Quentin was born," he went on conversationally. "But it was clear to me that we ran too great a risk of bringing more monsters into the world. When he didn't die, I decided I would make his life as comfortable as possible, but I wouldn't do anything to extend it by so much as a day. There's no point to it. So don't come to me with any more tales of proven research and medical breakthroughs. You don't waste money on a losing proposition. That's one of the first rules of business, Ms. Kendall, and it serves pretty well as a pattern for life."

I could not believe what I was hearing. "Quentin's not a monster," I whispered. "He's—he's a sweet and loving and intelligent and—"

"And ruined and useless and dying child," he finished. "Give it up, Ms. Kendall. Nothing you say will convince me."

He came to his feet in a single lithe movement and strolled across the room to where I stood, rooted to the floor. "Though your affection for him is touching," he added, in that purring voice that was more frightening to me than his cruel, hammer-edged tones could be. "I see a soft and warm-hearted soul beneath your rather severe exterior."

"I don't—" I said and shook my head. I was still in shock. I couldn't move or really think. *Where's Francis?* I found myself wondering. If he was standing outside, surely he had heard this shift in the conversation; surely he would step back inside at any moment. "But Quentin—"

Now Duncan Phillips took my frozen hand in his and carried it, with exaggerated and terrifying tenderness, to his chest. "Your concern for my son does you great credit," he said. "But you should turn your attention to those who are still among the living."

"I can't," I said, shaking my head again. "You're—I can't."

"I've never gotten a chance to really talk to you," he said, reaching up his free hand to stroke the back of my head. I tried to twist my hand free, but his grip was shackle-tight, and I could feel myself starting to tremble from a sense of overwhelming dread. "All I know about you is that you like books— and my son, of course. Surely there must be more to learn."

Where was Francis? "I don't wish—I want to keep our relationship on a purely professional level," I said in a small, constricted voice. "Please don't—"

"I don't like professional relationships," he said and crushed my body against his. His mouth was on mine, bruising and savage; his arms were locked around me so tightly that I felt my ribs give way. Blood galloped through my head and adrenaline ignited through my veins. I wrenched free, choking and coughing, scratching at his arm to make him drop my hand, which he still clutched in his. He jerked me back toward him, laughing, but I swung my awkward left fist at him and connected wildly with the bones of his face. He was still laughing; he still did not drop my hand.

"Well, well," he said. "A little fire in the straight-laced schoolmistress after all."

I was panting. "Let me go, you fucker. How dare you call your son names? You're the monster in this house."

"At least I'm honest about what I want," he said. He seemed unutterably amused. "You pretend to be some ice queen when you're talking to me, but you're playing femme goddess with all the men on my staff and bringing whores in to tantalize my son—"

The door opened behind me, and I thought, *Francis. Thank God.* Then Quentin's voice said, "Dad."

I don't know what emotions Duncan Phillips experienced as, in molasses-slow motion, he dropped my hand and we both turned to face the door. Not just Quentin there, stony-faced but calm, but Bordeaux behind him, hand on her little shoulder bag, fingering what I was sure was a tiny gun that would fire through the glittering mesh cloth. And behind them, the ranks of the cavalry, Bram and Francis and even Dennis, all staring inside, all of them haloed with horror, all of them gazing between me and Quentin and Duncan Phillips, and all of them looking as though their hearts were shutting down.

"Dad," said Quentin again. "I need Taylor. Are you done with her?"

There was a moment's silence. Then, "Quite done," Duncan Phillips said in a dry voice. "You don't need to return her to me."

And then, for the first time, Quentin looked at me. I could read nothing in his face, which was usually so open and expressive, so full of energy and excitement. "I was waiting for you."

"Sorry," I answered. "I wanted to talk to your dad a moment. But I'm all through with him."

And we left the weapons room, a parade of us, absolutely silent, heading without any discussion to the elevator, and Quentin's room, and a margin of safety. Bram took my hand as we walked down the hall, and through my fingers he could feel my shaking, so he transferred my right hand to his right hand and put his left arm around my shoulders. Bordeaux was behind Quentin's wheelchair, and both of her hands rested on his shoulders. I thought,

Those of us who need comfort are getting it, though I wasn't sure there was enough comfort anywhere in the world to erase from my mind the memory of that last quarter hour.

Inside Quentin's room, everyone started murmuring at once. Bram shut the door a little too forcefully and stood with his back against it, glaring impartially at the world. Bordeaux drew me over to the window and by sunlight examined my face for evidence of bruises, touching her fingertip to the corner of my mouth. Dennis was swearing, quietly and inventively, to no one in particular. Quentin sat absolutely still and said nothing.

"I'm so sorry, Taylor," Francis said in a remorseful tone of voice. "There was a call from the front gate—I was only gone for three minutes—it is entirely my fault—"

"Not your fault at all," Bram said shortly. "We should have gotten down there more quickly."

Bordeaux pulled me to the couch and we sat down side by side. I looked over at Bram. "How did you know to come at all?" I asked.

"I was showing them the security systems," Bram said bleakly. "Bordeaux and Quentin. Dennis joined us a few minutes after you walked into the study. We saw the whole conversation."

I put my hand to my mouth. I'd been hoping Quentin had just had the misfortune to enter the room at the very tail end of the episode, catching his father's denunciation of his girlfriend and maybe his assault on me. "Heard it all? About—the new program?"

Bram nodded. Dennis slammed his fist into the wall, leaving a grapefruit-sized hole in the plaster. "That absolute fucking son-of-bitch," he raged. "God, I would see that man dead in the nastiest way possible—"

"Dennis," Francis said quietly. "Quentin."

Dennis looked over at the pale, quiet figure. "I'm sorry, man," he said. "Sorry you have to have a dad like that. Sorry he's such a lousy excuse for a human being. Not sorry I said it."

"It's all right," Quentin said.

"No, it's not all right! Asshole stands there and says things like—things no one should say—"

Francis crossed the room and laid his hands heavily on the other man's shoulders. "Dennis," he said in a firmer voice. "Shut up."

I had enough control of myself now to come to my feet and walk over to Quentin. I knelt beside him and took his hands in mine. "I'm sorry, baby," I said, peering up at his set, closed face. "I'm so sorry you saw that. If I had known what he would say—if it had occurred to me you would be watching—Quentin, I'd have done anything in the world to keep that from happening to you."

He squeezed my hands and leaned forward to kiss my cheek. "It's okay,

Taylor," he said. "He's said all that before. He's said it to my face."

There was silence in the room for a minute. "Oh, how I wish that weren't true," I whispered.

Dennis was cursing again, but he'd grown a little calmer. He'd sunk to the floor and was nursing his punching hand against his chest. Francis disappeared into the bathroom at the end of Quentin's suite and brought Dennis a cold wet washcloth. Bram had passed a hand over his face and stood there like a statue of pain. Bordeaux pulled out a pack of gum and offered it all around. No one accepted.

"Well," she said, "unless there's something we can do about Quentin's dad, or something we can do to make Quentin forget about his dad, I don't see that any of this moaning and moping is helping anybody."

Bram dropped his hand and gave her a cold and level look. "There should be something we can do," he said.

She shrugged. "Seems to me we're all doing what we can just by being here. Quin'll be okay. He's known his dad a lot longer than any of you have. He knows how to cope." She gave us all her dazzling smile, and I saw gold glitter wink along the creases around her eyes. "He's just worried about Taylor and the rest of you going off the edge. Settle down a little and he'll be fine."

Quentin gave my hands a shake and smiled at me with a hint of liveliness. "You listen to her, Taylor, all right? She's a smart girl. She knows what I'm thinking. It's you I'm worried about."

So with that mandate, I had to pretend to recover. I gave him a tremulous smile and came shakily to my feet, pulling my hands free. "Okay, well, I can act like a normal person if everybody else can," I said. "Though I'm not too sure I can get through an actual lesson today."

"I think we should all get out of the house," Dennis said. "Go out for a beer." He glanced at Quentin. "Ice cream."

"Great place up at the campus," Bordeaux offered.

"I need to stay at the front door," Francis said.

Bram crossed the room to the intercom on the wall and punched in a series of numbers. "I'll get Hastings to watch the door for a couple of hours," he said. "You're coming with us."

And so, in the strangest end to the strangest afternoon I could remember spending for about a hundred years, the six of us fled the house and crammed into one of the estate cars and drove out looking for treats. Evanston was too far to be practical, but we found a Victorian Ice Cream Shoppe & Parlor in Palatine, and we all crowded into a small booth to study our menus and debate our choices.

Funny how dread and terror can metamorphose into hilarity. The simplest sentences seemed riotously funny, the most innocent observations became targets for ridicule. I could not remember ever laughing so hard, or liking any group of people so much, or feeling, at times, such a strange and joyous sense of hope and reprieve. How could that be? Grim things had happened and no solution had been offered, and the world, at this moment, was far more dismal than it had been this morning, when I had thought Duncan Phillips might at least agree to consider ways to extend his son's life. The only thing I could see that was casting any bright light was this circle of fellowship, and I did not think it would be bright enough for long enough to illuminate our way beyond this hour.

But this hour was what we had, and we made use of it. We laughed too much and we ate too much, and when we climbed back into the car a couple of hours later, I believe all of us still felt a lingering glow of happiness.

CHAPTER TWENTY-ONE

I WAS STILL IN BED WEDNESDAY MORNING WHEN MY EARFONE chimed, and Bram was on the other end. Despite the flirtatious interactions at the mansion, the dinners in Hawaii, we had never gotten in the habit of calling or texting on a regular basis. It was like we were still circling each other, figuring each other out, interacting only in person and then stepping away to take refuge in emotional distance.

So I was surprised to hear his voice on the phone. Surprised but pleased. "Hi," he said. "I didn't even get a chance to talk to you yesterday, what with one thing and another."

I snuggled against my pillow to enjoy the conversation. "I noticed."

"I've missed you," he said. "I've been thinking about you."

"I missed you, too," I said. "Oh! And I never thanked you for the roses! They're marvelous."

"How was your birthday?"

"Nice. Dinner at my mom's with some friends and relatives. A few trinkets and emails and phone calls. And roses."

"I got a rose, too," he said. "From someone. Very mysterious. Kind of pressed between some pieces of cardboard and smelling—huh. Now that I think about it, it kind of smelled like you."

I giggled. "How did you find that poem? I can't believe you just knew it off the top of your head."

"It's a poem? I thought it was a song."

"It's a song?"

He began singing in an exaggerated opera-star fashion. "'Drink to me only wi-ith thine ey-eyes and I-I will pledge with mine . . .' The bit about the roses is the second verse."

"Huh. I did not know that it had ever been set to music. It's a 17th-century poem by Ben Jonson."

"Oh. Well, my mom used to sing it all the time."

"How was your visit with your family?" I asked.

"Good. Laney seems happy. Her ex-husband has finally disappeared off the face of the earth and her oldest daughter's about to enroll in college, and these were two miracles she never expected to witness, so she's doing well. We stayed up till two in the morning talking Friday night. She wants to meet you."

"She—so I guess you covered your personal life a little in this conversation."

"Sure. Don't you talk about me with your brother?"

"No, but he's found out all about you anyway. He came over Saturday night to count the roses."

Bram laughed. "I hope he was satisfied."

"He seemed impressed."

"Anyway, I wanted to check in on you and see how you were doing after yesterday."

"Not great," I admitted. "How about you?"

"Not great. Want to go out and talk about it? Tomorrow or Friday, maybe?"

"I can't tomorrow," I said regretfully. "I have a party in Atlanta."

"Well, then—no, wait, I can't Friday. Damn."

"Saturday?"

"That seems so far away."

I was sure he could hear the smile in my voice. "Well, I'm free tonight if you can be spontaneous."

"Are you kidding? I'm the most spontaneous guy you ever met. Let's do it!"

I think I might have squealed. "Let's! This will be the highlight of my week. After the roses."

"You just never know. There may be more roses where those came from."

"I'll have to be thinking of what I can give you in return," I said.

He laughed, and I felt my whole face go red. That was not what I had meant. "I'm sure you'll come up with something," he said. "I'll pick you up at six."

By two, a chilly rain had moved in, and the weather forecast said it would last through midnight. I texted Bram. *Kind of an ugly day to go out. If you just want to hang out here, I'll cook dinner.*

He responded in less than a minute. *I was thinking along the same lines. Want me to bring a pizza?*

Even better! I answered. *I'll make a salad.*

Deal.

Of course, this meant I had to straighten the living room, scrub down the bathroom, and put away the seven pairs of shoes that littered the apartment. But I was humming with happiness as I did it.

At five, I laid out two outfits on the bed and tried to decide between them. A floaty sleeveless sundress or a pair of tan khakis and a soft, slouchy green shirt that flattered my face. I texted photos of each to Marika.

Bram's bringing pizza over. What should I wear? I asked. Her first response was a string of exclamation points, her second said *Call me the minute he leaves,* and the third added *Wear the dress.* So I did.

Bram arrived exactly as the clock struck the hour. Rain had plastered his hair to his head and turned his navy shirt almost black, but he'd wrapped the pizza boxes in his jacket so our dinner was safe.

"*Two* pizzas," I said. "That seems ambitious."

"Wouldn't want you to go hungry."

I'd set the table with the plates that weren't chipped and the silverware that matched. I'd considered and rejected candles, which seemed to project romantic expectations, but set out a bottle of wine, which could go either way. I wasn't nervous, exactly, but I was fluttery, a little off-balance, but in a good way. Bram seemed as rock-solid as ever.

"I'm actually starving," I said.

"Me too."

We talked easily over the meal, avoiding for the moment any conversation about Duncan Phillips and concentrating on happier topics. My birthday dinner, his visit with his sister, a few funny stories about episodes in our pasts. We only ate one of the pizzas, but we finished off the wine.

"I have another bottle," I offered. "Or a beer, if you'd rather."

He had sprawled back in his chair, looking as relaxed as I'd ever seen him. "Maybe one beer," he said.

I fetched bottles for both of us. "So how's Quentin?" I finally asked.

"Hard to say. He seems the same as always, but he doesn't want to talk about what happened yesterday. And Bordeaux has stuck close to him all day, watching him every minute. So I think *she's* a little worried about him, but when I had a chance to ask her, she said, 'He'll be fine.'" He shook his head. "So I don't know."

"I'll be back on Friday. Maybe we can do something special. I don't know what."

"Everybody seemed to like the ice cream."

"Maybe we could go back to the beach?"

"Not if it's still raining."

"Well, we'll think of something."

He gave me a serious look. "I'm a little worried about you coming back to the house, to be honest."

No point in pretending I didn't know what he was talking about. "Trust me, I will never again in my life be stupid enough to be alone in a room with Duncan Phillips."

"I thought you had already learned that lesson."

"I had, but Francis was right there—"

"I'm not sure Francis could have stopped him," Bram said quietly. "I'm thinking maybe I need to be the one to meet you at the gate and escort you through every hallway."

"It's not like I'd *mind* having you around all the time, but it seems a little extreme."

His expression was even more grim. "Under any other circumstances, I'd tell you not to come back. Not to risk yourself in what is clearly a dangerous environment. But my worry for you is just *this much* less than my concern for what would happen to Quentin if he never saw you again." He held up a hand, his finger and thumb just a quarter inch apart. "So all I can do is try to keep you safe."

I leaned forward and placed my hand on his wrist. "Bram. I'll be careful. I won't take a step from the gate unless you're right beside me."

"I was thinking," he said. "I could teach you a few self-defense moves. Might be useful."

"I suppose. Sure. Right now?"

He glanced around. "We can push the coffee table back—and get that butterfly statue out of the way—make a little room to move around."

So we rearranged the furniture in the living room, and Bram carefully walked me through a few defensive strategies. The goal was not to disable my attacker, he said; the goal was to get away. Hit, kick, distract, do anything I could to get free, and then run like hell. A purse could be a weapon if I threw it in someone's face hard enough to temporarily blind him. A scream could rouse a household.

But if I *was* unlucky enough to be physically caught, he said, there were a few tricks I could use to break someone's hold. He showed me how to twist my arm from a hard grip, how to employ a knee or a heel or an elbow.

"It's important not to panic," he said, standing behind me, his cheek brushing against mine. He had one arm around my waist, and he held my wrist with his other hand. "It's important to remember what leverage you have and use it to break away."

I leaned back so that my head grazed his shoulder. I could feel the slight scrape of his stubble against my skin, smell the faint clean scent of his soap. "What if I don't want to break away?" I murmured.

He tilted his face closer to mine. I could feel the shift in the grip of his hands, I could sense when the attacker's trap became the lover's embrace. "You better keep fighting," he said, "unless you're sure the person who's holding you is safe."

"I'm pretty sure."

"You have to be positive."

I wriggled in his arms, and he loosened his hold enough to let me turn. I lifted my hands to lay them on his shoulders. "I'm positive."

He watched me for a long moment, his dark eyes scanning mine, his face completely sober. "Big step," he said.

I couldn't hold back my own smile. "Why do I get the feeling you usually move faster than this?"

He acknowledged this with a small grin. "You're right. Once I make up my mind, I don't waste much time."

"Why so cautious with me?"

"You know why."

I sighed. "Quentin."

"You and I start dating and then break up, maybe you get so mad you never want to see me again. You won't even come to the house anymore because you don't want to risk running into me. I don't want Quentin to lose you because I messed up."

Now I lifted my hands to his cheekbones, cupping his face. "What makes you think I won't be the one to mess up?"

"I've got two busted marriages behind me. You've only got one."

"And a few other disastrous short-term relationships."

"You're not making your case any stronger."

Impulsively, I stretched up to kiss his mouth. He responded hungrily, pressing one hand against the back of my head to lock me into the kiss. I slipped my arms around his neck and fitted my body more tightly against his. He was the one to pull back.

"All right," he said a little breathlessly. "Maybe you could convince me."

I laughed against his lips. "What if I promised," I whispered, "I *promised* not to let anything interfere with my relationship with Quentin? No matter what happens between us, even if I come to *hate* you, which I don't think I will, I will still stay in Quentin's life for as long as he needs me? Will that be good enough for you? What if I say I'll hurt you before I hurt Quentin?"

His response was a breath of laughter. "I'm sure all your friends would tell you that's a terrible bargain to make."

"I'm not asking *them* for their opinion. I'm asking *you*."

He kissed me again. "I think it's the best deal anyone could offer me."

"Well, then," I said and lifted my mouth to his again.

We stood there maybe fifteen minutes, kissing, clinging to each other, rubbing against each other just to get a sense of how our bodies responded. Bram seemed in no hurry to move on to the next phase, but I could feel my heart growing impatient as my body tingled with nerves.

"Mmm," I finally said. "Time to go to the bedroom. Time to take some clothes off."

"No rush," he said but he followed me without protest.

This early on a midsummer evening, it wasn't quite sunset, but what little light was left in the stormy sky barely had the strength to make it through the gauzy curtains. I was just as happy to be in near total darkness as I pulled the sundress over my head, slipped out of my underthings, and dropped to the bed. The cotton coverlet felt cool against my bare skin.

Bram was beside me in a moment, pulling me back into his embrace. "You're so warm," I said, running my hand up and down his arm. "Should I turn down the air conditioning?"

"I'm fine," he said. His own hands were playing down my back, gently exploring. "I'm happy."

"You have such impressive muscles. I've noticed that before."

"Have you?"

"When we were swimming."

"Huh. I never thought to look at your body when we were all in the pool."

I swatted him on the shoulder. "That's a lie."

"That is most definitely a lie."

"But this is better."

"And you want to know the best part about being in bed with you?"

I held my breath. "What?"

He lifted an arm and felt along the headboard. "I can take a sip from your fancy little water reservoir system."

I started laughing helplessly. I could see just well enough to observe him as he found the spigot, sat up a little, and took a swallow. "I was so thirsty," he added.

"This was *not* what I expected from you at this moment, I'll be honest. Goofy humor."

He ostentatiously wiped his mouth and dropped back to the pillow, turning onto his back. "What were you expecting?"

"A little more focus. I thought you'd be, shall we say, more goal-oriented."

From the sound of his voice, I could tell he was grinning. "I *am* goal-oriented. But this—" He waved a hand to indicate the bed, the room, the apartment, everything. "Is part of the goal. The whole experience. Not just a few minutes at the end."

I rolled closer and lifted my body to cover his. His arms instantly went around my back with satisfying pressure. "It's going to be more than a few minutes," I whispered against his mouth, "but it's going to start now."

⁓

So often that first time with a new person is awkward, uncertain, maybe uncomfortable. *Did he like that, am I responding the right way, should I be clearer about what I want?*

But everything was easy with Bram. He noticed all my nuances, he gave clear signals of his own. He was appreciative and mirthful—more lighthearted than I had ever seen him. And our bodies fit together with exquisite precision.

Afterward, we curled up together, face to face, hands still roaming, mouths still occasionally meeting, but mostly lost in our own thoughts. Outside, true dark had fallen and the city lights had come on; the room was actually brighter than it had been when we first walked in.

"What are you thinking about?" Bram asked after a while.

I sat up enough to prop my chin on his shoulder. "A line from a poem."

He snorted with laugher. "Of course you are."

"It's by William Stafford. It *seems* like he's describing how hard it is to climb up a mountain and how people tell him he probably can't do it. But *really* he might be describing what it's like to write a poem. And the last line is, 'Made it again! Made it again!'" I peered down at his face. "That's what I always feel like after good sex. Made it again."

He kissed me and drew me down beside him. "You," he said, "are like no one I've ever met in my life."

"Eh. Hang out in a few English departments and you'll find a lot of people who spout quotations at you under the most extraordinary circumstances."

"It's not just the poems," he said. "It's the whole package."

"Well, I'm glad to be unique in your experience."

"So when can we get together again? Not tomorrow, not Friday. How about Saturday?"

"I'm free."

"And Sunday?"

"Ooh, we could spend the whole *weekend* together."

He was smiling. "That's kind of what I was thinking."

"You could stay the rest of the night, if you wanted to," I offered.

"I would," he said, "but I have to leave by five. I don't want to wake you up."

"I bet I could fall back to sleep."

He tightened his arms around me. "Then I'll stay. I'd rather be here than anywhere else in the world."

CHAPTER TWENTY-TWO

I headed down to Marika's early on Thursday, because we had a full day planned. I had texted her around midnight when I got up to use the bathroom, just so she didn't worry, but I saved all the details about the date to share over a late breakfast.

"You really like him," she said when I was done.

"I really, really do."

"I mean, I never would have pictured you with a military guy, a cop, but I like how solid he sounds. And I like the two divorces."

"You *do?*"

"He's gotten all his mistakes out of the way. He's going to do it right this time."

"Maybe. I hope so." I sighed. "I hope I do it right this time, too."

After the meal, we headed back to Peachtree Promenade to have our temporary face jewels reapplied. This time I had both rubies glued along the curve of my right cheek, so they winked and sparkled when I smiled. Marika had a pink sapphire set at the corner of her mouth and a pearl placed at the corner of her eye.

"We look stunning," she pronounced.

Back to her house to get it ready for guests. She lived in a rambling old mansion that her grandmother, who had been loaded with money, bought for Marika when she moved to Atlanta. Most of the property surrounding it had long ago been sold off to developers, so town houses, condos and little brick bungalows filled in the rest of the neighborhood. So it was pretty hard to miss Marika's place.

Inside—well, if you'd ever met Marika and you walked through the front door, you'd instantly realize you'd found her home. First, there was the butterfly motif on wallpaper and floor rugs and hanging mobiles and dishware. But the opulence of style, the richness of texture, and sheer hedonistic abundance of *things* were what really marked the place as Marika's. Red velvet settees sat a few degrees from tapestried chaise lounges, and overstuffed pillows were piled on chairs, sofas, piano benches, the floor. In every room, vases overflowed with flowers, some real, some silk. The windows were covered by layers of curtains—flimsy lace sheers topped by thick colorful drapes, with swaths of contrasting fabric looped over the rods. The carpets were thick and luxurious. Crystal knickknacks graced every flat surface. The air was scented with perfumes too various to catalog.

Marika and I moved through the rooms, arranging candle groupings, tossing red silk scarfs over fringed Victorian lampshades, predetermining an ambience that Marika said would only become visible once night fell. We also cleared off the tables that would hold food platters, made sure there was plenty of toilet paper in the bathrooms, checked the ice supply, and called the caterer about a dozen times. This all took longer than I could have imagined, and it was nearly four in the afternoon before we could turn attention to our own beauty routines.

It was while we were admiring our jeweled faces in the mirror that Marika said, "I guess I should warn you. Axel might be here."

"What? I thought you stopped talking to him weeks ago."

"I thought so too, but then we had a couple of conversations that were pretty civil, and I told him about the party. He said he'd like to see Erika and a few of the other guys, so I said he could come."

"You know Jason'll walk out."

"Do you think so?" she said anxiously. "Because I want Jason to have a good time."

"Well, don't tell him Axel's coming. 'Cause he might not show up, and if he does, Jason might not notice him. It's a big house."

Marika sighed fatalistically. "Not that big."

"Not as large as, say, Duncan Phillips' palatial estate," I agreed, "but surely large enough to—"

"Oh!" she exclaimed, turning away from the mirror where she was watching herself apply lipstick. "What does everyone think about the news?"

"What news? News about Duncan Phillips?"

"Yes! It's all over social media that he's engaged."

"Engaged! To whom? Since when?"

"Apparently, he's been dating some actress for a while. She's blonde and maybe twenty-five years old. Big smile. Doesn't look very bright."

I snorted. "Yeah, I suppose that tracks. Don't all rich assholes date dumb blonde actresses?"

"Well, if the rumors are right, Duncan Phillips has broader tastes than your average billionaire. A couple of years ago, everyone thought he was involved with the CEO of some California tech company. She was a smart forty-something brunette, so not quite the stereotype." Marika added another coat of lipstick. "Of course, no one ever knows for sure, because he's so secretive about his personal life. I was really hoping you'd be able to come up with some good gossip for me, but you've been a major disappointment in that area."

I spread my hands to signify complete ignorance. "I know nothing. We never talk about him at the house. I wonder if Bram or Francis have heard about the new fiancée."

"Maybe it's not true," she said. "You know they'll say anything online."

We were done with our toilettes a little before seven. Tonight, Marika was wearing a soft rose-colored flapper's dress instead of her usual signature red. It had thin spaghetti straps and row after row after row of crystal-beaded fringes, and every time she moved, she glittered like Richard Cory.

I was wearing sapphire blue, a simple sheath dress whose only glory was its lustrous color. Marika had swept my dark hair up into a chignon, held in place by sapphire-tipped pins. She'd also done my makeup, a little more dramatically than I would have liked, but I had to admit I looked striking.

"Where are all the guests?" I demanded. "We cannot keep all this raging beauty to ourselves."

Almost on the words, the doorbell rang. "Par-tay!" we cried in unison and scrambled for the door.

The house quickly filled with people, only about half of whom I knew. Some were friends from high school, some from college, some from the neighborhood; some were from Marika's office, or Erika's; a few were hangers-on who got invited who-knew-how. Jason and Domenic arrived together a couple of hours after the event was in full swing and proceeded to monopolize all my friends who had been mad for them in high school. Usually, girls don't care for your younger brother and his friends, but Jason and Domenic were different. They had always drawn attention, and they'd always loved it.

I spent way too much of my evening talking to a mousy woman named Sylvia McAllister, whom I could scarcely remember from college. I was pretty sure she had lived down the hall from me in the dorm, and that I had found her annoying then. From what I could catch of her words over the music and the continuous low buzz of conversation, I was guessing I wouldn't find her much more interesting now. Most of her conversation consisted of complaints about her incompetent boss, domineering husband, and inconsiderate neighbors. She'd hoped to forget these troubles and have fun at the party, but all she could think about was how much she disliked teleporting and how fearful she was that she would get lost at Olympic Terminal. I tried to keep a sympathetic expression on my face, but my inner voice kept saying, *What a heezling*. When I found a chance to turn her over to another college friend, I quickly stepped away.

I had much more fun visiting with Erika, who talked faster than anyone I had ever met, and Jodie and Calico and Azolay (not my cousin) from high school. I also had a great time flirting with a couple of guys from Marika's office whom I knew from running into them at Braves games.

"Next time you're here visiting Marika, we should all go to a game together," one of them suggested.

A voice in my head said, *Sorry, I'm seeing someone.* But I just smiled. "Sounds like fun."

I scarcely saw Marika until late in the evening, when I found her frowning at food selections set out in the darkened dining room. "What's the matter? Are we going to run out?" I asked.

"I think someone might have walked off with one of the caterer's platters."

I looked vaguely out into the sitting room. "Maybe someone just moved it," I said. "Should we start a search?"

"Nah, I don't care. As long as everyone's happy." Like me, she glanced toward the big crowded room, where candlelight and shaded lamplight made all the guests' faces appear animated and angular. "And everyone seems happy, don't you think?"

"Completely. The party is absolutely marbro." I spotted Jason and Domenic deep in conversation with three women my age, all of them married, all of them listening with adoration to whatever the guys were saying. "Look at them. It's like they're hypnotists or something."

Marika watched them for a while with a half-smile on her face. She seemed, for the moment, unwontedly pensive. Domenic stood up suddenly, illustrating a point with a wide sweep of his hands. He was dressed all in black, of course, and his long hair was caught back in a braid tied with a bright yellow ribbon. I swear I had seen a gold inset on his cheek when he first walked in, and I wasn't sure it was temporary.

"I've always had such a crush on him," Marika said softly. "My whole entire life."

"Me, too."

She rounded on me in complete revulsion. "Taylor! *Yuck!* That's disgusting! That's *incest!*"

"I didn't mean *Jason.*"

She calmed instantly. "Oh. That's all right, then."

"Wait a minute."

Now she turned motherly and cautionary. "You shouldn't have a crush on Domenic, Tay. He's not a nice guy."

"Hold on. You're in love with Jason? You mean, for real?"

"I mean, I adore Domenic, he's the best friend in the world, but he's going to hurt every woman who ever comes into his orbit."

"I have a crush on Domenic the exact way you had a crush on Davey Kittering in eighth grade," I said impatiently. "I'd never want to date him, ever ever ever, but I'm glad he's in the world."

"And now you have somebody *much better* in your life."

"So much better," I agreed. "But let's get back to the main point. You're in love with Jason?"

She nodded. She was as serious as I'd ever seen her, even a little sad. "I thought you knew."

"I—" I shrugged. "I thought he was practically your brother. Like you're practically my sister."

"No."

I thought a minute. "You should tell him."

She laughed a little wildly. "Oh, right. Just think how weird *that* would be for the rest of our lives. He'd call and say, 'Hey, Taylor, me and Domenic are going out for pizza, wanna come?' and you'd say, 'Sure, let me call Mareek,' and he'd say, 'Oh, better not. I feel so awkward around her ever since I found out about this big gaudy torch she carries for me.' It would never be the same."

I thought about all the girls Jason had ever dated—nice girls, wicked girls, smart girls, stupid girls—and how any time I'd asked him to explain what had gone wrong, he had just shrugged and said, "Just not what I wanted" or "Not what I'm used to." Who was he used to but Marika and me? "I think you should tell him."

"No. And you can't either."

"We'll talk about this in the morning," I said.

A sound caught her attention and she turned her head. "Was that the doorbell?"

It must have been, because some woman I didn't recognize hurried over to admit a latecomer. An exchange of greetings at the door, and she stepped back so I could see his face.

Axel.

"Looks like your evening just got better," I said.

"Maybe no one will notice him."

At that moment, Jason looked up, as if sensing our attention on him or, who knows, scenting the presence of a hostile invader. He looked straight at Axel, now talking with Jodie, came to his feet in one unhurried movement, crossed the room in about eight strides, and punched Axel in the face.

Jodie screamed. Marika screamed, too, then ran over to try to stop the fight. I missed some of the action, because there was a sudden shouting crowd around Jason and Axel, who appeared to be going at it with a fierce exchange of blows. Domenic was standing nearby but had made no attempt to interfere, so I assumed Jason wasn't being pummeled to death. Within a few minutes, the other party-goers had separated the combatants, though Axel, pinned against the wall by some of Marika's officemates, continued to shout invective at my brother.

No one was holding Jason back. He shook his head, resettled all his clothes, and looked around for Marika. She spoke first.

"Jason, you have to apologize."

He glared at her—Jason, who was usually so cool and so collected. "Get him out of here."

"It's my house! I can invite anyone I want."

"Fine," he said and headed toward the door. Axel aimed a kick at him as he passed, but Jason ignored him.

"Jason! Wait, Jason!" Marika wailed, running after him with her crystal fringes flying. The door closed behind them.

Those of us left in the room looked at each other and wondered who would be the best companion in a little gossipfest.

Axel shrugged free of his captors and brushed his tangled hair out of his eyes. "Where's the beer?"

He disappeared. Jodie and Azolay and Calico enveloped me.

"What was that all about?"

"Why does Jason hate Axel so much?"

"Do you think Marika's left her own party?"

"I hope Jason's not really mad."

By the time we had talked this all over in low and excited voices, the party had more or less reasserted its own rhythm, despite the fact that the hostess had not reappeared. I supposed it was now up to me to make sure everyone was comfortable and cared-for, so I canvassed the rooms, smiling, inquiring after everyone's well-being, and noting who was off in a dark corner with whom. Axel had found consolation almost immediately with a statuesque brunette whom I did not know, but she seemed awfully sympathetic to the grievances he was detailing in her ear.

Everyone, in fact, seemed just fine except sad little Sylvia. When I circled back through to the front hallway, she was standing near the door, clutching an empty wine glass and looking miserable. "Something wrong?" I asked.

"I have to go," she said. "I wanted to say goodbye to Marika, but I can't find her."

"She does seem to be missing. I'll tell her you left."

She made no attempt to depart. "I have to go," she repeated somewhat desperately.

"What's the matter?" I asked as gently as I could.

She looked like she was about to start crying. "I'm afraid to teleport by myself. I've never done it alone. I mean, my husband brought me here to-night, and I said, 'Oh, I'm sure I'll know someone who will be going home at the same time,' but no one looks ready to leave and I—I guess I'm just afraid."

I managed to tamp down my uncharitable surge of disdain. "You want someone to walk with you to the neighborhood gate?" I asked. "I'll do it."

"No, I want someone to come with me to Olympic Terminal. I'll be fine once I get to John Wayne Station, I've come home from there lots of times, but Olympic is so big—"

"I'll be right back."

I found Domenic holding hands simultaneously with two women and feeding them some bullshit line about how to increase their libido or their psychic powers or some such thing. I'd been right before; he did have a gold graft on his cheek. Looked fabulous.

"I'll be gone for a while," I told him. "I have to make sure Sylvia gets home safe. You're in charge."

"I'm right on it," he said with a lazy smile

"Knew I could count on you," I said and returned to the door. Sylvia was watching me with apprehension. "Let's go," I said.

Her face cleared. "Oh, you'll come with me? Thank you *so much*. I know it's an imposition—"

"I can't walk too fast in these shoes, but other than that, we're good to go."

We stepped outside into the scented Southern air, still warm and dreamy at what must have been very close to midnight, whether before or after. I looked around but saw no sign of Jason and Marika. Either they were hiding somewhere in the back yard, or they'd taken a very long walk—or they'd snuck back inside through a rear door and were somewhere in the house hashing things out. I could hardly wait to hear the story.

"So. Taylor. Tell me what you've been doing lately," Sylvia invited. Her voice sounded falsely brave as if, even with my imposing presence, she feared the shadows on the streets.

I smothered a sigh. Half an hour. It couldn't take much more than that. "I'm still teaching at Sefton, and I've been doing a little tutoring on the side—"

There was no one at the local gate when we arrived. Sylvia, it turned out, didn't have a transit pass in her thumb chip and seemed worried about the expense when she asked what I thought the fare would be. Just to hurry things along, I presented my own thumb chip, pushed her through the door, and punched in the appropriate numbers.

"As soon as you close the door, hit this 'go' button and you'll be sent to Olympic," I told her. "Step outside of the booth and wait for me. I'll be along in a few seconds."

"Okay! I'll be waiting!" she trilled. A small flash, and she was gone.

I squashed an ignoble impulse to turn around and head back to the party. Instead, I stepped in the booth, hit FOLO, and found myself instantly in Olympic Terminal. Poor Sylvia was standing as close to the door as she possibly could.

"Here I am," I said brightly. "Let's find the California gates and look for John Wayne Station."

Ten minutes later, we had found the right portal and she was stepping inside. She assured me she had enough money in her account to cover the next jump, but I agreed to wait until the system actually accepted her payment before I headed back to Marika's. I was never in my life so glad to see anyone disintegrate behind the glass of a teleport door. Once she rematerialized in Orange County, she was on her own.

I retraced my route, not exactly ecstatic about walking alone down Marika's street in my thin sheath dress and my high-heeled shoes. However, I made it safely, no terrors to chase me back. I heard Marika's antique grandfather clock strike a single note as I walked through her door—twelve-thirty? one? one-thirty? It was the least helpful chime of them all—and I looked around to see if I could assess what I had missed.

Most of the tableaux appeared unchanged, except Axel and the brunette were missing and Marika was back. She was talking to Calico and laughing, and she seemed unreservedly happy. I didn't see Jason anywhere.

I walked up behind her, grabbed her arm, and pulled her away from her conversation in mid-sentence. "What's going on?" I demanded.

"Taylor! Where have you been?"

"I told Domenic. Taking Sylvia to Olympic. What's going on? Where's Jason? Where's Axel?"

"I don't know where Axel is," she said airily. "Jason left. But everything's fine."

"Everything's fine how?"

"I mean, he's not mad any more. Can we talk about this tomorrow?"

"Oh, you better believe it."

"Right now we both need to circulate," she said and returned to her conversation with Calico.

The rest of the evening became progressively fuzzier as I got wearier and the people around me got drunker. I sat next to Domenic for a while, his arm around my waist and my head against his shoulder, as he described to a fascinated circle of women some ancient Native American ritual that I was pretty sure he had manufactured on the spot. When he briefly lost his audience—three went for drinks, one went to the bathroom—I stretched my head up and whispered in his ear.

"What do you think's going on with Jason and Marika?"

"Could this be love?" he demanded, hand to heart, thunderstruck.

"Be serious. What do you think?"

"Dunno. He's always been crazy about her, but I don't think he realized it until a year or so ago. I mean, anyone could tell."

"I couldn't tell."

"You're his sister. You're stupid."

"You're stupid," I said sleepily and closed my eyes.

I don't know if I actually fell asleep there on the couch, but I do know that the party seemed to have fizzled to a close by the time I opened my eyes. Marika was moving through the almost-empty rooms, picking up discarded plates and pushing fallen cushions back into place. A few people were still standing around talking in small groups, but she ignored them, and most of them appeared to be edging toward the door. Domenic, bless his heart, was filling a plastic trash bag with napkins and bread crusts and other pieces of garbage. The grandfather clock struck three.

I shook myself and climbed unsteadily to my feet. "What can I do to help?"

"Just look like you're cleaning until everyone leaves. Then we're going straight to bed."

It was another half hour before the last guests had departed, Domenic had kissed us and headed out the door, and we were upstairs brushing our teeth.

"I've turned off my EarFone, and I am *begging* you not to wake me up before eleven tomorrow," I called out from the guest bathroom, just down the hall from hers.

"Right back at you," she said. "See you in the morning."

⟲⟳

It was actually closer to noon the next day when I woke up and heard Marika moving around downstairs, so I padded down to see what was available for breakfast. The house was a complete disaster despite our half-hearted efforts last night, and I foresaw a long ordeal of cleaning ahead. Fortunately, I would not be able to stay for it all; I had to be at Quentin's in about three hours.

"Morning," I said, flopping down in one of the kitchen chairs.

She handed me a glass of orange juice. "How'd you sleep? Are you hung over?"

"Slept great. Nope, no hangover. I only had two beers."

She laughed. "Me too. So who was drinking all those beers and leaving all those bottles all over my living room?"

"Your inconsiderate guests."

She sat across from me at the table. "It was a good party, though, wasn't it? Erika had fun, anyway."

"It was good until the fistfight," I agreed, "and until the hostess vanished for, oh, an hour. What happened?"

"Well, I guess Jason saw Axel walk in and—"

"I mean, between you and my brother."

She glanced down at her hands, clasped loosely around the base of her glass. Her hair was barely combed, so it was even wilder than usual; her red bathrobe was made of silk and velvet. Marika never looked like an ordinary woman.

When she looked up again, she was smiling. "I told him."

"And?"

"You were right. He feels the same."

"So he—so you—I mean, are you going to be my sister-in-law or something?"

She laughed gaily. "We didn't get that far. We just talked about—everything, really. Things we liked about each other, things we'd noticed—we remembered some of the strangest things, the smallest details, things that had happened years ago. He remembers the dress I wore to junior prom! I mean, he was only thirteen then. He remembers the name of every guy I've ever dated." She shrugged. "Of course, I could list his girlfriends in order and by year, so I guess that's not so surprising. But what *was* surprising was—this sense of connection. It goes so deep. I can't explain it." She took a sip of her orange juice. "It was the most marbro thing ever."

I started laughing. "You don't even know what the word means."

"I do now."

Well. This was an event that could not be covered in one conversation, so we recurred to it multiple times during the next couple of hours as we made a stab at reordering the house. A little after two, I had to quit to put on real clothes instead of the pajamas I had worn since I borrowed them from Marika last night. I gathered the rest of my stuff and got ready to go.

"Sorry to leave you with such a mess. Want me to come back tonight?"

"Oh, I'll be fine. Jason's coming over."

"I don't know if I'll be able to take this for long," I grumbled. "My little brother making someone all googly-eyed. It's kind of gross."

She made a prim face. "Don't you want me to be happy?"

"Well—yeah—but with Jason? I don't know."

She shoved me toward the door. "Go. Have fun. Give my love to Bram."

I decided not to answer that, just waved goodbye and set off down the street. A little less spooky in broad daylight, I had to admit.

Olympic Terminal was crowded, and I had something of a wait before I could step into the gate for Chicago. Then O'Hare, as always, was packed with people, and there were long lines at all the local ports. I would have been impatient anyway, but today I was almost jumping out of my skin. Bram would be there at the mansion. We wouldn't have more than a few minutes to talk, and I knew he was busy tonight, but I would *see* him. He would smile at me. We would both remember—

I shook my head. A few minutes before three, it was finally my turn to enter the booth. I typed in my personal code for the Phillips mansion and punched the "go" key.

And was confused and disoriented to find myself stepping out of the port, not in the formal foyer, but at the security gate a quarter mile from the house. There were people everywhere—guards, and uniformed policemen, and reporters loaded down with cameras and mikes. Rows of ambulances

and cop cars lined the drive as far as I could see, lights flashing, figures leaning from their windows to shout at people attempting to cross the wide lawn.
This was no journalistic frenzy caused by the announcement of the billionaire's impending nuptials. This was something much worse.

I stood there, stupefied, staring around me, until a security guard grabbed
my arm and pulled me out of the way. I knew she couldn't be one of Bram's
people, because all of his hires were men.

"Ma'am? Please step to one side. You'll need to give me your name and
your reason for coming here. Ma'am?"

I stared at her, scarcely registering her face, which she was trying hard to
mold into an impassive professional expression. Disaster had unfolded at the
Phillips mansion, that much was certain. I opened my mouth, but I couldn't
even bring myself to ask a reasonable question. Unbidden, the Wordsworth
lines came rushing into my head, modifying themselves, terrifying me:

Oh mercy, to myself I cried, If Quentin should be dead!

CHAPTER TWENTY-THREE

"MA'AM? YOUR NAME AND YOUR REASON FOR COMING HERE?"
The voice jarred me back to reality. "Taylor Kendall. I'm Quentin's tutor."
I looked at her, focusing on her young face, willing myself to seem sane and
sincere. "Bram Cortez will vouch for me."

The name registered with her, but she merely nodded. "Were you expected here today at this time?"

"Yes, three o'clock every Friday. What happened?"

"You have your own door code for the house?"

I gestured. "Yes, usually I go straight there, but today—" And for a moment I thought, *Oh, no. Bordeaux's already at the house on my code. That's why
I was rerouted.* But Bordeaux was much more scrupulous than that; she knew
better than to appropriate my code on my assigned days. "I don't know why I
ended up here," I finished lamely.

"All visitors are being sent to the security gate," she said. "A precautionary
measure."

"Can you tell me what happened?"

She practically gaped at me. "Haven't you seen the news?"

I'd never bothered to turn my EarFone back on after disabling it for the
night. It was more astonishing that Marika had also failed to do so, since she
practically lived on the digital plane, but she had clearly been too involved in
her own messy life to check the chaos in the outside world. I could scarcely
suck in enough air to breathe out a single syllable. "No."

"Duncan Phillips has been murdered."

I stared at her; for a moment, my surroundings seemed to dissolve into
an unreality not unlike teleport transmission. Not just *Duncan Phillips is
dead.* But *Duncan Phillips has been murdered.* You don't toss out pronounce-
ments like that unless you're awfully sure. Unless it's official.

"Murdered," I repeated. "But who—but how—why did—when did—"

"We don't know most of the details. But since you've got your own door
code, I'm sure the police will want to talk to you."

"Since I've—why would that—"

"Let me just call out to the house."

I stood there and shivered while she spoke into a phone implant, got instructions, and nodded sharply. She waved over a policeman who was driving something that looked like a golf cart.

"Take her to the house. She needs to talk to Siracusano."

As the cop drove me down the crowded drive between police cars and journalists, I imagined my face being transmitted out onto all the live video feeds and internet news sites. Would reporters be speculating about the "mysterious dark-haired woman being escorted to the grand house by police authorities"? I hoped my mother wasn't watching the news. Though Marika probably was.

The cop took me inside, where we were met, thank God, by Francis. I couldn't help myself; I threw myself into his arms. "What happened?" I cried as I pulled back. "Quentin's dad has been murdered? Do they know who did it?"

Francis looked straight at me. "Someone who had access to the house."

"Come this way," the young cop said, pushing between us and edging me down the hall."

I moved along with him, but I was still staring back at Francis. "One of us?" I demanded. He nodded.

"This way, please, ma'am. They should be waiting in the library."

"They" turned out to be Bram Cortez, whom I was mortally glad to see, and a large man in an expensive business suit. He had gray hair still edged with black, features as bluff as a boxer's, huge hands, a bulky body under his Italian jacket, and a firearm strapped to his belt. I saw his intent brown eyes assess me quickly, once, and file away all visible information.

I wanted to fling myself into Bram's arms, too, but I knew that this wasn't the forum. Actually, I wasn't sure we were supposed to know each other; I wasn't sure exactly what the setup was here. So I nodded at him, my face very serious, and held my hand out to the big man.

"I'm Taylor Kendall. Quentin's English tutor."

"Tony Siracusano," he said. His grip was warm and completely enveloping. I would have bet he was strong enough to crack my fingers without even trying, though he did not, at this moment, appear to be trying. "Homicide detective with the Chicago PD. Let's sit down."

We took our places at a table in front of an impromptu high-tech control room the cops had set up in the middle of the library. Banks of monitors showed video feeds from several views of the house, while a couple of other screens were tuned to television stations and internet sites. All the sound was down, so people spoke and gestured and reacted like ill-taught mimes, unable to convey their points. There was also an array of other equipment completely unfamiliar to me, as well as an untidy pile of papers and pens and photographs. One of the photos featured me.

I was sure I was supposed to wait for Siracusano to open the investigation, but I spoke first anyway. "Please tell me what's going on," I said. "I was out late last night, and I never heard the news this morning, and until I arrived here, I had no idea—what had happened."

Detective Siracusano glanced at Bram, as if checking whether anyone could really be that stupid, then spoke in a calm, dispassionate voice. "Someone teleported into this house around one a.m. this morning, went into Duncan Phillips' study, and shot Mr. Phillips dead. From what we can tell, this individual came to the house with a specific agenda—to commit murder."

I tried to keep my voice as cool as his. "Who are you considering suspects?"

"People with access to the house. Specifically, those who live and work at the Phillips mansion, and those who have their own door codes."

"That includes me."

"It does." Siracusano gestured at his notes. "The last time you were here— the last time anyone *knows* that you were here," he corrected himself, "you had a nasty argument with Mr. Phillips. Which was witnessed by five other people and caught on security monitors. We have had an opportunity to view the recording. It looks like an unpleasant encounter." His hard brown eyes watched for any flicker of emotion on my face. "Is that the last time you saw Duncan Phillips?"

"Yes, it was," I said sharply. "No, I didn't come back to the house in the middle of the night and kill him. I don't even know how to use a gun."

"There are a lot of fingerprints and DNA traces on this particular weapon. Possibly some of those are yours. You'll need to be printed and scanned before you leave today."

"But I—" I put my hands to my head. I was confused and shaking and completely disoriented. Was this the place where I was supposed to say, "I won't talk to you without my lawyer present"? I had a terrible feeling it was. "I didn't kill him. I wasn't even in Chicago last night. I was at a party in Atlanta. There must be fifty people who can give me an alibi."

"Atlanta's not so far away," said Siracusano, "by teleport."

I opened my mouth to reply—and then I froze. No doubt my face drained of color. If it had been possible to look a fraction more guilty, I'm sure I would have managed it.

Because I'd been at an international teleport terminal last night, probably just around the time Duncan Phillips was meeting his death. How hard would it be for Siracusano and his team of detectives to figure that out for themselves?

"Well," I said, in a voice that sounded feeble even to me, "I never left Atlanta last night."

Siracusano was watching me unsympathetically. "I'm sure you understand that we'll be checking into that."

"Of course." I tried to pull myself together, and I allowed myself a quick look at Bram. "I still don't entirely understand. Why don't you know who did it? Don't you have security monitors on all the time?"

"Monitors were off," Bram said briefly. "Not too hard to jam the system if you know what you're doing."

I had a sudden brief memory of an afternoon expedition with Quentin and Dennis as we snuck off to take an unauthorized tour of Duncan Phillips' holographic gallery of mistresses. Quentin had dismantled the system under Dennis' supervision and I had watched. I wouldn't have been able to replicate that trick to save my life—though possibly no one would believe that—

And surely Bram Cortez knew how to jam his own monitors, and Francis knew literally everything about this house—

"Oh, my God," I said as the implications became clearer. "Oh, my God."

Bram nodded. "Exactly."

"Who else do you suspect?" I demanded.

"A lot of people."

"What about his new fiancée?"

"She was at a publicly broadcast charity event last night," Siracusano said. "She's not on the list."

I spoke a little too eagerly. "Wait—don't you keep a record of the door codes that have been used? Won't that tell you who was here last night?"

"They were temporarily wiped out when the monitors went down," Bram said in a careful voice, "but we believe the information is still in the system."

"That will solve everything then, won't it?"

Siracusano still watched me with that level, unwavering regard. "It might," he said. "We'll have to wait and see."

I nodded, trying to appear casual, trying not to reveal just how alarmed I was. I turned to Bram and attempted to change the subject. "How's Quentin taking all this? Is he okay? What's going to happen to him? He's an orphan now. Does he have a guardian?"

"He's nineteen, Ms. Kendall," the cop reminded me. "In two years, he'll have attained his legal majority. He might be able to convince the court that he doesn't need a guardian."

"Quentin does," I said. "Is he all right? Where is he? Can I see him?"

"Quentin Phillips will remain in this household, which will be run just as it has been, until we sort everything out," Siracusano said.

Bram gave him a glance that I interpreted as dislike. I wondered if they'd known each other back in Bram's cop days, and whether that would work for or against me—and the rest of our friends. "Quentin's a suspect, too," Bram told me.

Siracusano looked irritated, but I had already figured that out for myself. Nonetheless, I said, "Not Quentin! He couldn't possibly have done something like that."

"He saw your fight with his dad," Bram said. "And his dad said some pretty harsh things—about Quentin. Motive enough, if that's what you're looking for. So he's basically under house arrest."

"I don't think we need to give Ms. Kendall a list of suspects and their possible motives," Siracusano said icily.

Bram shrugged. "I'm sure she's already guessed. There are five primary suspects, and we all had access to the house, and we all witnessed the fight with Duncan Phillips. Which gives each of us the same motive for killing the bastard."

I pretended to be shocked. "Does that mean *you're* under suspicion, too?"

"Ms. Kendall, until we're able to reconstruct the security systems, everyone on the planet is under suspicion," Siracusano said. "It's true we think it was someone who had access to the house, which means someone who had a personal door code and a good idea of the layout of the place. But in my experience, there are a lot of ways for people to get information that you would much prefer they did not have. Duncan Phillips was a powerful guy with a lot of money and a lot of enemies. And someone we may not even have thought of yet could very well have wanted to kill him. You and your friends are all on the list—but it's not a short list."

"What do you want me to do?" I asked.

"I want you to be printed and scanned before you leave. I want you to stay in the Chicago area until further notice."

"Taylor's job is in Houston," Bram said quietly. "Financial hardship to restrict her movement."

Siracusano looked at me. "Ms. Kendall?"

I shook my head. "Summer break. I should be fine for a few weeks. And if a meeting comes up, I can always videoconference in."

Siracusano was taking notes. "All right. If you need to go to Houston, or anywhere else, contact my department and someone will escort you." He fixed me with his intent eyes. "Other than that, you're not to leave the city. Do you understand?"

I nodded wordlessly. I was all out of words anyway. "Where do I go for the scan?"

Bram was on his feet. "I'll take you." He glanced at Siracusano as if expecting a challenge, but the big man merely shrugged. "I'll be back in a few minutes."

I followed him out of the room and down the hall toward the elevator. When we were relatively clear of the possibility of spying eyes, he did a sudden pivot and took me in his arms. I hugged him back somewhat convulsively. My eyes were shut and my shoulders were locked in a permanent hunch and I felt completely battered.

"Oh, Bram," I said into his shoulder. "What in the world happens now?"

I felt him shake his head above mine. "I don't know. I can't imagine what Siracusano's investigation will turn up. I don't even know what I should hope for. But I can't even think about that as clearly as I should. I keep wondering—what about Quentin? What happens to him?"

I nodded into his shirt. "He can't live by himself, even if he gets legal emancipation. And, anyway, we couldn't possibly leave him alone after this."

"I'm moving in. For a while. Francis has rooms here. Dennis will still come by, and I assume you will, but I don't think they'll let anyone else camp out here. So for the moment he's taken care of, but—"

"What about his aunt?" I asked. "Does she know? Maybe she's his legal guardian now, has anyone checked?"

"Francis talked to her this morning. But she's in Australia and she just had back surgery, so she says it'll be a month before she can travel. And I don't think Quentin can just pack up and move to the Outback. Anyway, he has to stay here while he's still a suspect. So I think it will be a while before everything's sorted out. We'll just have to hold tight."

"I'm so afraid," I whispered against his chest.

His arms tightened; I felt him drop a kiss on the top of my head. "I'm not afraid yet," he said. "But once they start pointing fingers, I have a feeling I'll be terrified. I can't imagine who would have done this. I mean, I know the possibilities, but I just can't believe—" He shook his head again.

I lay still against him and didn't answer. But I already had a strong suspicion of who the killer was. There were five of us on the list. Five of us with the exact same motives, the same means, and pretty much the same opportunities—and some of those five, at least, had wanted Duncan Phillips dead for a long time. But no one had made a move to destroy him until this week, after my little fight with him. Nothing Duncan Phillips had said then had been new, nothing that Bram and Francis and Dennis and Quentin had not heard before. Nothing that would have made them lose their cool enough to seek him out in the dead of night and kill the man they had already hated for so long.

But Bordeaux had heard this diatribe for the first time, and Bordeaux had had reason to come calling late at night when no one else was awake. And Bordeaux had access to the house, keying in a code she only used when she knew I would not be present—a code that only I knew she possessed. And Bordeaux, I was very sure, could take care of herself—and anyone else she cared about.

I would die before I offered this speculation aloud.

"So what do we do now?" I said, still speaking to his chest.

"We get you scanned. And then, if you're up to it, you go upstairs and say hello to Quentin. And we carry on the best we can, until we find out something that we can't endure. And then we fight."

I lifted my head and attempted to smile. "Sounds good."

He kissed me, his mouth hard and swift on mine. "I know we had plans tomorrow night," he said. "And I want to be with you more than I can say. But—"

"I know," I said. "We can't."

He kissed me again. "Soon. When things are all better."

"Soon," I echoed. But I imagined it would be a very long time before things were *all better*.

CHAPTER TWENTY-FOUR

THE FINGERPRINTING WAS QUICK AND PAINLESS, SINCE ALL I DID was lay my fingers on a sensor and watch an interior light flash beneath my hands a few times. I also consented to a mouth swab as a way to contribute a DNA sample to the lab. I assumed this meant that, for the rest of my life, I could engage in no criminal behavior, since I was well and truly in the police records now. I had no plans to carry on illegal activities in the future, and I knew I was not guilty of this particular crime, and yet the gathering of evidence against me made me a little nervous. As if I had testified against myself, been tricked into a confession. What could I be convicted of now?

"My DNA is probably all over the house," I told the indifferent technician. "I don't know exactly what this will prove." He shrugged and just had me sign a release form.

I was glad to escape the dining room, which had been set up as a police lab, and climb into the elevator, kissing Bram goodbye at the door. "I'll call you later," he said, and I nodded.

Upstairs, I hesitated a moment outside Quentin's room, wondering what I could possibly say. *Oh, Quentin, so sorry your dad's dead.* Not remotely true. But I had to say *something*.

My knock was answered by Bordeaux, who looked more grave and adult than I had ever seen her. She was dressed in a close-fitting navy shirt and trousers of some slinky material, sober by her standards, and her hair was free of ornaments. Her open, happy face looked drawn and tired. Even her jeweled insets could not muster a sparkle. "Taylor," she said, and hugged me. "I'm glad you're here."

I crossed the room to kneel beside Quentin and wrap my arms around his lanky body. "Oh, honey," I said with my cheek next to his, "I simply do not know what to say."

"Yeah, no one does," he replied. "And I don't know what to say or feel. It's just the strangest thing."

I released him and found a seat on the couch, Bordeaux plopping down next to me. "Tell me," I said. "What happened? When did you find out? Just start from the beginning."

Quentin shook his head. Like Bordeaux, he looked older and more serious than I had ever seen him, but not shattered. Shocked but not sad. Certainly, he would not miss his cruel and careless father—but oh, what a way to lose him.

"I didn't know anything until Francis and Bram came up here this morning. I guess one of Bram's security guys saw my dad's body on the camera sometime in the morning."

"I thought the cameras were out."

He nodded. "They were, but nobody knew that until the morning shift came on. Then someone spent an hour fixing them—and then somebody saw the—saw my dad. And told Bram. Who I guess called the cops in."

I couldn't bring myself to directly ask the most obvious question. *Quentin, was it you who cut the cameras so your girlfriend could sneak in during the night?* "Anyone have any idea why the cameras went down?" I said casually.

"The big mean cop says someone tampered with them," Bordeaux said, her voice betraying her low opinion of Siracusano. "But Bram says they go down all the time without a reason, and that's what the tech guy said, too. So it could have just been random lucky chance." She glanced at me, her face and voice completely unrepentant. "Lucky for the killer, that is."

"Bordeaux," I chided.

She spread her hands. "Well, we can't pretend that anybody's sorry Duncan Phillips is dead. Even Quentin isn't pretending that. I just wish he'd died a little less—spectacularly."

"When did *you* hear about it?" I asked her. Still indirect.

"Around noon, about five minutes after I woke up. I went out with a bunch of girls from my dorm last night and woke up with a headache, so I didn't go to my first class." She rolled her eyes to convey a sense of utter disbelief. "The minute I turned on my feeds, that was the first thing that came up. 'Duncan Phillips found dead at home.' And I thought, 'Oh, God. The world has just turned upside-down.'"

Not the carefully thought-out alibi and skillfully manufactured emotional reaction I would have expected from a murderer.

"I don't even mind that he's dead," Quentin said in a low voice. "What I mind is what they're saying. About who killed him."

"Siracusano said it could be anybody," I said quickly. "Some old enemy, a professional killer, even."

"That's what he's *saying*, maybe," Quentin said. "But what he *thinks* is that it's one of the six of us with access to the house."

"I heard five," I said. "You, me, Bram, Francis, Dennis."

"Me," Bordeaux added. I looked at her and she shrugged. "I had access, too."

"They don't have to know that," I said quickly.

She shook her head dismissively. "They'll figure it out."

"But you—they'll be more suspicious—"

"This is what I can't stand," Quentin said.

"Let's talk about something else," Bordeaux said.

I couldn't imagine another topic of conversation that could hold our attention for more than a minute, but at that moment there was a distraction as my EarFone went off. "Taylor," I said.

It was Marika. "Taylor! Have you seen the news?"

"I'm at Quentin's."

"Then you—then he—Taylor, what's going on?"

"It's Marika," I said to Quentin before answering her question. "Don't know yet. Cops are here, reporters are here, and everyone's under suspicion. What are they saying on the news?"

"Just that he's been murdered and there are a lot of suspects and the police are—wait. Are *you* a suspect?"

"Yeah."

I heard her address someone else in the room. "Taylor says she's a suspect! Can you believe it?" My brother's voice said, "Put her on speaker."

"Look, I can't talk about it right now," I said before she could transfer to the aux. "Tell Jason I'm fine. I'll call you later."

"How's Quentin?" she asked.

I smiled over at him. "Quentin's doing better than I expected, but he's got all his friends around him."

"Well, tell him I'm thinking about him and—I don't know, tell him to call me if he needs anything. I mean, what could I do, but tell him that anyway."

"I will. I'll call you tonight. Bye." I disconnected and said, "Marika sends her love and says call her if you need anything."

"How about a Braves shirt?"

"She already gave you one!"

He glanced at Bordeaux. "Mmm. Tell her I gave it to somebody else."

I started laughing. Shouldn't have, but I did, and it actually felt good. "Tell her yourself." I let out a big sigh and momentarily covered my face with my hands. "Oh, kids, what a dreadful day. Let's do what we can to just get through it."

❧

I stayed with Quentin until about five, long past my usual allotted hour. We needed something to occupy our surface attention, so the three of us played video games as the hours crawled past. We said very little, but conversation was not the point. Solidarity was the point. Comfort was the point. The only real goal was surviving the day.

Dennis arrived just as I was thinking I could not endure the strain much longer. I had never been happier to see him.

"I made it past the gauntlet downstairs," he said breezily, crossing the room to look out the window. Quentin's view was of the back part of the lawns, normally not open to the public, but even here a few intrepid reporters had set up cameras and were sending off broadcasts. "Do you think I look all right? I knew I'd be on camera, so I dressed with special care."

"You look like a shasta queen, but you always do," Bordeaux said. "I think they'll be loving you."

Dennis turned from the window, eyes alight with malice. "Hey, I hadn't thought of that! 'Gay therapist kills the father of his boy lover.' That would make good copy."

Quentin abruptly jerked his wheelchair across the floor and through the doorway into his bedroom. The three of us looked after him.

"He doesn't like all the suspicions floating around," I said in a quiet voice. "He doesn't even like joking about it."

"Joking is my way of coping," Dennis said, his eyes still on the bedroom door. "But I'll try to restrain myself around Q."

Bordeaux rubbed her eyes. "I'm so tired," said the girl who never seemed to be sapped of energy. "I'm gonna say goodbye to Quentin and then take off for a few hours."

I stood up. "I have to go, too. How long are you staying, Dennis?"

He waved a hand, dismissing us. "As long as he needs me. Go. He won't be alone."

We each hugged him, then Bordeaux disappeared into the other room to murmur a few words to Quentin. I wanted to think of something hearty and cheery to say, but no appropriate words occurred to me. I waited in silence until Bordeaux emerged, and we left together, heading for the elevator.

It occurred to me that, with Duncan Phillips dead, I didn't have to make sure I had an escort every time I walked the halls of this building. It was a strange thought in the middle of an utterly strange day.

"I'm worried about Quentin," I said.

"Me, too. But I think he'll be all right. He looks pretty frail, but he's a tough kid. Lived through the kind of pain you and I can't even imagine."

"And no matter what that damn Siracusano says," I burst out, not meaning to say it, "I don't believe Quentin could have murdered his own father."

She shook her head and pushed the elevator button. "Oh, no. He didn't do it."

She spoke with such certainty that I could not help thinking she had corroborating evidence. Her own actions, maybe. "I've never thought about killing someone," I said slowly. "I mean, sometimes I'm walking down the street and I hear footsteps behind me, and I wonder what I'd do if someone attacked me. I'm sure I'd fight. If I had a weapon, I'd probably use if it I thought my life was in danger. But to walk into a guy's house and pick up a gun and shoot him dead? I don't think I could do it."

"I could," she said.

The elevator doors opened and we stepped inside.

"I mean, I could kill someone who was attacking me," she added, as the car went down. "Or someone who deserved to die. A murderer or a torturer. I could shoot someone like that, no problem."

"Duncan Phillips was neither of those things."

She smiled at me, completely at ease. "I know."

We rode in silence until the car paused on the ground floor and we stepped out. Bordeaux came to a halt in the marbled hallway and said, "Taylor."

I stopped and looked at her.

"I don't want any more payments."

I considered a moment. "For seeing Quentin?" She nodded. I said, "Does that mean you're going to stop coming by?"

She shook her head. "No. I'm never leaving Quentin. I just don't want to be paid for it anymore."

Because she loved him and didn't want to be his zydeco girl, or because she'd killed his father and felt too much guilt? "What happens if you need money?" I asked as delicately as I could. That would hurt Quentin worse than knowing what she had been to him—knowing she would be the same to another young man.

She shook her head again. "Well, right now I don't. And if things get tight—I guess I'll find a job. Can't be that hard."

"I'm concerned about you, too, Bordeaux," I said impulsively.

She gave me a jaunty grin, which, as far as I could tell, was completely genuine. "Don't worry about me. I can take care of myself."

Nothing much to say after that. We resumed our walk to the portal gate— which apparently could be used to send us away from the house, though it wouldn't accept our arrival—and were shown out by a uniformed guard who watched us with undisguised suspicion. Francis was nowhere in sight. I let Bordeaux precede me, then allowed the teleport mechanism to fling me home—where, though I arrived as always in one piece, I felt like I had not completely reassembled from the transfer.

⁓

Jason and Marika were inside my apartment when I arrived, cooking dinner and making themselves at home. "Hey, who gave you the key code?" I asked in mock irritation as I found them consulting over a recipe book.

"Charlotte Brontë's birthday," Marika said, not looking up from the page.

"Everybody knows that."

Jason came over to hug me. Something he rarely does. He must have been as worried about me as I was about everybody else. Nice, for a change. "Tell me everything," he said.

"No," Marika countermanded. "Wait until we're eating dinner and we can all hear everything at once."

I pulled up a chair at the dining room table, since clearly I wasn't expected to help with meal prep. Jason sat next to me, but Marika stayed in the kitchen. "What are you guys doing here?" I asked.

"I wanted Marika to come see Mom." He gave me a droll look. "You know, she's always asking to meet my girlfriends."

"Oh, this is going to be too weird," I responded. "What did she say?"

"She doesn't know yet. I'm bringing Marika over tomorrow for lunch. She's spending the night with you."

"Sure, of course."

"And maybe tomorrow, too. 'Cause I don't think Mom's up to having us spend the night together at her place."

I held up both hands in a *stop* gesture. "Yeah. Right. Please. I'm not quite up to it yet, either."

"Better get used to it," he said.

"I've got a lot of other things to think about at the moment."

He leaned forward, all serious and protective. "Tay. You have to start wearing your WristWatcher."

It was the last thing I'd expected. The little wristband communicator had been Jason's Christmas present last year, but I'd barely taken it out of the box. It had a tiny display screen and voice-activated text capability, but its most salient feature was that it was supposed to be untraceable. He had given it to me as a joke, because we had always loved cloak-and-dagger games. I'd used it to send him a few messages and then put it away, because it was too clunky for everyday use. I preferred my EarFone.

"Why?" I asked.

"So I can stay in touch with you."

I touched the side of my head. "You can always call."

He shook his head. "EarFone can be tracked and monitored. Even if you're not using it, anyone who's looking for you will know where you are."

I stared at him. I felt unexpectedly cold. "But—so what? Why would I—"

He flung up a hand. "If you're a suspect in a murder case, maybe the cops shouldn't always know where to find you."

I shook my head. "This is crazy."

"It can't hurt to wear the WristWatcher. And check it."

"I don't even know where it is."

"Well, let's look for it."

We searched the apartment while Marika finished cooking, and we ultimately discovered it on the top of the closet where I stored my Christmas decorations. After we charged the dead battery, we spent a little time testing it, Jason dictating nonsense messages and me replying with equal absurdity. Seemed to work just fine.

Over the meal, which was excellent, I told them everything I knew about the murder. Many details had already made it onto the news sites, so nothing I said surprised them.

"And they clearly already have the murder weapon, because they're in the process of checking it for fingerprints and DNA residue," I said.

Marika nodded. "Oh, yeah. It's a little Trellin-X laser, outlawed a few years back. It was part of Duncan Phillips' private collection. Which I guess he kept in some room where everyone in the world could just walk in."

I was staring at her. "Trellin-X? But—I handled that gun."

Jason's eyes were on me, lancet-sharp. "And why, exactly? When have you ever touched *any* gun?"

I twisted my hands in the air—exculpation, explanation. "I was in the gun room one day with Quentin, and he took this laser off the wall and wouldn't put it away. And it scared me, so I grabbed it from him and hung it back up. I mean, that was weeks ago. I suppose Francis or somebody could have cleaned all the guns by now and my traces would be gone, but—well, the way things are going, I wouldn't count on it."

Marika was cleaning her plate with her usual gourmand's satisfaction. "I don't see what you're so worried about. I mean, you were at my house last night. Everybody knows you were there. How could you even be a suspect?"

I bit my lip and looked at Jason. "You two were gone, so you don't know if I was there all night or not," I said slowly. "But Sylvia McAllister wanted someone to go to Olympic Terminal with her. She was afraid. So I said I'd go." I hesitated and then continued, "Not only that, she didn't have a transit pass, so I paid her way."

Jason's mouth formed a silent whistle, but Marika was still unimpressed. "Yeah, but how long were you gone? Thirty or forty minutes? That wouldn't be enough time to go from Olympic to O'Hare to a local gate and do it all in reverse to get back to my place. I mean, every time I head into Chicago, it takes me more than an hour to get where I want to be and you'd need another hour to get back. If people saw you coming and going—"

I felt like I was digging my own grave, lifting each spadeful of dirt with a swallowed grunt and climbing deeper into the muddy hole. "The Phillips mansion has a private terminal," I said quietly. "All I'd need would be a direct gate from Olympic. One quick jump there, one quick jump back. Easily could have done it in forty-five minutes."

Marika stared at me, finally horrified. "You don't want to be telling anyone that," she said.

"Oh, I won't have to. Lieutenant Siracusano is more than capable of figuring that out on his own."

"You need a lawyer," Jason said abruptly.

"I don't know any lawyers," I snapped. "Do you?"

"I know someone in Atlanta, but I think you want someone local," Mareek said.

"Domenic might know one," Jason said. "I'll call him."

I glanced around the apartment as if just noticing that someone was missing. "Where is Domenic, now that I think about it?"

"Work," Jason said. "Picked up extra night shifts at the Evanston hospital for the next week. But I'll leave him a message."

I rubbed my forehead with my fingers. "I don't want a lawyer. I don't want to be a suspect. I don't want to think about any of this."

"Well, you are a suspect and you have to think about this," Jason said. "And you really do need a lawyer."

⌇

After that, conversation stuttered to a halt. A great flood of exhaustion washed over me. Last night I had been up too late, and today I had had too much strain; I would not be able to function much longer. Jason sensed it and got up to leave as soon as the meal was over. He kissed Marika goodbye (I couldn't watch) and hugged me again before he stepped out the door. Marika and I cleared the table, then I made up the couch into a bed for her.

"Anything else you need, you know where to find it," I said through a yawn.

"Tu casa es siempre mi casa," she replied.

"Don't wake me up in the morning," I advised, heading toward my bedroom. "Even if it means leaving without saying goodbye."

"Hey, Taylor?" she called just before I exited.

I turned to face her, absolutely certain of what was coming. That's how well I know her. "No. I didn't kill him."

"Would you tell me if you had?"

I considered that for a moment. I tell Marika everything, sooner or later, though sometimes I keep things private until I trust myself to speak about them. She knows that about me and rarely presses for information, even when she can tell I'm not being completely open. But that's the thing; she can always tell when I'm withholding. "I don't know," I said at last. "I guess it would depend on whether or not I thought it would get *you* in trouble. You know, aiding a murderer and all that."

"I wouldn't tell anybody. Even Jason."

I laughed. "Well, I appreciate your loyalty, but it's wasted in this instance. I didn't kill Duncan Phillips."

She watched me from across the width of the room, her wild hair foaming around her shoulders, her big eyes dark and sad. She said, "But you know who did."

CHAPTER TWENTY-FIVE

MARIKA AND I WERE EATING BREAKFAST SATURDAY MORNING WHEN I got a call from Bram. I'd heard from him late the night before when we were both too tired to do more than whisper a few words of worry and affection. But I could instantly tell from his tone of voice that this would be a different kind of conversation.

"This is Bram Cortez," he identified himself, his voice formal, carrying a warning note. I wondered if Tony Siracusano was sitting nearby, listening in—or already monitoring my calls.

"Hi. What's up? How's Quentin?" No need for me to act guilty or strange. Not yet, anyway.

"Quentin's about as you might expect. But doing all right."

"I was thinking about coming over today to keep him company."

There was a small pause. "I'm not sure that's a good idea," he said and did not explain why. Because I was under suspicion? Because Quentin was under suspicion? Who was he trying to keep safe?

"What's happened?" I asked directly.

"Your DNA was found on the murder weapon. A Trellin-X laser owned by the victim."

I nodded, though he couldn't see me. "I handled that gun once. When Quentin and I were looking at his father's collection."

"That's what Quentin told Siracusano."

"But I guess I can't prove that that's the only time I picked up that gun. Any gun."

"There are still a lot of other traces on it," he said. "We haven't identified them all."

"Well, in this day and age, anyone who commits a premeditated murder and doesn't wear gloves is just plain stupid," I said. Marika, who was lifting a coffee cup to her mouth, paused to give me a look of amazement. I went on, "I would think anyone whose prints are on the gun is *less* likely to be your suspect than someone who didn't leave any evidence behind."

"That's assuming it was premeditated," he said. "Could have been someone who came in at that hour to make some kind of top-secret deal. And that person got into an argument with Duncan Phillips. And whoever picked up the gun shot him on the spur of the moment."

I kneaded the base of my neck. I could feel a headache coming on. "Is there anything else you can tell me?" I asked. "Do I need a lawyer?"

"That might be wise."

His careful, indifferent tone left me even more convinced that Siracusano was listening. "I wish I could be there," I said, meaning with him, meaning with Quentin. Hoping he knew how to interpret the vague words.

"I'll call you again when I know something more," he said and disconnected.

I found that I was clutching the edge of the table as if trying to keep myself from collapsing to the floor. Marika set down her coffee cup and watched me. Neither of us said anything.

⤬

Domenic called about an hour after Marika had left for the lunch date with my mother. I had declined the offer to join them. The world was already too strange.

"What the hell's going on with you?" were Domenic's opening words. "I leave you alone for five minutes and you're off shooting people."

I had to wonder what Siracusano might think of *that* bit of byplay. Maybe he hadn't started monitoring all my calls yet, just the ones from Bram. "I didn't shoot anybody. Jason thinks you might know a lawyer. Seeing as how you know all sorts of people."

"Woman I dated a couple of times last year was a hotshot attorney with some criminal law outfit. I'd recommend her."

"Does she have warm feelings toward you, or is she one of those people you dumped without a word after the first night you slept together?"

I could hear the grin in his voice. "No, man, she broke up with me. Said she was too busy for a relationship."

"And you said, 'But wait! I'm too shallow for a relationship! We'd be perfect together.'"

"You know, I don't have to help you out here."

"Yeah, you do, or Jason would never speak to you again. He's up at my mom's today, by the way, introducing Marika as his girlfriend."

"Looking to be sort of a pivotal week in the lives of the Kendall siblings," Domenic observed.

"So what's this woman's name and how do I find her?"

"I'll call her for you and get back in touch."

"Thanks, Domenic."

"Anytime you're wanted for murder, you just count on me."

The next call came from Caroline Summers. "Taylor? Thank God. Are you all right? I saw the news."

"I've been afraid to watch," I said. "What are they saying?"

She sounded genuinely upset, rocked hard from her normal icy poise. I suppose sensational news about one of her direct reports would unnerve even the calmest woman. "That Duncan Phillips was shot and they think it was by someone who knew him. Taylor, the news sites are running all sorts of speculative stories. They're naming suspects and they're giving odds on who the likely murderer might be."

"Oh, shit," I muttered. "Look, Caroline. I know this is bad. I mean, I didn't kill him, but the fact that I'm entangled in a murder investigation is just—I'm sure the dean is upset—"

"He called me this morning."

I was silent for a beat. "Does he want my resignation?"

"Of course not. Unless, of course, it turns out you had something to do with it."

"If I had something to do with it, I imagine I'd be in jail before the next semester," I said baldly. "But if he's concerned about how things look—"

"I think he's more concerned about losing the money Duncan Phillips donated every year," she said with a flash of her usual cool. "He seems more interested in the reading of the will than the apprehension of the killer."

"Just what I love," I said. "People who behave entirely in character even in the face of catastrophe."

"Look, Taylor, I have to go to Houston tomorrow evening and I probably won't come back until the middle of next week. Is there anything you need? Anything I can do?"

Just believe in me, I wanted to say, but that sounded so melodramatic that I couldn't bring myself to voice the words. "I don't think so. Thanks for calling, Caroline."

"I'll talk to you in a day or two," she said and hung up.

I stared at the walls for a few minutes and thought I might go mad. How do you occupy yourself when you think you're about to be accused of a heinous crime? I was too jumpy to read a book or watch TV. Doomscrolling through social media sounded like the worst idea ever. Shopping, my usual palliative, didn't appeal at all. I made another phone call.

"Hey, Quentin," I said when he answered. "How are you doing this morning?"

"Hi, Taylor," he said, sounding pleased to hear my voice. "Oh, I'm—you know, things are pretty weird. I talked to my aunt, though."

"Yeah? The one in Australia?"

"Yeah. She says she wants me to come live with her once everything's settled down here."

"And do you want to do that?"

"I don't know. I don't think so. It's so far away, and I'm afraid I'd never get to see you and Bram and Dennis and Francis again. And Bordeaux."

My heart absolutely broke for him, but I tried to keep my voice light. "Well, hey, I've always wanted an excuse to go to Australia! I'll come visit you. I bet everyone else would, too."

"Yeah," he said, sounded young and uncertain. "Bram says you're not coming over today, though."

Why? Why was I not to come over? "I've got some things to take care of here," I said.

"Bram says the police are monitoring your calls."

I opened my mouth, then shut it hard. "Well," I finally managed, "I guess that means I should be careful what I say."

"Bram says they're monitoring mine, too," he added.

I was sure Lieutenant Siracusano was happy to learn, as he audited this conversation, exactly how much information Bram Cortez had supplied to the primary suspects. But I was pretty sure Bram had told Quentin specifically so the news would be passed on to Dennis and Bordeaux and me. "I guess we should *all* be careful, then," I said.

"Yeah, and did you know your EarFone could be used as a locator device?" he asked. "So if you're trying to hide from someone and you have it turned on—even if you're not using it, Bram says—people can find you."

"Gosh, maybe I should turn mine off," I said lightly. But I felt sick with fear. Why did Bram want me to know that? I had thought Jason was overreacting. Maybe it was a guy thing, cops and robbers, intergalactic space war, all those macho childhood games they played. Think of the worst-case scenario and act accordingly and with great bravado.

"If you turn it off, I won't be able to call you," he pointed out.

"Call Marika. She's going to be visiting Chicago for a while, so she can get me a message."

"Sure, I could do that."

"So what are Bram and the cops doing today, do you know?" I asked. "Or do they tell you?"

"I think they're looking through the computer records. They got some of the information back early this morning. Door codes and stuff. So I guess pretty soon they're going to know who came in Thursday night."

Which should have been good news for me, since I hadn't come to Duncan Phillips' house early on the morning in question. But if Bordeaux had . . .

"Okay, well, I wish them luck," I said, since I couldn't think of anything else to say. "I've got to go now, but let Marika know if you need anything, all right, buddy?"

"All right. Bye, Taylor."

I had scarcely disconnected when the chime sounded in my ear again. "Get off the damn phone," Jason said furiously.

"What? What's wrong?"

"I told you—don't use the phone. Put on your WristWatcher."

"Look, I'm just sitting here in my house. If anyone was looking for me, that's where they'd start, anyway."

"Right. Turn off the phone, put on your WristWatcher, read what I've sent you."

"How's it going with Mom?"

"Great. She cried. She thinks we're getting married."

"Are you?"

"We'll think about that after we've cleaned up this little mess you've gotten yourself into."

"That is so unfair."

"Turn it off, Tay. For real. Bye."

So I disconnected and powered down, which made me feel strange. Isolated and alone, adrift and on my own in a world suddenly peopled by threats and terrors. I was used to being able to establish contact with someone by speaking a few words aloud into thin air. Now, everyone I knew and loved and trusted seemed separated from me by unfriendly distances. I felt like I'd snapped a lifeline, and I didn't think there were too many left to keep me afloat.

I picked up the WristWatcher, which I'd left on the dining room table last night, and strapped it on. Only then remembering to check for the message Jason had sent. With a groan, I saw that he had sent it in code, so I had to find the stupid sociology book and flip through its pages.

"Go to Domenic's," was the note I finally deciphered. "His key code is 7-1-1-5."

I didn't bother to encrypt my reply, though I made it vague enough that only Jason would understand it. "Does he know about this?"

The answer came back in seconds, so Jason was obviously sitting there waiting for me. "Yes. Go."

"Tonight," I replied, because I wasn't about to spend a whole day just sitting in Domenic's high-rise downtown apartment, waiting for the world to implode. I'm never really comfortable at Domenic's. He's decorated with black leather furniture and chrome accents and strange lighting, and every time I'm there I look around and wonder who has been seduced where. When I said this to him once, he laughed and said he usually kept women out of his place, preferring to romance them on their own turf. Somehow, this didn't make me feel better.

While I was contemplating exactly how to pass the hours before trundling over to Domenic's, the doorbell rang. My last unexpected visitor had arrived with roses in hand, but an instinctive reaction of trepidation led me to expect a much different caller this time. I was right. When I opened the door, I found Lieutenant Siracusano before me, his bulk mostly blocking my view of two younger cops standing behind him.

"Ms. Kendall," the big man said. "Had a couple more things I wanted to ask you. Can we come in?"

I felt the blood frisk madly through my body, a yelping little terrier of an adrenaline response. "Don't you need a search warrant to go through my house?"

"Yeah," he said. "I wasn't planning on searching. But I can get the warrant, if you like."

I did not step back from the doorway to admit him. "What do you want?"

"Just wondering what you were doing at Olympic Stadium Thursday night. Or rather, Friday morning. Thought you were supposed to be at a party."

I swallowed against a dry throat. "I *was* at a party. Most of the night."

"According to the records generated by the credit system at Olympic Terminal, your thumb chip was presented there around 12:40 Friday morning. Do you have a recollection of using it then?"

I nodded, unable to speak.

"So, there's no problem with your account? There's been no duplication or unauthorized use of your chip?"

I shook my head.

Siracusano watched me with those unwavering dark eyes. Behind him, his attendant cops peered at me over his big shoulders, fascinated by the sight of this potential killer. "What were you doing at Olympic Terminal at that hour, Ms. Kendall? Where were you going?"

I found my voice, small and choked though it was. "A friend from the party was nervous about teleporting by herself. I accompanied her to the station—watched her get in her gate—and went back to my party. I didn't come to Chicago."

He held out a small recorder for me to speak into. "And I'm sure you have that friend's name and address?"

"Her name is Sylvia McAllister. She lives in California. I can get her address and phone number and everything."

"Good," he said. "We'll be needing that information."

"I didn't come to Chicago and kill Duncan Phillips."

Siracusano didn't answer that, just pocketed his recorder. "We'll be in touch," he said and swung away from the door. Neither he nor his companions looked back at me as they marched down the hall.

I went inside and packed an overnight bag. Left a message for Jason—

Following the plan. Tell M I need Sylvia's address—and headed out the door for Domenic's.

⤳

That was a strange day, a strange night, alone in Domenic's apartment worrying about my life. I arrived a little before five in the evening, my duffle bag slung over my shoulder and a bag of groceries in my arms. Domenic never stocked any food in his refrigerator. I'd stopped at a store in my neighborhood since—if Siracusano was tracing my purchases—I didn't want my thumb chip registering anywhere near my secret hideaway. As I checked out, I requested fifty bucks in cash just so I could make a few sundry purchases in the future without leaving an electronic record behind. I was pleased that I thought of this. I was less pleased that I had to haul a bag of groceries with me through two teleport gates and down the crowded streets to Domenic's place.

Where, truth be told, I didn't feel all that safe. After I'd put away the perishables, I stood at the window of his apartment and looked at the panoramic view of Chicago spread out before me. Soaring glass buildings, squat dirty brick ones, neon signs, sidewalks, streets, cars, buses, L trains, people—viewed from this perspective, it was a layered, textured, industrious ant farm metropolis.

When the lights came up as darkness fell, it would be a glittering black ballroom of a city. Easy to hide in, you might think. Too big to be tracked through. But Siracusano must know everything about me by now, the addresses of all my family members, the addresses of all my friends. How long would it take him to figure out where I was?

I turned away from the window to the chilly comfort of Domenic's apartment. He had laid towels and sheets on the black leather sofa, an inviting gesture, and placed on the coffee table the operating instructions to his entertainment center. I turned on his computer and visited a few news sites, all filled with hyperbolic accounts of the Duncan Phillips murder. Pictures of me were everywhere, most of them snapped yesterday when I rode in the golf cart from the gate to the house, but a few of them culled from old sources. My official Sefton ID photo was posted, for instance, as well as a couple shots from formal university functions that had been covered by the Houston press. In none of them, I thought, did I look particularly murderous. I particularly liked the one of me standing next to Nancy Ortega at some dinner where she had won a writing award. I looked caring and warm and supportive, I thought. Not at all homicidal.

Photos of Bram and Francis and Dennis also appeared throughout the reports, though images of Bordeaux and Quentin were conspicuously absent. Because they were legal minors, I supposed, and protected by law from defamation. I couldn't keep myself from reading the personality profiles accompanying some of the photos, about my one divorce, Bram's two, and Dennis' "stormy relationship with a well-known Chicago-area clothing designer." In fact, I learned more about Dennis' personal life from these reports than I ever had from him, though I dismissed most of it as fabricated. Certainly, details about my own "spectacular financial disasters and complete emotional breakdown following the end of a contentious four-year marriage" were completely made up. I wondered if Danny was reading these passages right now. I wondered if he thought I was capable of murder.

I wondered if any of the people I knew were capable of murder. I thought several of them might be.

I shut off the computer.

As the hours dragged by, I flashfried a light dinner and forced myself to eat it. I turned on the television and surfed for distraction, watching about five minutes each of fifteen or twenty shows. I picked up books and put them down. I took a long shower, using many of Domenic's expensive skin-and-health-care products. Eventually, for lack of anything else to do, I stretched out on the couch and tried to sleep.

Instead, I spent a long time staring at the moving pattern of lights on the ceiling. I wanted desperately to call Marika or Jason, to hear a friendly voice soothe me with promises that all would be well. I wanted to call Quentin, just to say I was thinking of him, worrying over him, would rearrange the world, if I could, to make him happy.

More than anything, I wanted to talk to Bram Cortez. I wanted to hear his voice, deep and rumbling in my ear, have its low echoes filling up the dreadful accusatory silence. I wanted to ask him why, through Quentin, he had warned me to keep my distance. Was it because he feared for my life and freedom and couldn't figure out how else to keep me safe? Or was it because he thought I might have killed Duncan Phillips?

I wanted to ask if *he* was the one who had done it.

I didn't want to ask. I didn't want to know. But I was so hungry for the sound of his voice that I actually curled up on the couch in pain.

I couldn't call him. I couldn't talk to a soul, couldn't jeopardize my fragile safety with any kind of unencrypted communication. I was alone, in danger, and afraid, and the world had never seemed like such a hostile and perilous place.

⸰

Morning surprised me. That's because, lying awake and watching the hours flip slowly past, I had become convinced the night would never end. I had also believed I would never sleep again, so the fact that I had been wrong on both counts made me sit up in wonder. It was nearly ten, in fact, so I had slept a good long while. I had the vaguest memory of hearing Domenic come in sometime in the very early morning hours. He had crept up to me in the dark and kissed me on the cheek, then turned away without speaking and headed to his bedroom. I had slept much more soundly after that.

Shaking my head to clear it, I got up and contemplated my options. I simply could not spend another full day in this apartment, staring out the windows and slowly going mad. Plus, I didn't want to risk waking Domenic, who had put in a full night working at the Evanston hospital. I decided I would have breakfast here and then head out for the day. Chicago's a big city, after all—how hard could it be to amuse myself for a few hours? So I ate, dressed, left a note for my host, and departed.

Domenic's place was close to the heart of the city, so I headed over to the high-end shopping district on Michigan Avenue. It felt good to be strolling along on this pretty Sunday morning, dodging pedestrians and admiring the buildings, a careless hybrid of the very old and the strikingly new. In high school, Marika and I had taken a class called Chicago Architecture, which had consisted mainly of field trips to the Loop to gawk at the elegance and craftsmanship of the old brick structures. Couldn't remember a single thing I'd learned except to always look up when I passed one of those 19th- and 20th-century edifices—note the changing detail that marked each story, the graceful points of the Gothic windows, the ornamentation at the rooflines, the unexpected gargoyles. Our teacher had had no respect for the fantastical glass and metal confections created in the last hundred years, though Marika and I had been enthralled with the curving lines and disorienting reflections that broke the city into a thousand moving parts. To this day, when I walk downtown, I lift my eyes to the tops of the skyscrapers, and I always see something beautiful.

But glimpses of inspired architecture couldn't keep me occupied for long, so my next stop was the Art Institute. I found a special exhibit of Pre-Raphaelite art, so I lost myself for a while in the dreamy romantic figures in their faux medieval pursuits. "'I am half-sick of shadows,' said the Lady of Shalott," I murmured, feeling a certain sympathy for the imprisoned heroine who threw caution to the winds and rushed out to meet her doom.

Done with art, I still had hours of daylight left, so I slipped into a LucaPlex to watch a double feature. Usually at one of these cinemas, I feel physically transported to another place, another persona; the full-body effects are enough to make me forget who and where I am. But today my mind drifted and my senses did not respond. I did not believe I was running through the forest or ejecting from the spaceship or blowing away my enemies with my high-tech weapons.

Though it would have been nice to blow away my enemies, I thought.

I looked at the screen and pictured Siracusano melting in agony. The smile made my face feel strange.

My WristWatcher vibrated two separate times while I sat in the darkened theater and watched the movies. Jason was either checking in or offering more dire news. I didn't get up; I stayed seated until the last starship whirled through the last wormhole, and then I left with the hundred or so other movie-goers who had thought this might be a pleasant way to spend a Sunday afternoon.

In the main lobby, a massive construction of mirrors and pulsing lights, I found an unoccupied bench and sat down, pulling out my code book and a scrap of paper. Sure enough, Jason's first message was all numerical, and I had to figure it out word by word. But when I finished and read back the message, my heart stood still.

"Q called M. Your door code used Thursday night. Cops looking for you. Respond."

CHAPTER TWENTY-SIX

CINEMA PATRONS BRUSHED BY ME, TALKING AND LAUGHING, APOL-ogizing when they bumped into my knees. Disembodied voices announced that seating would begin in five minutes for theatres 14, 17, and 25. The lights seemed to pulse and recede, pulse and recede, far more slowly than in their earlier strobe effect. I thought I might faint. I placed my hands on either side of my body on the cushioned seat and closed my eyes.

Your door code used Thursday night. Cops looking for you.

This was the nightmare sprung to life. What could I do? Where could I go? If they were checking my phone records, they would quickly come across Domenic's name; it wouldn't be long before they searched for me at his apartment. And if they did find me there, cowering behind his black leather couch, wouldn't that make me look just as guilty as my DNA traces and my door code and all the other circumstantial evidence piling up against me? Maybe, but once I had a lawyer to help me, I could deal reasonably with the police. Now was not the to surrender to the cops. Now was the time to flee.

I opened my eyes. Everything flickered, which upped my panic quotient until I realized the effect was caused by the frenetic lobby lights. Probably the whole world would look better once I got out of this place.

I stood, then remembered to check for the second message. This one had not been encoded. "TAYLOR ANSWER ME ARE YOU ALL RIGHT?" I dictated a brief reply: "Got both messages. I'm trying to decide what to do." Then I pushed through the early-evening date-night crowd, all fresh young teenagers and well-groomed professionals, and stepped out onto the Chicago streets.

It was a little after seven, still light enough to see, but late enough so that all the streetlights and building lights and neon signs had come on. Pedestrians crowded past me, eager and oblivious; cars moved by more slowly, caught in traffic, horns sounding, voices calling, noise and irritation and excitement seeming to rise up organically from the streets and sidewalks. The whole world was ablaze and in motion, and I was heading back to Domenic's to hide in darkness and silence.

The corner where Michigan crossed Chicago Avenue was such a popular spot that it featured three teleport booths right in a row, though at the moment there were about fifteen people waiting to use them. I fell numbly behind the last couple in line, two young Hispanic men nuzzling each other with great affection. Until I could figure out where else to go, Domenic's place still seemed like my best option, but what would I do once I got there? Scan the headlines to see how reporters were currently handicapping the Great Duncan Phillips Suspect Race? Was I still considered the most likely killer, or had someone pulled ahead of me while I wandered the city? Which would be worse, learning that I was still the leading candidate—or discovering that that horrific honor had passed to someone I cared about?

My turn to step into the portal, and by rote I punched in the transfer numbers. I had exited onto the sidewalk at the other end before I realized I had automatically keyed in the most familiar code—the one for my own neighborhood. I took two steps away from the booth, stopped dead, and half-pivoted back toward the terminal before I consciously registered what I was seeing before me.

A silver Mustang, parked at the curb. Two men leaning against it, watching me.

Terror stabbed me in the throat.

"Taylor!" Bram shouted, but Siracusano didn't waste time with greetings. He lunged toward me, flinging his big body across the ten yards that separated us. I whirled and dashed back into the booth, slamming the door shut just as his hand scratched across the glass. No time to think of Domenic's code. I jammed my thumb against the NEXT button and felt myself flung across the city between two heartbeats.

I caught my footing and peered out. Where was I? I couldn't even see a street sign.

Five people waited impatiently to use my booth. Over their shoulders, I could see some tumbledown brick apartments, rusted cars lining the rubbled street. Close enough to the Hot Zone to be dangerous. Not someplace I wanted to linger. NEXT.

I found myself back in downtown Chicago, in the middle booth of a row of teleport stations. Just as I thought it might be a good idea to lose myself in the crowded city streets, the door on the neighboring portal opened, and a large man dashed out. I shrieked and slammed the NEXT button again.

Rematerialized somewhere else, getting another straitened view of an indeterminate high-rise neighborhood. I took a moment to breathe. Had that been Siracusano? Had he hit the FOLO button and caught up with me on my second stop? Had he seen me? Would he shove his way past the waiting commuters, jump in the booth I had used, follow me again?

Dear God, dear God . . .

I punched NEXT, felt myself dissolve and reassemble, then paused a split second to get my bearings. Rogers Park, I thought; I was pretty sure I recognized the metal spine of the southbound L tracks. A long line of night revelers waited for their turn in the booth.

I hit NEXT and moved on.

A discreetly lit station on a green, quiet street. I guessed I was somewhere in the northern suburbs, Winnetka or Highland Park. No one waiting to leave this neighborhood. Why would they? No terrors here. But this was a big enough station that it boasted three booths. Just in case the man I'd seen had been Siracusano, just in case he was still trailing me, I scurried out of this gate, slammed the door on the adjoining one, and pushed NEXT again.

Oak Street Beach. The lake was already dark, forsaken this early by the scarlet kiss of the westering sun. A few students played volleyball, black silhouettes dancing against the sinister gray of the water.

NEXT.

O'Hare, crowded and noisy. Tempting. No. But I took the opportunity to change booths.

NEXT.

Downtown again, cars and pedestrians and somewhere a frantic shouting.
NEXT.

A warehouse district. Spooky and silent. One or two stark lights giving the great buildings a hulking, ominous presence.

NEXT.

A flash of red brick; could have been anywhere in the city.
NEXT.

Rush Street. The smell of booze, even through the closed glass door. Laughter. Insouciance. Untroubled youth.

NEXT.

The lobby of some giant glass-fronted corporate office building. Empty. Big enough to change teleport booths.

NEXT.

Another well-maintained, verdant neighborhood street. No one was waiting to use the teleport booth, so I took the chance of stepping outside to catch my breath and try to figure out where I was. I thought I could glimpse the curve of the lake through a scrim of trees, so I might be back in one of the northern suburbs, maybe Lake Forest or Kenilworth.

I found it hard to believe that Siracusano could have tracked me through all my random jumps, but I felt too exposed and vulnerable to stand here long, trying to put my thoughts in order. I could feel myself shaking with stress or the systemic shock of disintegrating and reintegrating a dozen times in as many minutes. Had they ever done studies on how often a body could survive teleport within a short period of time without completely refusing to cohere again? Had I exceeded that limit?

I needed a place to rest and think. I wondered how close I was to the grounds of the Bahá'í temple in Wilmette. The gorgeous building, with its white stone walls and swooping arches, was set in the middle of lush, manicured lawns. Maybe I could crawl beneath one of its dozens of ornamental bushes and just lie quietly for an hour.

Although . . . Wilmette wasn't that far from Evanston. And maybe, just maybe, I had access to a haven there.

My memory played back Caroline's voice from yesterday's conversation. *I have to go to Houston tomorrow evening and I probably won't come back till the middle of next week.* I remembered exactly where her condo was—and I remembered her door code, too. It was my mother's birthday; how could I forget?

Surely Caroline wouldn't mind if I made my way to her condo and turned her place into a small, brief refuge. As long as I wasn't really the murderer, of course.

I didn't care if she minded. I had no other options.

I forced myself back into the booth to make one more brief jump to Caroline's quiet neighborhood. Trying not to appear too furtive, I exited the portal and headed quickly up the street, wishing my footsteps didn't sound so loud. I couldn't help glancing nervously over my shoulder as I checked for approaching cars. But those that passed by were filled with passengers who showed no interest in me. And none were cop cars. And none were silver Mustangs.

I resisted the urge to run as I covered the last block to Caroline's red-brick condo. With as much nonchalance as I could muster, I typed 1-1-2-4 into the outer keypad, and the door unlocked. Thank God she had had no reason to change her code since the day I had been here last.

The day I had picked up the information about applying for a job with Duncan Phillips. Oh, what a long time ago that seemed like now.

The same combination opened the door to her condo, and I quickly slipped inside. I shut the door and sagged against it, taking several deep breaths. *Be calm, be calm, now is not the time to panic.* Even if the cops were staking out Domenic's place—and my mother's and Jason's and Marika's—surely they couldn't keep track of every acquaintance I might have in the world? Surely it would occur to no one that I might come here?

I took another deep breath and then lifted my head, looking around. Caroline's place was exactly as I remembered it. Big open rooms, just now shuttered against the night. A low-wattage desk lamp had been left on, and it faintly illuminated the glass and metal furnishings, the cool neutrals of the sofa and carpet, the almost antiseptically clean spaces that in my place were filled with boxes and newspapers and junk. Caroline's condo looked just like Caroline.

"Thank you," I whispered to the ambient air. "You've saved my life."

When I was certain the world would not suddenly explode with gunfire—or dissolve around me as my body began to reflexively teleport—I took a few steps deeper into the room.

Better send Jason a message, tell him where I was. I pulled out a sleek silver dining room chair, which turned out to more comfortable than it looked, and perched on the very edge. I didn't want to mess anything up. Hardly a way to show gratitude.

Since I had to encrypt the message, I first spent a few minutes flipping through my sociology book and writing out numerical sequences that I could dictate into the WristWatcher. I was too exhausted to go into much detail, so I just said I was at a friend's and gave him the address, spelling out the street name letter by letter. Let him decode for a change and see how much fun it was.

After I'd sent the message, I started to relax. To tell the truth, I was starting to feel hungry. All the expenditure of adrenaline on terror, I supposed. I'd had popcorn and soda at the theater, but it wasn't exactly what you'd call a meal. I was sure it wasn't safe for me to order a food delivery, but I absolutely could not add to my iniquities by raiding Caroline's refrigerator.

To distract myself, I stood up and began moving around the rooms, examining items one by one. In one corner of the dining area was an open display unit holding four levels of colored glass curios in remarkable shapes. One appeared to be an aquarium tenanted by exotic fish. Others were floral arrangements of lush blossoms, vases in cascading colors, Mardi Gras masks, great feathered birds. All fragile, all beautiful, all devoid of any practical use. *Just the sorts of things Caroline would collect,* I thought.

In the living room, I checked the bookcases, floor-to-ceiling ebony shelves inset with mother-of-pearl motifs. I was afraid to pull out any volumes to get a closer look because they all looked like first editions in stiff, crumbling binding with faint gold lettering on the spines. Her specialty was the 19th century, so I was not surprised to see a full set of Dickens, a selection of Wilde, all of Thackeray—and, by God, a complete edition of the original O.E.D., volume by volume. I wondered what fortune she had spent on that.

Everything else within view was similarly exquisite, rare, and fabulously expensive. How had Caroline afforded such treasures? She was a few rungs higher than I was on the academic ladder, but her salary simply could not have been great enough to cover all of these bounties. Maybe she was independently wealthy and only taught for the joy of it, or maybe she had a rich relative with excellent taste who liked to shower her with gifts.

Or maybe she stole things. I fantasized about that for a moment, the icy and polished Caroline plotting to spirit copies of *Jude the Obscure* from antique bookstores, perhaps wearing big puffy caftans under which to conceal her purloined treasures . . .

I shook my head. Now I was turning giddy, a second and even less desirable reaction to stress and reprieve. I would have to chance a quick trip out to pick up food and essentials, or my mind would skitter into lunacy.

Maybe I should find a way to conceal my features before I left the condo. Would police have issued warrants for my arrest already? My face was all over the news sites. Any zealous citizen on the street might recognize me and alert the cops to my presence. I had to make some effort at disguise.

Although I felt squeamish about it, I sorted through Caroline's hall closet, but didn't find any hats or shawls. I headed back to the dining room, where a marble-topped sideboard stood on spindly bronze legs. Maybe Caroline had a nice lacy table runner that I could use as a headscarf if I tied it creatively enough. I rifled through the top two drawers, finding only old-fashioned fountain pens, pressed handmade paper, a wooden box containing a set of tableware made from real silver, and a few embroidered doilies that would not serve my purpose.

Well, hell. I closed the drawers and stood frowning down at the marble surface, wondering what to do next. The arrangement of items laid out there made me smile. I remembered noticing them the last time I was here and thinking they were very unlike Caroline. The cross-stitched piece had probably been done by a niece or goddaughter, the wooden horse might have come from the same source, and the small glass globe on the tripod—who knows, a friend with a sense of humor might have thought Caroline needed a crystal ball.

A car prowled by outside, its headlights glancing through the room and igniting a blaze inside the glass globe. Actually, it was more occluded than ordinary glass, denser, with dozens of slanting interior planes that formed galaxies of buried color.

I could not resist picking it up to examine it more closely. Even in the low light, it retained its brilliant sparkle. I made a wizard's gesture with it, holding it before me as if expecting it to flare with visions, then bringing it back coquettishly against my cheek.

My eyes narrowed with a flash of *déjà vu*; where I had seen that gesture before? I extended my hand again with the globe in my palm, then brought it back to cradle against my face.

I had seen somebody make that exact same motion recently, offering and reclaiming a bright opal treasure—

Opal.

I nearly dropped the globe in my sudden haste to put it back, and it rocked unsteadily a moment in its golden base. I backed up a few paces, my hands across my mouth. Opal, yes, it could be an opal. I had seen jewels just about that size and shape on display in Duncan Phillips' hologallery. He gave them as parting gifts to all his ex-mistresses, after he sculpted them in light—

Caroline had set up my job interview with Duncan Phillips. She had said the offer came through the dean, but perhaps it had been mentioned to her directly, in an intimate setting, one night over dinner or in the bedroom—

And I had seen her sobbing in her office, begging me to tell her how to endure the loss of love. *Didn't you want to get even with him? Didn't you want to hurt him back?* she had asked.

She must have spent some time in the mansion during their affair, must have known at least some of its rhythms and routines. She would have known where to find Duncan Phillips late at night and where the loaded guns were arrayed on the wall. But how had she cut off the monitoring system and blocked the cameras?

And how had she snuck in, using a private door code, since surely her own (if she'd ever had one) had been discontinued after the breakup?

I use the same door code for everything, I heard my voice say. *Charlotte Brontë's birthday.*

Oh my God. Oh my God. Oh my God.

I backed up a few more paces from the glittering jewel, now taking on, in the erratic light, a baleful, malevolent glow. Had she sent me there, introduced me to the household, simply to have a way in when the need for murder arose? Surely not. Surely she had been happily enough in love with him when she directed me his way, for it had been weeks later that I found her weeping and hysterical. What had occurred to push her over the edge, what had made her suddenly and violently decide the world could not support his presence for another hour?

The new fiancée. Whether or not the news sites had the story right, Caroline had heard the announcement about the young blonde actress. She'd seen photos of them together, laughing and happy, and all her hot anger had cooled into an icy spike of hatred.

And as for how she'd thwarted the camera—well, Dennis knew how to short out the system, and he'd taught Quentin, and no doubt any number of enterprising young felons could be found to teach an apt student a trick that appeared relatively simple.

So she'd guessed the gate code, and she'd developed the motive, and she'd obtained the means when she slipped into the house late Thursday night, pulled a gun off the wall, and shot Duncan Phillips.

Suddenly her condo did not seem like such a safe place after all.

I had just reached that conclusion and spun toward the exit when there was a small beeping as the key code was punched in. The door opened, and Caroline walked in.

The light from the hallway caught me in a perfect beam, leaving her a startled shadow just six feet away. She gasped when she saw me but, being Caroline, did not scream. Being Caroline, she assessed the situation coolly and came instantly to the obvious conclusion.

"Taylor! You must be hiding from the police. I saw a video monitor at O'Hare, and your face was all over the screen."

She doesn't know what you suspect; she doesn't realize she has anything to hide. Good, good. Play your part now. Be the wrongly accused fugitive.

"I'm so sorry to have showed up here like this," I said, my voice shaking and raw. "The police were waiting at my apartment—and I didn't think, I just ran. I didn't know where to go. I remembered that you'd said you'd be out of town and I remembered where you lived—I'm sorry, I know I shouldn't have just walked in like this—"

"No, don't apologize, of course you can come to me," she said. She stepped inside and closed the door, locking it. Only then did she flick on the overhead chandelier, quickly dialing it down to a low level to prevent anyone on the street from seeing in. "I can't imagine how dreadful your situation must be."

"Caroline, I didn't kill him," I said desperately. "I know it looks bad, but I didn't do it."

"No, I'm sure you didn't. I would never believe that of you."

"But the police think I did."

She came closer, dropping her purse and briefcase on the glass table and frowning at me, as if trying to read the explanation in my face. "But why? I didn't hear all the details." She made a sudden irritated sound and held her hands up as if warding off a big sloppy dog. "I spent two hours at O'Hare trying to get to Bezos, but all the long-distance teleport gates were down so I just came back. But the whole time I was at the terminal, I kept catching glimpses of you on the television monitors. What in the world is going on?"

"I swear it's all just circumstantial evidence. Duncan Phillips was killed with one of his own guns late Thursday night. I was in Atlanta then—but I spent a little time at Olympic Terminal, and they can prove that. And my DNA traces were on the gun. And apparently my gate code was used at the mansion that night. All that adds up to the fact that I *could* have been at the mansion right when he was killed."

Her frown deepened; she looked as though she was reconsidering her earlier quick profession of faith in my innocence. She was a better actress than I was. "Taylor. That's pretty bad."

"Yeah, I know."

"Did you go to his house that night?"

"No. But I'm not sure how I can prove it."

"Well, then—did someone else have your gate code?"

You did, you cold bitch. "I don't *think* so?" I said, because I was certainly not about to betray Bordeaux to Caroline. "But I know people hack passwords all the time. Maybe someone stole my code?"

She shook her head. "Taylor, this doesn't sound good. But I'm sure the

Chicago police department will figure it out."

"I hope so."

"Now," she said a little more briskly, "Do you want some tea? Why don't you take a seat and I'll put on the kettle?"

"Thanks, Caroline," I said gratefully, sinking into one of the silver chairs. "I don't know—I realize I shouldn't have come here—I didn't know what to do—"

"Please. Stop apologizing. I'll be back in a moment."

She disappeared into the kitchen and I sat at the table, wondering wildly what I should do. Run for it? Bolt out the door and race for the teleport booth, screaming for help as she chased after me? Would she chase after me? What would she do? Did she believe me? I mean, obviously she knew I hadn't killed Duncan Phillips, but did she believe that I had innocently stumbled into her condo, having no clue that she was the murderer? That seemed too farfetched, or it would to me if I'd had a guilty conscience.

Maybe, even now, she was in the kitchen poisoning my tea.

What was I going to do?

She came back into the dining room, carrying an old-fashioned silver tray laden with delicate rose-patterned teacups on matching saucers. "Sugar? Milk?" she asked, setting the tray on the table. "And are you hungry? I've got fresh bagels in the kitchen."

"Starving," I admitted. "No milk or sugar."

"Cream cheese on your bagel?"

"That would be divine."

"Let me just get some placemats out," she said, turning to the marble-topped sideboard.

I was looking at the door, calculating the distance from my chair, so I did not at first notice the quality of her silence. But suddenly, realizing she had frozen in place, I glanced over at her still figure. She was standing with her back to me, gazing down at the sideboard, examining all of her treasures, seeming to know by some phosphorescent residue of my hands that I had touched her glittering globe—

I had left a lace doily on the marble countertop.

My heart contracted as I saw the frilly little circle of netting neatly spread over the cold stone. Stupid, careless, how could I have been so dumb? She seemed to be working it out as she stood there, eyes fixed on the still-life arrangement—doily, dragonfly, horse, opal—guessing what I knew about Duncan Phillips' women, about her, what I had found in her condo and what I had pieced together.

I did not even breathe until she spoke again.

Which she did without even turning around to face me. "Charlotte Brontë's birthday," she said in an uninflected voice. "Your door code to the Phillips house."

"Yes."

"You use the same password for everything."

"Yes."

"When did you know?"

"When I saw the opal. About five minutes before you walked through the door."

She nodded, still not looking at me, and stood silently for another few moments.

And then spun to the nearby display case, grabbed one of her art-glass vases and smashed it against the marble sideboard as she dove past. I screamed, scrambling to my feet, *too late, too late.* I felt the wicked edge slice across my left shoulder, felt the flesh part as smoothly as two eyelids opening. I screamed again and dashed for the door, holding my skin together, feeling the blood leak through my fingers. I could not solve the lock and I rolled away from the door as she leapt for me again, as graceful as a fencer with a foil. The glass edge tinkled against the wood but only splinters fell away. She whirled and stalked after me, weapon upraised.

"Caroline!" I cried, backing away from her, bleeding all over her carpet, searching for weapons. "Caroline, stop! Stop!"

In the living room now—couch pillows in my hands—flinging them in her face, aiming at her eyes. She dodged, pivoted to follow my progress. I reached blindly to a table behind me—a lamp—a book—a paperweight. I threw them all amid great crashes of glass and metal. The base of the lamp hit her hard across the chin and she shouted something at me, primal, wordless—

Then she lunged for me again, knocking me to the floor, slashing at my face while I tried to slap her hands away. She cut my cheek, she sliced at my throat, and both of my hands were bleeding. I was screaming, she was screaming, the teakettle in the kitchen raised a frantic shrieking, and the pounding at the door grew first louder and louder and then fainter and fainter as the world blurred and whirled away.

CHAPTER TWENTY-SEVEN

THE FIRST VOICE I RECOGNIZED WAS JASON'S. "WE HAVE TO TAKE her to a hospital."

"We will, sir. There's an ambulance outside and they're bringing in the gurney. But she's stable now. She's in no danger."

"She's in a coma! And she's bleeding! She could bleed to death—"

"She's unconscious, sir, but I don't believe she's in a coma. And we've got the bleeding under control."

I heard my brother swear under his breath and move a few paces away, toward the sound of other voices murmuring in the background. "Are you the security guard who's in love with my sister?" he snapped.

"Yes." Bram's voice. Not a second's hesitation at the outrageous question. "We've got to get her to a hospital."

"We will. Just a couple things to wrap up here."

Now Caroline was speaking, as calm and collected as always. "I didn't mean to hurt her. That was just a moment of panic. I would never hurt Taylor."

Siracusano next. "But you did mean to kill Duncan Phillips, is that right?"

"I didn't plan to murder him," she said coolly, "but I did."

Several voices spoke at once in response to that little admission. I couldn't make out what any of them said. I felt myself slipping in and out of the scene, my senses growing sharper, then dimmer, in a strange wave-like succession. I seemed to be lying on the floor and I hurt all over, more sharply in some places than others. I didn't think it would ever be possible to open my eyes. The paramedic (or so I assumed him to be) had assured my brother that I was in no danger, but I wondered almost idly how badly I'd been hurt. Would I be disfigured? Would I be paralyzed? In movies, injured people were always asked to move their extremities in order to prove their muscles still responded to their wills. I curled and uncurled my toes, clenched and loosened my fingers. Everything seemed functional. The paramedic was probably right.

I was so tired then that if my eyes had been open, I would have shut them.

Suddenly there was a fresh batch of noises across the room. I heard the front door opening, people moving around the space, new voices asking questions.

Then familiar voices spoke almost over my head. "We're bringing Caroline Summers downtown," Siracusano said. "You'll take care of Ms. Kendall?"

"I'll take care of her," Jason interjected.

"We'll handle it," Bram said tersely.

"I'll want a statement from her tomorrow."

"You'll fucking leave her alone!" Jason swore. "After the things you accused her of—"

I could imagine Siracusano's heavy, impassive stare traveling from Jason's face to Bram's. "We're off, then," he said, and I heard the sounds of several bodies making their way through the door.

More footsteps crossed to me; people knelt on either side of my body. "We're just going to move her to the gurney and then we'll take her to the Evanston hospital," the paramedic explained. "Are you going to meet us there?"

"Yes," Bram and Jason replied in unison.

It was the most immense effort of my life to lift my eyelids and try to focus, first on the fair, furrowed face to my left, and then on the darker, sterner face on my right. Jason and Bram. "I'll be okay," I whispered.

"Tay!" Jason cried, bending down to peer at me. "Can you hear me? Are you all right?"

"Well, I've been better."

"Don't talk," Bram advised.

"She'll talk if she wants to," Jason said fiercely. "Do you hurt? They shot you up with morphine."

"I would have expected better—of morphine."

Bram's arm flashed across my vision as he pushed Jason back from me. "Don't make her talk," he said, just as fiercely. "Let's get her out of here."

I was too tired to protest. And there was no time to argue, anyway, as the paramedics elbowed their way to my side and began lifting me to the stretcher. In moments, they were carrying me outside and hoisting me into an ambulance with its carnival red-and-white lights. I shut my eyes against the kaleidoscope.

The ride to the hospital was a jumble of unsteady motion and rough bumps and static over the radio, voices raised in indistinguishable calls, sirens flaring in and out of range. It couldn't have taken more than fifteen minutes to reach our destination, where my eyes were jarred open as I was unloaded from the ambulance. I tried hard to keep them open and take in the events unfolding around me. The medics rolled me in through great glass doors, and I could see both Bram and Jason awaiting me on the other side. I realized they must have teleported over.

I closed my eyes again, let myself drift on a sea of sound and motion. I felt myself wheeled down hallways, then raised from the gurney to a hospital bed. Someone grabbed my arm and wrapped it with an inflatable cuff, and someone else began examining my recent wounds. I could sense the presence of multiple people hovering over me and the great glaring intrusion of a bright overhead light, but I was able to ignore it all until something touched too hard on the gash across my neck.

"Owww!" I cried as my eyes flew open. There were about five people in the room, but my gaze focused on the face closest to me, dark and unearthly beautiful and framed by a flowing mass of black hair.

"It's an angel," I whispered. "I've died and gone to heaven."

Domenic laughed. "No chance, sweetheart," he said. "You've sinned and gone to hell."

"Oh, well," I said, feeling my eyelids drop again. "As long as you're here with me."

I felt his hand rest briefly against my cheek—not, I was sure, a medical assessment. "I won't leave you for a minute," he said. "You can close your eyes."

There's no such thing as sleep in a hospital, though I'll admit the drugs went a long way toward negating the irritating effects of the constant noise and the hourly interruptions. I still felt like hell when I more or less woke up in the morning, responding to the invasion of a cheery little nurse who looked no older than my freshman students.

"Good morning, Taylor," she chirped, consulting a computer screen to learn my history and check my vital signs. "How are you feeling?"

"Like I had my throat cut last night," I said. "How are you?"

The sound of my voice triggered movement in a corner of the room, and Jason uncoiled into my line of sight. "Taylor? You awake?"

He was instantly at the side of the bed, gazing down at me, looking more serious and more adult than I'd ever seen him. Clearly, he had not slept any better than I had, and his cheek bore the corrugated imprint of the fabric from the chair where he must have spent the night. His eyes were gray with exhaustion and his skin was pasty with worry, but the smile that crossed his face was like a splash of sunshine.

"You look terrible," he said.

"Were you here all night?"

He nodded. "Domenic came in for a while when his shift was over. He just left, in fact."

The nurse seemed pleased with whatever numbers were registering on the monitors. "Do you want to try to go to the bathroom?" she asked. "I can help you."

"God, yes. Jason, you just sit here for a moment."

Five minutes later, I was back in bed, and my brother and I were alone.

I took a long sip of water from a bedside cup, then sank against the pillows with a groan. "Have you told Mom?" I demanded.

He scrunched up his nose. "Well, a little bit. I mean, she'd seen your face on the news, no way she didn't know what was going on. So I told her you were helping the police find the real killer, and you got slightly injured during the apprehension of the suspect—"

"When did you start writing true-crime melodrama?"

"And that you were in the hospital, but you'd be fine. She didn't really calm down, though, until I told her Domenic was here, and then she said, 'Oh, Domenic will take care of her,' and she wasn't worried any more. But she's coming over this morning, of course."

"So what happened?" I demanded. "When did you get to Caroline's? How did Bram get there? I mean, the last thing I remember is Caroline coming at me like something out of 'Psycho,' and the next thing I know the room is full of people, and you and Bram are having a fight."

"Soon as I got your text message, I headed for the nearest teleport booth. It just seemed wrong to have you out there by yourself, and I decided I should come hang out with you. And I guess your little cop buddy figured that was exactly what I'd do, because he had Mom's place staked out, and he followed me. I didn't know he was following me, of course, because I had no idea what he looked like.

"And I arrived at that woman's place just in time to hear *you* screaming, and *her* screaming, and glass crashing all over the place. And I was pounding on the door, trying to break it down, and all of a sudden this guy comes tearing around the corner and just *slams* into the door. I mean, it practically shattered. Took the two of us another couple minutes to break it open and when we did—"

He stopped and shuddered. I could imagine what a hellish vision that had been, a homicidal maniac wielding an art-glass stiletto as blood spumed up from my sprawled body. I was just as glad not to have witnessed it from their perspective.

"Anyway, he practically broke her neck jerking her away from you, and I was calling the paramedics while he got her under control. Actually, she kind of froze up as soon as he grabbed her. It was like she suddenly realized what she'd done and just—I don't know—didn't want any part of it. It was so bizarre. I mean, one minute she was this shrieking lunatic, and the next minute she was sitting there so calm and quiet she could have been in church."

"That's the Caroline I know," I said. "That second one."

"So who is she, anyway? How did you figure it out? And once you figured it out, how could you be so stupid as to go there and confront her?"

I sighed. "Oh, that's not how it happened," I said, and I explained the whole story. He shook his head in disbelief at the end of my recital.

"Strange," he said. "The whole thing is hardly credible. But at least it's all over now."

"She confessed, didn't she? I heard her say it. That she killed him."

"I heard her, too. I suppose she could hire some fancy lawyer who tries to prove the cops coerced a confession, but—not our problem anymore. You're not the chief suspect, and that's all that matters."

I said, "And any day that begins with not being a murder suspect has just got to be a good day."

∿

I sent Jason home to sleep, even though he'd planned to wait for our mother's arrival. "I can handle her on my own," I assured him, and he was so tired he agreed after only three protests.

After he was gone, the nurse found twenty minutes to peel off my bandages and help me to the shower, though the first experience of looking in the mirror was ghastly. I had small cat-scratch cuts all over my face, a few deep gouges along my neck at points that apparently did not house vital arteries, and three long slices on my left arm, my right shoulder, and my right ribcage. My hands were a mass of criss-crossed gashes. Flakes of dried blood flecked my face like glitter and streaks of it hennaed my hair. I was pale as a corpse and the circles under my eyes looked like actual bruises.

Against all this carnage, the ruby insets on my cheek looked frivolous and out of place.

"I think a quick glance is all I need," I said, turning from the mirror and stepping into the shower.

Amazing how much better I felt once I came out, bleeding slightly along the deeper wounds but clean and soapy-smelling. The nurse rebandaged all the dangerous cuts, gave me clean scrubs, and helped me back to bed, where I slept for the next two hours.

When I woke up, my mother was there, using actual cards to play gin rummy with Marika. I closed my eyes quickly, but that seemed cowardly, so I opened them again. "Hi, guys," I said.

They came to their feet so fast that the cards flew everywhere, and in seconds the two of them were hanging over my bed.

"Oh Taylor, oh honey, oh you look so dreadful—"

"Lord, she could have cut your throat."

"Sweetheart, how are they treating you? Has Domenic been here? I knew you'd be fine as long as they let Domenic take care of you."

"You wouldn't believe what the gossip sites are saying about Caroline. Discarded mistress with a mental health problem—they're digging up old boyfriends and even her therapist to talk about her instability—"

"Have you been eating? When are you going home? You'll come and stay with me a few days, I'll fix up your room."

"I gotta say, Tay, you look like shit."

I closed my eyes again, but this time I was laughing.

～

They stayed two hours and cheered me immensely. It didn't even seem too weird when talk turned to Jason and they spoke his name with equal affection. I would get used to it, surely I would get used to it, my brother and my best friend being lovers. I just didn't want the sorts of details one might normally ask for.

I napped again after they left, but sleep was beginning to seem pretty tame. Which was why I was sitting up on the side of the bed, my feet dangling over the edge, wondering if I had the courage to try to walk down the hall on my own, when Bram came striding in around four in the afternoon.

"I don't think you're supposed to be getting up," were the first words out of his mouth. "Has the doctor been here? Have you asked anyone when you can get out of bed? I think you should lie back down."

I stared at him with a great deal of resentment and a soupçon of anger. Nearly a full day since my desperate duel with a killer, and this was the first I'd seen or heard from him. "When did you turn into my mother?" I said in a hostile tone of voice. "I'll get up if I feel like it."

He didn't answer that, merely watched me push myself to my feet and stand there shakily for a moment. On my previous visits to the bathroom, nurses had supported me the whole way, and the world hadn't seemed quite so dizzying. "Okay, well, I don't really feel like it," I said, and sat down again.

Bram tried to hide his smile. "But I'm glad to see that you're showing your usual sass and spunk."

I felt very cross, though I'd tried hard to be sunny with all my other visitors. "Next you'll be calling me 'saucy' and 'perky,'" I grumbled. "I can do without the glib descriptions."

"I think I'm going to step outside," he said, "and try this all over again from the beginning."

He turned for the door, but I said, "No, wait. I'm sorry. It's just been— well, you know—kind of a rough day or two."

He came close enough to bend over, put a hand under my chin, and tip my face up for a gentle kiss. I immediately felt ten times more cheerful than I had since Friday afternoon.

"May I?" he asked and settled himself next to me on the bed. He wrapped his arm loosely around me, and I leaned into his shoulder. A hundred times better.

"I know," he said quietly. "It's been worse for you than for anybody. And there was nothing I could do to shield you."

"When did Siracusano start considering me the main suspect?" I asked. "Was it just when he found the door codes or—"

"Since Saturday," he said. "When he found your DNA on the gun. And then with your thumb chip showing up at Olympic—and the door code—I mean, he didn't seem to be looking anywhere else."

"Did you believe it?" I asked in a small voice. "Did you think I'd killed him?"

He pulled away so he could put his hands on my shoulders and turn me to face him. "No," he said, looking down at me so seriously that he seemed to be trying to reinforce his words with his intensity. "I didn't think you were capable of killing anyone, even Duncan Phillips, and especially not at one in the morning when you'd have had to sneak back in to do it. Siracusano thought there was motive, but it wasn't enough of a motive. If you were going to kill him, you'd have done it right there in the study Tuesday afternoon."

"Although I'm glad he's dead," I said.

"Oh, yeah. I'm going to be celebrating the anniversary of that day for years to come."

I settled back against his shoulder and his arm came around me again. "I knew you wanted him dead," I offered. "I remembered what you'd said at the pool one day. But I didn't think you'd done it. I didn't think you'd hurt Quentin that way."

"Glad to hear it."

"But who did you suspect?"

He was silent a moment. "Bordeaux."

"That's who I figured, too!" I exclaimed. "But what did you think when my door code showed up?"

He glanced down at me. "What I'd always figured. That you'd given it to her and she'd used it. I mean, everybody in the household knew that. But I don't think anyone would have told Siracusano."

"She said she was going to."

"Yeah, and I bet she would have. Tough girl, that one."

"I adore her."

He smiled. "Don't we all."

I slumped against him, still tired, but determined to stay awake and finish the conversation. "Caroline never crossed my mind," I said. "I ended up at her place 'cause I thought I'd be safe. Weird."

He kissed the top of my head, pressing his lips for a long moment against my hair. "God. Not something I want to go through again—seeing that scene—" He lifted his head and shook it. "Cool customer, though, once she calmed down. She went down to the station and made a statement and hasn't once recanted or altered a single detail. Never once tried to change her story."

"What will happen to her?"

I felt him shrug. "Go to jail, get bail, get a lawyer, go to court. I imagine it will be the trial of the century."

I was silent a moment, mulling things over. "I still can't take it all in," I said. "I'll need some time for it to make sense. Meanwhile, I guess, I just try to heal and put some normalcy back in my life."

"When are they releasing you?"

"I'm hoping it will be tonight."

"Tonight! I don't think so!"

I couldn't help laughing. "You know, I think the only reason they kept me overnight was that they couldn't get me to wake up. I can't believe that they always let people stay in the hospital when all they have are a few flesh wounds."

"I'm going to talk to your doctor before I leave."

"I want to go home. I want to be with my friends. I want to go see Quentin."

"Quentin's in the hospital, too," he said.

I jerked away from him, wired with a sudden alarm. "What? What happened? Why didn't you—"

"Shhh, shh," he hushed me, and drew me back into his arms. "He's at Northwestern General. Undergoing the first round of tests for the new Kyotenin program."

I pulled away again, still staring. "What? I thought his father—"

"His father's dead," he said callously. "Saturday, Francis and I took Quentin downtown to enroll him in the program, and today he went in full-time. We still have legal medical authority over him—and that won't change until his aunt arrives, so I guess we'll have it for a while. So we figured, act now while we can. Once he's in the program, no matter how she feels about it, it'd be harder to yank him out. We didn't want to waste any time."

I thought about this a moment. "An honorable plan of action," I said a little doubtfully, "but kind of ruthless."

He shrugged. "At times I can be a ruthless guy."

I looked up at him, searching his face. "What's going to happen to Quentin, Bram? Who is this aunt of his? What's she like? I know it's only two more years before he's of legal age, but that could be a long two years."

He nodded. "I know. I've thought about it a lot. I don't know what her plans are—I don't know how she feels about Quentin. I do know she hasn't fought too hard for him since his mother died. I do know that Dennis and Francis and I have done more for him than anybody he ever met—until you came along, and Bordeaux. And I think maybe we should be allowed to keep taking care of him."

"What do you mean?"

He shrugged. "I want to see if there's a way I can win legal guardianship. Only if Quentin wants it, of course—and he's old enough, and of sound enough mind, that I think a court would listen to him and place him with the guardian he chose. We'd appoint a whole board of trustees to take care of his money, so no one would think that was what I was after. And then he could continue to live in the house that he knows, and he could continue to be surrounded by the people who love him and—I don't know, I just think it would be a better life for him than going off to Australia with someone who's almost a stranger."

I was still watching his face. "That's a big responsibility," I said quietly. "To take on the care of a dying boy."

He nodded. "I know. So even if I win custody, it might only be for one or two years, and they could be really bad years. But they might be good years. This new program could maybe give him another decade—longer—no one knows. He might even outlive me."

I thought of all the shadows lurking in Quentin's life, the specter of mortality haunting him from the day he was born—and everything this man had done to try to cheat those shadows. "What a gift," I said. "Not death, but love."

"What?"

"Nothing. I'm just—you're an amazing man, Abramo Cortez, and I'm pretty sure I love you."

He smiled but did not, as I expected after my declaration, kiss me again. "Of course," he said, focusing his gaze on the wall across the room, "I'd be more likely to win custody of Quentin if I was married. You know. Sometimes people look askance at bachelor guardians."

Now I wrenched away, violently and completely. "Are you asking me to *marry* you?" I demanded.

"Well, not yet," he said, unperturbed by my sharp tone. "We don't know each other all that well—"

"We've only slept together once!"

"Right. We'd have to practice that a little more. And you've never met any of my family members, and let me tell you, they might be enough to drive you away right there. And of course, I've only ever met your brother, and he struck me as a little volatile, so I'm starting to wonder if maybe there are sides to your personality I haven't seen yet. I mean, I don't want to be too hasty—"

I hauled off and smacked him on the arm. Not as much force behind the blow as I would have liked, since wrestling with a crazed murderer the day before had left me weak, but enough of an impact that he would get my drift. "I think you're lucky you found *two* women to marry you. I wouldn't be counting on *three*."

He ostentatiously rubbed his arm. "And then there are your violent tendencies, which you've managed to conceal until now—"

"Keep talking like this, and you'll see some violent tendencies—"

"But all in all, I'm thinking, well, here's a woman I think I don't want to live without," he summed up. "So what I want is for us to spend enough time together getting to know each other so that it does make sense when I ask you to marry me. At the moment, that's all I'm asking."

Now he turned to look me full in the face. He was smiling, but his expression was still serious. He wore the air of a man who has spoken as directly and honestly as he knows how and now is just waiting to hear how the universe receives his proposition. As for me, I felt trembly and goofy and shy as a high school heezling who just got asked to prom by the captain of the basketball team. *Because the birthday of my life/Is come, my love is come to me . . .*

"That sounds good," was all I managed to say, a woefully inadequate reply to such a heartfelt offer. "That's what I want, too."

Now his smile grew broader, warmer, even a little teasing. "See?" he said, flicking my nose with his finger. "We think alike. A very good start."

I lifted my arms and put them around his neck, and he cradled me against him in a tender embrace. "Take me home, Bram," I whispered in his ear. "And then you'll see just how good it can be."

His reply to that was not verbal. Not much of the ensuing hour was, though it isn't easy to express your affection while perched on a hospital bed, gowned in scrubs, and waiting for the nurses to burst in. But there would be time for that. There would be plenty of time. No reason, now, to fear the oncoming days or encroaching nights or the long, dull strand of years. I kissed him, and the world grew light; I breathed in so much luminous air that I glowed from the inside. Words failed me and thoughts failed me, briefly, but long enough, and I realized that the silent language of love contained a poetry all its own.

ABOUT THE AUTHOR

Sharon Shinn has published 32 novels, three short fiction collections, and one graphic novel since she joined the science fiction and fantasy world in 1995. She has written about angels, shape-shifters, elemental powers, magical portals, and echoes. She has won the William C. Crawford Award for Outstanding New Fantasy Writer, a Reviewer's Choice Award from the *Romantic Times*, and the 2010 RT Book Reviews Career Achievement Award in the Science Fiction/Fantasy category. Follow her on Facebook at SharonShinnBooks or visit her website at sharonshinn.net.

OTHER TITLES FROM FAIRWOOD PRESS

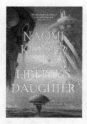

Liberty's Daughter
by Naomi Kritzer
trade paper $18.99
ISBN: 978-1-958880-16-6

The American Writer
by Jack Cady
trade paper $19.99
ISBN: 978-1-958880-17-3

The History of the World Begins in Ice
by Kate Elliott
trade paper $20.95
ISBN: 978-1-958880-19-7

Two Hour Transport 2
ed. by NIB, Ramona Ridgewell
& Keyan Bowes
trade paper $18.99
ISBN: 978-1-958880-20-3

Egyptian Motherlode
by David Sandner & Jacob Weisman
paperback $18.99
ISBN: 978-1-958880-21-1

Storm Waters
by Kat Richardson
trade paper $18.99
ISBN: 978-1-958880-22-7

Beyond Here Be Monsters
by Gregory Frost
trade paper $18.99
ISBN: 978-1-958880-15-9

Substrate Phantoms
by Jessica Reisman
trade paper $18.99
ISBN: 978-1-958880-23-4

Find us at:
www.fairwoodpress.com
Bonney Lake, Washington

Printed in the USA
CPSIA information can be obtained
at www.ICGtesting.com
LVHW041746231024
794637LV00005B/68

9 781958 880258